Yours, Mine, Ours

Sinéad's previous novels

The Baby Trail
A Perfect Match
From Here to Maternity
In My Sister's Shoes
Keeping it in the Family
Pieces of My Heart
Me and My Sisters
This Child of Mine
Mad About You
The Secrets Sisters Keep
The Way We Were
The Good Mother
Our Secrets and Lies
Seven Letters
About Us

Stories you'll care about, characters you'll love

Yours, Mine, Ours

SINÉAD MORIARTY

SANDYCOVE

an imprint of

PENGUIN BOOKS

SANDYCOVE

UK | USA | Canada | Ireland | Australia
India | New Zealand | South Africa

Sandycove is part of the Penguin Random House group of companies
whose addresses can be found at global.penguinrandomhouse.com.

First published 2022
001

Copyright © Sinéad Moriarty, 2022

The moral right of the author has been asserted

Set in 13.5/16pt Garamond MT Std
Typeset by Jouve (UK), Milton Keynes
Printed and bound in Great Britain by Clays Ltd, Elcograf S.p.A.

The authorized representative in the EEA is Penguin Random House Ireland,
Morrison Chambers, 32 Nassau Street, Dublin D02 YH68

A CIP catalogue record for this book is available from the British Library

ISBN: 978–1–844–88538–1

www.greenpenguin.co.uk

Penguin Random House is committed to a
sustainable future for our business, our readers
and our planet. This book is made from Forest
Stewardship Council® certified paper.

For my own beautiful, imperfect, wonderful family

Every family has a story to tell — blended families just have more chapters

I

Anna closed the door softly and tiptoed downstairs to where her sisters were waiting with a bottle of wine, opened, on the kitchen table.

'Well?' her older sister Anita asked.

'He's asleep.'

'Thank Christ for that, I thought he'd never sleep. You know, Anna, much as I love my nephew, he's a right handful. Too like his father, although hopefully he'll grow out of it. I don't know how you keep your patience.' Angela poured Anna a large glass of wine. 'Get that down your neck. You've earned it.'

Anita leant over and squeezed her sister's hand. 'It'll be okay, Anna, kids are resilient. Jack will get used to the change.'

All of Anna's siblings had names beginning with A. Her two sisters and her four brothers. For some unknown reason, her mother and father had decided that this was a good idea. They had been slagged mercilessly in school about it – Anthony, Albert, Anita, Anna, Alex, Angela and Adam.

'Jack worships his dad.' Anna's voice shook. 'He keeps begging me to get back with him. I hate seeing him unhappy.'

'He'll still see Conor, just a bit less,' Angela said. 'But at least now when Jack does see his dad it'll be quality time. Sure Conor was always out and about at the weekends. Now he'll have to stay at home and look after Jack and Grace. It'll be good for him and for the kids. He'll have to be less of a selfish git, and about time too.'

Anna rubbed her eyes. She was exhausted. Leaving Conor was the best, and hardest, thing she'd ever done. She'd expected the kids to be upset, but while Grace seemed to accept it and not be too surprised, poor Jack was devastated.

'You deserve happiness. You deserve to be with a man who adores you. James treats you the way you should be treated,' Anita said.

'Conor did love me in the beginning,' Anna reminded her.

Angela snorted. 'The only person Conor has ever adored is himself. If he could have sex with himself, he would.'

'To be fair to him,' Anita said, 'he was mad about Anna when they were going out. He was there for her when she was sick – I'll always like him for that – but when he banjaxed his knee and his football dreams ended, he changed.'

It was true: Conor had been brilliant to her when she'd had glandular fever and been in bed for six months. They were only nineteen and had just moved in together. Conor was training every day, playing with a local club, and hoping to be scouted, and given a contract with an English football club. Every day he had helped her shower, dress, made her breakfast, and when he came back from training, he'd cooked her dinner and looked after her. He had been so patient and caring, it had convinced her she had made the right decision, even though everyone said they were too young to be moving in together – not least her four protective brothers.

But then, just when he'd been approached by Derby County and offered a chance to play for them, he'd injured his knee badly, and after three failed surgeries and hundreds of hours of physio, he'd had to retire from football.

'Everyone has to deal with disappointment in life,' Angela said. 'He just never got over it and still feels sorry for himself. It's ridiculous, and you're a saint for putting up with him for so long.'

Was she a saint? No. She was a woman who had married a man she cared about and felt sorry for. A man who had shown up for her when she was sick. When Conor asked her to marry him, one drunken night shortly after his retirement from football, she'd said yes, even though she'd known in her heart it was the wrong thing to do. But how could she have said no? Conor's dreams had been shattered, and he kept telling her she was the only good thing left in his life. She couldn't kick him when he was down. He had been there for her, and now it was her time to be there for him.

'Anyway, you're done with him now. You've met James, he's mad about you, and your life is about to change,' Anita said.

Anna smiled. 'Yes, it is. Cheers to that.'

'Unfortunately you'll never be totally rid of Conor because of your kids. You'll be co-parenting for some time yet. But you'll figure it out. And don't worry about Jack. He'll come around, eventually,' Angela said. 'Besides, you've given your marriage seventeen years. It's time to stop thinking about Conor and the kids and focus on yourself for once.'

'Absolutely,' Anita said. 'I'm delighted you're so happy, even though I do think you and James are moving in together a bit quickly.'

Angela nodded. 'Agreed, but I suppose she's older and wiser now, so she knows what she's doing this time.'

Anna bristled. She knew her family thought she was moving too fast with James, but she was sure. She was head over heels in love, he would be a brilliant step-dad and she'd be a good step-mum to his daughter. Everything was going to be fine. Jack would come to like James when he got to know him, and Grace got on with everyone.

Angela topped up their glasses. 'Come on, tell us about meeting James's ex-wife. What was she like?'

Anna smiled. 'She was cool, calm and kind of patronizing.'

'She sounds like a bitch,' Anita said, with a grin.

'No, she isn't, she's just . . .' How could Anna explain Ingrid? She wasn't a bitch, she was just all about her job and Bella. She had no interest in Anna except to meet the woman who would be Bella's step-mother.

'She's one of those women who is *soooo busy*. You know, the ones with the big jobs who think no one else's is as important or valuable. She's a bit intimidating, to be honest. I felt like I was in a business meeting. She told me what Bella liked, what her schedule was, how many hours a day she needed to study, and then she said she had to go to a *very important meeting*.'

'Did she ask you anything about yourself, or your kids?' Angela asked.

'Not really. She asked me if I had kids and when I said I had two, she said, "That's a pity. It would be much easier if you didn't." Then she fired questions at me about their ages and if they were academic or not. It felt like a job interview, which, in a weird way, I suppose it was.'

Anita laughed. 'Good luck with her. She sounds like a force to be reckoned with.'

'Well, James did warn me of that,' Anna said. James had described Ingrid as intense and determined, but she hadn't quite appreciated what he'd meant until that conversation.

'Oh, God, one of *those* women.' Angela rolled her eyes. 'It's all about them. They're only interested in people who are more successful than them or useful to them in some way. Spare me!'

'I hope you told her Grace is a genius,' Angela said. 'Let her put that in her pipe and smoke it.'

'I may have mentioned that she's a straight-A student.' Anna grinned.

'And what did she say to that?' Anita asked, as she grabbed another bottle to open.

'That it would be good for Bella, that Bella would benefit from that positive influence, that Bella had the potential to be an A student too . . . It was all about what my kids could do for Bella.'

'I hope for your sake that Bella's more like her dad than her mum,' Anita said, filling their glasses.

Anna shrugged. 'I suppose you'd have to sort of admire

Ingrid. She's so focused on her daughter's well-being and future success that nothing and no one is going to get in her way. Although I do feel sorry for Bella. The pressure she must be under is huge. I did like that Ingrid was nice about James. She said she was glad he'd met me because he was lonely.'

Angela snorted. 'It sounds like James has had the luckiest escape ever. I'd say she had that poor man scheduled to within an inch of his life. They probably even scheduled sex. He must be so relieved to be with someone as lovely as you.'

'What does Ingrid look like?' Anita wanted to know.

'She's small, dark brown hair, attractive, very put together.'

'What do you mean?' Angela asked.

'Smart, her clothes are beautifully tailored.'

'Is she skinny?'

'She's slim, but a bit curvy too.'

'Oh, for God's sake, you're hopeless at describing her. I'm googling her.' Anita took out her phone.

The sisters bent over to look at Ingrid's profile. Angela and Anita provided a running commentary. 'Very conservative . . . boring . . . chunky legs . . . good hair . . . no supermodel . . . cankles . . .'

Anna laughed. She loved her sisters: they were so loyal.

Anita put her phone down. 'Explain to me what James saw in this average-looking woman with a God complex.'

Anna shrugged. 'He says they got on well and they dated. Then Ingrid decided it was time to get married and he sort of went along with it, and then Bella was born and he was head over heels about her so he stayed in the marriage. I can obviously relate to that. Although he said they pretty much lived separate lives for a number of years until Ingrid met Denis and left.'

'Denis the billionaire?' Angela asked.

'Yes. Well, multi-millionaire as opposed to actual billionaire.' Anna grinned.

'We googled him before you came down – he's no looker but he has that millionaire shine, which makes those men attractive. I know it's shallow, but millions in the bank is a turn-on. I'd like to meet a Denis,' Anita said. 'I could get used to a life of luxury.'

'You'd never leave Paul. You're like two peas in a pod,' Anna said.

'I dunno, yachts, penthouses, designer clothes . . . I mean, I could be persuaded,' Anita said, with a laugh.

Anna shook her head. 'Money means nothing. When you meet the right man it's just . . . well, amazing.'

'Oh, God, you're so loved up it's sickening.' Angela playfully punched her sister's arm.

'I'm delighted for you. To Anna and James, may you live happily ever after in your new blended family.'

They all raised their glasses and clinked.

'To my new family,' Anna said.

2

Conor stood, arms crossed, watching his wife struggling with a heavy box. James put down the suitcase he was carrying and went to help her.

'Thank you, darling.' Anna smiled gratefully at him.

James carried the box into the house.

Anna turned to Conor. 'Thanks a lot. I know this isn't easy but standing there glaring at everyone isn't helping.'

'You're the one who wanted to move, not me,' Conor said, shaking his head. 'None of this was my idea. I was perfectly happy. You're the one who walked out on me and forced me and the kids out of our home.'

Anna glanced around to make sure Jack and Grace weren't within earshot. 'You know perfectly well that our marriage was over before I met James. Stop rewriting history. I'm sick of being blamed for everything, Conor. Please try to make an effort for the kids. You're upsetting them.'

'To hell with this.' Conor dumped a plastic box full of Jack's Lego on the path and headed towards his car.

'Dad?' Jack called. 'Where are you going?'

'Sorry, mate, I've got to go. I've a job on,' Conor lied.

'You said you were going to help,' Grace called after her father.

Conor shrugged. 'I brought over loads of your stuff. The home-wrecker can help with the rest.' He pointed to James, who was coming out of the front door.

Grace flushed. James studiously ignored the comment and bent to pick up a desk.

Anna resisted the urge to shout at her husband. She needed

to keep things as calm as possible for the kids. Conor was her past. James was her future. But Conor had a way of getting under her skin. She wanted to laugh at his lie about a job. He hadn't taken on any new mechanic jobs in months. He'd used her meeting James as the perfect excuse to lie on the couch all day watching sport and playing Grand Theft Auto. He was too 'heartbroken' to work, apparently. The scraps he'd bothered to do in the previous three years since he'd been fired by the garage as 'unreliable' had barely kept him off the couch, but now he was doing absolutely nothing. Nothing but wallowing and feeling angry with the world. Their relationship had been rocky for years, but then Anna had met James, which had scuppered it for good. She had spent those eight months since falling for James sleeping on the couch, biting her tongue as Conor slated her. He'd called her a bad mother, a cheat, selfish, uncaring, but she'd bitten her tongue and taken it. After eight long months of nastiness, she and James had decided it was best to move in together so she could leave the toxic environment.

Was she a bad mother? Was she selfish? No. To hell with him. Anna had given Conor almost twenty years of her life and he had sucked her dry. The first year of their marriage had been all right – he was still gutted about his football career and was partying a lot, but then Grace had come along and he was besotted with her. Until he'd realized that babies actually needed to be looked after twenty-four/seven and that his wild-boy lifestyle would have to change. Conor was a man-child and he would never grow up. Not even the arrival of Jack had made him more responsible. In a way, it had made him worse: he went out more, came home later and worked even less.

Anna had tried, she really had, but eventually, she couldn't take it any more. She had been going to leave him anyway, she had already reached that decision, but meeting James had made it a lot easier. She looked over at him, heaving Grace's desk through the front door. At first glance, James wasn't really her type, although Anna wasn't sure she had a type. She'd never had the chance to figure out what it was because she'd met Conor when she was eighteen and had been dazzled by his cheeky charm and good looks. While Conor was all tanned skin, dark hair and brown eyes, James was pale, with sandy hair and blue eyes. But what blue eyes! Gorgeous deep blue ones that had melted Anna's heart. Love, Anna had thought when she'd met James. This is what love feels like.

James caught her eye and smiled at her. She beamed back. 'You okay?' he mouthed.

She nodded. Yes, she was okay. More than okay. She was truly happy for the first time in years.

'*Muuuuum*, why do I have the smallest bedroom?' Jack tugged at her arm.

'It's not small, it's just smaller than the others because the girls need desks in their rooms to study. You can do your homework at the kitchen table, like you always do.'

'It's not fair, just cos I'm the youngest,' Jack grumbled. 'And how come Bella gets the biggest room?'

'Because she's coming into the family on her own, so it's hardest for her. You and Grace have each other so we have to be extra nice to Bella.'

'I don't like her. She's so grumpy.'

'Come on, Jack, you've only met her twice. Give her a chance. We all have to make an effort to get along. It'll be fun having another sister.'

Jack frowned. 'Bella's not my sister. Dad said she's no relation to me and I don't even have to speak to her if I don't want to.'

God, she could kill Conor. 'Bella is your step-sister. We'll all be living together and we need to be nice to each other.'

Jack frowned, his hazel eyes narrowing, and he kicked the ground with his scuffed trainer. 'I've no one to play with. I miss our old house. I've no friends here in this stinky place.'

Anna forced herself to stay positive. 'I know you miss your old friends from the neighbourhood, but you'll make new friends here. And when you go to stay with Dad, his new apartment is near the old house, so you can still see your other friends.'

Jack pulled a face. 'It's not the same. I wish you'd never met James.'

Anna reached over and hugged her son. 'I know it's hard, sweetheart, but it'll all work out, I promise.'

At that moment, a large black Range Rover pulled up outside the house. Anna hugged Jack a little tighter and exhaled deeply. Grace came out to collect another box, but walked over to join them when she saw the car.

The three of them watched as Bella stepped out wearing a white mini-dress that was like a second skin, silver wedge-heeled trainers and huge sunglasses, despite the heavy clouds and lack of sunshine.

'Seriously?' Grace muttered, under her breath.

'Be nice,' Anna whispered.

'That's what she's wearing to lift boxes?' Grace looked down at her tracksuit bottoms and T-shirt.

Anna walked towards the car, plastering a smile on her face. 'Hello, Bella,' she said, putting out her arms to hug her new step-daughter.

Bella shrank back. 'It's even smaller than I remembered.' She pointed at the house.

'We'll make it a lovely home,' Anna said brightly.

James bounded out of the house and rushed to his daughter. 'Hells Bells,' he said, hugging her. Bella squirmed, but he held her tightly and she half smiled.

Ingrid came around from the driver's side, took Anna's hand and crunched it in a firm shake. She was wearing a tailored navy trouser suit, with very high heels, and perfectly applied make-up.

'Hello. God, it took us ages to find this place, it's very far out,' Ingrid noted.

'It's only four miles from the city centre,' James said.

'Miles away from Bella's school, though,' Ingrid replied. 'You'll have to leave early to get her in on time.'

'We will, don't worry,' Anna reassured her.

'Well, I have a conference call at two. James, you need to unload the boot.'

'Okay. Bella, help me out,' James said.

Bella snorted. 'I'm not dragging suitcases around. This is a brand-new dress.'

'Bella, you have to help,' James said.

'Oh, leave her, James,' Ingrid said, waving her hand. 'I don't want her injuring herself carrying those heavy bags.'

James bit his lip and went to the boot. Anna followed him to lend a hand.

Ingrid clicked her keys and the boot opened to reveal six huge designer suitcases and two big boxes.

'That's just some of her clothes, her schoolbooks and study reference books. I've bought two sets of all her books so she doesn't have to carry them between houses. I'll have the rest of her things couriered over later. Don't forget she has a strict study schedule and I want it adhered to.' Ingrid looked at Anna. 'Homework from four till six. Dinner and down time six till seven. Study from seven till nine. Every week night. After that, she can do what she wants.'

Anna nodded. James could sort that out: she wasn't going to force Bella to study for hours every night. There was no need for that crazy schedule. Grace was top of her class and she didn't work that hard. Bella was fourteen, for goodness' sake.

Ingrid glanced down at her huge watch. 'I have to go. Come on, James.'

'You could help, Ingrid. We'd go faster if you did,' he said.

'I hurt my shoulder last week. Denis got this new personal trainer who made me lift weights that were far too heavy.'

Of course she has a personal trainer, Anna thought. Ingrid

lived in a different world. A world where there was someone to do everything for you.

James heaved the last box out of the boot and half dropped it onto the pavement. 'I presume that's the books.'

'Yes, I got her a few extra on exam technique from the UK, which should help her to do better.'

Bella rolled her eyes and muttered, 'For fuck's sake,' under her breath.

This was Tiger Mum on a whole new level. Anna stifled a smile.

'Ingrid, Bella is fourteen,' James reminded his ex-wife.

'Almost fifteen, and it's never too early to start learning good exam techniques. Competition for college places is fierce these days. Bella needs to get ahead of the curve.'

James turned slightly and winked at Bella, who grinned back.

'Right, well, I have to go. Bye, darling, see you on Sunday.' Ingrid kissed Bella's cheek. Without a backward glance, she climbed into her huge car and hurtled out of the estate.

'Wow, she really is formidable,' Anna muttered to James.

'That's one word for her.' James grinned and they cracked up. He put his arm around Anna and kissed her cheek as they watched Ingrid's car whizzing away. 'The day she left me was the best day of my life until I met you, which made that day pale into insignificance,' he whispered into Anna's ear.

'Thank God our exes are gone. Now it's just us.' Anna snuggled into his arms. 'I'm sorry about Conor. He's so impossible at times.'

'Don't worry about it,' James said. 'It's hard on him. I'd be gutted if I lost you.' He kissed her lips.

'Oh, my God, can you snog later, please? I need to unpack,' Bella drawled.

'I'm starving,' Jack shouted from the hall.

'I can't find my laptop,' Grace called, from her open bedroom window.

'I wish they'd all go away so we could go to bed and christen our new home,' James muttered, into Anna's ear.

'Oh, God, me too.' Anna groaned at the thought.

'*Daaaaaad!*' Bella snapped.

James reluctantly pulled back from Anna and began to drag his daughter's suitcases into the house.

3

Grace sorted her room out, tidying everything away neatly. Putting order on her bedroom made her feel like she had some control, when she actually had none. When she'd finished, she went to help Jack. He was sitting in the middle of his room surrounded by clothes, Lego boxes, books, footballs, football annuals, posters, cards and his favourite teddy.

'Do you need help?'

'I don't know where to put everything.' Jack looked as if he was about to cry.

Grace gave him a side hug. 'Come on, I'm brilliant at organizing.'

They began to put away his things, side by side, companionably.

'Grace?'

'Yeah?'

'I want our old life back.'

'It's going to be okay.' Grace tried to comfort her heartbroken brother.

'I wish we didn't have to live here.' Jack fought back tears.

'Me too. It's very far out.'

'I hate James.'

'Ah, Jack, give him a chance. We don't really know him yet.'

'I wish Dad and Mum were together,' he said quietly, as he shoved a stack of T-shirts into a drawer.

Grace paused. Did she wish that? If she was being honest, she didn't really. The last couple of years at home had been pretty grim. Her parents barely spoke to each other. Mum was always at work, taking on extra shifts to pay the mortgage and the bills, and Dad was either flaked out on the couch or off with his friends. Occasionally, if Mum hadn't prepared dinner before she left in the morning, her dad would 'cook' – he'd order chips from the local chippy and throw on some sausages. But it was her mum who checked their homework, helped with school projects, went to parent–teacher meetings, shopped, cooked and cleaned. The only thing her dad did was bring Jack to football. He only did that because he was obsessed with it. That was how he bonded with his son. As for Grace . . . well, he brought her to the movies. Movies he wanted to see but, still, it was nice to spend time with him and he always bought her loads of treats.

But the atmosphere at home had been awful. Her dad had worked less and less, so her mum was always worried about money and tired from working overtime. And then one day Grace noticed her mum was humming in the car and smiling to herself. She was happy and cheerful, and there was a lightness about her that Grace hadn't seen before.

Grace never imagined it was because she'd met someone. She didn't think her mum was the type to have an affair. Anna was so straight and sensible. But then her mum had come home, told Conor she'd met someone and she wanted to break up, and he'd gone nuts. Her mum had stayed for months, trying to get Conor to see that it was best for everyone, and to help Grace and Jack get used to the idea. Grace thought it was pointless, though. Her mum would never convince her dad that breaking up was a good idea, while she and Jack were never going to like moving house and living with another man. That was why Grace had gone to her mum, after yet another shouting match between her mum and dad, and told her that she needed to stop waiting for the right time to move out and just do it. Anna had burst into tears and thrown her arms around Grace. It was awful but necessary: they couldn't go on living the way they were.

Grace was actually relieved when her parents finally broke

up properly because she had hated living in such a tense environment, but she agreed with Jack: she did not want to live here, miles away from school, her friends and her old life. Anna had explained to them that they could only afford a four-bedroom house if they moved further out. Grace was glad to see her mum happy but she hated the move, and she was pretty sure that Bella wouldn't become the sister she'd always wanted either, no matter how many times Anna tried to sell it to her. They'd only met a few times at awkward dinners, with James and Anna trying to be super-happy and positive about them all moving in together. Grace hadn't warmed to Bella at all. She seemed like a spoilt cow, and spent all of her time with her face stuck in her brand-new iPhone.

Grace unpacked Jack's books. Most of them were her old ones – *Harry Potter*, *Percy Jackson*, *Diary of a Wimpy Kid* – and placed them on the shelf in the corner of his bedroom. She felt sorry for her little brother. He was only nine and this was awful for him. He worshipped Conor and thought he was the best dad in the world. He didn't see the irresponsible, selfish side of his dad yet – he was too young. Grace had only noticed it in the last few years, but it had made her think less of him. She hated coming home from school and seeing him on the couch, watching TV and eating junk food. She was embarrassed and annoyed that he wasn't out working like other dads. She wished he'd work harder so her mum could work less.

During one of her parents' recent, late-night arguments, Grace had heard her mum shout, 'Jack was supposed to be a Band-Aid baby, but it didn't bloody work, did it?'

Grace had googled 'Band-Aid baby' – *a child conceived to strengthen a faltering relationship*. Poor Jack, born to fix a marriage that was doomed. Grace felt that, as his older sister, it was up to her to help him cope with all this change. 'Come on, Jack, let's finish your room. Where do you want the Mo Salah poster to go?'

She helped make his room as tidy and cosy as she could.

They could hear music blaring from Bella's next door. As they were putting up Jack's last football poster, Anna called them down for dinner.

The kitchen was humming with activity and delicious smells. Anna was setting the table and James was cooking.

'Wow, Mum, you've unpacked all the kitchen stuff already.' Grace was impressed.

'James helped. We wanted it to be nice for our first dinner.'

Grace had to admit, it felt really homely and warm and inviting. It was a relief not to be having dinner with her parents snapping at each other.

'Why do you have the good plates out?' Jack asked. 'We only use them on Christmas Day.'

Anna smiled. 'Because this is a celebration dinner.'

'Of what?' Jack was still grumpy.

'Of our new home and our new blended family.' Anna kissed his cross face.

James placed a big pot of chicken curry in the middle of the white-and-blue checked tablecloth. 'Thai green chicken curry *à la* James.' He beamed at them.

'Is it spicy? I hate spicy.' Jack was not easily pleased.

'Your mum told me that, Jack, so I made a separate one for you with no chillies.' James put a plate of steaming, chilli-free chicken curry in front of Jack.

Bella shuffled into the room, staring at her phone. She was orange-brown from heavily applied fake tan. Her knuckles were a deep shade of mahogany.

'I made your favourite, Bella.' James smiled at his daughter.

She glanced up from her phone, looked into the pot, and said, 'I'm pescatarian.'

James frowned. 'Since when?'

'Since yesterday.'

'Why?'

'I was going to go vegan, but Saffron said it's way too hard. So then Portia said we should all give up meat and chicken. Fish is, like, a really good source of B-complex vitamins, vitamin A and vitamin D, so it's, like, really healthy.'

James looked deflated. 'I wish you'd told me. I made your favourite curry as a celebration.'

Bella raised her over-plucked eyebrows. 'Celebration of what exactly?'

'Of us being together in our new home.'

'I didn't ask for this and, frankly, I think this whole thing is a nightmare. As far as I'm concerned, this is something to be endured. I don't want a new family. I don't want fake siblings or a fake mother.'

'Me too, me too,' Jack shouted.

Me three, Grace thought.

'Bella!' James's tone was firm. 'Don't be rude. I know this is difficult, but if we all try hard, we can make it work.'

'Your dad's right, Bella. We do appreciate that all of this change isn't easy for you kids, but if we all try to get along, we can have a great time together.' Anna smiled at her.

Bella rolled her eyes, her eyelash extensions fluttering. 'Great time? Are you mad? You and my dad are in your little love bubble and the rest of us just have to do what we're told. While you two hold hands and stare into each other's eyes, like a pair of sappy teenagers, us kids have had to move miles away from our friends and schools, not to mention decent shops, cafés and restaurants, to this suburban dump.'

Yikes. Grace watched her mother's face redden.

'Bella, apologize to Anna,' James snapped.

'For what? Being honest?' Bella snapped back.

Grace was watching her mother closely. She would never, ever have let her or Jack speak to her like this. How was she going to react to her new step-daughter being so rude?

Anna placed a hand on James's arm. 'It's okay, we're all a bit tired and emotional tonight. Let's just eat the delicious meal you prepared.'

James kissed her cheek. 'Thank you, darling.'

Jack made vomiting noises.

Bella sat at the end of the table scrolling through Instagram on her phone.

James handed her a plate of rice and some soy sauce. 'Sorry, but I don't have any fish.'

Bella ignored him.

'Put down your phone now, Bella, please.'

She continued to ignore him.

Anna cleared her throat. 'I understand we all need to get used to each other and that we have different rules, but I do have one rule that is set in stone. No phones at the dinner table.'

Grace held her breath.

Bella didn't look up.

Anna reached across to take the phone from Bella's hand. Bella gripped it. Anna tugged. Bella resisted. A tug-of-war ensued. Grace watched as her mother's jaw set and she ripped the phone from her step-daughter's hand.

Fake-smiling, Anna placed the phone beside her, face down on the table. 'Sorry, Bella, but, as I said, no phones at dinner-time is a rule that will not be broken. It's a break for all of us from technology and a chance to chat together and talk about our day.'

'Well, my day was absolutely shit. How was yours?' Bella folded her arms across her chest.

'Bella, that's enough,' James said.

Grace shovelled chicken into her mouth to stop herself laughing. To be fair, Bella was just saying what all the kids were thinking.

'Shit shit shit,' Jack whooped. 'Yes, my day was shit too.'

'Jack! Stop that.' Anna raised her voice. 'No cursing.'

'Bella cursed.' Jack pointed at her.

'Yes, but you're not to.'

'Why can she say "shit" and I can't?'

'Because it's rude and ignorant to curse,' Anna told him.

'Charming,' Bella drawled.

'Bella, Anna's right,' James said, 'cursing is ignorant. It's just laziness. Use proper words to describe your feelings.'

Bella sat back. 'Okay, then. My day was crap, rotten, manky, pain in the face, awful, depressing, and it all round sucked. I am now living in Kipsville with a step-mother who thinks she can order me about. Sorry, Anna, but I already have a bossy mother and I sure as hell amn't putting up with another.'

With that, Bella snatched her phone and stormed out of the kitchen.

When Anna walked in Grace was hanging fairy-lights around her bedposts. Her room was tidy and organized.

'This looks great, sweetheart, and thanks for helping Jack with his. Dinner was a bit tense, wasn't it?'

Grace wrapped the last section of lights around the left bed-post and looked up. 'I thought you wrestling Bella for her phone was pretty funny.' She grinned.

'I probably should have left it for tonight, but you know how rude I think it is to have phones at the dinner table.'

'I know, Mum, but you're not her mother. I don't want James telling me what to do and Jack doesn't either.'

'I'll try talking to her tomorrow morning when she's calmed down and is more reasonable.'

'She's never going to agree with you, Mum. You're wasting your time. She's spoilt rotten. She's a pain in the arse.'

'Ah, now, Grace, Bella's not used to having siblings or lots of people around. She's used to having her dad to herself when she's with him. For the past three years she's had every second week with him on her own and suddenly she has to share him with all of us. It's hard for her.'

'It's hard for me too, Mum,' Grace grumbled.

'I know, and I'm sorry it's all so . . . well . . . full-on. But it'll settle down. We'll find our rhythm. You do like James, don't you? He's the nicest man I've ever met.'

'He seems nice, but I don't really know him.'

'You'll adore him, Grace. He's really amazing,' Anna gushed.

Grace didn't want to talk about how wonderful James was. She'd had a long day, she was tired and had a headache. She wished they could have rented a smaller place closer to their old lives. Her mum was being needy and wanted Grace to say how brilliant everything was, but it wasn't. She just wanted her to go away now and leave her alone.

'I'm tired, Mum. I'm going to bed now.'

'Okay, darling, sleep well and thank you for all your help.' Anna kissed her daughter's cheek and left the room.

Anna stepped onto the landing and heard music blaring from Bella's room. There was no way Jack would be able to sleep through that racket. She took a deep breath and knocked twice, waited a few seconds and went in.

Bella was dancing around the room in her underwear. She screamed when she saw Anna.

'Sorry! I knocked.'

'Have you heard of privacy?'

Anna held her hands up. 'I did knock, twice. Sorry to give you a fright.'

Bella quickly pulled on her dressing-gown. 'What do you want?'

'I just came to say goodnight and wondered if you could lower your music or maybe put on earphones. Jack's next door and he's trying to get to sleep. I'd really appreciate it.'

Bella looked at her designer watch. 'It's, like, nine o'clock.'

'Yes, he goes to bed at nine.'

'Seriously?'

Anna nodded.

Bella fished out her earphones. 'Jesus, it's like a prison here.'

'Thanks so much. Sleep well.' Anna retreated from the room before she snapped at her step-daughter.

She made her way downstairs wearily. It had been a long and emotional day. James was waiting for her in the lounge. Resting on a large box – their coffee-table hadn't been delivered yet – she saw a candle, two glasses and a bottle of Prosecco.

'I thought we should have our own private celebration.' James handed her a glass. 'To my beautiful, gorgeous, patient Anna. Cheers to our new home and our new life together. I can't wait to spend every day with you.'

Anna melted into his arms. It was worth it – James was worth all the upheaval. They drank, kissed, drank and kissed some more. By the time the bottle was finished they were running up the stairs, giggling like teenagers, pulling each other's clothes off. They collapsed onto their new double bed and quickly got naked. Anna wrapped her legs tightly around James as he entered her.

'Oh, yes . . . yes . . . Oh, God, yes, Anna . . .' he moaned as she licked his ear.

'Mum?'

They froze. Jack was standing in the doorway.

Anna yanked the duvet over their naked bodies. 'What's wrong, pet?'

'I can't sleep. I hate my new room. I miss Dad. I want to sleep with you.'

'Oh, Jesus, not right now,' James croaked.

Anna pulled out from underneath him as he groaned.

'What are you doing?' Jack asked.

'We're just hugging, sweetie,' Anna said. 'Now, can you pass me my dressing-gown? It's hanging on the back of the bath-room door.'

Jack went to fetch it and handed it to her. She quickly covered up. On the other side of the bed, James was pulling on his boxer shorts and T-shirt from the floor.

'Now, snuggle in.' Anna moved back to let her son climb into her side of the bed. Jack climbed in beside her.

'Are you not going to try to settle him back in his own bed?' James asked.

'No. When Jack can't sleep, he always comes to sleep with me. I did it with Grace, too.'

'We never let Bella sleep in our bed. Ingrid heard that it developed neediness. We always settled Bella back in her own bed.'

Anna wasn't surprised to hear that. Ingrid was a frosty cow. 'Well, I always let the kids get in with me if they wake up in the night or can't sleep.'

James sighed and got back into bed. But Jack had taken up all of Anna's side, so she was now on James's. There was little or no room left for him.

He clung to the edge of the bed until Jack's wriggling drove him downstairs onto the sofa. James spent a fitful, uncomfortable first night in his new home.

4

James woke up with a crick in his neck. He'd forgotten to bring his special memory-foam pillow downstairs with him after being caught mid-sex with Anna. It had taken him a while to find a spare duvet among the still-packed boxes and when he went upstairs to get his pillow, Jack was face down, dribbling into it.

Hopefully the boy would stay in his own bed tonight. James didn't fancy another night on the uncomfortable sofa. He ran a hot shower and tried to wash away the tiredness. He had a full day of lectures and three one-on-one tutorials today. He needed to be alert. Trying to get a lecture hall of students enthused about economics required energy and motivation.

He was drying himself when Jack barged in.

'Uhm, I'm in here, Jack. Could you use the other bathroom, please?' James covered himself with his towel.

'What's the big deal? My dad doesn't mind if I pee when he's in the bathroom.' Jack proceeded to wee in front of James, who turned his back.

'Well, I kind of do mind. I think it's something you should do in private.'

'You're so weird.' Jack turned, dripping urine all over the floor. 'And, anyways, I saw your willy last night.' Jack padded out of the en-suite bathroom, leaving a speechless and mortified James to finish drying himself.

Parenting boys was very different from parenting girls, James thought. He'd have to try to get used to it, but they were a different species. Bella would never, in her wildest dreams, come into the bathroom when he was in it. Then again, Bella had never walked in on him and Ingrid having sex. Then again, he hadn't had a very active sex life with Ingrid, so the chance of her walking in on them mid-climax had been slim.

James got dressed and went downstairs. Anna was making school lunches.

'What would you like in your sandwich, Bella?' she asked.

'I want sushi,' Bella said. 'And there's nothing to eat for breakfast,' she added.

'There's cereal and toast. What do you normally have?' Anna asked.

'Natural yogurt, berries and organic muesli.'

'I'll try to pick some up later. But I'm afraid I'm not going to be able to produce sushi for your lunch.'

'Well, I'm not eating a sandwich. I'm not a five-year-old kid.'

James winced. Bella was being rude again. He didn't want another argument, but he needed to step in. 'I usually give Bella vegetable wraps with hummus or sushi for lunch.'

Anna looked at him. 'Well, I don't have any of those. I have multigrain bread, ham and cheese.'

Bella sighed. 'I'll just have a banana and some grapes.'

James went over to Anna. 'Could you pick up some sushi on the way to school? There's a place on the way.'

'James, my first patient is booked for nine thirty. I have to get the kids to two different schools across town. I'm not sure I'll have time for sushi pick-ups.'

'Please, darling, just for today? I just don't want her going to school hungry.'

Anna exhaled. 'Fine.'

James kissed the side of her neck. 'You're an angel. Thanks. I'll make it up to you tonight,' he whispered.

Anna smiled. 'I look forward to it.'

'Have a great day, kids.' James waved cheerily as he made his way to the front door. He stood outside and took a deep breath.

He'd have a quiet word with Bella later. She needed to make an effort with Anna. He wanted Bella to love her as much as he did. He knew she would once she got to know her step-mother better.

Anna knocked on the bathroom door. 'Bella, we have to go. We're all going to be late.'

'I said I'll be down in a minute. Stop harassing me.'

Anna kept her voice steady. 'Well, please hurry up.'

Grace and Jack were in the hall. 'Sorry, guys, Bella's almost ready.'

'She's been in the bathroom for twenty minutes,' Grace grumbled. 'I told you I have an early meeting with my science teacher about my project. I need to be on time, Mum.'

'I know. I'm trying to hurry her up.'

'I'm sick of this.' Jack marched upstairs and kicked the door. 'Hurry up, you're going to make us late. Are you doing a massive poo or what?'

The bathroom door burst open. 'Oh, my actual God, can I not have *any* privacy in this bloody dump?'

Anna and Grace giggled.

'At least he got her out,' Anna murmured.

Bella thumped downstairs, fully made-up. She looked ridiculous, Anna thought. Her eyelashes were caked in mascara and she'd overdone the blusher, too. Grace stood beside her, naturally gorgeous and fresh-looking.

'Right, let's go. I can't be late for work.'

'You should just get a driver to bring us to school like my mum does,' Bella said.

'You have a driver to bring you to school?' Grace was shocked.

'Yeah. My mum is way too busy so George drives me.'

'Cool,' Jack said.

'Well, I'm the driver in this house,' Anna said.

They drove in silence. Traffic was awful. Grace began to fret about being late.

'You're freaking out about being late for a meeting about a science project? I'd want to be late for that,' Bella said.

'Well, I don't. It's kind of a big deal.'

'Since when is a dorky science project a big deal?' Bella snorted.

Anna tensed. 'This one is. Grace has been chosen to represent her school at the Science Expo.'

'What's a Science Expo? Olympics for science geeks?'

'No,' Grace snapped. 'It's a national science competition.'

'That is my idea of hell. I feel sorry for you.'

'I like science,' Grace said.

Bella looked genuinely shocked. 'Seriously?'

'Yeah.'

'No, but for real?'

Grace sighed. 'Yes, Bella, for real.'

'Grace is really good at it. When you're good at something, you tend to like it. What's your favourite subject, Bella?' Anna asked.

'I pretty much hate them all.'

'You must like something. English? PE? Choir?' Anna persisted.

'I like drama.'

No surprise there, Anna thought. 'That's very creative. Are you doing any plays this year?'

'We're doing *Grease* as our school musical.'

'Are you hoping for a good part?' Grace asked.

Bella shrugged. 'I guess. I mean, whatever, but yeah.'

Anna smiled to herself. Bella's feigned nonchalance wasn't fooling anyone. The girl clearly wanted a main part. Anna hoped she'd get one. It might cheer her up and make her less difficult to live with.

Grace and Jack climbed out of the car. Their schools were

on the same road, which from their old house had been a lovely short walk. Still, Anna was sure she'd get used to the commute.

Anna quickly turned the car around and headed towards Bella's school. She tried to make conversation, but Bella stared at her phone and was non-responsive, so she gave up and turned on the radio.

It was eight fifty when she got to the sushi shop. Anna handed Bella five euros and told her to hurry.

'I'm going to need more than this.'

'How much is sushi?'

'I'll need ten euros at least and I want to get a lemon sparkling water, too.'

Anna fished in her bag for more money. She handed Bella twenty euros and got no thanks. She watched through the window as Bella strolled around the shop, looking at the shelves, taking her time. The clock was ticking. Bella was going to be late for school and Anna was going to be late for work. She beeped the horn. Bella ignored her but slowly made her way to the till.

Anna turned to her, when Bella finally climbed back into the car.

'What?'

'Can I get the change?'

Bella handed her two euros.

'Is that it?'

'Yeah, I got some rice cakes too.'

'Fine.' This girl was going to bankrupt her with her expensive tastes.

When they got close to Bella's school, she told Anna to pull over. 'I'll get out here.'

'I can drop you to the door.'

'I'd rather get out here.' Bella undid her seatbelt and jumped out of the car.

'Bye, have a nice day, you're welcome . . .' Anna muttered, as she headed into more traffic on her way to work. The cars coming from Bella's school were all shiny Land Rovers, Mercedes, BMW X5s. Anna's Golf was dwarfed by monster SUVs.

Bella went to St Alban's, considered the best girls' school in the country and way out of Anna's budget. Still, she was glad Grace didn't go there if Bella was an example of the girls who did.

Anna arrived at the surgery with three minutes to spare. She rushed through Reception and into her room. She took off her coat, sanitized her hands and pulled fresh paper down over the examination bed.

She had always loved her job as a practice nurse, and working in this GP clinic was a dream, but in the last few years, when she'd had to take on so much overtime, the shine had begun to wear off. But then James had walked into the surgery just over a year ago and everything had changed.

She remembered him hobbling in on crutches. It hadn't been love at first sight, but she'd found him attractive straight away. His eyes were so blue you couldn't miss them, but it was his personality that she'd really fallen for. He was kind and funny, warm and thoughtful.

While she cleaned, examined, sutured and dressed the wound in his foot – a deep gash he'd got from standing on broken glass – he had chatted away to her. Anna had loved the way he lit up when he talked about his daughter: he was so proud of and affectionate about her. Anna had mentioned in passing chit-chat that she liked yellow tulips. When he came back to have his dressing changed and his wound checked, he'd arrived with a bunch 'to cheer up your room'. Her heart had begun to melt. Over the next few weeks, as James kept coming back, even though his wound was healing perfectly, she had fallen for him, hook, line and sinker. They talked about everything. He'd told her about Ingrid leaving him for Denis two years before. How he had been relieved when she'd left, but sad for Bella. He explained how they had made it work, fifty/fifty custody and always putting Bella first. She'd found herself opening up to him, too. She'd admitted that she was living with Conor but that they were no longer together as a couple and hadn't been intimate for more than two years.

On the sixth appointment, when James's wound had completely healed and he had no excuse to come back, Anna had been bereft. She'd never see him again. She thought James might like her, but she wasn't sure. He was a warm, friendly man but maybe she was imagining their chemistry.

But then, on that last day, he'd turned to her as he was about to leave and said, 'I don't know if this is inappropriate or not, but I'd really like to see you again. I was almost thinking of standing on broken glass on purpose so I could keep coming. Can I take you out to dinner?'

Anna had felt a joy inside that she hadn't felt in for ever. She'd thrown her arms around him and said yes. It was completely spontaneous and very unprofessional of her to hug a patient in her room. 'Just so you know, I don't do this with all my male patients,' she'd said, embarrassed.

'Any chance you could cancel your next patient so we could take this further?' James had asked.

'I really wish I could, but I can't. I'm already behaving very out of character.'

He'd kissed her then, deeply, passionately, and she'd felt her body awaken with a desire she hadn't felt in years. She smiled to remember it.

Now Donna the receptionist came in and handed her a cup of coffee. 'You looked all stressed when you arrived. I thought you'd need that.'

'You're an angel.'

'Mrs Peabody is here, but she can wait until you've had your coffee. I'm dying to hear, how was night one in the love shack?' Donna winked at her.

'It was lovely, although a bit chaotic. We're all just getting used to each other.'

'I had a step-dad I hated. It's not always easy, but I'm sure your kids will get on with James. He seems a lovely bloke, not like the jerk my mother brought home.'

'Did you grow to like your step-dad at all?' Anna was really hoping Donna would say yes.

'Nope. Still hate him.'

'I'm ready, Nurse.' Mrs Peabody banged on the door.

'Good luck with her!' Donna giggled as she left the room.

Anna welcomed Mrs Peabody in. 'How are you today?'

'Well, obviously awful or I wouldn't be here now, would I? Ridiculous question.'

It was going to be a long day. Anna had five smears, six blood tests, two post-op suture removals, five flu vaccinations and an ear syringing booked in. She closed her eyes and thought about getting back into bed tonight with James and finishing what they'd started last night. She just had to keep reminding herself that he made everything worth it.

5

Conor lay on the couch, looking around his poky apartment. He missed his old house. He missed his kids and he missed Anna, even though she'd ruined his life.

How was it fair that she'd had an affair, left him, forced him to sell the house and he was the one who'd ended up in a crappy apartment? And she kept going on about being so generous to him. Generous? She was living in a four-bedroom house – granted, it was miles out, but still – while he was in a shoebox. She banged on about being the one who'd paid the mortgage for the past few years, but so what? Her job paid better than his. Being a mechanic wasn't as lucrative as being a practice nurse. If he'd earned more, he'd have paid the mortgage. Women loved to talk about equal rights, but they didn't like it when it came back and bit them in the arse. He was entitled to half the house, so why was she making out like it was a big deal, like she was being so kind to him?

Anna was such a nag, too. Always on at him to take on more work. He needed his chill-out time, and a chance to go to the gym: it was good for his physical and mental health. And all those arguments about him going out for pints with the lads on the weekend! She really had turned into an old woman. He wouldn't miss her constantly being on his back about work and spending more time with the kids.

Still, though, it was very quiet now. He was hungry and he hadn't made it to the shops yesterday, so there was only cereal to eat and he had no milk left. He heaved himself off the couch. He'd have to get some food in. He'd pick up some frozen pizzas for dinner and see if Pete was free to call over for some beers and a game of Grand Theft Auto.

His phone rang: Mr Holland. He muted it. He'd be banging on about his crappy car not being fixed yet. Conor had been feeling too low to work today. He'd get around to it later. Besides, he had the money from the sale of the house so he was good financially for a while. He deserved a bit of me-time after what his ex had put him through.

Later that day, Pete and Mandy called over. Mandy brought a freshly cooked lasagne and Pete had a six-pack of beers. Conor would have preferred to see just Pete. Mandy was a bit of a handbrake. Still, the lasagne smelt really good and he'd been living on frozen food and takeaways, so he was glad to eat something freshly made. He missed Anna's cooking.

'Cheers, Mandy,' he said, scooping a forkful of lasagne into his mouth.

'If you're anything like Pete in the kitchen, you'd starve.'

Conor grinned. 'Pete's probably better than me. Anna always did the cooking. Before she became a cheating bitch.'

Mandy stared at him. 'Hang on now. Anna was a brilliant wife to you, Conor.'

Conor put down his fork. 'Oh, really? A brilliant wife who had an affair, left me, sold my house and only gives me the kids every second weekend?'

Mandy pursed her lips. 'To be perfectly honest, Conor, I think Anna was a saint to put up with you for so long. I'm sorry, but I'd have kicked you out years ago. Plus, you didn't ask for joint custody. You were happy to have them every second weekend, so don't change history now.'

'Ah, here, Mandy, give the guy a break,' Pete said.

Conor downed his beer. 'All women are ball-breakers. What's

wrong with you? Can a guy not have a bit of fun with his mates without being nagged into an early grave?'

'We have no problem with you having a bit of fun, but you were out nearly every Friday and Saturday night with your mates and, let's be honest here, Anna was the one working day and night to pay the bills. She was the one who deserved a night out.'

'She could have come to the pub with me,' Conor said. 'I asked her to loads of times, but she always said no.'

'Go to the pub and sit with a bunch of lads drinking pints and talking about football and cars? What an offer.' Mandy rolled her eyes.

Conor cracked open another beer and took a long sip, he was beginning to feel a bit woozy and Mandy was really starting to piss him off.

'I was a good husband and a good dad. I was never unfaithful to Anna. I loved her,' he said, slurring his words a little.

Pete raised an eyebrow. Conor prayed that Mandy didn't spot it. For God's sake, you couldn't compare a drunken one-night stand with a full-on affair. Conor had slipped up once – okay, twice – but Anna had had a relationship behind his back. She had betrayed him. She had humiliated him. He'd never have done that to her. He loved her. She was his person. He'd always loved her. Maybe he could have shown it more, but she knew. And she'd broken his heart and didn't care.

'I don't know what to do without her.' Conor's voice caught in his throat. 'We've been together since we were eighteen. I want her back. I want my life back.'

Mandy leant over and patted his hand. 'I know this is hard for you, Conor, but sitting around feeling sorry for yourself isn't going to help. You need to focus on work and the kids. They'll get you through this. It's hard for them, too. You need to try to be positive for them.'

Conor slammed down his beer. 'Why? Why do I have to be

positive when she's ruined our lives? Why do I have to pretend to be happy when I'm miserable?'

'Because you're a father and your kids need their dad. Seeing you moping about, unshaven in a messy apartment, isn't going to help them.'

'She's right, mate,' Pete piped up. 'You need to get yourself together for Grace and Jack.'

'Who's going to be there for me? No one! I have no one.'

'I'm here for you. All the lads are.' Pete slapped him on the shoulder.

'Yeah, but you've all got wives or girlfriends,' Conor grumbled.

'Well, then, we'll just have to find you one,' Pete said. 'Drink up and we'll head out.'

'Head out where?' Mandy wanted to know.

Typical bloody Mandy! She'd ruin their buzz. Conor wanted her to sod off so he could hang out with Pete by himself.

'For a beer or whatever.' Pete shrugged.

'No dodgy nightclubs or strip clubs, please, and don't be late. You're getting up with the kids tomorrow. I need a lie-in.'

Women! Conor thought darkly. Always nagging and wanting things and not letting you have fun. Maybe he was better off without Anna. Maybe he'd meet some amazingly hot super-model type who, unlike his wife, actually wanted to have sex with him.

'Yeah! Let's go, Pete. Let's have some fun.'

They all put on their coats. Mandy headed towards her car as Pete and Conor walked to the local pub to get their order in.

The last thing Conor remembered was doing shots in a strip club. Then the world went blank . . .

'Morning!' a high-pitched voice sang in his ear.

Conor peeled his eyes open. Where was he? He looked left and right and his eyes fell on a framed picture of the kids. Oh,

35

yeah, this was his new apartment. But . . . who was beside him? He peered over as two mascara-smudged eyes stared back at him. He hadn't a clue who owned them.

Conor tried to pull back the memories from last night. He vaguely remembered going to Starbutts, then a hot dancer and then . . . it all got hazy.

'I'd kill for a skinny cappuccino. Would you nip out and get one, please?' the annoying voice said, slicing through Conor's brain.

He pulled himself up into a seated position and looked at the girl beside him. Jesus, she was no hot young thing. She was older than him, her make-up was plastered on and stuck in clumps in the wrinkles around her eyes. Her teeth were stained from smoking. How had he ended up bringing her home? How drunk had he been? Paralytic, clearly.

'Chop-chop.' She clapped her hands. 'I need my caffeine and you owe me for calling me Anna three times last night.'

Conor wanted her out, now. He smiled apologetically. 'Really? Sorry. About that . . . Look, my kids are coming over this morning.' He pointed to the photo frame. 'So, I need you to go.'

Her face darkened. 'Oh, I get it, shag and go. No coffee, no breakfast, you've had your bit of action. Yeah?'

Conor stood up and pulled on his boxer shorts. 'Look, I just have to protect my kids, you know how it is. Can you leave now, please?'

She climbed out of the bed, her huge breasts swaying, and began to get dressed. Conor looked away. He wished with all his heart that it was Anna who was sharing his bed with him. He missed her body and her smell and . . . and everything.

He ushered the woman out of the door. As she was leaving, she turned to him. 'My name, which you've clearly forgotten, is Lisa. You spent most of last night slating your ex-wife to me but shouted her name when we were having sex. You're clearly not over her, but I'm not surprised she left you. You're a self-pitying arse and a rubbish shag, too.'

Conor slammed the door shut and fell back onto the couch. He held his head in his hands and cried. He cried for his old life, the one he hadn't appreciated, the one he hadn't fought for or done enough to save. He cried for his broken marriage, and he cried because he was desperately lonely . . . and hung-over.

6

Bella pressed the button for the penthouse and examined herself in the mirrored walls of the lift as it whizzed her up to the top floor of the Kildare Hotel. She was delighted to be staying with her mum and Denis for the week. Denis's hotel was super-luxurious and the three-bedroom penthouse was amazing. Life in that crappy house with her dad and her step-family was a nightmare. Grace was a dork and Jack was the most annoying kid ever. As for Anna, she followed Bella around the whole bloody time asking her really irritating questions and being over-friendly.

Her dad seemed to think that because he was in love with Anna, Bella was supposed to love her too, and be thrilled to be part of her family. No, thanks, Bella thought. I would never, ever choose to hang out with those people.

The lift doors slid back and Bella stepped into the reception area of the penthouse. Her feet sank into the soft cream carpet. Everything was so nice and plush and perfect. She felt her anxiety disappear. She called her mum. Ingrid appeared, with her phone glued to her ear. She waved, then went back into her home office and shut the door. Bella put her bag into her bedroom and lay down on the king-size bed, luxuriating in the space. She had a crappy single bed in her dad's new house and she hated it.

She picked up the soft cashmere blanket that was lying across the bed and wrapped it around her, breathing in the scent of the huge bouquet of fresh lilies on the chest of drawers. Through the floor-to-ceiling window she could see the rooftops of the city against a crisp blue sky. Bella pulled out her phone and scrolled through Instagram. Saffron had posted a selfie posing in her new Victoria's Secret bikini. She looked amazing. Super-slim and really tanned. Bella looked down at herself. She had her mother's chunky thighs and big bum. She hated them.

Her mum said it was all about tailoring, that you had to wear tailored clothes to hide your flaws and accentuate your good points. But Bella was nearly fifteen. She couldn't wear tailored trousers and skirts. She wanted to wear skinny jeans and mini-dresses and leggings and crop tops, like her friends, but she always felt fat in them. Her mum said that was her shape and there was nothing she could do about it, but Saffron said you could change your shape: you just had to focus. Saffron was always skinny, but now Portia had lost weight and had a hot body, too. Bella was the only one of the three with fat legs.

She'd have to focus on changing her shape. Her new step-sister being so gorgeous didn't help. Tall, skinny and naturally tanned, with huge brown eyes, Grace was stunning. But Bella thought Grace didn't know she was good-looking. She made no effort. She had really boring clothes and didn't even wear make-up. Like, seriously!

Ingrid knocked on the bedroom door and came in. 'Hey, how are you? How was your first week at your dad's?'

Bella sat up against the mounds of soft pillows. 'Horrendous. I don't want to go back, Mum. Please, can I just stay here?'

Ingrid shook her head. 'Sorry, Bella, your dad and I have joint custody, and Denis and I work from London every second week so I'm afraid you have to spend it with your dad.'

'But Anna and her kids are awful. I hate it there.'

'Come on now. Anna seems fine, a bit eager maybe, but nice enough. Your dad seems happy.'

'Yeah, he is. They're all over each other – it's so cringy. Every time you walk into a room they're kissing or hugging. It's really uncomfortable.'

39

Ingrid frowned. 'That sounds a bit over the top. They don't need to shove it in your face. I'll talk to your dad.'

'Thanks, Mum. What's for dinner? Can we order that amazing superfood salad and watch a movie?'

Ingrid looked up from her phone. 'Sorry, darling, Denis and I have a business meeting. Order whatever you like from room service and make sure you tell them what you want for your school lunch tomorrow. The chef can do sushi.'

Bella was disappointed. She wanted to spend time with her mum. She'd been dying to get back to the penthouse and talk to her about her week, but Ingrid was as busy as always.

'Okay. Will you be late? We could have dessert together.'

Ingrid didn't look up from typing. 'I don't know how late we'll be. It's one of Denis's biggest investors, so we'll probably be late-ish. I'll see you for breakfast.'

Bella flicked through the channels. There was nothing on Netflix that she wanted to watch. She'd seen almost every show. Ingrid and Denis were always out at business dinners, so she spent a lot of time watching TV alone. She wandered around the penthouse, picking things up and putting them down. It was so clean and uncluttered, unlike her dad's house, which was crammed full of stuff. Every room there felt cluttered. Anna had even put up a full wall of photos in the kitchen. Lots of her and her kids, but lots of James and Bella too. Some were really embarrassing, of Bella when she was ten and eleven and really ugly, before she discovered fake tan, eyelash extensions and make-up. Bella wanted to take them down, but her dad had said no way. He loved every photo and she wasn't to touch them.

The only good thing was that none of Bella's friends would ever see them because she would *never* invite anyone to that house.

There were only two photos in the penthouse. One was a

black-and-white portrait of her and Ingrid that had been professionally taken. They both looked good in it. The other one was Denis with his daughter, Claire, on Denis's yacht. Thank God Claire had been twenty-two when Ingrid had met Denis, so Bella wasn't forced to live with her. Claire lived in London and in the three years Ingrid and Denis had been together, Bella had only met her six or seven times. Claire was a bit rude to Ingrid, but she was nice to Bella and gave her some of her designer bags when she got bored with them, which was usually after about two weeks of owning them. Ingrid thought Claire was ridiculously spoilt, but Denis adored her and liked spoiling her. He was super-generous to Bella, too. Ingrid tried to stop him sometimes, but Bella loved it.

She used to think Denis was a bit cold and distant, but now she'd experienced Anna following her around, in her face trying to be super-friendly step-mum, she appreciated Denis a lot more. He was always busy so he left her alone most of the time, which she now realized was actually kind of great.

Bella needed to post something on Instagram. She needed to post something cool. She wandered downstairs to the lobby, snuck into the bar without the manager seeing her and posted a photo of herself holding a half-drunk pink cocktail that someone had left behind.

Just an average Sunday night #highlife #cocktailhour #funfunfun

Then she got the lift back up to the empty penthouse and went to bed.

Bella woke to the smell of coffee and freshly baked croissants. She had a long shower in her en-suite bathroom using all the gorgeous Jo Malone products the hotel provided. It was another world from her dad's bathroom, where she now had weirdos beating on the door and shouting to get in while she had to shower quickly with crappy non-branded shower gel.

She put on the fluffy white dressing-gown hanging on the

back of the door and went in to have some breakfast. Ingrid and Denis were sitting opposite each other. Denis was reading the newspaper and Ingrid was on her phone.

'Morning, darling,' Ingrid said. 'Coffee?'

'Yes, please.' Bella sat down and held out a beautiful china cup.

'Hey, Bella, how are you?' Denis glanced up from his paper. But before Bella could answer, he said, 'Christ, Ingrid, did you see what this fool is proposing now? Higher tax rates. As if we're not being fleeced enough. We may end up moving to London full-time. I'm sick of handing over so much of my earnings to an inept government.'

'If you move to London fully, I'm coming too,' Bella said, through a mouthful of warm, buttery croissant.

Ingrid smiled. 'We're not moving anywhere. Denis loves living here. He just likes giving out too. By the way, did you finish that project you were given last week?'

Bella nodded.

'Which important figure of history did you choose?'

'Barbra Streisand.'

Ingrid's coffee cup hung in the air. 'What?'

'She's famous.'

'For singing songs!' Ingrid was incredulous.

'Exactly.'

'Bella, your teacher would expect someone who actually changed the world – Martin Luther King, Nelson Mandela, Rosa Parks, Daniel O'Connell . . . Barbra Streisand is a ridiculous choice.'

Bella bristled. Her mother always criticized her when it came to school and she hated it. She was never smart enough, studious enough or successful enough in exams. 'Well, I think music is important and she has an incredible voice.'

'She has a nice set of pipes on her, but she hardly changed the course of history,' Denis said, from behind the newspaper.

'Really, Bella, I'm disappointed. It was a silly choice. You won't get good marks for it. You need to impress your teachers, not underwhelm them.' Ingrid frowned at her.

Bella felt stung. She'd spent ages on the project and she was pleased with how it had turned out. She loved singing and thought Barbra Streisand had the most incredible voice.

Denis put down the paper and picked up his buzzing phone. 'Right. Let's get a move on. We have that meeting with the bank.'

Ingrid finished her coffee and stood up. 'George will be waiting at eight thirty. Don't be late, Bella. I want you in school on time and I want to see more focus. The next time you get an assignment, talk to me before you choose your subject matter. This is an important year. You need to put your head down and do well in your exams.'

'Listen to your mother,' Denis said, winking at Bella. 'She's the real brains in this relationship. Her financial advice got me the funding for this hotel and the others I've bought since. She's the sharpest accountant I've ever dealt with.'

Ingrid smiled. 'To be fair, you were doing pretty well before you met me, but thanks.'

They left for their meeting and although Bella had only planned to eat half a croissant and a bowl of fruit, she ended up eating two because she was so angry.

She messaged Portia from the back of the Mercedes on her way to school: *Ugh, ate two croissants at breakfast, feel fat and bloated.*

OMG that's a total pig-out. Just skip lunch.

Bella looked at her sushi box. She knew she'd be hungry by lunchtime, but Portia was right: she needed to skip a meal to make up for breakfast or her fat thighs would get fatter. When she got to school, she dumped the sushi box in the bin.

7

Anna dropped Grace and Jack at school and drove to work. She sang along to the radio. Bella was with Ingrid this week and the morning had been smooth and uneventful. No one had argued and they had left on time and . . . she'd had great early-morning sex with James. Jack had actually slept a full night in his own bed. Things were looking up.

She felt lighter than she had in years. Light and happy. The constant pressure of worrying about everything was gone.

For most of her marriage with Conor, it was Anna who had fretted about everything. Now that she was with James, she had gained a new perspective. She had wasted so many years arguing with Conor, begging him to take on more work. She had even threatened to give up nursing and see how he liked having no money, but how could you do that with two kids to look after? It was all very well to want to take a stand, to force your lazy-arse husband to work because you needed more money and because he should want to pitch in and help, but there were two innocent children involved and she didn't want them to miss out on anything. She wanted them to have a decent home, be able to go on school trips and not worry about money.

She knew her breaking up with Conor had been hard on them, but she had partly done it for them. She didn't want them growing into adulthood thinking that her marriage was 'normal'. She wanted Grace to be with a man who worked and helped pay bills and mortgages. She wanted her to be with a man who was a grown-up, a decent partner, a team player. She wanted Jack to grow up to be a responsible adult, who understood that hard work was an important part of life. She wanted him to be a good husband, who shouldered responsibility and was a partner to his wife, not a burden.

James was all those things, he had all of those qualities, and Anna hoped that living with him and seeing how considerate and trustworthy he was would set a good example to her children.

She sang along to the radio as she pulled into the clinic car park.

Chrissie was waiting for her in the little kitchen with coffee and a fresh pastry. Although technically her boss, Chrissie and her husband Tony had been incredibly good friends to Anna through all the years she'd worked at their clinic. They had held her up on days when she was really struggling with life. Chrissie had encouraged her to leave Conor. She was the one who'd said, 'It's not good for your kids to think that this is how relationships are supposed to be. It's not a partnership. It's you carrying everything while he sits back.'

When Anna had met James at the clinic, Chrissie had been delighted for her and told her to go for it. She'd been so supportive and kind. Anna didn't know how she would have got through without Chrissie and Tony's support, not to mention all the extra hours and salary rises they'd given her so she could pay her bills. The clinic had been Anna's safe place when things at home were toxic.

'Yum, thanks.' Anna bit into the cinnamon roll.

'So, how's it all going?' Chrissie beamed at her. 'Are you still in the honeymoon period?'

'Kind of.' Anna smiled. 'James is wonderful, and Grace and Jack are adapting, slowly, but they're trying. Jack actually slept in his own bed all night last night, which was great.'

'And Bella?'

Anna paused. 'Bella's tricky, but she's a teenager and it's hard for her. I'm going to take her out and do something with her, try to connect a bit.'

'Good idea. How's James getting on with your two?'

'Grace would get on with anyone and she's making a real effort for me, bless her, but James is struggling a bit with Jack. You know how Jack is about his dad. He thinks Conor's the Second Coming of Christ. He has him on a pedestal. Jack resents James for what he sees as breaking me and Conor up, although I've explained to him a thousand times that the marriage was over before James came along. It's hard for him, though. He's only a little kid. James knows he has to be patient with him.'

Chrissie sipped her coffee. 'Do the two girls get on? It must be strange to have someone your own age suddenly living in your house.'

'Yeah, it's hard on both of them. They're very different, so I'm not sure how close they'll ever be, but hopefully in time they'll get on. James and I also have different rules around phone use, bedtimes and all that. We need to sort it out.'

'Is he more easy-going about it or are you?' Chrissie asked.

Anna smiled. 'He definitely gives Bella a longer leash than I give my two. She's constantly on her phone, but when I try to talk to him about it, he doesn't seem bothered by it. I did get him to agree to a dinner-table ban, but she's on it at breakfast and she has it in her room at night, which I think is a bad idea.'

'That's going to be difficult,' Chrissie said. 'Different parenting styles are always contentious. When we went on holidays with friends last year, we saw how hard it was. As a couple with no kids we really got a bird's-eye view. One couple were like James, very relaxed about phone use, but the others weren't at all. It caused quite a lot of problems – arguments between the parents and their kids and a lot of tension between the two couples, too. I can't imagine what it's like when that conflict is in your own home.'

'I know,' Anna said, with a sigh. 'But it's important to have boundaries. I mean, I was trying to get Jack back to his own bed the other night and I could hear Bella chatting on her phone. It was two in the morning. That has to be bad for any kid. You and I know the amount of teenage anxiety out there – we have proof of it in the clinic every day. But I just can't get James to see that.'

'To be fair, a lot of my friends' husbands are more laid back about technology use than their wives are. You probably over-worry because of all our teenage patients. But it must be hard when you're not on the same page,' Chrissie said.

'You're right, I probably am over-cautious because of the kids we see coming in here. James is just more laissez-faire. We'll need to meet halfway. He's not a worrier and I, unfortu-nately, am.'

Chrissie smiled. 'That's a good thing. I think it's great to have an optimist about the place. He'll balance you out. It'll be good for you.'

'Well, all the kids will be gone this weekend, so I'll be able to broach the subject with him. We can talk about it calmly and figure out a compromise.'

They had an entirely child-free weekend coming up. Anna would talk to James about it then. They could iron out their little niggles and afterwards, hopefully, spend lots of time in bed having uninterrupted sex. She couldn't wait. James all to herself: it would be absolute bliss.

8

Jack stood at the window, hopping from one leg to the other, staring out. James hoped Conor would be on time to pick up the kids. He was dying for time alone with Anna and a weekend of peace and quiet. Grace was completely independent and polite whenever she was around, but Jack was a bit of a handful. James wasn't used to boys. He'd only had Bella and she'd been easy. When she was nine, if he'd needed an hour to correct student papers, he'd just handed her an iPad and she'd happily play on it for an hour. But Jack never sat still. He was hyper and never stopped running, shouting, jumping or bouncing his football off the walls, furniture and stairs.

'I can't wait to spend the weekend with Dad. He's the best fun. We're going to get pizza and play Fortnite and FIFA, and tomorrow he's taking me to my football game and a movie after. It's going to be epic.'

'That sounds great, Jack,' James said.

'Way more fun than here,' Jack grumbled.

James ignored the dig. A red sports car, which had seen better days, came hurtling down the road.

'It's Dad!' Jack whooped. 'He's here.'

Conor threw the car onto the kerb outside the house. Music blared from the open window. He climbed out, wearing tight jeans and a very tight white T-shirt that showed off his bulging muscles. He was in good shape, James had to admit. He looked down at his own arms. Grading essays didn't get you much muscle. Maybe he should start going to the university gym at lunchtime. He didn't want Anna looking at her ex and comparing the two of them. James reckoned Conor was bloody good in bed – he oozed masculinity and virility. He wondered if he needed to up his game to keep Anna satisfied.

Anna opened the front door. Jack raced out and jumped into his dad's arms.

'Hey, buddy, there's my champ.' Conor swung Jack around.

Grace picked up her backpack and kissed her mother. She waved at James.

'If you need me, call me,' Anna said to the children.

'Why would they need you?' Conor snapped. 'They'll be with me having a brilliant time. Right, kids?'

'Yeah,' Jack shouted.

Grace looked less sure.

'Drop them back for dinner on Sunday, seven o'clock. Okay?'

'Yes, Hitler.' Conor rolled his eyes and Jack giggled.

Anna reached for James's hand and squeezed it.

'Don't let him get to you,' James said.

They watched as the car drove off.

James laid his head on the pillow and grinned. This was what he had missed, him and Anna . . . alone. The only night Jack hadn't insisted on sleeping with Anna because of bad dreams, scared, too hot, too cold . . . they'd tried to have sex, but it had had to be quiet, non-headboard-banging, non-verbal sex because the walls were paper thin and Jack's room was next to theirs.

'That was fantastic.' Anna kissed James and snuggled into his chest.

'What was Conor like in bed?' James asked. He couldn't help himself: the man was a walking muscle machine.

'What?' Anna sat up.

'Well, he's very fit-looking, you know. He was practically exploding out of his T-shirt earlier.'

Anna laughed. 'He may be fit, but Conor's idea of sex is all about his pleasure. He didn't really believe in foreplay. He

49

wanted to be satisfied quickly, with minimum effort, and then he'd go straight to sleep.'

James wanted to punch the air. He knew it was childish for a forty-two-year-old man to be delighted that his partner's younger, fitter ex was bad in bed, but he was absolutely thrilled.

Anna kissed him. 'You, on the other hand, are a very generous and considerate lover.'

James grinned. 'Delighted to hear that.'

'And,' Anna rested her head on his chest, 'the best thing that's ever happened to me. Honestly, I don't think I knew how deeply unhappy I was until you walked into my life.'

James held her closer. 'And I didn't realize how lonely I was or what love really felt like. No disrespect to Ingrid, but we were never in love. We liked each other a lot, got on well and decided to get married. But it was never a big romance. There was never anything like the depth of feelings I have for you.'

Anna kissed him again, more passionately this time. Then she pulled back and asked, 'How was Ingrid in bed?'

'We had scheduled functional sex.' James grinned.

Anna burst out laughing and rolled on top of him. 'How about I show you the opposite of functional?'

James laughed and held her close as they kissed, deeply, and desire flooded his body.

James placed the tray on the coffee-table. Anna looked up from the newspaper. She was wearing a cute pink-and-white-striped pyjama top and shorts. Her hair was messy and she looked younger than thirty-seven – could have passed for twenty-seven. She was gorgeous. James thanked God for giving him this second chance at happiness. Until the day he'd walked into the GP clinic where she worked, he'd thought he was happy. Not high-on-life-happy, more like content. He loved lecturing, he loved economics, as geeky as that made him, and he loved Bella.

He went on occasional set-up dates, but they rarely led to anything.

Then he went to the GP surgery after hurting his foot and the minute Anna had turned and smiled, his heartbeat had quickened. For him it was fireworks at first sight. Even in her nurse's scrubs, of navy trousers and top, she was radiant. Part of him wished he'd met her before Ingrid and before she'd met Conor. That they had been without the baggage of exes and children. Then again, he wouldn't have had Bella and, after all, their baggage and life experience had made them the people they were today.

Having spent eleven years with Ingrid, whose idea of affection was a kiss on the cheek and sex every second Friday night at 9 p.m., James loved how affectionate Anna was. She was always hugging him, kissing him and holding his hand. He felt wanted and cherished. He was exactly where he was meant to be. This woman was his soul-mate.

Anna looked down at the tray. 'Oh, James! All my favourites. *Pain au chocolat* and a cappuccino. You are amazing.'

He sat down beside her and they raised their mugs. 'Cheers to our first weekend alone in our new home.' They clinked.

James picked up the Review section of the newspaper and they sat side by side reading. Anna curled her bare feet under his thigh and all was good with the world.

Later that day, as Anna was in the bath relaxing before they headed out for a romantic dinner, James received a call from Ingrid.

'Hi – is everything okay?' he asked. Ingrid never called him when Bella was with her, unless Bella had forgotten something.

'I need to talk to you about Anna.' Ingrid, as usual, cut straight to the point. She didn't believe in chit-chat and hated small-talk: she considered it a waste of oxygen.

'What about Anna?' James didn't like the sound of this.

'Bella told me you're all over each other like horny teenagers and it's making her uncomfortable.'

James burst out laughing. 'What?'

'It's not funny, James, she's quite put out. You need to remember that this whole blended family living under one roof was your idea, not Bella's. She's been dragged across town to live with three strangers. The last thing she needs is to have to watch you behaving like a randy sixteen-year-old. Save your public displays of affection for the bedroom.'

'Oh, for goodness' sake, stop being so ridiculous. Anna and I aren't having sex on the kitchen counter. We may have kissed or hugged a few times but we're very conscious of the kids. Bella's being dramatic. She's just taking time to settle in.'

'She's a young girl who's been thrown into a situation she never asked for. Just be mindful of that and paw each other when she's not around.'

James rolled his eyes. 'Bella's used to change. Remember when you left me for Denis? That was a pretty big adjustment.' He decided to remind his wife that it was she, not he, who had caused the first upheaval in Bella's life. 'She got used to that and she'll get used to this too. Anna is a beautiful, warm, affection-ate woman, who makes everyone around her feel loved and cared for. Bella is lucky to have her in her life, and her kids are nice too.' Jack was still very much a work-in-progress, but he wasn't giving Ingrid any ammunition.

'I didn't ring for an argument or to dig up the past. Can you please just tone it down in front of Bella? It's not a big ask.'

Ingrid was relentless, and James wanted to get her off the phone. She was ruining his chill-out day with Anna. 'Fine, I'll try to keep my hands off Anna, but it won't be easy.' He grinned as Ingrid sighed.

'Try harder,' she said, and hung up.

He called up to Anna: 'Are you still in the bath, darling?'

'Yes.'

'I might join you!' He peeled off his shirt as he headed for the stairs.

'Come on in.' She giggled.

As James reached the top of the stairs there was a loud thump on the front door. Cursing another interruption, he ran back down, pulling on his shirt.

He opened the door to find Grace and Jack on the doorstep. Conor was behind them.

'Hi – what's going on?' James asked. 'You're twenty-four hours early. Did you get the days mixed up?'

'I'm not feeling well. I don't want to give the kids whatever it is I have, so I'm dropping them off early.'

Conor looked fine to James. In fact, he was the picture of health. James wanted to tell him to take his kids and sod off. They had an arrangement. Conor took the kids every second weekend and Ingrid had Bella every second week. It meant that James and Anna would be alone only every second weekend and it was precious. He wanted and needed more time with Anna. But then he looked down at Jack's unhappy face. 'Well, we're supposed to be going out for dinner.'

'Yeah, I heard. Sorry to ruin your romantic evening.' Conor smirked at James, who had a strong urge to punch him.

'I see. Well, maybe if you feel better tomorrow you can take them for lunch,' he said, through gritted teeth.

'Maybe.' Conor backed down the driveway. 'But I wouldn't count on it.'

James refrained from shouting, 'You've ruined my night, you selfish prick.'

He held the door open and Jack shuffled past followed by Grace, who was looking at her phone.

James went up to tell Anna. She jumped out of the bath, covered with bubbles. 'Sick, my arse. He's such a selfish git. I bet he just wants to go out with his mates and is looking for an excuse. He couldn't even stay in for one Saturday night with his own kids.'

James decided not to tell her that he strongly suspected Conor had done it to ruin their dinner plan. She didn't need to be more upset. Instead, he handed her a towel. Anna dried herself roughly and threw on her dressing-gown.

'I bet Jack's upset. Is he?'

'He didn't say anything, but he seemed a bit down. Why don't we get them pizza and Grace can babysit Jack while we go out?'

Anna frowned. 'There's no way I can leave them alone now. Conor's let them down and they need me. I'll cook them something nice and we can watch a movie together.'

James sighed. 'Right. I'd better cancel the restaurant booking.'

Anna reached out to him. 'Sorry, darling. We can try again in two weeks' time.'

'Sure.' James tried to hide his disappointment. He loved that she was a good mother and that she was so caring of her kids, but he had really been looking forward to a romantic night out. He was being selfish. He shook himself and went downstairs to talk to Jack.

The boy was kicking a ball against the freshly painted kitchen cabinets. James winced as the doors shook. 'Your mum will be down in a minute. She's going to cook something nice and we can all watch a film.'

'I don't want to watch a stupid film with you. I want my dad.'

'I know, Jack, but he's not well, so . . .'

Jack walloped the ball against the door again.

'Can you go easy with the ball there, Jack?' James tried to keep his voice light. 'I understand you're disappointed, but we can still have a nice night.'

Jack kicked the ball even harder. 'You don't understand anything. You're stupid and annoying.'

BANG. The ball went higher this time and knocked against a glass bowl on the counter. It teetered, wobbled, then fell and smashed into a thousand pieces on the tiled floor.

'For Christ's sake, Jack, stop kicking the bloody ball!' James shouted.

He bent down to scoop up the shards of glass.

Grace appeared at the door. 'You don't have to shout at him. He's only nine,' she said.

James cut his hand on a piece of glass. 'I'd asked him calmly several times to stop, but he didn't listen and now there's glass everywhere.'

Anna came in. 'What's going on?'

'Nothing. It's fine.' James grabbed a brush and swept the remaining glass into a dustpan.

'James shouted at me and cursed at me,' Jack announced.

Anna looked at James. 'What?'

'No, I . . . It was . . . He wouldn't stop kicking the ball and I was worried something would break, and it did.'

'He said, *For Christ's sake, Jack*,' Jack said.

'He's nine and he's upset,' Anna muttered, glaring at James.

'I was worried that he'd break something and, well . . .' He held up a large chunk of glass.

'It's just a bowl,' Anna said.

'He could have hurt himself,' James said.

Anna bit her lower lip and turned to the kids. 'Why don't we leave James to clear up? I don't want you to cut yourselves. Let's pop down to the shops to get treats for the movie.'

Anna didn't look back as she led her kids out of the house. James stared at his cut hand and sighed.

9

Anna held out her cup while her younger sister poured more tea into it. Her older sister, Anita, was painting her nails at the kitchen table.

'Do you have to do that now? It's stinking out my whole kitchen,' Angela grumbled.

'Yes, I do actually. I'm going out with Paul's new boss and his much younger wife. I need to make an effort.' Anita skilfully applied nail polish to her left hand. 'I even bought a new black dress. Paul said it's very sexy. He must be desperate for sex because it's far from sexy. It's big and baggy to hide the extra stone I've put on.'

Anna and Angela laughed.

'Poor Paul. Just shag him and put him out of his misery.' Anthony, their oldest brother, piped up from the fridge, where he was rummaging around for something to eat.

'There's nothing decent in there. I've biscuits here,' Angela called over to him.

'Paul knows that the deal is no sex until he gives up smoking.' Anita shook the nail-polish bottle.

'But he may never be able to give up cigarettes,' Angela said.

Anita grinned. 'Here's hoping.'

'Jesus, women!' Anthony groaned.

The sisters cracked up.

'But don't you miss it?' Anna asked.

'Sex?' Anita asked. 'Not really. Sex with Paul was always a bit wham-bam-thank-you-ma'am. I've always preferred cuddles.'

'And what about what Paul likes? Does he not get any say?' Anthony defended his brother-in-law.

Anita turned to him. 'He can have lots of sex when he gives up the cigs. Well, not lots, but some.'

'I love sex. Raunchy, sexy sex,' Anna said.

'Jesus, I'm not able for this.' Anthony pulled the lid off a yogurt and began to eat it.

'Did you actually just say "sexy sex"?' Angela snorted.

'Look at you, all loved up and ripping the clothes off James. Enjoy it while it lasts.' Anita grinned across the table at her.

'Are you at it all the time?' Angela wanted to know.

'Whenever we can,' Anna admitted. 'Although it's harder lately with the kids around.'

'Ladies, less detail, please,' Anthony remonstrated.

'Shut up! You might learn something,' Anita said.

'Maria and I are very happy in the bedroom, thank you very much,' he replied.

Angela sighed. 'I remember the days when I wanted to rip Tom's clothes off. Now I mostly want to punch him in the face. Even the way he chews his food irritates me.'

Anita laughed so hard she missed her nail and painted her hand instead.

'Angela! Tom's great,' Anna said.

'I know he is, and we do have good sex. He's just annoying me at the moment because he said he'd finish tiling the bathroom. It's been three weeks and he still hasn't. It's like living in a student squat upstairs.'

Anthony scraped the bottom of his yogurt pot. 'Women are mental. You want to punch him for chewing loudly.'

'Yeah, I do. He chomps.'

'To be fair, he does chew loudly,' Anna said.

'Jesus!' Anthony shook his head. 'It's not easy being a man, these days.'

'Go on anyway. How's it all going with James, apart from the great sex?' Anita asked.

Anna put down her teacup. 'Good. We had a tricky weekend, though. Conor dropped the kids home a day early.'

'Pillock.'

'Dick.'

'He's doing it to wreck your head. Do you want me to have a word with him?' Anthony offered.

Anna smiled at her protective older brother. Anthony was always looking out for his sisters. He was the rock of the family. Like Anna, he had married his childhood sweetheart. Unlike Anna, his marriage had turned out well. He was still happily married after twenty-five years, and they all adored his wife, Maria.

'No, but thanks. Not yet anyway. So, my romantic dinner date with James was scuppered. He said he didn't mind, but I could see he did. Moving in together with our kids has definitely been more of an adjustment than I'd thought.'

'What did you expect, Anna? Everyone in that house has had their lives upended. It was never going to be easy.' Anita blew on her nails to dry them.

Anna bristled. 'I know that. I'm not completely delusional, but I thought . . . well, I guess I imagined it'd be less tricky.'

'It'll get easier. It's very early days.' Angela tried to reassure her.

'So, why did Conor drop them home early?' Anthony asked.

'He said he wasn't feeling well, but I saw him later on Mandy's Instagram in a bar. He'll never change.'

'He did it to interrupt your weekend alone with James. I know how blokes' minds work,' Anthony said.

'Thank God you left him. You were too good to him.' Anita wriggled her wet nails.

'How were the kids about it all?' Angela asked.

'Jack was gutted. He'd wanted to spend the whole weekend

with Conor – you know how he worships him. Grace was quiet, but I think she was okay.'

'So you stayed in with the kids instead of going out to dinner?' Angela shook a few more chocolate digestives onto the plate in the middle of the table.

Anna nodded. 'I couldn't leave them and go to dinner. Jack was really upset. He insisted on sleeping with me, so James had to sleep on the couch.'

Angela held up her half-eaten biscuit. 'Hang on a second. Your romantic dinner was ruined and then James got shoved onto the couch? That's not fair.'

Anna frowned. 'What was I supposed to do? My nine-year-old son was crying. I can't just dump him in his bed and let him cry himself to sleep. He's confused and upset. He needs to feel secure and loved during all this upheaval.'

'He also needs boundaries, Anna,' Anita said. 'If you let him sleep in your bed, you'll never get him out. Settle him in his own bed, but don't let him kick James out.'

'Having Jack in your bed is going to be some passion-killer.' Angela sipped her tea.

'They're right. James needs to sleep in his own bed in his own house,' Anthony said. 'Make sure it doesn't become a habit. Maria was too soft on our Ellen and she was in our bed every other night for years.'

Anna rubbed her eyes. She was tired – sharing a bed with Jack wasn't easy. He wriggled around and made it difficult to sleep, but how could she not let him stay with her when he was so upset?

She decided not to tell her sisters and brother that Jack had been in her bed five times in the past week. It was only temporary – he just needed reassurance. She was sure he'd settle soon.

'How are James and Jack getting on?' Angela asked. 'I'm sure the bed-hopping can't be good for their relationship.'

Anna fidgeted with her phone. 'Well, Jack is acting up a bit and James isn't used to boys. He's used to a daughter who spends her whole time on social media. I think Jack's energy is a bit overwhelming for him.'

'Sure that kid is like something on speed,' Angela said.

'Ah, he's just full of beans,' Anthony defended his nephew. 'Boys like to be constantly on the go.'

'Not easy for James, though,' Anita said, 'if he's used to a quiet, peaceful house. He's in for a big change.'

'I was thinking maybe they could do something together to bond, like maybe go to the park and play football or something. I was going to take the girls out and try to get to know Bella. She's not the easiest kid to get along with – and the fake tan, oh, my God! Grace doesn't wear it so I'm not used to it. It's ruined my towels and sheets.'

'Don't talk to me about that muck,' Anthony said. 'Ellen and Katie are constantly putting it on. It stinks – and they look like they've been rolled in cheesy Doritos.'

They all laughed.

Then Anna asked the question to which she needed an answer. 'We're struggling a bit on the boundaries issue. Like, what do we do when it comes to disciplining each other's children? James gave out to Jack last night for breaking a bowl, and I didn't like it. But if I don't want him to discipline Jack, I can't take Bella's phone away from her at mealtimes, can I?'

'Good luck with that! It's a minefield,' Anita said.

'I wouldn't tolerate anyone other than me giving out to or criticizing my kids,' Angela said.

'Jesus, I'd hand mine over to anyone who offered.' Anthony chuckled. 'I'd love someone else to deal with two hormonal teenage girls.'

'I think if a kid, any kid, is living under your roof, you have the right to set rules and have boundaries,' Angela said. 'Sure if everyone living under one roof had different rules life would be chaotic. You and James need to be on the same page if this is going to work. The kids need to see a united front.'

'Yeah, but you have to tread softly. You wouldn't like some random woman telling your kids off, Angela,' her sister said.

'I'm not some random woman,' Anna reminded them.

'Well, to whatshername with the cankles, you are.'

'Ingrid.'

'Does she have cankles?' Anthony asked.

'Yeah and chunky thighs. James traded up with our Anna,' Angela said.

'I'd take cankles over chunky thighs,' Anthony said.

'Oi, I have chunky thighs,' Anita said.

'I'm saying nothing.' Anthony held up his hands.

Anita punched his shoulder. 'Anyway, Anna, to Ingrid, you're a virtual stranger disciplining her kid. Just like James is a virtual stranger disciplining his kids to Conor. No one likes that, but you're going to have to figure out a way to make it work.'

'It was never going to be easy, Anna. We told you that,' Angela reminded her. 'We also told you to take more time before moving in together.'

Anna didn't want a lecture from her younger sister. 'It's fine. These are just teething problems. James and I love each other. We'll figure it all out. It's early days.'

Anna pushed her concerns to the back of her mind. If they all made an effort, her blended family could work. It was never going to be easy, but the good things in life were worth fighting for, and Anna was a fighter.

10

Grace bit her nails as her mum drove to the print shop. She had two weeks to perfect her project before having to present it to her three science teachers. She'd been thrilled when she'd been chosen to represent the school at the Science Expo competition, but now she was more nervous and stressed than excited. If she won the Science Expo, she'd go forward to the Global Science Fair in America. Mr Kettering, one of her science teachers, thought she had a really good chance with her project to neutralize the lactose in milk using a specially made capsule, but what if she failed? What if they didn't think it was good enough? What if she let everyone down?

Anna reached over and pulled Grace's hand away from her mouth. She hadn't even realized she was chewing her nails. 'Grace, I don't want you to get too stressed about this project. If it's too much, you can back out.'

Back out? What was she talking about? There was no way Grace could back out. Her mum just didn't get it. This was a huge opportunity, and if she did well, she could get a scholarship to a university in America. Previous winners had gone to the best universities all over the world. As soon as she had finished school, in three years' time, she was getting the hell away from here. She was sick of looking out for Jack and worrying about her mum and her dad all the time. She wanted to be free of all the responsibility and immerse herself in science. No baggage, no history. Just Grace.

'I'm worried it's all getting a bit much for you,' Anna said.

'It's fine, Mum. It's all under control. I just need ink to print so I can work on it all day.'

'Actually, Grace, I want you to take the afternoon off.'

Grace stared at her. 'What? No way, I can't.'

Anna pulled into the car park outside the shopping centre where the print shop was. 'Grace, I'm taking you and Bella out for a treat.'

'What treat?'

'Well, I thought a manicure would be something we could all enjoy.'

'You mean Bella would enjoy.'

'Well, yes, but it'll be good for you too. It'll stop you biting your nails.'

'I don't want to go for a stupid manicure! I'm too busy. You go with Bella on your own.'

Anna sighed. 'I wanted the three of us to spend some quality time together. I think we need to make an effort to get to know Bella better. You're kind of sisters now and I want you two to be friends.'

Grace turned to face her mother. 'Let's be clear. Bella and I are not sisters in any way whatsoever. If you want to get to know her better for James's sake, fine, but I don't. She is a random person who has been dumped into my life. I didn't choose her and I don't want, or need, to be friends with her. How would you like it if I came home with an annoying rude woman the same age as you and said, "This is Jane. You'll be living together from now on and you must be sisters and best friends."'

'I understand that this is difficult, and you're right, it's particularly hard on you having a girl the same age as you living with us. But James is so lovely and I'm sure Bella is underneath it all. She's probably just being a bit prickly because she's struggling with all the upheaval, too. We need to be kind.'

'Knock yourself out, Mum. Be as kind as you like – go for a full spa day with Bella – but I want to study.' Grace snapped off her seatbelt and headed to the print shop.

Anna rushed after her. 'Grace, please. I promise it won't be more than an hour out of your day. Can you just do this one thing for me? Please, love?'

Grace knew her mother would keep asking until she gave in. Anna was relentless when she wanted you to do something. In a small way, Grace did want to try to get to know Bella better: she wanted to see if she really was just a spoilt cow or if there was a nice side to her. Also, Grace was glad that her mum was happy with James: she deserved it.

'Okay, one hour and no more. I'm doing this for you, so you owe me.'

Anna threw her arms around Grace and hugged her. 'Thank you, my gorgeous, generous girl. What did I do to deserve a daughter like you?' She covered Grace's face with kisses. 'I love you, I love you, I love you.'

Grace laughed and pushed her away. It was great to see her mum so playful again. She always used to be busy working, and at the weekends she was doing cleaning, laundry, grocery shopping and cooking batches of food for their week's dinners. She also spent a lot of time arguing with Conor. Grace loved seeing this fun side of her mother – she was like a different person with James, lighter, more carefree and just . . . happier.

She hated losing study time, but maybe if they tried with Bella, she'd stop being such a pain and things at home would be easier. Grace would welcome that – she wanted peace and quiet. She'd lived with enough conflict for a lifetime.

Ingrid kissed Bella's cheek. 'See you next week. Study hard.'

Bella rolled her eyes and climbed out of the car. She pulled her monogrammed Louis Vuitton suitcase, a Christmas gift from Denis, up the short path to the front door. Yippee, another week with her freak step-family.

She rang the bell. No answer. She rang again.

'Who are you?' Jack's voice said, through the letterbox.

'It's Bella. Open the door. I forgot my keys.'

64

'How do I know it's really you and not some paedophile who wants to kidnap me, take me away and sell me as a slave?'

'What are you on about?'

'Mum said I wasn't allowed to open the door to anyone, ever. She said there are bad people out there who want to kidnap kids. She said they pretend to be people you know and they offer you chocolate and sweets or ask you to help them look for their dog or cat and then throw you in the back of a van and abduct you.'

'I don't have any sweets or chocolate, I don't have a van, and I don't want you to help me look for any animal. I live in this house, you idiot. Open the bloody door.'

'You could be a bad person pretending to be Bella.'

Bella put her hand on the doorbell and rang it for a good twenty seconds. She heard her dad shouting, 'Who is it, Jack?'

'It's someone who says she's Bella, but I don't believe her.'

'Dad!' Bella shouted. 'Open the door.'

'I can't. I'm up on a stepladder, painting.'

'Well, tell this thick fool of a child to open it.'

She could hear Jack shouting, 'Mum said I'm not allowed to open the door to anyone if I'm on my own.'

'But you're not on your own. I'm here and it's Bella.' James sounded exasperated. 'My hands are full here, Jack. Can you please open the door?'

Jack snorted. 'You're not going to be able to fight off kidnappers if you're up a ladder.'

Bella punched the door. 'It's starting to rain. Open the door or I'll kick the fucking thing down!'

'Bella said the F-word,' Jack shouted.

'Language, Bella,' James called.

'Are you kidding me?' Bella screeched. 'I'm standing in the rain being refused entry to my own bloody house.'

She heard movement on the other side.

'Don't open it,' Jack said.

'Move aside, Jack. I'm letting my daughter in.'

The door opened and Bella stormed in, rolling her suitcase over James's foot.

'Ouch.' James winced.

Bella ignored him and glared at Jack. 'You are the most annoying kid I have ever met. I hope someone does kidnap you.'

'Ah, now, Bella, there's no need for that,' James said.

'Oh, yeah?' Jack shouted. 'Well, I hope you die and get eaten by worms and spiders and cockroaches and —'

'That's enough, you two.' James raised his voice. 'Come on now, be nice to each other. We're family.'

Bella snorted. 'That halfwit is not related to me in any way.'

'Yeah, well, I've got a sister and she's nice and you're mean and grumpy, and my mum says you're spoilt and rude.'

The front door opened behind them and Grace and Anna walked in, smiling. Their faces dropped when they saw the scene in front of them.

'Your mother said that about me, did she?' Bella said, glaring at Anna.

'Said what?' Anna said, glancing at Jack.

'That I'm spoilt and rude,' Bella said. 'Charming to hear you're talking about me behind my back, Anna, when you're doing all the super-friendly step-mother act to my face.'

Anna's eyes widened. 'I didn't say that about you. Jack, you shouldn't say things like that. You'll upset Bella.'

Jack shrugged. 'Well, she is rude. She said the F-word to me just now.'

'What?' Anna said. 'For goodness' sake, Bella, he's only nine. Tone down your language.'

'He locked me out!' Bella shouted. 'He's a bloody nightmare to share a house with.'

Anna took a deep breath. 'These new living arrangements are hard on everyone. James and I appreciate that, but we wouldn't have moved everyone in together if we didn't feel it was worth it. Come on, guys, with your help we can make this a happy home.'

James stepped forward and put his arm around Anna's shoulders. 'Anna's right. We know it's a big change for you all. We're not saying you have to become best friends overnight. But we do want everyone to make an effort, and if we all try our best, it'll work.'

Bella looked at her dad. He was clearly desperate for this crappy situation to work, but it just didn't feel like something that ever could. They were all so different. She could see how much he loved Anna. She'd never realized how lonely he was until he'd fallen for her. She wanted her dad to be happy – he deserved it. She just wished she didn't have to be dragged into his new romance.

Anna placed her hand on Bella's arm. She tried not to pull away, although she wanted to. 'Bella, I really want to get to know you better and for us to be friends so we can all live together amicably. I'm not trying to be your mum, but I do want to create a happy home for all of us.'

'Fine,' Bella said. 'Whatever.' She pulled away.

'Great. I'm going to take you and Grace for a manicure later today. I thought it would be good for us three to spend some time together. Are you free?'

Bella sighed deeply. Anna reminded her of a pleading puppy and her dad was looking equally desperate. She didn't have the heart to refuse the stupid manicure. 'Okay.'

Anna came downstairs and sat beside James at the kitchen table. 'Jack's really upset. He said Bella was mean to him.'

James sipped his coffee. 'There were two of them in it.'

'Bella's nearly six years older than him.'

James held up his hands. 'I understand, but he was refusing to let her into her own house.'

'He was just following my rules.'

'Come on, Anna, he knew it was Bella. He was doing it just to annoy her.'

Anna didn't want to argue with James. She felt it was more important than ever for them to try to spend the day bonding with their step-children. 'I'm taking the girls out at three p.m. for an hour. How about you and Jack go to the park and have a kick about?'

James stared at her. 'Football isn't my strong point. Could he help me finish painting the hall ceiling?'

Anna chewed her bottom lip. Was he that clueless? Jack with fresh paint and a brush would equal carnage. Damnit, she really wanted them to do something today as a bonding exercise. 'Okay, then. How about the zoo or a museum or . . . or . . .'

James reached for her hand. 'I have an idea. How about we all go to Trinity and show the kids around? Grace could have a look at the science department, Jack could run around the playing fields and Bella could take selfies with the statues.'

Anna laughed.

'And then we could go for lunch in town together.'

Anna beamed at him. 'I love that idea. You're very clever, Professor.' She kissed him.

'Get a room,' Bella drawled, from the kitchen door.

James pulled back, making Anna feel awkward, like a teenager whose mother had just caught her snogging a boy.

'Dad, can you give me a lift to town? Change of plan. I'm meeting Saffron and Portia.'

'But you said you'd go out with Anna and Grace,' James said.

'I did, but my friends are going shopping so I'd rather meet them.'

'Well, we've had a change of plan, too,' James said. 'Forget the manicure. Anna has suggested that we have a family day instead.'

Anna put on her cheeriest voice. 'We're going to visit Trinity. Grace and Jack have never been. Your dad's going to show us around. I thought it'd be fun.'

Bella stared at her blankly. 'No, thanks. I'd prefer to meet my friends. You guys go ahead without me.'

Part of Anna wanted to say, 'Okay,' but she had to try to get to know her step-daughter. 'It'll be nice for us to spend the day together.'

'I have to spend every second week here. Why do I need any more time with you or your kids?'

'Bella, Anna's making an effort and you need to make one too. We're going to Trinity today as a family.' James's tone was firm.

'I have a family and I didn't ask for a step-family, so why should I be forced to do stuff I don't want to do with people I barely know?'

'Because that's how you'll get to know Anna, Jack and Grace. We all need to get to know each other better. I'll drop you to see your friends afterwards, okay? That's fair, isn't it?'

'Come on, Bella, it'll be fun.' Anna tried to encourage her.

Jack came into the kitchen and thankfully interrupted them. 'I'm starving.'

'Hey, Jack,' James tried to cajole him, 'we're all going to visit Trinity College today. You can check out the gym and the pool and the sports fields.'

Jack stopped dead in his tracks. He looked at Anna. 'No way. I don't want to go to some boring college.'

Anna bent down and looked directly into his eyes. 'Jack, James has kindly offered to show us around the campus where he works. It'll be really cool to see it.'

'No, it won't,' Bella and Jack said, at exactly the same moment.

'See?' Anna said, with a fake wide smile. 'You're bonding already.'

11

As they walked through the front gate of Trinity, James tried to engage the children with some history about the university he loved. 'When Queen Elizabeth the First was on the throne of England she wanted to strengthen England's control over Ireland, so Trinity College Dublin was granted a royal charter to open, in the 1590s.'

'Can I go now? I've heard all this before,' Bella said.

'No, Bella, this is a family outing,' James reminded her.

'I'm bored,' Jack said, bouncing the football that Anna had allowed him to bring, despite James's protests.

'Can we see the science department now?' Grace asked.

'Absolutely. Let's just walk across the front square and I can tell you a little more about the history of the university.'

Anna linked James's arm as they moved over the cobbles. 'Maybe keep the history part short and sweet. Jack has the attention span of a gnat,' she whispered.

Maybe he needs to bounce balls less and listen more, James mused silently.

'Okay, so a lot of very famous people have gone to Trinity College.'

'Any footballers?' Jack asked.

'Not that I know of, but Wolfe Tone, the leader of the 1798 rebellion against British rule, came here, and Oscar Wilde, the writer and playwright and –'

'Never heard of them,' Jack huffed.

'Well, Ireland's two female presidents, Mary Robinson and Mary McAleese, studied here. Maybe Bella or Grace will be the next president of Ireland.'

'Or Jack,' Anna added.

'Yes, of course, or Jack.'

'I don't want to be a boring president. I want to play for Liverpool. My dad nearly played for Derby and I bet he would have been transferred to Liverpool but he bust his knee.'

Liverpool, my arse, James thought. 'That's bad luck,' was what he said. 'Trinity has a good football team. If you come here, you could play for them, Jack.'

'I've never heard of them,' Jack said.

Bella took a selfie and began typing into her phone.

James turned his attention to Grace. 'That's where I roomed with my best mate when I lived on campus. It's great fun. You get to live right in the centre of town.'

'That would be cool,' Grace said.

James spotted Jarlath Hogan and waved him over.

'Hello, James, having a family day out? I didn't realize you had three children.'

'They're not all mine – well, they are my family . . .' James fumbled, trying to find the right words to be sensitive to everyone's feelings. 'Bella is my daughter and this is my partner Anna and her two children, my step-children, Grace and Jack.'

'Lovely to meet you.' Anna shook his hand.

'Guys, this is my colleague, Jarlath. He's head of genetics and microbiology. I'm giving them a tour of Trinity,' James explained.

'Lovely. Do we have anyone interested in the sciences here?' Jarlath asked.

'Actually, Grace is going to be representing her school at the Science Expo. Her project is really something.'

'Really? Good for you, Grace. Tell me more?'

Grace filled Jarlath in.

'Wow! That sounds absolutely fantastic.' Jarlath was clearly impressed. 'I think you have a very good chance of winning. That idea could really take off.'

'She's passionate about science,' Anna said.

'I can see that. Maybe we could get you in to meet some of our students and chat to them about your project.'

'That would be great,' James enthused. He felt really proud of his step-daughter.

'Seriously?' Grace's face flushed.

'Absolutely. You're inspirational.'

'I'd love that.'

'It's so kind of you, thank you.' Anna beamed at him.

'Dad!' Bella snapped. 'I'm meeting the girls soon, we need to go.'

James held up his hand. 'In a minute, Bella. That sounds great, Jarlath. I think Grace has a big future in science. I'll email you her details and we can set something up.'

'Sounds good. It was lovely to meet you, Grace. I can't wait to hear more about the project and watch your star rise. Bye, everyone.'

James put his arm around Grace. 'I think you have a fan there. Jarlath is not easy to impress, so well done.'

Grace blushed. 'Thanks, I'm blown away.'

Anna linked James's other arm. 'Thanks for bringing up Grace's project. That was brilliant of you.'

'When you've all finished your love-in, can we get the hell out of here?' Bella scowled.

'Yeah, I'm bored and hungry,' Jack complained.

'In a minute. I want Grace, and all of you, to see the Science Gallery.'

'More science? Are you joking?'

'Yes, Bella, and, no, I'm not. It'll do you good to see what the students here have created. It's pretty cool.'

James led the way, chatting to Anna and Grace, while Bella and Jack shuffled behind.

Anna looked back, then waited and walked with Jack and Bella.

'So, Grace loves science and Jack loves football, what's your passion, Bella? What do you love to do?' she asked her step-daughter.

'Shop.' Bella smirked.

'Apart from shopping?'

The teenager shrugged. 'Mum's always on at me to study harder and be successful like her, but I find school boring.'

'What about sports?' Anna asked.

'I don't like sports. I hate sweating. We do Pilates on Mondays at school, and that's okay, I guess.'

They had reached the entrance to the Science Gallery. James and Grace were waiting for them.

'You mentioned before that you like drama. Who's your favourite actor?' Anna asked.

Bella rolled her eyes. 'Are you going to ask me what my favourite colour is next? I feel like I'm on a bad date.'

Anna burst out laughing. 'A very bad date. Sorry, I know I'm asking a lot of questions. I'm just trying to get to know you better.'

'Why?'

'Because you're James's daughter.'

'So what? Just because my dad likes you doesn't mean I have to.'

'Bella!' James said.

'It's okay, James. She's allowed to be honest,' Anna said. Then, turning back to Bella, she said, 'I'd like us to try to get on – it'll make life nicer at home. I don't see why we can't all be friends.'

'I don't want you to be my friend. You're my dad's random girlfriend. I don't need to like you or get on with you, or your kids. You can stop all this fake interest. Honestly, you're wasting your time. I have a mother and a father. I don't need or want a fake family.'

Anna was speechless.

'You don't have to be so rude,' Grace said. 'Mum's just trying to be nice. This isn't easy on any of us.'

'I don't want her to be nice. I don't need her to be nice. I just want her to get out of my face.'

'That's enough, Bella,' James snapped. He was embarrassed that his daughter was behaving so badly. Bella was never normally rude to people. He hated that Anna was seeing this awful side and not the daughter he loved, the caring, funny, enthusiastic Bella.

'You're obnoxious,' Grace said.

'Well, you're just a loser,' Bella retorted.

'At least I don't go around looking like an Oompa Loompa,' Grace replied.

'At least I have a personality and don't embarrass myself by being a science nerd and sucking up to my dad and his colleagues about my "amazing" project.'

'Oh, yeah? I'd much rather be obsessed with Instagram and have zero ambition.'

'I do have ambition.'

'Really? Ambition to be able to put on fake tan properly or to take the perfect selfie?'

'To be an actress,' Bella hissed.

'Well, you certainly have a dramatic side.'

Anna put herself between them. 'Stop it now, girls. There's no need for anyone to be nasty. Come on, we're all living in the same house and we need to find a way to get along.'

James stepped in, too – he had to try to salvage the day somehow. It was turning into a disaster. 'Anna's right. We understand that this situation is going to take some getting used to, but snapping at each other won't help. Come on, girls, it costs nothing to be nice.'

'I'm bored and hungry,' Jack said.

'Maybe we should go for a nice lunch,' Anna suggested.

'I haven't seen the Science Gallery yet,' Grace reminded her.

'Sorry, of course. We can go for lunch after that.'

'I don't want to go to the stupid Science Gallery. I want food.'

'I think you'll enjoy it, Jack. The Science Gallery is where science and art combine to make some very cool things. There's a very interesting exhibition on at the moment. Some of the students have made a robot that can complete a Rubik's Cube in less than one second.'

'That's amazing.' Grace was impressed.

'I hate Rubik's Cubes. Mum got me one. They're too hard.' Jack bounced his ball loudly.

'I hate them too,' Bella agreed.

'Well, Bella, let's be honest, you didn't try very hard to figure it out. If I remember correctly, you gave it about twenty minutes.' James laughed.

'So science and technology are not my vibe,' Bella snapped. 'Sorry to be such a let-down to you, Dad. Maybe you should just swap me for Grace and pretend she's your genius science daughter.'

'Bella! You're not a let-down! Stop that. Yes, I'm proud of Grace, but that doesn't make me any less proud of you.'

'Doesn't feel like it.' Bella stormed into the Science Gallery, looked around and walked over to a mannequin that was wearing an elaborate ballgown made entirely of tin cans. She began to take selfies.

James knew there was no point in talking to her when she was like this. He'd talk to her later, when she'd calmed down and would actually listen to him. He took Grace and Anna to meet the two students who had created the Rubik's Cube robot.

Out of the corner of his eye, James could see Jack kicking his football against the wall. He looked at Anna. 'He needs to stop. He can't kick a ball in here – there are too many objects for him to damage.'

'Sorry, I'll talk to him.' Anna went over and James watched

as she tried to reason with her son. But he kept kicking the bloody ball.

James walked over and hissed, 'Anna, come on. Just take the ball out of his hands, or get him outside. He's going to damage something.'

'Leave it, James. I'm dealing with it.'

'But you're not. He's still kicking it.'

'I know how to manage my own son.'

'Do you?'

'Yes.'

Anna turned to Jack. 'Come on now, hand over the ball. There are lots of fragile exhibits here, Jack. We don't want to knock anything over. Okay?'

'One last one.'

'Okay, but that's it?'

'No, Anna,' James hissed.

Grace was engrossed in conversation with the two students when they heard a huge crash. Everyone in the gallery spun around to see the mannequin lying on the floor surrounded by her tin-can ballgown in smithereens.

'*Noooooooo!*' the female student screamed, as she knelt down among the tatters of her project.

'Oh, my God.' The two students who had been talking to Grace ran over.

'I'm so sorry,' Anna said to the girl, who was sobbing at her ruined exhibit.

Jack's ball rolled among the scattered cans.

'Get him out of here,' James ordered. Turning to the students, he said, 'I am beyond mortified. What can I do to help?'

'Nothing. It's destroyed.' The student sniffed.

'How could you let your son bring a ball in here?' another student asked James. 'Like, seriously, have you no respect?'

'He's not my son . . . I didn't want . . . I'm so sorry. I completely respect and admire what you've achieved.'

'He's my son.' Anna's voice had an edge to it. 'And he's just a kid. I'm so sorry about what happened. Can I pay for damages or repairs?'

'Just go,' the student said. 'You've done enough damage.'

They stepped outside, the cold air hitting them like a slap in the face.

'That went well,' Bella said. 'I can't wait for the next fun family outing.'

'Shut up, Bella,' Grace snapped.

'Jesus Christ, Anna!' James was so enraged he could barely get the words out.

'It was an accident,' she insisted.

'I told you to take the ball from him. This is my workplace. He just destroyed something they've worked months to create.'

'What do you want me to say? That you were right, I should have taken the ball sooner?'

'He shouldn't have left the house with the bloody ball. You should never have let him in there with it. For God's sake, you're his mother.'

'Oh, I know I am. And you were very quick to deny being his father.'

James did feel a bit bad about that, but Jack had just humiliated him in his workplace and, technically, he wasn't his son.

'Well, he isn't Jack's dad, just like you're not my mother,' Bella said.

'The point is, Bella, that if we all keep thinking like that, we'll never be a family.' Anna sounded exasperated.

'But he's not my dad,' Jack said, clinging to his ball.

'He's your step-dad, though,' Grace pointed out.

'Jack needs to go back in there and apologize,' James said.

'No, he doesn't. I've apologized and I've offered to pay for damages. There's nothing more we can do, James. Jack going in now, while they are all so upset, is not going to help. I'll get him to write them a note. It's very unfortunate, but it's done. We need to calm down and move on.'

'If you don't teach a child to face up to the consequences of their actions, how can they learn from them?'

'Really, James? You're preaching to me about parenting when your daughter is rude to me all the time?'

While they continued to argue, Bella leant over to whisper into Grace's ear, 'I give it a month before they break up and we can all go back to our lives.'

Conor opened the fridge. Not a lot going on in there. He'd meant to do a grocery shop, but then Pete and Deco had called in and he'd gone to the pub to watch the football instead. He pulled out his wallet. Twenty euros. He'd taken out a hundred yesterday. How had he only twenty left? Then he remembered the bet he'd put on the horse-racing, the protein powder and vitamins he'd bought from the gym. He'd have to slow down on his spending: the money from the sale of the house wouldn't last for ever.

He had two cars to fix, but he'd been fobbing off the clients. He'd get to it next week. He needed to generate cash. He'd forgotten how bloody expensive everything was. He'd relied on Anna to sort out the accounts, bills and all that stuff. She liked being in control and, besides, she earned way more than him so it made sense for her to pay the bills.

Conor tidied away the beer bottles and made up the beds in the kids' room. It was more of a box-room, really – he'd just about been able to fit bunk-beds and a small wardrobe into it. He missed the old house. This place was cold and impersonal. Anna had really screwed him over, breaking his heart, then taking away his home.

The doorbell rang. Conor buzzed the kids in. He opened the door and Jack ran up the last few stairs and jumped into his arms.

'Hey, buddy, I've missed you.' Conor hugged his son tightly.

'Me too, Dad. I can't wait for my match tomorrow. We're playing St Killian's and they're really good.'

'You'll beat them, no problem. Have you been practising your shooting?'

'Yep. James tried to save a few of my goals in the garden

yesterday, but he didn't even save one of my bad shots. He's crap.' Jack chuckled.

Conor threw back his head and laughed loudly.

Anna and Grace came up the stairs. 'What's so funny?' Anna asked.

God, she looked good. Conor wanted to reach out and touch her. He wanted to beg her to come back.

'I told Dad about James being a crap goalie.'

Anna frowned. 'That's not nice, Jack. He was making an effort.'

'Sounds like he failed at it,' Conor said.

Anna ignored him. She did that a lot. She'd ignored him when he'd begged her to stay. She'd ignored him when he'd said he'd change. She'd ignored him when he'd told her she was ruining his life . . .

'Jack's football gear is all packed. Grace needs to work on her project, so maybe you could take Jack out and give her a couple of hours of quiet.'

Conor bristled. Who was she to come here and tell him what to do with his kids? He didn't dictate to her when they were in her house. She'd walked out on him, so she didn't have the right to come here now and order him about.

'We'll do whatever we want to do. I don't need your input.'

'I'm just saying Grace needs space to work.'

'And I'm just saying back off.'

'Stop it, you two. I'm so sick of your arguing. I thought the separation would end all of this. It's fine, Mum, just go. I'll fig-ure it out.' Grace sighed and pushed past her father into the apartment. Jack followed her.

'Any other orders you'd like to give me?' Conor asked.

Anna sighed. He hated that sigh. It was a real you're-irritating-me sigh.

'Conor, I'm just filling you in on what's going on. You know how important this science project is to Grace.'

Yes, he did know. He wasn't stupid. He knew it was a big

deal. He didn't need his ex spelling it out to him on his door-step. 'Why don't you go home and nag your professor?'

'I'm not nagging you. I'm trying to talk to you. Anyway, please make sure the kids are home by six p.m. tomorrow.'

'I'll see.'

'How are you feeling by the way?' Anna asked.

'Fine.'

'Good. You were so unwell last time you had them, I was worried that you might have caught some really nasty bug. But after you dropped them home early, I happened to see photos of you in the pub at Pete's birthday party on Mandy's Instagram page.'

Damnit. Conor had felt bad about that, but he was really low and Pete was his best mate and he'd needed a blow-out. Most of all he'd wanted to mess up Anna's romantic weekend with James.

'What – are you stalking me now?' he asked.

'No, Conor. I have much more interesting things to do, thanks. Mandy and I follow each other on Instagram and I saw photos she posted of Pete's party. And imagine my surprise when I saw you, poor, sick Conor, in the thick of it. I see nothing's changed. Still putting yourself before anyone else.'

Conor clenched his fists. He knew he had been selfish, but he didn't need a lecture from the woman who'd had an affair and broken up his life. 'I dunno, Anna, you're the queen of putting yourself first. Let's not forget that you were shagging another man while married to me. You broke our family apart, so I really don't think you're in any position to be lecturing me.'

Anna reddened. Good: he wanted her to feel guilty. 'I'm not proud of having an affair, but I did not break this family up, Conor. Don't you dare say I did. I tried everything to make our marriage work. Everything.'

'You think whatever you want, Anna, but we both know the truth and so do the kids. Your affair destroyed our family.'

Anna's eyes welled. 'I am not the reason, Conor, and you're a bastard for putting that on me.'

'The truth hurts, Anna. I just hope he was worth it.'

Conor closed the door. He looked through the peep-hole and saw Anna wiping her eyes. Good. He'd cried rivers over the break-up while she was all loved up with that prick.

Conor tapped gently on the bedroom door. 'Grace?' He opened it. His daughter was hunched over her laptop, surrounded by papers and folders. 'I've ordered pizza and it'll be here in a minute. Come on, take a break now. You've been locked up in here all afternoon.'

Grace didn't want pizza: she wanted peace and quiet. She wanted one bedroom with one desk, not having to drag her stuff between two bedrooms and two homes. She wanted parents who didn't argue and no step-sister. She wanted everyone to leave her alone so she could focus on her work and get a scholarship to a university in the US.

Grace wanted to eat something healthy. Something that would give her energy. Pizza would just make her tired and sluggish and she needed to be alert to get a few more hours' work in.

'I'm serious, Grace, you need to take a break,' Conor repeated.

Grace reluctantly closed her laptop and went into the kitchen-living room where Jack was playing Fortnite.

'Right, turn that off, Jack. Let's get some plates out,' Conor said.

Jack turned off the game just as the pizza was delivered. They sat around the tiny kitchen table.

'So, James is rubbish at football, yeah?' Conor bit into a large slice.

'The worst,' Jack said. 'Then again, you're a football legend, so I guess I'm used to the best.'

'I'm no legend, but I could have been a professional.'

'It's such bad luck that you got injured, Dad,' Jack said.

'Yeah, it was. But now you can be the first professional foot-baller in the family, eh?'

"Yes!' Jack high-fived his dad.

Grace picked the cheese off the top of the pizza and pushed the heavy base to one side.

'How's your mum doing? She seemed kind of stressed earl-ier. Is everything okay?' Conor addressed this to Grace.

'She's fine,' Grace said loyally. She knew what her dad was up to. He wanted Anna's relationship with James to fail.

'Well, she's been a bit grumpy and she doesn't like Bella. I hate Bella, too.'

'Jack!' Grace glared at her little brother.

Conor grinned. 'So she doesn't like Home-wrecker's daugh-ter. That must make things awkward.'

'She's still getting to know her. We all are,' Grace said diplomatically.

'What do you think of her?' Conor asked.

'She's a bit spoilt, but she's okay.'

'Liar!' Jack shouted. 'You said you couldn't stand her.'

Conor laughed. 'So everyone hates Bella. Interesting. And how do you guys get on with Home-wrecker?'

'His name is James,' Grace said. She hated him calling James 'Home-wrecker', and it was bad for Jack to hear it all the time. He'd never get on with James if Conor kept accusing him of ruining their lives.

'I hate him.' Jack gazed up at his dad, who winked at him.

'He's fine.' Grace didn't want to hurt her dad's feelings or be disloyal to her mum.

'Seems like a tosser to me, and your mum doesn't look happy.'

Grace tried to change the subject. 'So what time is your match tomorrow?' she asked Jack.

'Ten thirty kick-off,' Jack said. 'And I practised loads with Dad in the park today.'

'He was brilliant. He's going to score the winning goal, aren't you?' Conor ruffled his son's thick brown hair.

'Yeah!' Jack punched the air. 'Are you coming to watch, Grace?'

She shook her head. 'Sorry, but I've really got to focus on the project. But I bet you'll be amazing.'

Conor polished off the last slice of pizza and opened another beer. 'You need to chill out a bit, Grace. All that studying isn't healthy. You need to have fun with your mates. You're fifteen – you should be going to discos and kissing boys. You're gorgeous – boys would queue up for you.'

Grace felt herself blush bright red. Her dad was so embarrassing sometimes. She didn't want to talk about boys or whether they wanted to kiss her. She still hadn't kissed anyone. She was shy around boys. Her two best friends, Maddy and Juliette, had done some snogging, but Grace was waiting for the right boy. Maddy told her to kiss anyone to get that first experience over with, but Grace didn't want just anyone shoving his tongue down her throat.

'Oooh, I think I've hit a nerve,' Conor said, grinning at her over his beer can. 'Do you have a crush on someone?'

'Shut up. You're so annoying,' Grace snapped.

'Come on, Gracie, I'm only teasing you. I want you to have a fun childhood, not one with your head stuck in a book. You're only young once, enjoy it. Life can really suck when you get older.' Conor looked down at his beer.

'I'm sticking my head in my books so that I can be successful and have a brilliant life. That's the whole point.' Grace was exasperated by her dad's tiny, narrow view. She wanted so much more than he seemed happy to live with.

Conor held up his hands in surrender. 'No need to bite my head off. I think it's great that you're so smart. So, what's this big science project on anyway?'

'Do you really want to know?' Grace felt he was only asking to make up for teasing her.

'Yes, Grace, I do. I'm interested in your life. I'm your dad.'

'Okay. Most communities have a high percentage of people who are lactose intolerant, which means they don't produce the enzyme needed to properly digest milk. A lot of people can't afford to buy lactose-free milk or dairy-free options like soy or almond milk. So I've tried to create an affordable capsule that anyone can add to milk to neutralize its lactose. I'm trying to figure out a way to make it work at fridge temperatures up to thirty-seven degrees centigrade and equally well in low-fat and full-fat milk. The capsule I'm working on will be reusable, will neutralize the lactose enzymes in milk for up to a week, and it'll be affordable for everyone.'

Conor stared at her. 'That's incredible, Grace. I mean, you sound like an expert scientist. I felt as if I was listening to someone from Harvard. You've got your mother's brains, that's for sure.'

Grace was touched. 'Thanks.'

'Seriously, you're amazing. I'm very proud of you.'

'What about me?' Jack asked.

'Grace is the genius and you're the sports star.' Conor slapped him on the back.

Jack beamed.

'Right! Let's clear this up and watch *The Joker*.'

'I've got to work, but isn't *The Joker* a bit scary for Jack? Isn't it, like, a sixteen age rating?' Grace asked.

'Ah, he'll be grand. He's a tough nut.' Conor winked at Jack.

'I want to watch it. Stop being such a bore, Grace.'

'It might give him nightmares,' Grace whispered to her father.

'Chill out, Grace. You sound like your mother. He'll be fine,' Conor replied.

Grace was up four times in the night with her little brother as he woke, screaming.

13

Bella opened her eyes and stretched out her arms. The sheets were so soft, they were like a second skin. She reached over and pressed the button to raise the blinds. It was a grey London morning. She got out of bed and put on the dressing-gown hanging on the back of the bathroom door. She padded out of her room and down the corridor, to where she could smell freshly brewed coffee.

She felt happy for the first time all week. She loved being in London, away from her needy step-mother and those annoying children. She was delighted to be missing Jack's tenth birthday party. Just thinking about being stuck in that house with a bunch of hyper boys gave her a headache. She was looking forward to a day out with her mum. The shops in London had much better stuff than they did in Dublin.

Ingrid looked up from her phone. 'Morning. Did you sleep well?'

'Amazing.' Bella grinned. 'The beds in this apartment are incredible.'

'I know. Denis is going to get the same brand put into the penthouse in Dublin.'

Bella poured herself a coffee and added lots of milk. She didn't really like coffee, but she liked the idea of it. It felt sophisticated.

'How's school?' Ingrid asked.

'Fine. The auditions for *Grease* are next week.'

'Mm.' Ingrid's forehead crinkled. 'I'm not sure about that, Bella. I don't want you wasting your time on a musical when you need to be focusing on maths and science.'

Here we go, Bella thought. Another lecture about needing to study more. 'It's fine, Mum, I can do both.'

'Well, your latest exam results weren't exactly brilliant. I'll organize some grinds for you.'

Grinds! The last thing Bella wanted was more schoolwork. Her exam results hadn't been that bad. Her mother expected her to be as smart as she was, and it wasn't fair. Bella hadn't been born with a big fat bulging brain like her mother's. She didn't like maths – in fact, she hated it – but she could never admit that to Ingrid. Her dad knew and he tried to help her. He never put pressure on her, just said, 'Do your best.' But Ingrid was different: she considered anything less than a higher merit to be a failure. Bella needed to nip the grinds idea in the bud.

'Mum, I don't need grinds. I'll study harder and my Easter results will be better. I promise.'

'If they're not, you'll be having grinds all summer.'

Bella sipped her coffee and picked at a croissant. She didn't want to eat much before shopping. She didn't want a bloated stomach when she was trying on clothes. Saffron and Portia were so slim now. Bella was a bigger build, curvier, but she knew clothes looked better on you when you were slim. Saffron said no one should be over a size eight because clothes just didn't look good or hang properly if you were any bigger.

Bella was a size twelve. She wanted to be a size eight for her fifteenth birthday party in six weeks. She'd thought being a pescatarian would help her shift the weight, but it hadn't. She knew the sneaky bars of chocolate she ate didn't help. She'd have to try harder. She really needed to be skinny for her birthday and for the musical. She was determined to get the part of Sandy in *Grease* and Sandy did not have chunky thighs. Bella put down the croissant and drank more coffee. Portia said coffee was an appetite suppressant.

Denis walked in, dressed, as usual, in a suit. Bella had rarely seen him out of one. His idea of casual dressing was suit trousers and a work shirt with no tie. 'Morning, Bella, how's things?' he asked.

'Good, thanks.'

'Excellent.' Denis's phone rang.

Bella appreciated his hands-off attitude to her even more now that she'd experienced Anna's suffocating approach. He never tried to 'get to know' her. He never dragged her out to 'bond'. He left her alone. He was nice, friendly, but not all that interested in her, or in anything apart from his work, and that suited Bella fine. She didn't want another dad. Denis gave her amazing presents, had incredible apartments and penthouses for her to live in, and made her mum happy. He was the perfect step-father.

Denis left the room to take the call.

'How are things with your dad?' Ingrid asked.

Bella sighed. 'Dad's fine, but Anna's still stalking me. She keeps saying she wants to get to know me better. It's creepy and really annoying.'

'She sounds very needy,' Ingrid said.

'Yeah, she is. Dad's obsessed with her, though, but I think he finds her kids hard going, especially Jack. He's the most annoying child ever.'

Ingrid clicked her tongue. 'Well, you know your father. He's a hopeless romantic who doesn't think things through. I told him he was rushing into this and that he shouldn't move in with her so quickly. But he didn't listen.'

'I just wish I didn't have to live with her too.'

Ingrid patted her arm. 'It's only every second week and think of it as character-building.'

Every time Bella had to do something she didn't want to do, her mother told her it was character-building. 'Great, thanks, Mum.'

Ingrid smiled. 'Come on, Miss Grumpy, let's cheer you up with a bit of retail therapy.'

Bella grinned. 'Yes!'

Denis walked back into the room, his face like thunder. He held up his phone. 'That was Frank. They've come back asking for more. We had a bloody deal and now the greedy bastards want an extra three million.'

Bella watched her mother. Ingrid shook her head. 'They agreed with the figures we laid out. They verbally agreed to everything yesterday. I don't understand why they're suddenly coming back on this now.'

'I've called an emergency meeting for eleven a.m. in the boardroom. We need to go over the figures before then.' Denis stomped out of the room.

Bella's heart sank. Here we go, she thought. I'm going to be dumped for work again.

Ingrid turned to her. 'I'm sorry, darling. I had everything sorted out yesterday and my schedule was clear. But this is a huge deal and we need to get it over the line. Take my credit card and have fun. Don't go totally crazy, but treat yourself. We'll have dinner together, I promise.'

With that, Ingrid rushed off to help Denis sort out yet another big, important deal. Bella sank back in the chair. She admired her mum. She was proud that she was so successful and had this amazing life, but did success mean you always had to put work first, regardless of who you let down?

Bella stood at the counter in Selfridges and handed over the pile of clothes to the shop assistant. She watched the amount go up and up.

'That's eight hundred and ninety-three pounds, please.'

Bella handed over her mother's credit card. She knew she'd got a bit carried away, but so what? She'd been left on her own yet again and Ingrid had said, 'Treat yourself.'

She took a selfie at the main entrance to the department store, holding up all of her shopping bags.

Having the best time ever!! #shopaholic #newwardrobe #Londonfashion

Bella sent the post. Her feet hurt and she was tired from trying on clothes. She saw a Starbucks and went in to order a coffee. She sat at a table in the corner, alone. All around her were couples, families, friends . . . She was the only person on her own on a Saturday afternoon.

She was starving, but she didn't want to eat. The really cool Paige skinny jeans she'd wanted to buy were too tight and she'd felt gross trying them on. She needed to cut back seriously and finally lose weight.

As she sipped her non-fat cappuccino with no chocolate sprinkled on top, her phone buzzed. It was a message from her dad.

He'd sent a photo of him, Anna, Grace and Jack in the local pizza place. They were all sitting in front of delicious-looking pizzas and everyone was smiling. Bella felt a bit sick. They looked like a family. A perfect family. Her dad was grinning from ear to ear, gazing at Anna, who was beaming back at him. Jack and Grace looked like their kids. A pretty mum, a good-looking dad, a gorgeous teenage daughter and a cute-ish son.

Wish you were here. Missing you. Hope you're having fun with your mum in London. Dad xxx

Bella switched to Instagram. She scrolled through the hundreds of photos of people she followed. Some she knew well, others barely at all. Saffron had posted a photo of herself in denim shorts and a bikini top. She looked super-skinny and really hot. There were loads of comments and flame emojis underneath. Bella peered down at her legs. She'd never look like that in shorts. She had to do something about it. She couldn't control her parents' choices and their crappy decisions, but she could control her body.

She took a photo of her Starbucks cup. *Post shopping spree coffee! #lovetoshop #funnestdayever #Ilovelondon #creditcardmaxedout*

*

90

Ingrid watched Bella moving food around her plate. They were in a top-class restaurant and Bella was wearing a new dress and shoes she'd bought that day, but still she looked miserable. She'd spent a fortune on her shopping spree, which should have cheered her up. Ingrid felt guilty for backing out of their planned day together, but who was going to pay for Bella's shopping if she didn't work? Ingrid's mother had never handed her a credit card and said, *Go shopping*. Ingrid's mother had had hardly enough money to pay for schoolbooks. Bella had no idea what it was like to struggle, and Ingrid worried that she lacked drive because of it.

'Do you not like your fish?' she asked Bella.

'I'm just not very hungry.'

'My scallops are delicious,' Denis said.

'Did you have fun today?' Ingrid asked. 'Are you pleased with what you bought?'

'I got some good stuff.'

'Expensive stuff,' Ingrid commented.

'There's no harm in having a splurge,' Denis said, smiling at Bella. 'My Claire used to go nuts with my credit card when she was your age.'

Yes, and she's a spoilt, entitled bitch, Ingrid thought darkly.

'I have to say, Denis, you're a very cool step-dad, you really are,' Bella said. 'You never hassle me or ask me annoying questions. Anna being such a nightmare has really made me see how great you are.'

Denis beamed. 'Well, I'm delighted to hear it. Thank you.'

Ingrid smiled at Bella. 'That's lovely, Bella, and hopefully Anna will back off a bit soon. I can have a word with your dad about it.'

'No, he'll only get upset. I don't want that. Leave it, Mum. Anyway, Denis, how is Claire?' Bella asked.

Denis's face lit up. He was obsessed with his daughter. In his eyes, she could do no wrong. Ingrid marvelled that he couldn't see how entitled Claire was.

'She's fantastic – just made two million profit on a big property deal. She's a chip off the old block.'

Ingrid tried not to laugh. What a joke. Denis had handed his daughter six apartments in a very desirable area in London and told her she could keep any profit on the sale of them. The property market was extremely buoyant, so naturally Claire had made a profit. But any fool would have made the same amount. It was lucky timing, and the privilege of being handed six free apartments to sell. It had nothing to do with hard work or brains.

Besides, Ingrid reckoned that Claire had fried a lot of her brain cells with her cocaine habit. Denis thought it was just a little fun on the side, but Ingrid could see that it was a lot more than that. Claire was always high.

For a man who was so sharp in business and didn't miss a trick, Denis was blind when it came to his daughter. Ingrid worried that Bella would be over-indulged too, which was why she was so tough on her doing well in school. If she had a good education, she'd have a better chance at being successful and happy in life. Claire had dropped out of the private college her father had paid a fortune for her to go to and now 'worked for the family business' when she wasn't on holidays, partying or snorting drugs.

'Wow, that's incredible.' Bella was impressed.

Denis's phone buzzed. He glanced down. 'Frank says they've agreed to one million. I think that's worth considering.'

Ingrid placed an arm round Denis. 'Maybe we should talk about business later. Bella could probably do with a break from work chat.'

Denis put his fork down. 'I disagree. It's good for Bella to be around business conversation. It's how Claire learnt about business and look how successful she is. Bella is getting a priceless business education right here. Bella, if you listen and absorb what you hear, you could be a millionaire by the time you're twenty-three, like Claire.'

Unlikely, Ingrid thought, as Bella didn't have a parent who had six fancy apartments to hand over to her to flog.

'It's fine. I like listening to business chat, Mum,' Bella said.

Did she? Ingrid strongly suspected that Bella liked them to talk business because she could switch off and not have to get involved. She was worried that Bella was too like James, happy to be mediocre. Ingrid had begged James not to become a lecturer but to go into business. He had a brilliant mind, but he insisted that teaching was what he wanted to do. He lacked ambition, and it was one of the things that had broken their marriage. Ingrid couldn't understand why he didn't want more and strive for it. He was even smarter than Denis – he could have been hugely successful – but James was content in his safe, boring university world.

Ingrid wanted Bella to push herself, to be motivated and driven. Ingrid had always striven for more and she had achieved all of her goals. She had earned enough money never to have to worry and she enjoyed her job. She was a brilliant accountant and she knew it. She derived huge satisfaction from being the best at what she did. Her success had also allowed her to buy her mother a house and to help pay for private education for her four nieces and nephews. She wanted to encourage Bella to do better, want more and work hard to achieve it.

Denis continued to talk about business until their plates were taken away and they were handed dessert menus.

'Why don't you order something?' Ingrid suggested.

'No, thanks, I'll just have a coffee,' Bella said.

14

Anna hung the happy-birthday bunting across the kitchen. She loved making a big fuss on the kids' birthdays. Every year she went all out with decorations and balloons, with each gift individually wrapped, no matter how big or small. It was one of the few things she and Conor agreed on, that birthdays were for spoiling the kids. They didn't always agree on appropriate gifts, and Anna was hoping Conor hadn't bought anything crazy for Jack this year. The hopper he'd bought him last year had ended up with Jack breaking his arm after five minutes.

Jack had spent this birthday eve with Conor, who was due to bring him over at two, in time for his party. Anna had invited ten of Jack's schoolmates. She had set up a few party games in the garden and Conor had said he'd organize a football match. Anna had bought pizzas and Grace had helped her make a chocolate cake covered with Smarties and M&Ms. Jack was going to love it.

Anna was glad that Bella was in London with Ingrid and Denis. She didn't want anyone spoiling Jack's special day. When she'd finished decorating the kitchen, James helped her tie a long row of bunting between the two trees in the garden. 'It looks like a party grotto,' he said, laughing.

'That's what I'm aiming for.' Anna grinned.

James kissed her. 'I love that you're making such a fuss for Jack. I'm feeling a bit inadequate now. When Bella was younger, Ingrid and I usually just took her out for the day. She'd choose her gift and then we'd go for dinner. If she asked for a birthday party, Ingrid always persuaded her to take her friends to the cinema and out for pizza afterwards, so the house didn't get messy.'

Anna rolled her eyes. There was controlling behaviour and there was just plain selfish. Poor Bella had never had a proper at-home fun, crazy, unruly party. The kind of party every kid wanted. No wonder she was so uptight and demanding – she took after her mother.

'I wanted to make a special effort this year. Jack's still really upset about the separation, the poor pet. If you like, why don't you ask Bella if she'd like to do something at home for her birthday this year?' Anna suggested. 'You can hire these disco bubbles for the garden – it's kind of like a bouncy-castle disco for teens. We hired one for Grace last year and she loved it. She had so much fun.'

'That sounds brilliant, but I'm not sure how Ingrid will react to us throwing the party for Bella's fifteenth.'

'Why don't you suggest it?' Anna said. Come on, James, stand up to your ex, she thought. He was so decisive in his work life and with most things, but when it came to Ingrid, he always gave in to her, rather than rocking the boat. It annoyed Anna a little. Sometimes you needed to confront people, especially when it came to your kids.

Anna heard the doorbell and went to answer it. Angela was standing on the doorstep holding a big cake in the shape of a football. 'Oh, Angela, that looks incredible.'

'I know you've a cake made, but sure he's my godson, so I have to spoil him. It's chocolate biscuit cake with marshmallows, his favourite.'

'You are the best godmother!'

They went inside, and put the cake into the fridge. Then Angela helped them finish tying the last bunch of balloons to the hall door. As they were knotting the string, they saw Conor's car screeching to a halt outside.

Anna ran down the path to greet the birthday boy.

'Conor's such a tool,' Angela murmured.

'You took the words out of my mouth.' James grinned at her.

'Thank God she met you and left him. Honestly, she was miserable for so long, and it's lovely to see her happy.'

'Thanks, Angela. I know how much your opinion matters to her.'

Angela laughed. 'Anna never listens to anyone. We all told her she was moving in with you and all the kids too fast, but she ignored us.'

'I know it seemed a bit hasty, but it's working out well. Obviously we all have some adapting to do, but we're getting there.'

'We just want her to be happy. She deserves it.'

They watched as Jack jumped out of the car and ran up to his mum, panting.

'You'll never guess what Dad got me for my birthday?' He jumped up and down with excitement.

'What?'

'A BB gun!' Jack shouted.

'Well, he's really outdone himself this time,' Angela muttered.

'Are they even legal?' James was shocked.

Anna marched over to Conor, who was pulling the weapon out of the boot of his car. 'Are you joking? Do you have any idea how dangerous those guns are?'

Conor smirked at her. 'Here comes the killjoy. I knew you'd try to ruin his buzz. It's an airsoft BB gun. They're perfectly safe. I've taught him how to use it so he's not going to hurt any-one. Chill out.'

'He could take someone's eye out with it,' Anna hissed. 'It's irresponsible to give a gun to a ten-year-old. I had a patient in a few weeks ago who got hit on the eyelid with one and it wasn't pretty. They are incredibly dangerous.'

'Why don't you go and nag your new boyfriend, Anna? The one good thing about being separated from you is that I don't have to put up with your nagging any more.' Conor strode past her into the house, studiously ignoring James as he walked by.

James held out his arm and pulled Anna in. 'Don't let it ruin your day.'

Conor made his way to the back garden but was blocked by Angela.

'Hello, Conor, nice parking.'

'Look what the cat dragged in.'

'Still behaving like a teenager, I see.'

'Still sticking your nose into everyone's business, I see.'

'Don't use Jack to get at Anna. He's an innocent kid.'

'Since when is it a crime to buy your own son a present that he actually wants and likes?'

'When it's a weapon.'

'Give it a rest, Angela. Your Darren would be made-up to get one of these.'

'Oh, he would, Conor, but Tom wouldn't buy him one.'

'Unlike Tom, I'm no longer under the thumb of you Johnson women.'

'Anna was the best thing that ever happened to you, and you blew it.'

'She left me, Angela. She walked out on me.'

'She should have done it years ago.'

'Always so nice chatting to you, but I'm going to hang out with my son now.'

Angela let him past and moved over to where Anna and James were standing.

'Go, Angela.' James high-fived his sister-in-law.

'I've been dying to say that to him for years.'

'Remind me never to get on the wrong side of you.'

Angela laughed, then looked at Anna, who was fighting back tears.

'Anna, don't let him upset you. He's not worth it,' she said.

'He always does this – gets Jack a completely irresponsible present and I have to pick up the pieces when Jack hurts himself. He's such a dickhead.'

James rubbed her back. 'Look, we'll hide the gun as soon as we can and you can deal with it later. We can talk to Jack about the dangers of using it and make him see he's far too young for it.'

'Good luck with that conversation,' Angela said.

Anna sighed. James didn't have a clue about young boys. Jack would sleep with that gun in his bed. He'd never let her hide it, and if she did manage to prise it out of his hands, he'd hunt it down.

'There's nothing you can do right now, so plaster a smile on your face and deal with it later. Come on, sis, James and I are here for you.'

Within minutes, cars began to pull up, dropping off hyper-excited boys. Conor was in the back garden hanging a huge piñata from the branch of a tree. As the boys spilt into the garden, Conor handed them cans of Red Bull, high-fiving them. They flocked around him as he chatted to them, making them laugh, and within minutes had them all eating out of his hands.

A big kid talking to little kids, Anna thought bitterly. She never got to be Fun Mum because someone had to be a responsible adult.

James stood at the back door, watching Conor handing the energy drinks to the boys. 'Is he for real?' he whispered to Angela.

'Sadly, yes.'

'The kids will be high as kites. Red Bull is not a suitable drink for them. It'll make them even more hyper than they already are.'

'I'll see if I can make some of the cans disappear when the kids are distracted with the gun.'

The gun! James had no words. How could Conor have been so irresponsible? Jack was bound to hit someone with it. He'd have to make sure it was banned from the house. Anna needed to be stronger with Conor: she let him get away with too much. She should have taken the gun as soon as they'd walked through the door. It was an accident waiting to happen. James didn't want it anywhere in his house. Let Conor keep it in his apartment and let Jack shoot it at him, not at James or Bella, thank you very much.

They watched as the kids knocked back the Red Bull, then attacked the piñata with sticks. The donkey exploded and hundreds of sweets sprayed all over the garden. The over-caffeinated boys dived on top of them and began to add high doses of sugar to their already overactive bodies.

'Sweet Jesus, ten-year-old boys high on sugar and caffeine. Brace yourself, James, there's going to be carnage,' Angela warned him.

'How bad?' James felt his stomach drop.

'Judging by the quantities, I'd say extremely,' Angela replied.

'*Woo-hoo!*' Kyle yelled, as he swung on the new curtains in the living room. Splat. A piece of cake missed his shoulder and spattered chocolate icing all over the cream fabric.

'Missed me!' Kyle swung higher as the curtain rail creaked under his weight.

Jackson scooped another lump of cake from his plate and tried again, hitting Kyle in the face this time. In trying to duck, Kyle managed to pull the whole curtain rail off the wall.

'*Yeah!*' Timmy and Jude threw themselves onto the couch and began pounding each other with the cushions, until one burst and feathers flew everywhere.

'Cool!' they shouted.

'Push us, Dad!' Jack roared. Conor gave the mattress at the top of the stairs a shove, and Jack and his two best mates, Fred and Ron, slid down on it.

'James, watch out!' Angela shouted.

But James was so shocked by what he was seeing that he didn't move aside quickly enough and was sent flying.

He lay on the floor, his mug of tea in pieces all around him.

'Sorry Mr . . . What's his name?' Fred asked Jack.

'Home-wrecker,' Jack shouted. 'It doesn't matter. He's just my mum's boyfriend.' He was pulling the mattress back up the stairs for more fun and games.

'He's fine, lads. Come on, I'll push you again,' Conor called from the top of the stairs.

'Your dad is the best,' Ron gushed. 'He's so much fun.'

'Yeah, he's the greatest,' Jack replied.

James lay on the floor, in the house he was paying for, surrounded by a bunch of wired lunatics. He was covered with hot tea and broken pottery. In his living room, the curtains were on the floor. In the garden, a boy was vomiting into the newly planted rosebushes.

He closed his eyes and tried to block out the dread that was rising in his chest. If this was step-parenting a ten-year-old boy, he wasn't sure he was up to it.

Anna came out from the kitchen to see what was going on.

'James! Are you okay?' She helped him up, then picked up the remnants of the mug. 'Jack, sweetheart, I'm sorry but you can't slide down the stairs. It's too dangerous. Put the mattress back on your bed.'

'*Muuuuum*, it's fun. Just two more goes.'

Anna paused. 'Well, one of you has to stand at the bottom and shout if someone's passing so there are no more accidents.'

James was speechless. Was that it? Was she going to let her son continue? Was she not going to reprimand Jack for knocking him over? Was she not going to ask her ex-husband to stop pushing the mattress? Was Anna really okay with this crazy behaviour? This was his home, and her kid, his friends and her irresponsible idiot of an ex-husband were destroying it.

He breathed in deeply and swallowed the anger. The last thing he wanted was for Conor to see any discord between him and Anna. He knew the man would love that.

'What in the name of God happened?' Angela gasped. She had come through the back door and was in shock at what she saw.

'Jack and his friends knocked me down while I was holding hot tea – they were sliding down the stairs on a mattress in a party game that has been deemed fun.'

'Ah, come on. Anna, you need to put your foot down and stop this.'

'No, Aunty Angela. It's the best game ever!' Jack shouted.

'Yeah!' yelled his friend.

'It's the best party of my life.' Jack whooped.

'Let them have two more goes. I'll stand here and make sure no one else gets hurt,' Anna said.

'Anna, they're completely out of control,' Angela hissed.

'They'll all be gone soon and Jack is loving it. It's the happiest I've seen him since we left Conor,' she whispered.

Angela shook her head. 'Be careful. Kids need boundaries and you're letting him get away with murder.'

'It's one day, Angela.'

'Right. Well, I'd better change my shirt,' James said, through clenched teeth. 'I'm soaked in hot tea. Luckily, I like my tea milky or I might have had second-degree burns.' He rubbed at his wet shirt.

Anna patted his arm distractedly. 'Could you just sweep up the rest of the cup so none of the kids stand on any broken bits? Angela, could you take the pizzas out of the oven? They need to eat – it might calm them down a bit.'

Angela snorted. 'You'd need to feed them horse tranquillizers for that to happen.'

'Anna, you do realize that our curtains have been pulled down from the wall?'

Anna winced. 'I know, and I'm annoyed about that, but I can't start shouting at Jack's friends. He'd die if I gave out to them. I can't upset him on his big day. We can hang the rail back up later.'

Anna called up the stairs, 'Two more goes, Conor, and then I need you to put the mattress back and help me with the pizzas.'

Conor dumped the mattress on the landing and vaulted over the banisters, landing like a cat. 'Sod it, I'm starving, let's eat now, kids.'

'But, Dad, I want two more goes,' Jack said.

'We need to eat now so we have time to play with the gun.'

'*Yeaaaaaaaah!* The gun!' Jack's friends shouted.

Jack grinned and ran down the stairs after his father.

As he was passing by, Conor picked up a chunk of the broken mug. He looked at it and snorted. '*Educational Rockstar*. I'm embarrassed for you, mate. It's a good thing it's broken.'

James snatched the piece of mug from Conor's hand. 'It was a gift from one of my students.'

'Maybe you should have a mug that says Mr Grumpy-old-fart,' Conor taunted, as Jack and his friends giggled.

'Better than Juvenile Wanker,' Angela muttered, and James laughed.

The kids were in the garden, playing with the BB gun. They were marginally calmer now that they'd eaten the pizza. James, Anna and Angela had tidied the ravaged kitchen. Before she left, Angela had handed James a beer and told him to stand out-side: he needed a break from the madness.

James was standing on the patio, sipping the beer, trying to calm his fury at this fiasco of a party. He glanced at his watch. The parents would be there to pick up their kids any minute now. Thank God the party was almost over. Conor stood beside them, helping them aim the gun at empty Red Bull cans. He tickled them, slapped them on the back, wrestled with them, tackled them ... He shouted, slagged and generally entertained the boys. They loved him. They lapped up his jokes, cheesy one-liners and trash-talk.

He was very natural with them, James had to admit. He was a complete tool, but he was good with kids because he was a big one himself. James watched nervously as the boys took it in turns to shoot pellets. Potentially the gun was a weapon of mass destruction and James couldn't wait to get it out of their hands.

He rolled his neck to loosen the tension. Only a few more minutes and they'd all be out of his house. Then he could relax. Anna came up behind him and massaged the back of his neck.

'Are you okay? I know it's been a bit manic.'

A bit? The house was trashed and his back was throbbing after being slammed against the wooden floor when he was knocked over.

'I'm fine, but looking forward to saying goodbye to this lot.' He half smiled. 'I think next year we might have the party outside the house or in Conor's apartment.'

Anna frowned. 'No way. We always have parties at home. Look how happy he is.'

Jack was running around the garden, holding his BB gun over his head and roaring, 'Bullseye,' at the top of his lungs.

The doorbell rang. Anna went to answer it.

James watched as Jack lined up to take a shot. Conor whispered in his ear. Jack giggled. Instead of shooting the can of Red Bull, Jack turned and aimed the gun at James.

'What are you –'

James didn't get to finish his sentence before a pellet smacked him in the cheek. The pain was acute.

'What the hell are you doing?' he roared at Jack. 'You could have blinded me. Jesus Christ, what is wrong with you? You don't aim a gun at someone. Did you tell him to do it?' he shouted at Conor. 'Was this your idea of a joke? What type of arsehole tells their son to shoot at someone?'

'James!' Anna raised her voice to drown his.

James turned to see her glaring at him. Four sets of parents were standing beside her, witnessing the 'happy family scene'.

'The only arsehole here is you,' Conor whispered, as he pushed past James to greet Jack's friends' parents.

James closed his eyes and tried to ignore the throbbing in the side of his face.

'Oh dear. It looks like the new family set-up is a bit of a disaster,' James heard a mother whisper behind him.

'Dave, how's it going, my man? Denise, you're getting younger every time I see you.' Conor schmoozed the parents. 'Sorry about that. The new boyfriend can't handle a bit of rough-and-tumble.' Conor rolled his eyes.

'Sure, it's only a bit of fun,' Dave said to Conor. 'Yer man needs to chill out.'

I'd like to see how chilled out you'd be if you got shot in the face, James wanted to retort, but instead he pretended he hadn't heard the comment.

'Sorry, everyone, things got a little livelier than anticipated.' Anna's voice was high and strained. 'But I think the boys all had fun. They might be a bit hyper from sugar, but they were all so good and Jack loved it, didn't you, Jack?'

'Yeah. Thanks for coming and for all my presents,' Jack said.

'I want a BB gun,' one of the boys said to his dad.

'Over my dead body,' the father muttered, as he ushered his son out of the house.

Conor raised his voice over the kids' chatter: 'See you all soon, thanks for coming, kids. You were all brilliant, we had the craic, didn't we?'

'Yeah!' the boys all shouted, punching the air.

Conor high-fived them and joked around with them as they began to file out.

Nice of him to thank everyone for coming to my house and

trashing it, James thought. As they left, he could hear the boys telling their parents, 'Jack's dad is the coolest . . . funnest . . . craziest . . . best dad ever. He's so lucky.'

James sighed. How on earth was he ever going to compete with the 'funnest dad ever'?

15

Grace arrived home from the library to complete chaos. The house was trashed. Her mum and James were tidying up while Jack ran around in circles, completely hyper.

Grace looked at the curtain rail on the floor and the chocolate-stained cream curtains. 'Is this all from the party?' she asked.

Anna nodded. 'Your dad gave the boys Red Bull and they got a bit over-excited.'

'A bit?' Grace looked at the cushions strewn everywhere, feathers all over the floor, food crushed into the rug, drinks spilt on the wooden floors, sweet papers on every surface.

'It was brilliant.' Jack bounced up and down on the couch. 'The best party ever. Dad got me a BB gun and all my friends are so jealous. But narky James won't let me keep it here.'

James lifted the curtain rail from the floor. 'I got shot in the face, so I thought it best that the gun did not remain here.'

Grace noticed a red welt on the side of James's face. 'Oh, my God, was it sore?'

'Extremely, and only two inches from my eye.'

Yikes. James was seething. Grace could feel anger emanating from his pores.

'It was only a pellet. I was trying to shoot his beer bottle from his hand, but I missed. James shouted at me and called Dad an arsehole.'

'Jack, that's enough.' Anna mopped sticky Red Bull from the floor. 'James has apologized for shouting at you and you should never, ever aim the gun at anyone. It is very dangerous. You really could take someone's eye out with a pellet.'

Jack stormed out of the room, shouting, 'You're all so boring in this house. I want to live with Dad. He's way more fun.'

Grace watched him go. She couldn't believe her dad had bought Jack a BB gun. Jack was a clueless ten-year-old with no appreciation of danger. Was he mad?

'I'll take these to the dry-cleaner's,' James said, holding the curtains in his arms. He left the room and they heard the front door close.

'Is he okay?' Grace asked.

'He hasn't had a good day. He got knocked down, covered with tea, broke his favourite mug and then he was shot,' Anna said.

Grace looked at her mother and they began to laugh.

'It's not funny.' Anna giggled.

'But it kind of is.' Grace cracked up.

Anna wiped her eyes. 'Poor James, he has no idea how boisterous boys can be. Today was a baptism of fire for him.'

'I do feel sorry for him. Jack and his friends can be so annoying. Then again, so can Bella, so you've both got difficult kids to deal with.'

'And you're just perfect.' Anna kissed her forehead.

'Compared to those two I am.'

Anna finished mopping and they went into the kitchen, where Grace held a black bin bag open and Anna filled it with paper plates and other rubbish.

'How's the project coming along?'

'Good. I've finished my PowerPoint presentation, so I'll present to the teachers tomorrow and then, hopefully, they'll approve it for the competition.'

'Will you show me?'

'Now?'

'Yes.' Anna put down the brush and dustpan. 'The clean-up can wait. Your project is far more important.'

Grace was delighted to have her mother's full attention for once. She pulled out her laptop and began to present. She was in mid-flow when . . .

'Oh, my actual God, have we been robbed?' Bella exclaimed from the hallway.

Anna mouthed, 'Sorry,' to Grace, stood up and went to explain the mess to Bella. Grace switched off her presentation and closed her laptop. She'd almost had her mother's attention for a full five minutes.

James drilled the screws into the wall, making sure the right side of the curtain rail was secure. Anna held up the left as he moved to fix it to the wall.

'They'll have the curtains dry-cleaned by Wednesday.' James broke the silence.

'Great.' Anna let go of the newly hung curtain rail. 'Look, James, I'm sorry the party got a little out of hand. Boys can be boisterous – they have a lot of energy.' She held her hand up. 'And, yes, I know that Conor filling them with Red Bull didn't help and I obviously didn't mean for you to get shot, but I suppose I'm saying you're not used to boys and they're different from girls. Very different.'

James rubbed his sore cheek. 'I understand they're more energetic, but the carry-on today was out of control, Anna. A bit of fun is fine, but they were like a bunch of lunatics. Your ex is a total moron. Who gives young boys caffeinated drinks and vats of sugar? Not to mention a gun. Seriously?'

Anna understood that James was frustrated, but he also needed to get a bit of perspective on this. Yes, Conor was an idiot and, yes, the boys had got a bit hyper, but Jack and his friends had had a ball. 'Look, I'm not happy at all about the gun. I agree with you that it's completely inappropriate, but he's going to keep it at Conor's place, so you don't have to worry about being shot again. I know the house was messy, but the

108

boys had fun and Jack loved his day and, really, that's what matters most. He's been so upset about the break-up and I've been worried about him. Did you see how happy he was today?'

'I could have lost an eye, Anna.'

'But you didn't.'

'But I could have, and so could one of Jack's friends.'

'Yes,' Anna replied, 'but they didn't.'

Why did he have to go on about what could have happened, when all that did happen was the party got a bit rowdy? It was over now. No one had been hurt, the gun was in Conor's place and the house was clean again. James was a lot more pernickety about tidiness and calmness than Anna had realized. He really seemed to struggle with mess or any kind of chaos, but life was messy and chaotic.

James sank into the couch. He looked tired. Anna sat down beside him and took his hand. 'Thanks for helping to clean up. I'm sorry my son shot you and knocked you down. I will replace your mug. I'll get one that says *Superman Step-dad*.'

James's lips twitched. 'How about, *I survived being shot by my step-son*?'

Anna laughed, and James, thankfully, joined in. She snuggled into him. He ran his hands through her hair.

'It's harder than I thought it would be,' he said quietly.

'It sure is,' Anna replied.

'I love you so much, and I want to be with you no matter what. But we both bring baggage to the relationship.'

Anna couldn't speak. She was afraid that today might make James doubt their relationship. She loved this man. She loved him like she'd never loved anyone before. But he was right: they did have baggage, lots of it.

'I guess I'm just used to being with Bella. I grew up an only child and I have an only child. I'm not used to . . . to . . .'

'Chaos?'

'Yes.'

'And I grew up with six siblings in a small house in total bed-lam. We never had any privacy, we shared everything, and it was always loud and messy. It's what I'm used to. It doesn't really faze me.'

'But it does bother me,' James admitted. 'I even find the fact that I trip over Jack's bags, shoes and footballs every morning incredibly irritating.'

James wanted everything to be ordered, Anna thought. She wasn't like that. She was an organized person, but she didn't mind a bit of mess. She'd grown up in a busy house, full of people: if what you owned wasn't on your person, it was borrowed, broken or damaged. She'd shared a bedroom with her two sisters and they'd fought constantly over clothes, make-up, hairbrushes, shoes . . . everything. As for her brothers, they were constantly wrestling each other, roaring and knocking things over.

James was used to having things exactly as he liked them. He wasn't used to sharing his space with lots of people. He wanted everything put back in its place after use. He'd asked Anna if she'd mind keeping her creams and make-up to one side of the washbasin in their bathroom so that he could have his side clear for his shaving things. If she left her clothes hanging on the back of the chair in their bedroom, he'd hang them up before he went to bed and line up her shoes beside the wardrobe.

When James cooked, he tidied up as he went along so that when the meal was ready the kitchen was tidy. When Anna cooked, she threw all the pots into the sink and cleaned up after they'd eaten.

When James got up in the morning, he liked to have a long shower. Anna was in and out in three minutes. James folded his towel and hung it neatly on the towel rack. Anna usually left hers hanging over the shower door.

'What are you thinking?' James asked. 'I can see the little

frown in the middle of your forehead that you get when you're mulling something over.'

She smiled. 'I was just thinking how wonderful you are.' She fudged the truth. 'Taking on my two kids and all of our messiness.'

'Well, you took on Bella, who, much as I adore her, I know can be challenging at times.'

'We both took on a lot, but I think you're worth it.' Anna kissed him.

'Me too.' He kissed her back. The kiss became deeper and more passionate. Anna leant into James, feeling passion rising in her body.

'For goodness' sake, can you take your tongues out of each other's mouths for, like, five seconds?' Bella stood at the door, hands on her hips.

James pulled back. 'What is it, Bella?'

'What it is, Dad, is that your girlfriend's annoying kid won't stop kicking his football against the thin, crappy wall between our bedrooms.' Bella's face was red. 'If he doesn't stop soon, I'm going to get that BB gun and shoot him.'

Anna was very glad the gun was safely tucked away in Conor's apartment.

'I'll talk to him.' James began to get up from the couch.

Anna placed a hand on his arm. 'Let me go.'

'Make sure you come down with the ball or he'll just start again,' James warned her.

I know how to deal with my own child, Anna thought, irritated by the instruction. Besides, it was still his birthday and James had already shouted at and reprimanded him. He was only ten, for goodness' sake.

Bella stomped up the stairs ahead of her. 'If he doesn't stop, I'm going to get my scissors and puncture the bloody ball,' she snapped. 'It's like a zoo here.'

'There's no need for that, Bella.' Anna was firm. 'I said I'd deal with it.'

'Please do.' Bella went into her own room and slammed the door.

Anna could hear Jack thumping the ball against the wall. She was tempted to let him carry on for a few more minutes just to annoy Bella, but then she remembered she was supposed to be the adult. She went in. 'Hi, love. It's nearly your bedtime and I think we'll leave the football kicking for the garden. It's a bit loud for Bella on the other side of the wall.'

'I amn't kicking it hard,' Jack said.

'I know, pet, but it's annoying for her.'

'Grace doesn't mind.'

'Grace is used to it.'

'So Bella will get used to it.'

'Look, Jack, can you just stop for now? You've had a long day so why don't you get ready for bed?'

'I'm not tired.'

'Come on, Jack, it's almost ten. Go and brush your teeth. They need a good brush after all those sweets.'

Jack grinned. 'Dad's piñata was the best. It was ginormous.'

Anna smiled. 'It sure was.'

'And the BB gun is the best present ever.'

'You're a bit young for that, but I'm not going to give out. Just be really, really careful with it. Promise?'

He nodded. 'I will. I know James hates me now cos I shot him.'

Anna put her hand on his shoulder. 'James doesn't hate you, Jack. He just got a fright.'

Jack shrugged. 'I don't care if he hates me because I hate him. He's a home-wrecker and a nerd like Dad says he is.'

Anna fought the urge to shout, Your dad is a lazy waste of space.

'Jack, that's not fair or nice. James is not a home-wrecker.

You know Dad and I were not happy for a long time. James has nothing to do with us breaking up. We were already broken up when I met James.'

'But we were a family, all together, and then James came and you left Dad.'

'Your dad and I were only living in the same house because Dad had no money to move out. James did not break up me and your dad.'

'Dad says he did.'

Anna exhaled. 'Well, that's not true or fair. Look, your dad and I love you and Grace more than anything and we tried to stay together, but it didn't work. I'm sorry it didn't, but I'm so much happier now.'

'Dad isn't happy. He's sad.'

'He's fine, Jack. Your dad is absolutely fine.'

'I hate it here. I want you and Dad to get back together and for us all to be a family again. I don't care if you fight. I prefer you and Dad fighting to you and James kissing. Yuk.'

Anna's heart ached for her confused little boy. She knew he adored Conor. She knew he wanted them to be a couple, but the best decision Anna had ever made was walking away from Conor.

Anna took her son's sticky hands in hers. 'Jack, your dad and I will never get back together. I'm sorry, love, but that's never going to happen. I know this is hard on you, and I know living with James and Bella feels strange, but it's hard for them too. We all need to make an effort to get along. Will you try? Please?'

He shrugged.

'Come on, Jack, pretty please?'

He sighed. 'I promise not to shoot him again, but I don't promise to like him.'

That would have to do for now. Anna pulled her young son in for a hug and prayed silently that he'd grow to love, or at least to like, James.

16

After school that Monday, Bella laid out all her new clothes on her small bed and began cutting the tags off. She had gone a bit mad, but her mum had let her down and there had to be some upside to being on her own almost all weekend. She put on the skinny black ripped jeans and her new Marc Jacobs black satin bomber jacket with gold embroidered birds.

Bella tried to take a good selfie for Instagram, but she couldn't get the angle right. She needed help. She knocked on Grace's bedroom door.

'Yeah?' Grace called out.

Bella went into her room. It was so neat. Everything was tidied away. The only slight mess was her desk, which was covered with papers.

'Hi, can you help me out for a sec?'

'What is it?' Grace barely looked up from her laptop.

Jesus, did she ever stop studying and working on her dorky project? Like, did she even have Netflix on her computer?

'I just need you to take a photo.'

Grace stood up and followed Bella into her room. Her eyes widened when she saw all the new clothes. 'Wow! Is this all the stuff you bought in London?'

'Most of it. I left some over there.'

Grace picked up a red Zadig & Voltaire mini-dress. It would look amazing on her with her long legs and tanned skin, Bella thought. It was a bit tight on Bella, but she'd bought it because she was going to stop eating like a pig and lose weight, so it would fit perfectly soon.

Bella stood in the light of the window. 'Okay, this is my good side. You need to climb onto the chair so that you're photographing me looking up. It's way better and makes you look skinnier.'

Grace stood on Bella's desk chair and took photos as Bella pouted, turned and twisted this way and that.

'Just a few more,' Bella insisted, as Grace made to climb off the chair.

Grace took a few more photos.

'Hang on, let me have a look before you go. I need to make sure they're good.'

While Bella examined her photos, deleting most of them because they were horrendous, Grace held up a Nike crop-top hoody and looked in the mirror.

'Hi, girls.' Anna popped her head through the half-open door. 'What are you up to? This looks like fun.'

Anna seemed excited to find them together. Bella hoped she wasn't going to make a big deal of it and presume they were now best mates. She was so over-eager, it was cringy.

'Bella just asked me to take some photos for her Instagram.'

'Cool. Grace is actually really good at taking photos,' Anna enthused.

Is there anything Grace isn't good at? Bella thought.

'Well, I've found one that's just about okay. It's not your fault, Grace, it's my chunky thighs.' Bella sighed.

'You don't have chunky thighs. You're lovely,' Anna said.

Bella did not need her step-mother lying to her. 'Yes, I do. I inherited them from my mum. Grace is lucky. She has long skinny legs that look good in anything.'

'Yeah, but you're the one with the amazing wardrobe,' Grace said. 'Everything you have is so cool.'

Bella hadn't thought Grace was into clothes. She'd only ever seen her in either her school uniform or leggings or a tracksuit.

'You can borrow them anytime. I don't have to worry about you stretching anything because you're half my size.'

Grace was surprised. 'Really?'

'Yeah, sure. I've loads more stuff in the penthouse here and in the apartment in London. Borrow anything. My mum gives me tons of guilt money to buy clothes. I guess there's an upside to having a mother who is more interested in work than her daughter.'

'I'm sure your mum is just busy, and you're the apple of your father's eye,' Anna assured her. 'It's so kind and generous of you to offer to lend Grace your clothes, Bella. What a sweet girl you are. Isn't she, Grace?'

Could this woman be any more annoying? She didn't need Anna telling her how her own dad felt about her. Bella wanted Anna to get out of her room and her face.

'Thanks, Bella.' Grace smiled at her. 'I won't even bother to say you can borrow my clothes because your stuff is so much nicer than mine.'

'It's lovely to see you girls getting closer. I knew you'd get on when you got to know each other better,' Anna gushed.

There was a brief, awkward silence. 'Yeah, well, I need to get back to my project.' Grace put down the hoody and left the room.

Anna followed her out, much to Bella's relief. She closed her door firmly.

Anna leant against the door to Grace's bedroom. 'I know Bella has lots of lovely things, but life is not about material things, it's about love and fulfilment and experiences.'

Grace crossed her arms over her chest. 'Well, Mum, I'd love to experience the fulfilment of having some of those amazing clothes.'

'But, Grace,' Anna lowered her voice to a whisper, 'you heard her say they're guilt clothes because Ingrid works so much and doesn't pay her any attention.'

Grace wanted to say, You used to work night and day but

I never got guilt clothes. She didn't because she knew it would be hurtful and, to be fair, her mum had had no choice. Her dad only worked sporadically and Anna had had to work to keep them afloat. Still, though, Grace would have loved a wardrobe like Bella's.

'I think Bella offering to lend you her clothes is so nice. She's obviously decided to try to be friendlier. Isn't that great? We can all get on now and be like a family.'

Grace wanted to laugh. Was her mother completely delusional? Bella offering to lend Grace her clothes was a nice gesture, but it hardly made them best friends or 'sisters'. They were never going to be close – they were way too different. Grace wished her mum would stop being so needy about them all getting on. It was too much pressure. They were all still getting to know each other. She needed to relax and stop trying to force them all to be a big happy family. James would never be her dad and Bella would never be her sister. They were two people who had been forced upon her, and she tolerated them. That was it. End of story.

Anna left the girls and went to help Jack with his maths homework, which was her least favourite thing to do because he never listened.

She was trying to get him to sit still and concentrate when James came in from work. He kissed her hello and ruffled Jack's hair. 'Hey, kiddo.'

Jack patted down his hair and grumbled, 'I hate it when he calls me kiddo.'

James picked up Jack's football and boots from the floor and tidied them into a corner of the kitchen. He stacked the dishwasher with the dinner plates that Anna hadn't got around to doing. Then, after wiping the counter, he joined them at the kitchen table, eating the lasagne Anna had made for dinner.

Jack handed Anna the answer to the question.

Anna patiently explained to him where he had gone wrong.

'I don't get it,' he said, kicking the leg of the table.

'You're not concentrating, pet,' Anna scolded him gently.

'I hate maths. It's so boring. Who cares about it anyway?'

'Most of the world,' James replied. 'Being good at maths helps with everything.'

'Like what? Does it help with football? No.'

'Well, even footballers need to know how to manage their money, don't they?'

'They just pay someone to do it for them,' Jack replied.

'But what if that person is a crook and steals their money?' James asked.

'Duh, they're not thick, they don't hire crooks. Dad says school is a waste of time. He says learning a trade is way better. I want to be a mechanic like him, or an electrician like his friend Pete. You can be your own boss and only work when you feel like it.'

Anna hated the way Conor dismissed education and filled Jack's head with nonsense about only working when he felt like it. What a load of crap. Anna wanted the best for her children. She wanted them to go to university and achieve great things. Just because Conor hadn't gone to university and barely worked didn't mean his kids shouldn't. She didn't want them to be lazy or to cut off opportunities that could enhance their lives. Besides, Conor was hardly a role model of the hard-working self-made man. The last thing Anna wanted was Jack thinking that Conor's way of life was something to aspire to. She didn't like criticizing him to the children, but neither was she going to let her son waste his life.

'Jack,' she said, keeping her voice even, 'going to school and to college gives you lots of options. And, by the way, if you have a trade and are your own boss, you have to work extremely hard to build up your business and make it a success.'

'Dad said nerds go to college and real men get jobs.'

James laughed. 'I think you'll find that nerds also get jobs after college. Good jobs.'

'Exactly,' Anna agreed. 'That was a silly thing for your dad to say. Grace will be going to college and she's not a nerd.'

Jack giggled. 'She kind of is.'

'Jack, you need to concentrate and do your best. That's all I ask of you, your best. Now come on, let's do the sum again,' Anna urged him.

Jack tried to do it again, while kicking the table with his right foot as James tried to eat his dinner from a vibrating plate.

He got the sum wrong again. Anna looked at James. Maybe he could give Jack a hand with his homework. It would help them bond and, besides, Anna would be happy to hand over maths homework to someone else. It had been a tough day in work. Chrissie was off sick with flu, so they were all working twice as hard to keep the schedule running smoothly. The last thing Anna felt like doing was sitting there, staring at a maths book.

As James put his last bite into his mouth, Anna stood up and took his plate from him.

'James, would you try explaining the sum to Jack? You'll probably be able to do a much better job than me given that you have a degree in economics.'

James didn't seem thrilled at the prospect.

'Please, darling?' Anna wasn't giving up.

'All right. Let's have a look.' James moved over to sit beside Jack. 'The first thing we might do is stop kicking the table, so it doesn't move when we're trying to read and write.'

Jack whacked the leg of the table even harder.

James picked up the maths book from the shaking table and read the question. Anna busied herself at the sink, soaking the lasagne dish.

'Okay, so Liam has fifteen sweets, which he shares evenly with his five friends. How many sweets do they each get?'

'It's a stupid question. He should just eat them all.'

James chuckled. 'Good point, Jack, but in this case he shares. So, if Liam has fifteen, and he divides the fifteen by his five friends, how many sweets does each friend get?'

Jack walloped the table with his foot again. 'I dunno. Liam's a dork.'

'Come on, Jack, try and work it out.'

'I don't want to.'

Anna stayed silent, hoping James would get through to him.

'You need to divide fifteen sweets by five. You can do that. Come on, Jack, you're a smart kid.'

Was he, though? Anna wondered. Grace was naturally bright, but Jack had always struggled to apply himself. People said boys were different from girls and they were right. He also had a father who didn't encourage him to work hard or sit down with him and help with homework. She was hoping that James would be a good role model and show him that doing well in school mattered.

'Five,' Jack shouted.

'No, it's not five. Nearly right, but not quite. Think about it now, concentrate on the question. Come on, Jack, stop kicking the table and focus.'

Whack. The table shuddered.

'Jack, try,' Anna said.

'Go away, Mum,' Jack snapped.

Anna decided to leave the room. Maybe Jack would behave better if she wasn't hovering. She stood outside the door, listening.

'How many times does five go into fifteen, Jack?' James asked again.

Thump, thump, thump.

'You can use your fingers, if you like. Count to fifteen and we'll see how many fists of five it takes to get there.'

Thump, thump, thump.

'Come on now, you can do this.' James's voice sounded a bit weary.

Thump, thump, thump.

'Jack, please stop kicking and concentrate. It's important to get the basics of maths right or you'll fall behind.'

Thump, thump, thump.

'You're not trying, Jack, come on.' James's voice was tense now.

Thump, thump, thump.

Anna's stomach fell. This was not going to end well. She was about to go in when she heard . . .

'You're just messing now. Focus, Jack,' James snapped.

'I hate poxy maths and I hate you,' Jack shouted. 'You're not my dad. You're not allowed to tell me what to do. My dad said you're a home-wrecker and a – a tool and a – wanker.'

'Jesus Christ, I'm trying to help you here. Have some respect.' James was furious now.

Damnit. Anna rushed in. 'Okay everyone, calm down. I'll take over from here.'

James glared at Jack. 'I think an apology is in order, Anna.'

'I'm not sorry,' Jack said. 'Not even a tiny bit.' He began to cry.

'Anna.' James looked to her for support, but she couldn't give it. Jack was upset and she wasn't about to give out to him now. She knew it would only make things worse.

'Leave it, James,' she said quietly, ushering her furious partner out of the room and then going back in to try to teach her son how to divide fifteen by sodding five.

James was reading when Anna went into the bedroom. She got undressed, brushed her teeth then lay down beside him. She needed to get this right. She needed to explain to James why she was going easy on Jack and not reprimanding him the way she would normally.

'James, I know you're angry and I understand. Jack should not speak to you like that. It's unacceptable.'

James put down his book. 'It really is, Anna.'

She held up her hand. 'Let me finish. The reason I'm letting him get away with more at the moment is because he's really struggling, James. He's a little boy who is lost. He's up every second night because he's upset. He never used to wake up at night. I have to rock him to sleep because he's crying and begging me to get back with his dad. He needs time and patience, James. His little heart is broken.' Anna fought back tears. 'And it kills me to see him like that because *I* did that to him. I know it was the right thing to do, but I didn't think he'd be this devastated.'

James nodded. 'I'm sorry he's finding it so hard. I know he's only young, but, Anna, if you continue to let him be so rude to me, you'll be setting a precedent that will be impossible to work back from. If he thinks he can treat me with no respect, well, what happens when he hits puberty and his teenage years? It'll be ten times worse. This is my home, too. We're all living under this roof and everyone is trying to figure out how to fit in, but letting him be so disrespectful is only going to cause more problems down the line.'

Anna fiddled with her ring. 'I understand that, but can you please just bear with me for a few weeks while I try to work with him rather than give out to him? This is all new to me and I'm trying to keep everyone happy, give everyone attention and bond with Bella – she's not easy either.'

James shook his head. 'Look, I'll stand back a bit and give you the space to work on Jack, but I'm going to say something if he insults me. There have to be boundaries, but I will try to tread gently. And, yes, I know Bella's been rude to you and I've spoken to her about it.'

He reached for Anna and wrapped his arms around her. 'I know how hard you're trying to make this a happy home and I love you for it. Let's take it day by day.'

She kissed him. 'Thanks for understanding. I love you.'

'I love you more.'

'Thank God for that or you'd probably have run for the hills.'

They both cracked up laughing and held each other tight.

17

Anna sat outside the classroom, staring at the clock on the wall. Their parent–teacher meeting slot was six fifteen and it was now six thirty. Thankfully, the other parents' meeting had run on because Conor was still nowhere in sight.

She'd pulled out her phone to call him again when she saw him strolling down the corridor towards her.

'You're late,' Anna said.

'Chill out, these things always run over. I'm here now.'

He sat down beside her. The smell of his aftershave hung in the air. A smell so familiar to her. A scent she had once loved but had grown to hate. He'd used it once too often to try to hide the smell of alcohol seeping out of his pores after another big night out with the lads.

He was wearing a blue shirt that was tight to his body and his best jeans. He looked younger than his age and Anna knew that he got a lot of attention from women. He had a good body and lots of swagger – women loved that about him. But she'd had quite enough of his swagger, his aftershave and his lateness.

The other parents came out of the classroom and Mrs Higgins called them in. She beamed at them across her desk. 'What can I say about Grace? She's the most fantastic girl. You must be so proud of her. Her science project is quite extraordinary and we have high hopes that she'll win the national Science Expo and go forward to the Global Science Fair.'

Anna felt her heart soar. How had she got so lucky with Grace?

'We're very proud of her. She's a diamond,' Conor said.

'She really is,' Mrs Higgins agreed. 'The only concern with

Grace is that she could wear herself out. I have said to her that she needs to take breaks and have some fun, too. She's a very serious young woman, even more so lately, I find.'

Conor cleared his throat. 'Yeah, well, that's probably because her mother left me and Grace and her brother are now living with a strange man.'

Anna felt herself go bright red. She was mortified. Why did Conor have to air their dirty laundry in the middle of a bloody parent–teacher meeting? Did he even consider whether Grace wanted this to be public knowledge or not?

'James is not a stranger. He's my partner. Grace has experienced some upheaval over the past few months, but I'm doing everything I can to smooth things over and help her adjust. I think she's absolutely fine, and the focus of the project has probably helped her work through some of the . . . well, the changes to our family situation.'

Mrs Higgins nodded. 'Grace seems a very well-adjusted girl. I agree that the project is a positive focus and the kudos she's getting is helping to raise her confidence. I see her on a very successful road ahead.'

'I hope so. She deserves it. She works so hard,' Anna said.

'Yeah, but we need to make sure she has fun, too, like Mrs Higgins said. All work and no play,' Conor said.

'I know that,' Anna cut across him, 'but I think that after this competition she'll be able to relax a bit.'

'She can't relax with that rotten step-sister around. She hates her.'

'No, she doesn't,' Anna snapped.

'Yes, she does. And Jack is miserable and keeps begging me to take him full-time.'

'Could you please stop airing our problems here?' Anna hissed. 'This really isn't the time or the place.'

'Right. I think the next parents are waiting, so I won't keep you.' Mrs Higgins stood up.

Conor jumped to his feet and headed for the door.

'Thank you so much.' Anna shook the teacher's hand. 'I'm very sorry about the personal side of things coming up . . . I . . .'

Mrs Higgins patted her arm. 'I've seen and heard it all in my thirty years' teaching. Grace is wonderful. Don't worry at all.'

Anna made her way to where Conor was waiting for her in the car park.

'Did you really have to bring up our personal life?' she snapped.

His face darkened. 'Yeah, I did, Anna. Believe it or not, your affair has affected your family. You walking out on me has upset our kids and turned their lives upside-down.'

Anna fought back tears. 'Stop blaming me for everything, Conor. For once in your life take responsibility. You were a shit husband. You don't do responsibility. While you sat around on your lazy arse, I worked double shifts to meet our mortgage repayments. I lay awake at night worrying about everything, while you just continued living your life the same way you've always done, worrying about yourself before anyone else.'

Conor stuck a finger in her face. 'Bullshit, Anna. Stop playing the martyr. *Poor Anna who got stuck with useless Conor.* I was there for you when you were sick. I lost everything when my knee blew out – I lost my dreams of being a professional footballer, I lost my hopes . . . everything. And all you did was nag me to get on with my life and put it behind me. I didn't want to have kids so young, but you did. You wanted to be a young parent, so I said okay. You got exactly what you wanted, Anna. I stood by you. I helped you raise Grace and then, when you wanted another kid, against my better judgement I went along with that too. You made decisions that affected my life regardless of what I wanted. You can rewrite history and play that poor-Anna card with your new boyfriend, but I was there, Anna, and you got exactly what you wanted.'

Anna felt as if she'd been slapped in the face. Conor was breathing heavily, raw rage emanating from his pores. Had she pushed him into having Grace early? Maybe, but Anna thought Conor didn't want to have a baby simply because he didn't want his freedom and fun to be hampered. She had also thought a baby would cheer him up and stop him getting depressed about his football career being over. She'd wanted to bring something positive to his life. And they'd had Grace, wonderful Grace. Conor had adored her the minute he'd set eyes on her.

And as for Jack, well, Conor was right: she had pushed for another baby. She hadn't wanted Grace to be an only child. She'd also thought that another child might get Conor to grow up a bit, and might save their marriage. Looking back now, it was naïve and stupid to think a baby would change anything, but she'd still had hope then. It was almost eleven years ago now, and she'd still loved Conor. She'd still thought she could make their marriage work.

'I didn't force you to stay with me, Conor. You could have walked away but, yes, you did stay and we have two beautiful children. I don't think I ruined your life, so why don't you stop playing the martyr card? Our kids are amazing.'

'True,' Conor muttered.

'Maybe I did push you to have Jack but I was trying to save our marriage. I was committed to our marriage, Conor. You can't say I wasn't.'

Conor took a deep breath. 'I know, and so was I,' he said. 'I didn't want to break up. I liked our life. I know it wasn't perfect, but it was us.'

'Come on, Conor, we fought day and night. The last few years were awful.'

'I know, but I . . . I just presumed it would get better. We're childhood sweethearts, we're not supposed to break up.'

'I tried, Conor, I really tried, but we weren't working. And now we have to find a way to get on and co-parent our kids.

Outbursts like that one in front of Grace's teacher are not help-ful,' Anna said, looking directly at him. 'So you get to humiliate me, great, and then what? What's the point?'

He shrugged. 'It just gets on top of me sometimes. It's hard to be around you. I miss you, Anna. It would be easier if I never had to see you, but I do because of the kids.'

Anna nodded. 'It's a really difficult situation, I agree. It's hard to know how to navigate it. But we won't find a way through if we keep taking pot shots at each other. That's get-ting us nowhere and it's bad for the kids to feel all this tension between us.'

She could see his shoulders dropping, the anger melting away from his body. He was listening to her, which was something.

Anna gave him a half-smile. 'We did something right, though. We have two fantastic kids and one of them appears to be a bit of a genius.'

'Well, she didn't get it from me.' Conor smiled.

'Okay, I'll take all the credit.'

They laughed together. It was the first time they had in years. It felt so nice. Conor reached out and put his arm around Anna. 'Truce?'

'Absolutely,' Anna said. Things would be so much better if she and Conor could meet halfway and stop needling each other all the time.

'How about I buy you a drink to celebrate our genius daughter?'

Anna didn't want to go for a drink with Conor, but it was a nice moment. The first in a very long time and she didn't want to break the spell. She had to think of Grace and Jack and what it would mean for them if their parents were friendly.

'Sure. Sounds nice,' she said.

Anna sat in a chair by the fire in the pub around the corner from the school. Conor stood at the bar. This was a big step forward for them. Anna smiled to herself. Things were going to be okay. It just took time.

Conor came over, handed her a glass of Diet Coke and sat down with a pint of Guinness. They sipped in companionable silence.

'Imagine if she wins the Science Expo,' Conor said. 'She'll go to America and then if she wins the Global competition, she'll probably get a scholarship to one of those posh universities over there.'

'Gosh, if she wins the Science Fair, she could well get a scholarship to Harvard or Yale in a few years' time. Wow, our little Gracie in an Ivy League university.'

'And Jack will play for Liverpool.'

Anna laughed. 'I'm not so sure about that.'

'Yeah, me neither, but a man can dream.'

'Jack needs to focus more on his schoolwork. He's falling behind in maths.'

'He's grand, leave him alone. Maths was never my strong point. He's a good kid. He's different from Grace.'

'True, it's hard for him to follow in her footsteps. She's set the bar very high. But Jack needs a range of choices so he can make the best of his life, you know? The only way to get that is through a good education.'

'I suppose,' Conor said, knocking back his pint. Anna had barely drunk half of her Coke. He went to the bar to get another.

He sat down beside her on the couch again, took a long drink from his pint and put his arm around her.

'This is nice. Us, chatting.'

'Yes, it is.'

'I miss this. I miss us. I wish things hadn't turned out like this. I miss our family, Anna. We were a unit, all of us together. I miss family dinners, sitting around chatting and laughing with the kids. It's bloody lonely in that apartment on my own.'

Anna held her glass a little tighter.

'We're good together, Anna. You and me. We're a good team. You're the strict parent, and I'm more the fun one. Our kids have a good balance. We're a perfect partnership. I know I've been a bit lazy lately and that put pressure on you, but I'll change. I'll be a better husband and we can get back to the way it was.'

Anna didn't say anything. Conor was leaning in a little too close for comfort.

'I love you, Anna. I love our kids. I love our family. I think I can forgive you. It won't be easy, but I'll try. I want us to be a family again. I miss you, Anna.'

He leant over and kissed her on the lips. Anna jerked her head back.

'Come on, babe, we're so good together.' He tried to kiss her again.

Anna pushed him back firmly. 'Stop it. Jesus, Conor, what are you doing?'

'Trying to kiss my wife,' he snapped.

'I'm not your wife any more.'

'We're not divorced so technically you're still my wife. Come on, I love you, Anna. I want us to try again. It makes sense, you know it does.'

Anna put down her glass. 'Conor, we'll never be together again. This is over. We are over. We were over years ago. You don't love me. If you did love me, you would have tried harder to make our marriage work. But you always put yourself and "the lads" first. I didn't want to be the strict parent, the nagging parent, the parent who had to take responsibility for every-thing, but I had to. You're a man who never grew up. I know that I enabled you. I took on all the responsibility and let you live your carefree life. But whenever I tried to get you to step up, we'd have a big argument, so I gave up. I realize now that I became someone I'm not. I'm not a nag, I'm not a bore, I'm not a weapon or any of the things you called me. I've found myself again and I'm so happy. I'm not constantly worried and stressed. I'm lighter and more joyful than I've been for years. I'll always have a place for you in my heart because you're the father of my children, but I'm in love with James. This is it for me, Conor. I love him. I'm really, really happy.'

Conor slammed down his pint. 'I give it a year. He's a dickhead and the kids hate him. So while you're so happy and in love, your children, who you always tell me are your first priority, are miserable. Who's the selfish one now, Anna? Who's putting their happiness first now? Who's the shitty parent now?'

'That's not fair,' Anna said quietly.

'The truth hurts.' Conor grabbed his jacket and stormed out of the pub.

Anna sat and stared into the fire. Was she selfish? Were the children really unhappy? Was she a bad parent? Was it so wrong to want to be happy? Was it so wrong to allow yourself to fall in love? Was it self-seeking to want to be in a relationship with someone you respect and love, who makes your life so much better in every way?

Anna sipped her drink and pushed away the negative thoughts. She would not let Conor get under her skin and make her question herself. She would not let him ruin her lovely life. She would not let him destroy her happiness any more.

She picked up her keys and went home to the man she loved. The man she wanted to spend the rest of her life with.

18

Anna held up a third dress.

'No,' Angela said.

'I give up,' Anna replied.

'What about that black one with the halter neck?' Anita asked.

'Too boring,' Angela said.

'She doesn't want to look like a slapper,' Anita replied.

'Yeah, but she doesn't want to look like a granny either.'

'Ingrid will be in something simple and classy. I can't be too jazzy.'

Angela rolled her eyes. 'You're way better-looking than Ingrid, with a better body. You have really good legs and she has stumpy, chunky ones, so we need to show your legs off.'

'Sssh! Bella's across the corridor in her bedroom!' Anna reminded them.

They ignored her.

'Not short mini-dress, though,' Anita said.

'Just above the knee,' Angela replied.

'Yeah.'

Angela got up from the edge of Anna's bed and began rifling through her wardrobe. 'This one!' She pulled out a fitted red dress, with spaghetti straps, that ended just above the knee.

'That's my sexy date dress.'

'So?' Both sisters stared at her.

'Well, it's Bella's fifteenth birthday party, I don't want to look like I'm trying too hard. You know, the slapper step-mum.'

'It's not like your boobs are hanging out and your knickers are on view.' Angela held the dress up to her sister.

'I think Ingrid will probably be in a conservative dress or trouser suit and I don't want to be standing there in my tight red dress.'

'But you've a great figure, so why should you hide it?' Angela pointed out.

'I kind of get what she's saying. How about this one?' Anita pulled out a navy dress. It was fitted and the same length as the red one, but it had cap sleeves and was more muted.

'Yes, that's better.'

'Boring,' Angela said.

'Not boring, but a bit more like "I'm the classy new bird,"' Anita said.

'What's the step-cow wearing?'

'Sssh!' Anna was terrified Bella would hear the nickname her step-aunts had given her.

'Unless she has bionic ears, she can't hear us,' Angela said.

'She has four different designer dresses and she can't decide which one,' Anna told them. That whole week Net-a-Porter boxes had arrived almost daily. Grace's eyes were out on stalks when she saw the dresses Bella had ordered. 'Honestly, I think it's obscene that a fifteen-year-old girl has a credit card with apparently no limit to her spending. I hate Grace seeing how spoilt Bella is. I tried to say it to James, that Bella should have a limit on her spending, but he got very defensive and said it was Ingrid who had given her the credit card and it was Bella's birthday, and if her mother wanted to spoil her a bit, then so be it. He never stands up to that woman.'

'Now hang on,' Angela said. 'James is a saint in my eyes after what I witnessed at Jack's party.'

'What happened?' Anita wanted to know.

'He got mown down holding hot tea and then shot in the face.'

'What?' Anita's jaw dropped.

'It was a BB gun.'

'He could have lost his eye, Anna,' Angela said. 'To be honest, I can't believe he didn't run out the front door and head for the hills after that. He was so good about it.'

'I presume Conor bought Jack the BB gun?' Anita asked.

'Of course, he did,' Angela said.

'They're dangerous, Anna,' Anita said.

'I know. He keeps it at Conor's and isn't allowed to bring it here. I've told him he has to be extra careful. But I can't control what goes on in Conor's apartment.'

'Yes, but you can control what goes on here and you let Jack get away with murder that day.'

'Come on, Angela, it was his birthday and you haven't seen how unhappy he's been. It was a joy to see him smiling and laughing.'

'Be careful, Anna,' Anita warned her. 'If you let him get away with murder now, he'll be a complete nightmare when he's older.'

'It was one day!' Anna was exasperated.

'It's not, though. You've been letting him sleep in the bed with you and spoiling him. I know it's because you feel guilty about leaving Conor, but you're going to have to set some rules and boundaries. It's not fair on James. This is his home too,' Angela reminded her. 'If I was physically assaulted and shot in my house, I'd be gone.'

'Look, we all parent differently,' Anita said. 'Sure Paul and I argue all the time over screen time and curfews for the kids, but we know we have to meet halfway. It sounds like James is getting a raw deal here, sleeping on the couch and Jack acting the maggot. You need to show Jack that it's not okay. You need to be firm about how he treats James, just like James needs to be firm with Bella about how she treats you.'

'It's just hard when your child is unhappy. You'd do anything to make it better.'

'I understand, but all kids need boundaries and you need to

be careful not to push James away while you're pandering to Jack,' Angela pointed out.

'She's right, Anna. Okay, I'm popping to the loo. Try on both dresses and we'll make a final decision,' Anita said.

As Anna was about to try on the navy dress Anita poked her head around the door and beckoned Anna over.

'What?'

'I think someone's sick,' Anita whispered, pointing to the bathroom door. The three sisters went into the corridor and stood outside the bathroom.

Anna put her ear against the door and heard someone vomiting. Grace and Jack were at their dad's and James had gone to meet a friend for a game of squash, so that left Bella.

Anna knocked gently on the door. 'Bella? Are you okay, love?'

'I'm fine.'

'Are you sick?'

'No.'

'Are you vomiting? Did you eat something or maybe pick up a bug at school?'

'I'm fine. Go away and stop stalking me. Jesus, can I not have some privacy in this house?'

Anna stepped back. 'If you need anything, I'm here.'

'I don't want or need anything from you except for you to leave me alone.'

The sisters went back into Anna's bedroom and closed the door.

'She's a real charmer.' Angela snorted.

'She's a piece of work,' Anita said.

'She's adjusting.' Anna tried to remain positive.

Anita rolled her eyes. 'She's rude and she shouldn't speak to you like that. You'd never let your two get away with that, and neither would we with our girls. She needs manners put on her. The cheek!'

Part of Anna agreed with her sisters, and she was embarrassed that they'd witnessed Bella being so rude and dismissive of her. But it all came back to the fact that Bella was part of James's package. If Anna wanted James, she had to accept Bella too.

'Seriously, Anna, you and James need to sort out your kids' behaviour. He needs to nip that in the bud,' Angela said. 'If you let her speak to you like that, it'll only get worse. That is disrespectful and this is your house. You wouldn't let Grace speak to James like that, would you?'

'No, but, as you pointed out, Jack has been pretty rude to James.'

'At least he has the excuse of still being young. Bella's nearly fifteen, and it's out of order,' Anita pointed out.

Anna tucked her hair behind her ears. 'It's complicated. I hate it when James gives out to Jack, so I'm slow to give out to Bella.'

'Manners are manners. There's nothing complicated about respect.' Anita was not letting go.

'We're all still getting used to each other and Bella is used to being an only child. Now she has to share her dad with me and two new siblings.'

'She's lucky to have you as a step-mum. She could have got a weapon,' Anita said.

'Very true, and Jack is lucky to have James as a step-dad. Your kids need to realize how lucky they are and start behaving.'

Anna groaned. 'I'm hoping they'll just wake up one day and see that we're nice step-parents. I think James could be such a good influence on Jack.'

'By the way, Anthony bumped into Conor the other day. He said he's playing the martyr card.'

Angela rolled her eyes. 'Pillock.'

'He told Anthony he was a broken man, then tried to say it was all your fault and that you had a fabulous marriage until James came in and broke you up.'

'He's unbelievable.'

'Yeah, well, he was barking up the wrong tree. Anthony told him to cop on and stop blaming you when he was a lazy git who never got off his arse to do a decent day's work and that he was lucky you'd stayed with him as long as you had.' Anita chuckled.

Anna grinned. Good old Anthony. Oldest brothers were the best. She decided to tell her sisters about the kiss.

'Brace yourselves, ladies. You're not going to believe what Conor did after Grace's parent–teacher meeting.'

'What?'

She filled them in on the attempted kiss.

'He did not!' Anita gasped.

'The cheeky git!' Angela fumed.

'What did you do?' Anita asked.

'Please say you punched him.'

Anna laughed. 'No, although I was tempted. I jumped backwards.'

'Why did you go for a drink with him?' Angela asked.

'Because I'm trying to get to a place with him where we can be civil and not have all this tension. He was being kind of nice and normal and he asked me. I thought I should make an effort and then he hopped on me.'

'You're too bloody nice, Anna, that's always been your problem,' Anita said, shaking her head.

'Far too nice,' Angela agreed. 'What possessed him to kiss you, though?'

'He said he missed me and then he lunged at me.'

'What did he do when you recoiled in horror?' Anita giggled.

'He was furious. He said I'm selfish and a shitty parent.'

'That's the pot calling the kettle black if ever I heard it.'

'Have you spoken to him since?' Anita asked.

'No, we've only communicated by text. I'm dreading the next time I see him.'

137

'Don't worry, it's his embarrassment not yours.'

'Men! Seriously, how delusional is he? Any word on Grace's competition?' Angela asked.

'She presents it next week, so cross all your fingers and toes.'

'I'm going home to kick my lazy lot up the arse. There's Grace changing the world with her science projects and Larry spends all day playing feckin' video games and staring at dopes on YouTube. He announced yesterday that he doesn't need to go to school any more because he's going to be a YouTube star. "Doing what?" I asked. "Just videos of me hanging out with the lads and stuff, showing my personality and banter," he says. Banter? He barely says three words a week. They'll be short videos, that's for sure. You'd have better banter with a donkey.'

The three sisters cracked up laughing.

Anita's watch beeped. 'Bloody fitness app. All it does is make me feel guilty every time I sit down. I think I'll get rid of it. Apparently I need to "get moving". If I don't do ten thousand steps a day, it torments me. It's like having a flea in your ear.'

'Life is too short for some stupid watch to be making you feel bad. Get rid of it,' Angela said.

'I agree,' Anna said. 'We don't need any more guilt. Well, I certainly don't. I feel guilty all the time about James and the kids and Conor and, well, everyone.'

'All this guilt is driving you crazy and making you pander to them all. Park the guilt, and when your kids or step-kids behave badly, call them out. You need to shed the past, Anna. You so deserve to be happy and don't you forget that.' Angela squeezed her sister's hand.

'Thanks. I'll try.'

'Well, I'd better move my arse or I'll be stalked by my watch. Wear the navy dress. It's gorgeous, and it shows off your figure without flaunting it.' Anita picked up her handbag.

'You're gorgeous in both,' Angela said.

Anna thanked them and walked them to the front door. She

waved them off and turned back inside. She silently thanked God that she was not an only child. She loved being from a big family. Her sisters and brothers were like a support network. They weren't all as close to each other as she was to her sisters, but they were always there for each other. She felt sorry for Bella – it was hard being an only child. She hoped she'd come to consider Grace and Jack as her siblings. It would be good for her, if only she could see that.

Anna went back upstairs to tidy up the dresses. As she passed Bella's bedroom she heard her talking on the phone.

'Yeah, I do have to invite them. Dad said I did. It's such a pain. Grace is like a mouse, she barely speaks, and Jack is the most irritating kid ever. As for my step-mother, she is such a drag.'

Anna closed her bedroom door to block out the negativity. She took ten . . . twenty . . . thirty deep breaths and tried to stay positive. It had taken her thirty-seven years to find James and true love. It would just take a bit more time and patience to find a happy balance in this new family unit.

19

Ingrid watched as Denis instructed the staff that everything was to run smoothly and that this was a very important evening for his step-daughter.

'It's her fifteenth birthday and I want her to have the time of her life. We need to make sure none of the kids sneak alcohol in. I don't need some litigious parent suing the hotel because their kid got drunk on their own vodka. If any kid is caught drinking, they're out on their ear, no second chances. I want champagne on ice for Ingrid and me and James and . . .' He turned to Ingrid. 'What's her name again? Angela?'

'Anna,' Ingrid reminded him.

'Oh, yes, Anna.'

Denis clapped his hands. 'Right, off you go.'

Ingrid flinched at Denis's sharpness. Sometimes she wished he'd be a little less harsh when he talked to his staff. He was right to demand high standards, but sometimes he came across as a bit too gruff. Although when she had mentioned it to him in the past, he'd said, 'I didn't make it to this level of success by pandering to my staff's feelings. If you want to work for me, you work hard and I pay well. End of.'

None of his staff worked harder than Denis, so he certainly set a strong example. He never, ever stopped working. Even in his sleep she'd heard him muttering about deals, issues, mergers . . . He was relentless, but she admired it. She loved his drive and found it very attractive. Striving hard for success was something she could completely relate to.

Ingrid and Denis went up to the rooftop terrace where the party was being held. Ingrid stepped out of the lift under a huge balloon arch and was greeted by hundreds of candles and fairy lights. It looked gorgeous, just as she'd instructed. The staff had done a great job. Tall tables were covered with silver cloths and a mirrored dance-floor had been laid down beside a small stage. Heaters pumped out warm air from all sides of the terrace, keeping the temperature pleasant. Bella was going to love it.

'It's perfect.' She smiled up at Denis.

'Everything you asked for? Nothing missing?' he asked.

'It's exactly what I asked them to do.'

'Good. I must say the new manager, Yvonne, is proving to be a very good hire. I might get her to sort out the Pilkington in London. It needs a strong manager. What do you think?'

Ingrid laid her hand on his arm. 'Let's have a glass of champagne and enjoy the gorgeous view.' She loved talking business, she loved being involved in every aspect of Denis's large portfolio of properties, but Bella was right, they did talk of nothing else.

They sat on one of the couches and a waiter came over to hand them each a glass of ice-cold champagne.

'Cheers,' Denis said. 'To a great party for Bella and to her wonderful mother.'

Ingrid smiled. 'Cheers to that, and to her ever generous step-father.'

'Hardly. You insisted on paying for it all.'

'Yes, but it is your hotel.'

'Our hotel, darling,' Denis said.

Denis always reminded her that they were a partnership, and Ingrid loved that. She hadn't wanted to remarry, but he'd persuaded her. He said he liked being married, that she was his match in every way and he wanted to do this one last time. After his two failed attempts, Ingrid was surprised Denis wanted to commit to her. She hadn't needed marriage to feel secure: she was happy being his partner. But Denis had insisted they get married, so in turn Ingrid had insisted that they draw up a pre-nuptial agreement. They were married in a register office in

London. Their two witnesses were Bella and Claire, although Claire was not enthusiastic about the union.

Ingrid sensed that Claire saw her as a threat, the woman who would 'steal' her father's money. That was why she had insisted on a pre-nup, because she didn't want Claire accusing her of being a gold-digger. Besides, Ingrid did very well for herself, thank you very much, and she didn't need Denis's money. Sure, his wealth was in a different stratosphere from hers, but while she enjoyed the finer things in life, they didn't make her world turn. Closing big deals and mergers and acquisitions did. Work was what gave Ingrid a high. It was why she and Denis got on so well: they were kindred spirits.

James had never understood her hunger to be successful, to chase the next big deal. He was content with his life as a professor, content with standing still. Ingrid had found it so frustrating. She couldn't understand his lack of ambition and drive. She had always wanted more, bigger, better, but James was happy with small, consistent and cosy.

If it wasn't for Bella, she reckoned they'd have broken up years earlier. Bella had been the glue, but even their wonderful daughter couldn't cover the cracks in their marriage. They grew apart and, in the end, when Ingrid met Denis, she knew he was the man she needed to be with. He was her match. James wasn't surprised when she left him – in fact, Ingrid thought he was secretly relieved. She'd told him to keep the house, but he'd insisted on selling it and dividing the proceeds evenly. Then he'd bought a small apartment in a nice area, a brisk twenty-minute walk to Trinity, and Ingrid had moved into Denis's penthouse and that was that.

Ingrid was glad James had met someone, but she was irritated by the stories Bella was telling her about James and Anna being all over each other in front of her, and Anna coming into her bedroom to try to get to know her better. For goodness' sake, could the woman not just leave poor Bella alone and get to know her in Bella's own good time? Neediness was so unattractive in a person.

'OMG!'

Ingrid and Denis looked up to see Bella jumping up and down.

'It's amazing, Mum, thank you.' Bella hugged Ingrid. 'And thank you too, Denis.' She hugged her step-father.

'It's all your mother's handiwork.' Denis heaped praise on Ingrid.

'It's absolutely perfect. I can't wait for my friends to see it.' Bella clapped her hands with glee.

Ingrid beamed at her. She was proud of her girl. She looked so lovely tonight in her silver dress and high heels, like a young woman. Too much make-up and fake tan, but all the girls at her age overdid it. She was radiant nonetheless.

Ingrid kissed her cheek. 'Happy birthday, darling.'

'Can I have some champagne?' Bella asked.

'Absolutely not.' Ingrid shut that down.

Before Bella could ask again there was shrieking at the entrance. Her friends had arrived. Ingrid and Denis stood back as hordes of squealing, screeching girls and loud boys poured onto the terrace.

Denis watched them like a hawk, making sure no one was sneaking alcohol into their soft drinks.

Anna squeezed Grace's hand as the lift came to a halt. Grace had begged not to go to the party, but Anna had insisted. It was important to James that everyone was there for Bella's big night. Grace looked so beautiful in her pale-blue skater dress and white runners. Anna hoped she'd have a good time and that Bella would be nice to her. She'd promised Grace that they only had to stay for an hour.

'I can't wait for Bella to see my present.' James beamed. He was so proud of it. He'd gone to so much trouble to source the tickets and had paid way over the odds for them. Anna hoped his daughter was really grateful.

The lift doors opened and they stepped into a wonderland.

'Wow,' Grace said.

'Awesome!' Jack's eyes zoned in on the bar, laden with fizzy drinks, and on the six silver mini-vans that were kitted out as a sweet shop, a burger bar, a pizza parlour, a sushi restaurant, a nail bar and an ice-cream-frozen-yogurt parlour.

She tried to hold him back, but James told her to let him go and enjoy himself.

'Go on, Jack, enjoy the party,' James said, smiling at him.

Jack didn't need a second invitation. Anna watched as he raced over to stock up on food and drink.

James scanned the room for Bella.

'There she is.' Anna pointed to Bella, who was shimmering in a stunning silver dress.

James went over to wish his daughter a happy birthday.

'I'm only staying for an hour,' Grace reminded her mother.

'At the most,' Anna whispered back.

James hugged Bella, then beckoned Anna and Grace over. At least Bella was smiling, Anna thought, that was a bonus. 'Happy birthday.' She kissed her step-daughter's cheek.

'Isn't my daughter the Bella of the ball?' James gazed adoringly at her.

'You look amazing,' Grace said.

'Thanks. You look fab, too, but you always look good,' Bella said. 'Three guys have already asked me who you are.'

Grace blushed. 'Really?'

'Yeah.'

'That's so nice of you to say, Bella,' Anna gushed. 'What a lovely compliment. Isn't it, Grace?'

'Stop, Mum.' Grace was mortified.

'Yeah, like, whatever.' Bella bounced off to chat to her friends.

'What?' Anna asked, as Grace glared at her.

'Stop making a big deal about everything that Bella says. It's embarrassing.'

'Hey.' A young guy came up to Grace. 'So you're Bella's step-sister, yeah?'

'Yes.'

'I'm Zach.'

'Grace.'

'Do you want to get some food?'

'Okay.'

Anna watched as Grace and Zach, who had a large diamond stud in his right ear, went off to the food stalls. 'I'm not sure about Zach,' she said.

James laughed. 'She's getting food with him, not sleeping with him.'

'Yes, but one could lead to the other.'

James put his arm around her. 'Anna, relax. Grace is a beautiful girl. She's going to get attention from boys.'

Yes, but I don't want her getting stuck like I did, Anna thought. I don't want her married young and trapped.

'You're here.' Ingrid waved to them. 'Come and sit down.'

'We've been summoned,' James muttered.

Anna followed him to his ex-wife. Ingrid was wearing a tailor-made black tuxedo with a beautiful silk shirt. She looked very cool and elegant. Anna was glad she hadn't worn the sexy red dress. The navy one was definitely the right call.

Ingrid introduced Anna to Denis. She had been dying to meet him. She'd googled him with her sisters and there was a lot about him online. The successful multi-millionaire property developer, philanthropist and businessman. The ex-wives, the properties, the yacht, and the party-girl daughter, Claire.

He was more attractive in the flesh. In photos, he looked older than fifty-six. In the flesh, he could pass for fifty. He'd grown one of those designer close-shaven beards and it suited him. Anna wouldn't have called him handsome, but he was attractive. They were a very attractive and powerful-looking couple. They had the rich shine that wealthy people have.

'Lovely to meet you, Anna.' Denis offered her a glass of champagne, which she accepted gratefully.

'You too, Denis. I've heard so much about you,' Anna said.

'Have you?' Denis looked surprised.

Oh, shut up, Anna, you fool, she thought. She hadn't heard lots about him: she'd googled lots about him.

'What? Uhm, oh, well, you know, Bella says nice things about you.' Anna shoved the glass to her mouth to stop words cascading out. She always talked too much when she was nervous or uncomfortable and, right now, she was both.

'Gorgeous party, Ingrid. Very Bella.' James smiled.

'Thanks. The hotel staff did it all. I just gave them instructions. She seems very happy.'

They turned to look at Bella, who was surrounded by friends and laughing loudly.

Silence.

'So, how's business, Denis?' James asked.

'Good, thanks, very good actually. We've just acquired a hotel in Paris.'

'Congratulations, that sounds great.'

Silence.

Anna noticed that Denis didn't ask James how his work was going.

Grace came over and sat beside her mother.

'Denis, this is my daughter, Grace.'

Denis shook her hand.

'You've met Ingrid before,' Anna reminded Grace.

'Yes, hi.' Grace shook her hand.

'Hello, Grace, how are you getting on? You're in the same school year as Bella, aren't you?' Ingrid said.

'Yes, that's right.'

'Grace is representing her school at the Science Expo,' James

146

said. 'If she wins, she goes to the Global Science Fair in California later in the year. One of my colleagues, head of science at Trinity, was so impressed he's asked her to come in and tell his students about her project.'

Anna fell in love with James a little bit more as she watched her daughter flush with pride.

'Oh, my goodness.' Ingrid was impressed. 'That's fantastic, good for you, Grace. What's the project about?'

Grace filled her in, while Ingrid and Denis listened intently.

'That's ingenious,' Ingrid said.

'Come back to me if you need investment. That idea has legs. Everyone's looking for lactose-free products now,' Denis said.

Anna almost burst with pride. Here was her fifteen-and-a-half-year-old daughter impressing this power couple.

'You'll be a good influence on Bella,' Ingrid noted. 'Hopefully she'll see how successful you are and stop wasting all of her time on this silly school musical.'

Anna thought it was good that Bella was interested in something other than make-up and fake tan.

'She's very excited about it, Ingrid. Don't knock it,' James said. 'Getting the lead role of Sandy was a big deal for her. We need to encourage her.'

'I'd like to see less singing and dancing and more studying,' Ingrid replied.

'I've heard her singing in her bedroom. She's really good,' Grace said.

Ingrid shook her head. 'Singing isn't going to pay her mortgage.'

'Ingrid,' James's tone was strong, 'we need to support her.'

'I do support her.' Ingrid's tone was icy. 'Just not in wasting her time on pointless pursuits that will lead to nothing and eat into her study time.'

'Playing the lead in a school musical is good for her self-esteem, her confidence and fulfilment,' James said.

Anna wasn't sure Bella needed more confidence – she was about as confident a teenager as she had ever met. Anna glanced over at Denis, to see if he was feeling the tension too, but he was looking at his phone.

Denis stood up. 'Right, I've a conference call with the US in twenty minutes, so let's give Bella her present now.'

Denis spoke to Yvonne and, within seconds, was handed a microphone. They all walked over to the stage. Anna stood back with Grace, while Denis, Ingrid and James climbed up. Out of the corner of her eye, Anna could see Jack knocking back Coke and shovelling sweets into his mouth. He'd never go to sleep with all that sugar.

'Sorry to interrupt the party, but could I have Bella up here, please?' Denis's voice boomed across the crowd, silencing the chatter.

Bella walked up onto the stage and stood beside her step-father.

'Bella, your mum and I are very proud of you and we wanted to give you something you'd never forget so . . . for your birthday we're giving you four VIP all-access tickets to see Harry Styles. You'll also be meeting him backstage after the concert and going to the VIP after-party, which is being held right here on this terrace. You and your three guests will be staying in a suite at the hotel for the night of the concert.'

While Bella and her friends shrieked, Anna's heart sank. She looked at James. His face was white.

Bella threw her arms around Denis and Ingrid, and thanked them over and over.

'Now I'll hand over to your dad, who has a gift for you too.' Denis handed James the microphone. James refused to take it.

Bella turned to James, eyes shining. 'What is it, Dad?'

'Nothing.' James shoved the envelope into his pocket.

'Dad?'

'It's nothing, forget it. I'll give it to you tomorrow.'

'Give it to me now. It's my birthday party.'

'We can do it tomorrow, Bella. You'll have something to look forward to,' Anna said.

Bella ignored her. 'Dad, come on.'

James turned and stepped down from the stage. Anna could see the raw emotion on his face.

Bella followed him. '*Daaaad*, why are you being so weird? What's in the envelope?'

Denis and Ingrid had stepped down, too. Everyone was staring at James.

'Nothing. Please, just drop it.'

'For goodness' sake, James, stop making such a fuss and give her the present,' Ingrid exclaimed.

Anna wanted to slap her.

'Fine.' James snatched the envelope out of his pocket and handed it to Bella. 'It's two tickets to the same concert. Just normal, bog-standard tickets.'

'Oh,' Ingrid said.

'That's cool, Dad, thanks so much. Here, Grace, you can take these. I have the other ones.' Bella casually handed Grace the tickets her father had gone to so much trouble and expense to procure. 'Now everyone's happy!' Bella danced off into the middle of her clamouring friends, who all sucked up to her, vying for one of the golden VIP tickets.

Anna felt sick for James. Grace held out the envelope, not knowing what to do. Anna took it from her and put it into her bag. She whispered, 'Find Jack, we're leaving.'

'We probably should have communicated on the gift, James,' Ingrid said.

'It's actually worked out well. Grace gets to go too now. Right, I'm off.' Denis breezed off the terrace, his ear glued to his phone.

Ingrid turned to Anna and James. 'Denis is right, there's no harm done. Bella is happy and now Grace gets to go to the concert.'

Anna was so hurt for James that she couldn't stop herself

saying, 'James didn't buy the tickets for Grace. He bought them for his daughter. He moved mountains to get those tickets and he was very excited to give them to Bella. It's not easy for him to be usurped by Denis.'

Ingrid waved a hand in the air. 'No one's dead, Anna. We all had the same good idea. Bella is going to the concert and is delighted with her gift. That's all that really matters.'

Jesus, was this woman for real? Had she no compassion for how humiliated and hurt James was feeling?

'James's feelings matter, too,' Anna snapped.

'For goodness' sake, let's not blow it out of proportion. James is an adult not a child.'

'He still has feelings, Ingrid.'

When James spoke, his voice was very measured, and Anna could tell he was fighting back hurt and anger. 'We're leaving now, Ingrid. And going forward, the next time you and Denis decide to buy a big gift for Bella, I'd appreciate a heads-up.'

'Fair enough.'

James was holding Anna's hand so tightly that she thought he might break it. They gathered Grace, and a now completely sugar-rushed Jack, and made for the lift.

'Dad!' Bella ran over to them. 'Where are you going?'

'We need to get Jack home and, besides, you don't need your dad ruining your fun.'

'Okay. Well, thanks for the present and for being a great dad.' Bella hugged him. 'Thanks all of you for coming.'

The lift doors opened and they all stepped in while Bella rushed back to her friends.

In the lift, while Jack listed everything he had eaten and drunk to Grace, James leant in and whispered in Anna's ear, 'That's why I left her and why I thank God every day that I met you. Thanks for defending me in there. I couldn't love you more than I do right now.'

Anna nuzzled into his neck. 'I feel exactly the same way.'

20

Grace's hands shook as she hung up. She'd won. She'd won the Science Expo and her project was going forward for the Global Science Fair in California in six months' time.

She ran downstairs to tell her mum.

Anna, still in her nurse's scrubs, was taking freshly baked scones from the oven and chatting to Jack. Grace threw her arms around her mother from behind.

Anna turned, taken by surprise. 'What's that for?'

'Mrs Higgins called. I won, Mum. I won the science prize. I won!' Grace felt her voice rising.

'Oh, my God – Grace, that's incredible!' Anna's eyes filled with tears. 'I am so ridiculously proud of you.'

'Thanks.' Grace's welled too.

'We have to tell –'

As Anna said, 'James', Grace said, 'Dad.'

They stopped and looked at each other.

'Your dad, of course, Conor.' Anna fumbled over the words.

Grace tried not to mind that Anna had wanted to tell James before her father, but it stung. Was her mother so obsessed with James that she wanted him to know before Conor?

Grace rang her dad and filled him in. Conor whooped and roared and shouted and told her she was a legend and a diamond and how proud he was. 'You, Grace Mangan, are one in a million.'

Grace laughed. She loved her dad's enthusiasm: he always made a big fuss over every achievement, however small . . . or big.

'We have to celebrate this. I'm taking us all out to dinner. Even your mum.'

'Really?' Grace said.

'Absolutely. I'll book a table in Franco's, your favourite.'

Grace beamed. 'Thanks, Dad.'

'See you later, genius.'

Grace handed the phone back to Anna. 'Dad's taking us out for dinner.'

'Oh, I was going to do that.' Anna's face fell.

'No, with you too. Our family.' Well, our original family, Grace thought. And that's what she wanted. She didn't want James or Bella there. She wanted it to be the Mangan family only. No outsiders.

'Yeah, just us, no stupid step-family.' Jack punched the air.

'I'm not sure that's the best idea,' Anna said. 'Your dad and I aren't exactly seeing eye to eye at the moment.'

Grace sighed. 'Can you just behave like adults and have a nice dinner?'

Anna reached out and touched her daughter's arm. 'I'm sorry, of course we can. It'll be lovely.'

Anna dressed in jeans and a buttoned-up shirt. She didn't want Conor getting any ideas. She was dreading the dinner. She hadn't spoken to Conor since the night he'd tried to kiss her. They had only communicated via text. She wanted to give him a wide berth. It had been three weeks and she'd rather have waited at least another month before seeing him.

She went to get a fresh hand towel from the cupboard in the main bathroom when she heard someone being sick. 'Grace?'

Silence.

'Grace, are you okay?'

Grace came out of her bedroom. 'I'm here. Bella went in there after me.'

Anna knocked gently on the door. 'Bella, are you all right?'

'Fine.'

'Do you have an upset stomach again?'

'I just ate something and it must have been off.'

'Can I do anything for you?'

'No. I'm fine.'

'I'll just let your dad know you're not feeling well, so he can keep an eye on you.'

'Anna,' Bella's voice was sharp, 'there is no need to make a big deal. It's just something I ate. I'll be fine now.'

'Okay. I hope you feel better soon.'

Anna went downstairs to talk to James. He needed to know his daughter had food poisoning in case it got worse.

James went straight up the stairs, Anna following.

'Bella, Anna told me you're sick. Should I call the doctor?'

'JESUS CHRIST! Could that stupid cow shut the hell up? I'm fine.' Bella whipped open the door.

'Are you all right, pet?' James asked.

'For the millionth time, I'm fine. God, can you all get a life and stop zoning in on me?' Seeing Anna behind James, she shouted, 'Go out for your stupid dinner, focus on your own kids and stop snooping around me. I hate this fucking house.'

She stormed into her bedroom and slammed the door. They heard the lock click.

Jack pointed at the closed door. 'She said "fuck" again.'

'Sssh.' Anna hushed him.

'Why is she always so grumpy?' Jack asked.

'Oh, it's just hormones,' James said. 'Girls can be a bit moody when they're teenagers.'

Moody! Anna almost laughed. She was an overindulged pain in the arse whose father needed to tell her off once in a blue moon.

'She called Mum a stupid cow,' Jack said.

Yes, she bloody did, Anna thought, and James wasn't reacting to the insult or to the shouting or to any of his daughter's rotten behaviour.

'Yes, I know, Jack, but she's sick and upset. We all say things we don't mean when we're not feeling well.' James continued to excuse his daughter's behaviour while Anna bit her tongue.

'I don't,' Jack said. 'Grace doesn't.'

James stared at him, lost for words.

'Why don't you and Grace wait downstairs? I'll be down in a minute,' Anna suggested.

She went into her bedroom, James following.

Anna put on some lipstick.

'Poor Bella,' he said. 'I wonder what she ate? Nothing worse than an upset stomach. I'll keep a close eye on her.'

Anna had to say something. Her sisters were right: if she let Bella speak to her like that she was setting a precedent and things would only get worse. 'James, Bella can't speak to me like that. I wouldn't allow Grace or Jack to speak to you in that way. It's not acceptable.'

James bristled. 'Hold on now, the poor girl is feeling ill. I agree she was snappy, but I think we need to cut her some slack in this case and, besides, Jack is rude to me all the time.'

'He's ten.'

'She's sick.'

'She's rude to me when she's not sick too.'

'Fine. You talk to Jack and I'll talk to Bella about manners and boundaries.'

'Please be firm with her, James.'

'I will, but she's unwell, so it might have to wait until tomorrow.'

Anna zipped up her boots. 'I'd better go.'

'You look lovely.' James attempted a smile.

'Thanks.'

'It's a big night. Grace's achievement is really phenomenal. I'm so proud of her.'

'I wish you were coming.'

'Yes, but I'm not.'

'I'm sorry.'

James shrugged. 'Blended families aren't straightforward.'

'No, they aren't.'

'Have a nice time, but not too good a time. I don't want you spending too much time with your ex, looking at his muscly chest and comparing it to mine.'

Anna laughed. 'You don't have to worry about me and Conor spending too much time together. It'll be a miracle if we get through this dinner without arguing. As for his muscly chest, it never did anything for me. I prefer your more normal-sized one.'

James kissed her. 'Good answer.'

Anna hadn't told James about Conor trying to kiss her. There was no point – it would just have wound him up and made him uneasy every time she saw Conor. Besides, they had enough conflict going on inside the house without adding to it.

Conor was waiting for them. He was chatting to the very attractive hostess, making her laugh as they walked in. Always flirting, Anna thought. Conor needed attention and validation all the time. Anna blamed his mother. He and his brother Billy had been brought up by their single mum, Dolly, who thought the sun, moon and stars revolved around them. They were told every day how wonderful they were, gorgeous, talented, amazing . . . You name it, Dolly told them they were it. While it was nice to have a doting parent, all of Dolly's praise had given Conor and Billy, who now lived in New York, over-inflated egos.

Conor was dressed in a crisp white shirt, sleeves rolled up to show off his ripped forearms. The shirt was snug to his body and he was wearing tight jeans and white trainers. The whole outfit looked brand new. He was obviously spending the money from the sale of the house.

Anna hoped he wasn't getting through it too quickly. She was not going to support him if he ran out of money. They'd agreed on half the house and no more. He was on his own now: he had to start working full-time, not just whenever it suited him. She heard Angela's voice in her head: 'Anna, what Conor does with his money and his life is no longer your problem. You worried about him for nearly twenty years. Park him, the guilt and the worry. It's Anna time now.'

'There she is, my genius daughter.' Conor picked up Grace and swung her around. He introduced her to the hostess. 'Penny, this is Grace, who we're celebrating tonight, and this is Jack, my sports star, and that's my ex.'

'Hi, Penny, I'm Anna.' Anna ignored Conor's rudeness and shook Penny's hand.

'Nice to meet you.' Penny looked embarrassed at Conor's dismissive introduction. 'Follow me, guys. I've got you the best table in the house for your big celebration.' Penny showed them to a lovely table in the window, overlooking the city.

They ordered their food and a bottle of wine.

'I'm driving, so I'll have just half a glass,' Anna said.

'Well, I'm walking because I don't live in Timbuktu, so I can drink.'

As soon as the bottle arrived, Conor poured Anna half a glass and himself a large one.

'Cheers to our incredible Grace.' Conor clinked with Grace and Jack's glasses of Coke and Anna's wine.

By the time Anna had taken a sip, Conor had downed his glass and was pouring another. Oh, God, please don't let him get drunk. Anna crossed her fingers under the table.

Their food arrived swiftly and they all tucked in. The conversation was easy, everyone slotting back into their old familiar roles. This was what they knew. Conor teased and cajoled and was loud and funny. Jack hung on his father's every word, Grace laughed at some of Conor's jokes and rolled her eyes at others, and Anna sat back, keeping an eye on everyone, making sure things ran smoothly.

Anna watched her children as they tried to balance spoons

on their noses with Conor. They were so relaxed. She hadn't seen Grace being goofy in ages and Jack was laughing so much he was doubled over. It was infectious: she couldn't help but join in. They all laughed loudly as spoons clattered onto the floor.

Families at other tables looked over at them. Anna could see envy in some of their eyes. They looked like the perfect family: the beefy handsome dad, petite pretty(ish) mother, beautiful daughter and cute son all having a ball together.

Never presume, Anna thought. Never, ever presume you know what goes on. To everyone in the restaurant they appeared to be the happiest family in town. Little did they know they were broken, had been broken for a long time, and would never be fixed.

But this was great. This evening proved they could still have fun together and behave like a family unit when they needed to. Anna felt the knot in her stomach unwind. This was a huge step forward. Conor was obviously moving on, letting go of his anger and resentment. Maybe the attempted kiss had made him realize, once and for all, that their relationship was over.

Conor tapped the side of his almost empty glass and made another toast, slurring slightly. 'To my kids, the two best, most brilliant, coolest kids in the world. I love you, guys. I know your mum left me and says I can never do anything right, but I must have done something right because look at you two!'

Uh-oh. Anna jumped in. 'Yep, they are amazing, and Grace will be off to California with her project.'

'I'm a good dad,' Conor continued. 'I'm there for you, guys. I'm behind you. Okay, I admit that I could work a bit harder, and I will. But I'm a good dad and I love you, kids. I miss you. I really do. I want us to be a family again. We're great together, look at us.'

Anna wanted to punch him. It was Grace's night and he was ruining it. She could see Jack's eyes lighting up. No!

'Yeah, we are great. Let's be together again. Can we, Mum?' His sweet face looked up expectantly at Anna.

'Yeah!' Conor punched the air.

'This is such a special night for Grace. Such an achievement. Imagine, she'll be off to California representing her country.' Anna was desperate to change the subject and to remind Conor that this was all about Grace – no one and nothing else.

Conor drained his glass. 'There she goes, avoiding the subject again. She doesn't want us to be a family, Jack. She just wants that home-wrecker James.'

'Conor.' Anna stared straight at him, keeping her voice low and steady. 'That's enough. This is Grace's night.'

'Does the truth hurt, Anna?'

'Stop it. You're upsetting the kids.' She wanted to scream the words at him, but she knew only too well that when he was angry and drinking it was a volatile mix. She had to keep this calm and get them all through the meal without a major argument erupting. Grace would die if that happened.

Conor glared at her. 'I didn't upset the kids. You did. You walked out and dragged them with you.'

Anna's hands were shaking. As firmly and calmly as she could, she said, 'Let's please all try and remember that this is Grace's night. We need to focus on that and nothing else.'

'Easy for you to say in your swanky new house.'

'What would you like for dessert?' Anna asked the kids.

'Can we not all be a family again?' Jack's voice was low.

Anna took his hand. 'We are a family, love. We're just not a family that lives together. Dad and I will always be your parents and we love you and Grace to bits.'

'But if you love us so much, why won't you live with Dad like we want you to?' Jack's lip began to tremble.

Anna felt as if a knife was being stabbed through her heart. It killed her to see Jack's heartbreak, but she had to hold tight to what she knew to be true: she and Conor didn't make each other happy. He was immature and selfish. He turned her into a person she didn't like, always complaining and worrying. Leaving Conor and moving in with James had been incredibly difficult decisions and paths to take, but she knew in her heart that they were the right ones. Seeing how upset the kids were when she'd told them they were moving out had been a million times worse than she had imagined. Grace had told her, through tears, that she understood why, but Jack had been absolutely devastated. His dad was his hero. Now, it was still very new and raw, but in time, they would both see it had been the best choice for all of them.

Anna gripped her napkin tightly. 'We've talked about this, sweetheart. Dad and I love you guys so much and we always will. Dad and I still like each other and want to be friends, but we don't love each other any more.'

'But if you hadn't met James, you'd still love Dad,' Jack said. 'I hate James.'

'No, pet. James has nothing to do with this.'

'Of course he does. He *is* the reason,' Conor said.

Anna looked at Conor pleadingly. She felt close to tears. 'Come on, Conor, stop.'

'It's the truth.'

Grace slammed her hand on the table. 'Stop it, Dad. You're upsetting Jack.' She put her arm around her little brother. 'I'm older than you, so I notice more stuff. Mum and Dad were always arguing, they hadn't made each other happy for ages, long before Mum ever met James, so it's better that they don't live together. I know it's hard, Jack, but we'll get used to it. It's just going to take a bit more time.'

Thank you, God, for gifting me this incredible young woman as my daughter. Anna's heartbeat began to slow down.

Jack rested his head on his sister's shoulder.

Anna glanced at Conor. He was looking a bit contrite.

'Do you really think so, Grace? Do you not think they could love each other again?'

'No, Jack, not like husband and wife. They can be friends, though. If they both' – Grace glared at her father – 'make an effort to be nice to each other, they can love each other as friends and then we can do fun stuff like this together.'

'I just wish things didn't have to change. I want it to be like tonight all the time.'

'I know, Jack, but we'll get used to it. Remember when you changed school and you hated it at first? Well, you love it now. Change can take time. We'll be okay.'

Anna fought back tears. How had she and Conor created this mature, caring young woman?

'Dad's fine, he's just feeling a bit nostalgic, but he knows it's for the best too. He wasn't happy with all the arguing either, were you, Dad?' Grace looked directly at Conor.

Wow. Anna sat back and watched Conor's face.

Conor chewed his bottom lip and took a deep breath. 'Grace is right, Jack. Mum and I were not getting along and . . . well, it's not good for kids to be around arguing and so . . . I guess we'll just have to get used to our new normal.'

'And the important thing is that we love you, Jack. We love you and Grace to pieces.' Anna's voice shook with emotion.

Conor ruffled Jack's hair. 'Who couldn't love this kid? Come on, buddy, let's order every dessert on the menu and eat until we're so full that our stomachs explode food all over the restaurant.'

Jack smiled. 'For real?'

'Absolutely.'

They ordered everything, and Jack and Conor had a ball overeating sugar. Anna's anger towards her ex dimmed as she watched him make Jack smile again.

She reached under the table and squeezed Grace's hand. 'Thank you,' she mouthed. Grace nodded, then went back to her dessert.

The bill arrived and Conor made a big show of paying. 'This is my treat. I'm taking you out to celebrate our star, Grace.'

Anna bit her tongue. The only reason you're paying for dinner – for the first time in years – is because of the money you got from the sale of the house I worked day and night to pay for.

They left the restaurant. Conor hugged the kids and headed off alone. Anna decided to show Jack that she and Conor could be friends, so she called to him, 'Hey, hop in, I'll drive you home.'

Conor turned, looking surprised. 'But it's out of your way.'

Anna shrugged. 'Not by much. I'm happy to. You can sit in the back with Jack and see who can burp loudest from over-eating.' She smiled at him.

Jack giggled. 'Yeah, Dad! Let's do it.'

Anna felt good. She had done the right thing. Maybe now things would settle down and she could enjoy her new life with James.

21

James found Anna crying in the bathroom. 'Oh, darling, what has Conor done now?'

Anna shook her head. 'For once it's not him. Angela just called. Granny Ita died.'

'Oh, no, I'm sorry. She wasn't sick, was she?'

James couldn't keep track of Anna's family. There were so many of them. He vaguely remembered her saying that one of the grandparents was sick, but he was hazy on which one. His grandparents were all long dead. But he wanted to be sensitive and Ita was the one Anna mentioned most.

'No, it was so sudden. She had a stroke. She's never been the same since my mum died two years ago. Mum was her only daughter and she just couldn't cope with losing her.'

He put his arms around her. 'What can I do?'

'Can you pick Jack and Grace up from school and bring them home? I have to go to Anthony's house – we're all meeting there to sort out the arrangements.'

'Of course, no problem.' Damnit, they finished school at three thirty, which meant he'd have to cancel and reschedule his three o'clock lecture and his four-thirty tutorial.

Anna rested her head on his shoulder. 'Thanks, James, you're a lifesaver.'

He kissed her.

'Granny had a sharp tongue but a good heart. I loved her. Do you know what she said when she met Conor? "He's a charmer, but he'll never grow up."'

'Astute.'

'Very.' Anna sighed. 'Right, I'd better go. See you later and thanks.'

James stood outside the school gate waiting for Jack. He saw him running out with a group of other boys. They were all pushing and shoving, hitting each other with their backpacks. Had he done that when he was their age? James didn't remember being so physical with his friends. Maybe he was just a different type of kid. He saw another group of boys, walking behind Jack's group, who were talking and not feeling the urge to thump each other. That was me, James thought. I was definitely in the second group.

Jack's friends split up as they made their way to find their parents. When Jack saw James, his face fell. 'What are you doing here?' he demanded.

James put on his cheeriest grin. 'Hey there, Jack. Your mum couldn't pick you up so she asked me to.'

'Why? Why couldn't she pick me up?'

'Well . . . uhm . . .' James wasn't sure if he was supposed to tell the kids or if Anna wanted to tell them herself. She hadn't said. He couldn't think of a lie so he said, 'I'm afraid your great-grandmother died.'

'Oh.'

James watched closely to see if Jack was upset. 'I'm very sorry.'

Jack shrugged. 'She smelt of wee and she was always grumpy.'

Okay, good. He wasn't upset. They walked in awkward silence down the road towards Grace's school.

'Is Mum sad?' Jack asked.

'Well, I think she'll miss her granny, but she was an old lady and had a good life,' James answered.

'When's she coming home?' Jack asked.

'I'm not sure. She's gone to your uncle Anthony's house to organize the funeral. I said I'd do dinner. What do you fancy?'

'Pizza.'

'I was thinking I'd cook something.'

'I want pizza.'

James decided not to argue. 'Fine. We can order in.'

'Will I get a day off school to go to the funeral?' Jack asked.

'You'll have to ask your mother about that,' James said, as they approached Grace's school.

'I want to go and see Mum now.'

'I think she needs a bit of space to organize the funeral.'

'Well, then, I want to go to my dad's.'

'You're not due at your dad's until Friday.'

'I don't want to stay with you if Mum's not there. You're not my parent. I want to go to my dad's,' Jack insisted.

'Your mum wouldn't want the schedule being changed, Jack. She'll be home later. Hopefully she'll be back in time for some pizza with us.'

'I'm not going home with you. I'm going to my dad's.'

'Oh, come on now, Jack. No need for that.'

'NO! I'm not going with you! You're not my dad,' Jack shouted.

The parents congregated outside Grace's school gates turned around to stare at them.

James tried to grab Jack's arm to stop him running away.

'Get off me! You're not my dad!' Jack was bellowing now.

A man approached them. 'Is everything all right here?' he asked Jack.

'Yes, it's fine. Jack, stop it,' James said.

Jack wriggled out of his grip. 'He's not my dad and he's trying to force me to go home with him,' he shouted.

A woman approached them. 'What's going on?'

James was mortified. 'Everything is fine. I'm his step-father.'

'Is he?' the woman asked Jack.

'No. He's my mum's boyfriend and I hate him,' Jack said.

'Come on, Jack, stop it now.' James tried to laugh it off.

The woman took her phone out. 'Do you want to call your mum?' she asked Jack.

'Yes,' Jack said.

'No!' James put out his hand to stop the woman giving her phone to Jack. 'His mother's grandmother has just died. She is with her family. I'm taking Jack home.'

'You're not taking him anywhere,' the man interrupted. 'Either he calls his mum or I'm calling the police.'

'Look,' James held up his hands, 'this is a misunderstanding. Jack's mum asked me to pick him up from school. I'm taking him home for pizza.'

'The boy clearly doesn't want to go with you and he's upset,' the woman said. 'Call your mum,' she offered her phone to Jack.

The last thing James needed was Anna getting a call from Jack saying he was being forcefully held against his wishes – with her whole family witnessing the drama. He had to stop this.

'Please take your phone back. I don't want his mother bothered by this when she's trying to organize a funeral. Look, Anna and I have only been living together for a few months, and we're all still getting to know each other. Jack is just taking time to settle in.'

'I cannot in good faith leave this boy with you. He's upset.'

James looked around, sweat forming on his forehead. In the distance he spotted Grace walking out of her school gate, looking around for Anna. Thank God!

'Grace.' He waved frantically to get her attention.

She looked over and began to walk towards them.

'Who's this now?' the man asked.

'My sister,' Jack said.

'Are you forcing her to go home with you too?' the woman asked.

'I'm not forcing anyone to do anything. As I have already explained, I'm their step-father.'

'Where's Mum?' Grace asked.

'Great-granny has died and James is making me go home with him, but I want to go to Dad's and these people say I should go to Dad's. They said James can't make me go with him.' Jack was loving the drama.

Grace's brow crinkled. 'What are you talking about? Dad's probably out and we're supposed to go home to Mum's house. Well, Mum and James's house.'

'Do you know this man?' the woman asked Grace.

'Yes, he's my mum's boyfriend.'

'Your brother seems very keen to get away from him. Do we need to call the police or call your mother to come and get you?'

Grace was taken aback. 'No – and why would you call the police? Jack's just acting up.'

'Are you sure there's nothing more to this?' the woman asked Grace. 'We can help you if you need to get away. Is he harming you? Are you afraid of him? Your brother seems afraid.'

Grace burst out laughing. 'Oh, my God, no. If anyone's afraid, James is afraid of Jack. This is crazy. James is totally harmless.'

Harmless? Ouch, that stung. No one wanted to be harmless: it meant you were bland. Was he bland? James wondered. He hoped not.

'Jack, stop pretending you're afraid of James. Mum will be really cross if she finds out you've caused so much trouble.'

'Fine. James is not scary or mean,' Jack admitted to the woman. 'He's just really boring and narky. My dad's way more fun.'

Jesus, harmless and boring. James tried not to wince.

'All right then. We'll leave you to it.' The woman walked away.

'Good luck to you. It looks like you need it.' The man patted James's shoulder before walking off.

In the space of two minutes he'd gone from potential abductor to useless, pitiful step-father.

When they got home, Grace went up to her bedroom to do her homework. Jack lay on the couch and began to play on the Xbox.

'Jack, you need to do your homework now.'

'I'm too tired. I need to chill out a bit. I'll do it later.'

James knew that Anna didn't let Jack play video games until his homework was completed and checked.

'Come on, Jack, your mum always says homework first. It won't take long.'

'My dad lets me play after school.'

James tried to choose his words carefully. He didn't want another argument with his step-son.

'In this house we need to follow your mum's rules. So, turn it off and when you've finished your homework you can go back to it.'

Jack ignored him and continued to play his game.

'Jack, turn off the game.' James was firmer this time. He was fed up with Jack being antagonistic.

Jack continued to behave as if James was invisible.

'Jack, if you don't turn off the game, I'm going to have to take it from you. I'm asking you to be reasonable.'

Nothing.

James reached down and tried to pull the controller from Jack's hands, but the ten-year-old was too fast. Jack spun around and dived to the other end of the couch. James tried to get hold of Jack's arm, but he ducked under him. Losing his balance, James fell on top of Jack, who kicked and punched him. James tried to hold the boy's legs down, but they were kicking him black and blue.

Eventually, James wrestled the controller out of Jack's hands and stood up.

'You're a bully!' Jack shouted, as James rubbed his shin where Jack had kicked him particularly hard.

James tried to catch his breath as he tucked his shirt back into his trousers, noticing that Jack had managed to rip off a button. 'You need to go and do your homework,' he panted.

Jack crossed his arms. 'No. You're not my dad and you can't tell me what to do. I don't have to listen to anything you say because you are nothing to me. Not a parent or even an uncle or a granddad. Nothing.'

James was really fed up now. 'Okay, Jack, here's the deal. I'm the adult here and, while your mum is out, I'm in charge of you. So I'm asking you to do what your own mum asks you to do every day and get on with your homework.'

'You're not my mum.'

'Jack, just do your homework. The sooner it's done, the sooner you can play your game. You're just wasting time here.'

Jack gritted his teeth. 'My dad says I can play when I get home from school, so I'm gonna play.'

'This is not your dad's house. Your mum's rules are different.'

Jack stared straight ahead. James hesitated. Should he just leave him? Maybe he'd cool off and get bored.

'Right. Well, your schoolbag is in the kitchen, so come in and do your homework when you've calmed down a little.'

James was making himself a strong coffee when he heard the television blaring. Jesus Christ, the kid was relentless. He marched into the lounge. Jack was lying back, watching some football match. 'Turn it off, Jack.'

'No.' Jack gripped the remote control tightly.

Did he really have to have another bloody wrestling match with this kid? James tried to think of a way around him.

'Jack, I'm ordering your favourite pizza for dinner, but you can't have it until your homework is done.'

'I don't want your poxy pizza.'

What? Right. Enough was enough.

James marched over to the television and ripped out all of the plugs.

'What the hell are you doing?' Jack yelled.

'I have asked you calmly, over and over again, to do your homework, but that hasn't worked. So now, Jack, I'm telling you to go into that kitchen and start your homework before I lose my temper.'

'I'm calling my dad. This is child abuse. I'm calling ChildLine and the police too.'

'Go ahead, knock yourself out.' James called his bluff.

Jack ran into the kitchen and grabbed the house phone. He dialled Conor's number. 'Dad, help, James is attacking me and hurting me.'

Oh, Jesus.

'No, I am not,' James called, but Jack had hung up.

'Jack, why did you do that? Why did you lie to your father? I never laid a finger on you.'

'Yes, you did. Look at my arm.' Jack pulled up his shirtsleeve and showed James a very faint red mark where James had grabbed his arm to try to wrestle the controller out of his hand.

'I held your arm for about two seconds. Honestly, Jack, you're making a huge deal out of nothing. If you just did what you were bloody told, life would be a lot easier for all of us.'

Jack narrowed his eyes. 'Yeah, well, if my mum had never met you, my life would be brilliant. But she did and she left my dad and everything is shit now.'

'Stop using bad language and have some respect, please.'

'I hate you.' Jack ran out of the kitchen and locked himself into the downstairs toilet.

James decided to leave him in there. He had no idea how to handle him. He was being dictated to, tormented and harassed by a ten-year-old kid. In desperation he went to ask Grace for her help, but she was on a Zoom call with her science teacher.

James went back to the kitchen, poured himself a glass of

wine and gulped it down. This step-parenting thing was a mine-field. He ordered pizza in the hope that the smell would bring Jack out and maybe calm him down. He heard a loud knock on the front door. It was way too fast to be the pizza guy.

James opened the door and was shoved aside by Conor.

'Where is he? Jack? Jack?'

'Dad, I'm in here!' Jack shouted, from behind the locked door.

Conor grabbed James by the scruff of his shirt. 'Did you lock my kid in the toilet? Did you hurt my son? I will break every bone in your body if you put a hand on him.'

'I didn't touch him. He locked himself in the toilet,' James croaked, his breathing ragged from the chokehold Conor had him in.

The door opened and Jack came out. He ran over to his dad and wrapped his arms around him.

Conor crouched down. 'Did he hurt you?'

'Yeah, look.' Jack held out his arm where the red mark had almost faded. 'He threw me on the ground and crushed me and nearly broke my arm trying to get the controller.'

Conor's face darkened. 'He what?'

'No, I did not. Jack, don't lie.'

Conor walked over and dug his index finger deep into James's chest. It was surprisingly painful. 'Do not ever call my son a liar. Do you understand me?'

James felt a strange urge to laugh. This was all so farcical. Conor seemed to think this was a scene from a gangster movie. James needed to get control of the situation. He did not want a broken nose.

'Conor, I asked Jack to do his homework and he refused. So, after many calm requests, I took the controller from him and he fought back. There was about three seconds of pulling and pushing with the controller.' James lifted his trouser leg to show a large red welt on his shin.

Conor grinned. 'That's my boy.'

Jack smiled up at him. 'I kicked him as hard as I could, Dad.'

'Good man, Jack. Don't ever let him touch you or try to take anything from you.'

For the love of God. 'I just wanted him to do his homework,' James said.

Conor stepped closer to James, so they were almost nose to nose. 'Jack will do his homework when Jack is ready to do his homework and not when some wife-stealer tells him to. He is not your son and you do not get to give him any orders. Is that clear?'

James had had enough. 'This is my house, your son is in my care, and his mother's rules are that Jack does his homework before playing any games.'

Conor moved even closer. James could smell his breath. 'Do you feel good about bullying a ten-year-old? Does that make you feel big? Isn't it enough that you stole my wife and now you're abusing my kids?'

James stepped back. 'For Christ's sake, stop with all your lies and false accusations. I did not steal your wife, and I am extremely nice to and patient with your son.'

Conor grabbed James's shirt collar again. 'Listen here, you –'

But James snapped. He had had enough of this bullshit. He pushed back hard. Conor wasn't expecting the retaliation and stumbled, but then he caught his balance and charged at James, wrestling him to the floor.

'Get him, Dad, kick his arse,' Jack cheered.

James tried in vain to move the lump of hard muscle off him, but Conor was like a concrete block pinning him to the floor.

The front door opened, and Anna stood staring at the scene before her.

'What in God's name is going on?'

'James squashed me and now Dad is squashing him.' Jack

was jumping up and down with the excitement of seeing James being beaten up by his father.

James was mortified that Anna was witnessing him being completely dominated by her gym-bunny ex.

'Get off him, Conor.' Anna pulled Conor back.

James stood up and tried to rearrange his clothes. His shirt was now missing three buttons and had a rip on the shoulder.

Anna listened while each person told their side of the story. It was humiliating to have to stand in the hallway of his own house defending himself against a ten-year-old, who was very loose with the truth, and a beefy ex, who shouted random insults at will.

Grace came running down the stairs in the middle of all the commotion and told them all to 'cop on' and 'shut up' because she was on an important Zoom call and they were behaving like 'freaks'.

Eventually, Anna ushered Jack upstairs and Conor towards the front door. James went into the kitchen. He could hear Anna trying to calm Conor down.

'It's okay, I'll sort this out,' she said.

'If he lays a hand on Jack, I swear I'll kill him.'

'He won't. James would never hurt anyone. It's okay, Conor, you know I would never let anyone hurt our kids. You know that.'

'I hate that there's another man looking after them.' Conor sounded upset. So he did actually have a heart. He kept it hidden well, James thought.

'I know it's hard. Look, go home and calm down. I'll get Jack to call you before he goes to bed.'

'You'd better talk to that prick and make sure he knows never to touch Jack again.'

'I will. Now go and let me sort this out.'

James poured himself another very large glass of wine and went upstairs to change his shirt, bringing the bottle of wine with him. At this rate he'd be an alcoholic with no clothes.

An hour later, Anna came up. 'We need to talk.'

'Okay.'

'What happened today can't happen again. It was complete chaos when I got home. You have to figure out a way to connect with Jack. I know he can be tricky, but he's just a lively young boy and he has such big heart and a very sweet side.'

Really? Well, he hides it well. Very bloody well. James drank more wine as he tried to think of a response that wouldn't involve him telling Anna her son was a complete and utter shithead.

'I understand that you're not used to boys – they're boisterous and they can be difficult – but you're the adult and you let it get completely out of control. The last thing I need is Conor coming over and accusing me of being a bad parent.'

James tried to keep his voice steady, as he said, 'Anna, I rescheduled my day to pick up your kids from school. Your son accused me of kidnapping him in front of concerned parents, who were about to call the police. Do you have any idea how serious that is? Accusations like that can destroy a person's life. This is not some boyish prank, this is my reputation. Then, when Grace thankfully saved the day, we got home and I calmly asked him to do his homework and he turned into a complete monster, then called his dad and accused me, for the second time, of serious wrongdoing. This has to stop. You need to make it very clear to him how serious his behaviour is, that it is not acceptable and will not be tolerated.'

'I think maybe we should let things settle for tonight. You're upset and angry and so is Jack. Please remember that he is ten years old, James. He doesn't know what he's saying, or what it means. He was just lashing out. I'll talk to him in the morning and explain it to him.'

'I think you need to talk to him right now and be very clear about the seriousness of what he accused me of. You need to put your foot down. I know you feel guilty about the break-up, but this has been going on for months now and his behaviour is getting worse, not better. If you don't deal with it properly now, he is going to cause serious damage to me and, frankly, to us.'

Anna glared at him. 'James, he's a young boy who is traumatized by the break-up of his family. All he wants is for his family to get back together. He needs time to process and accept the situation. He needs us, the adults in his life, to cut him some slack and instead of reacting to his behaviour, to try to understand that he's just acting out because his heart is broken. You're very quick to react to him. I think if you tried to be more patient, things wouldn't be so volatile.'

'Patient!' James threw his hands in the air. 'I have been more patient than the Dalai fucking Lama.'

Anna shushed him. 'I don't want the kids to hear us arguing. Look, I know you're trying. I'm just saying, give it time. I can't have him calling Conor when he's upset. It's just going to make a bad situation a million times worse. I need you to help me, not cause more problems between me and Conor. I'm tired, I've had a crappy day, and I'm upset about my granny. I was hoping to come home to a nice, calm house. Instead, it was complete chaos. I'm going to check on him now – he was crying earlier. His mind is spinning. He just needs patience and reassurance that everything is going to be okay.' Anna walked out of the bedroom.

'So do I,' James whispered, to her back. 'So do I.'

22

Bella fidgeted the whole way through the funeral mass. James had had a hell of a job getting her to come. 'Why do I have to go to some boring mass about a dead woman I never met, who isn't related to me in any way?' she'd fumed.

But James had been firm. It was out of respect for Anna and that was that. He wanted Bella to make an effort. If he was asking Anna to discipline Jack more, he had to do his part and make sure that Bella tried harder too.

She sighed and wriggled around in her seat beside him. He had taken her phone to make sure she didn't look at it in the church. He wasn't surprised she was wriggling about: the mass had gone on for a very long time. Everyone seemed to want to say something about Ita or read a prayer or sing a song or play an instrument. Adam's youngest son, Brendan, was playing a very long, very off-key version of 'Ave Maria' on the flute, which was as painful as being stabbed in the eye repeatedly.

Up ahead of them, James could see Conor and Jack playing rock-paper-scissors while somewhere Schubert was turning in his grave, listening to his beautiful song being mangled.

Finally, with one last mis-hit note, the agony was over and five minutes later they all filed out behind the coffin. Outside the church, people queued up to hug and console Anna and her large family. James and Bella stood to one side. It all felt a bit awkward. James had only met some of Anna's brothers once and he didn't know the uncles, aunts and cousins. But Conor did. He was high-fiving and hugging the relations like a long-lost friend. He was right there in the thick of it. James looked around for Anna, but she was surrounded by a throng of people.

'Can we go now?' Bella asked. 'We're total outsiders here, Dad.'

James wanted to say yes, and she was right, they were outsiders, but he felt he had to stay. 'Not yet, I want to talk to Anna and see what the plan is for later.'

'I can see where Jack gets his hyperness from.' Bella nodded to where Conor was arm-wrestling a teenage cousin. 'Like, seriously, he's such a try-hard. Dude, you're old, deal with it.'

James laughed. 'Do you not think he's kind of a cool dad?'

'Are you kidding me? He's embarrassing. No one wants a dad who acts like he's *down with the kids*. It's mortifying. I feel sorry for Grace. How did Anna marry him? She's so serious and he's so cringy. No wonder she wanted to leave him. She's lucky she met you.'

James couldn't have loved his daughter more – she saw right through Conor and his antics. 'How did you get to be so smart?' he asked.

She grinned. 'Come on, I have two genius parents. Some of the genes must have landed.'

They heard Conor loudly calling, 'Hey, Angie, looking good, how are you?'

'It's Angela and fuck off,' she said, as she made her way towards James and Bella.

James tried not to show his delight at Conor being snubbed.

'Hi, guys,' Angela said. 'It's so nice of you to come.'

'Of course. Sadly we never met Ita, but we're here to support Anna,' James said.

'I know she appreciates it. How are you, Bella?' Angela asked.

'Finding this all a bit awkward, to be honest,' Bella said.

Angela laughed. 'Yeah, I get that.'

'We haven't met many of Anna's relatives yet, so we thought we'd stand back a bit,' James tried to explain.

'And Conor's here making a lot of noise, which doesn't help.' Angela smiled.

'No comment.' James grinned.

'James, right?' Alex came up behind his sister.

'Yes, hello. It's Adam, isn't it?'

'No, I'm Alex.'

'Oh, God, I'm so sorry.'

'Don't worry about it, there are far too many of us.'

'This is my daughter, Bella. Bella, this is Anna's brother.'

Bella smiled and said hello.

'We were just saying what a wanker Conor is,' Angela filled her brother in.

'Hang on, I didn't say that.'

Alex put his hand on James's arm. 'Don't worry, we all think that, but we have to put up with him for the kids' sake.'

'Of course, they come first,' James agreed.

'Still, it's very nice to see my sister happy with you,' Alex said. 'So, how are you getting on with the whole living together like *The Brady Bunch*, Bella?'

James prayed Bella would not be her usual honest and direct self.

'I'm not gonna lie, it's challenging. Jack can be a lot.'

Alex laughed. 'Yeah, he's lively, but he's a good kid. The break-up hit him the hardest.'

'We're all getting used to each other, but it's easier than it was, and Anna is . . . Well, you don't need me to tell you how fantastic your sister is,' James said.

'No, but it's nice to hear.' Alex smiled.

Anna came up to them and hugged James. 'Sorry, I wanted to come over ages ago, but I kept getting stopped by people.'

'It's fine, darling, we've been chatting to your siblings.'

'Mum.' Jack came over to her. 'Dad wants to take me for ice-cream.' Seeing James standing behind her, his face fell. 'What's he doing here?'

'James and Bella came to support us, Jack. They're part of our family now,' Anna said.

'No, they aren't.'

'Come on, sweetheart, be nice,' Anna said.

'I don't want the home-wrecker here.'

'What did you call him?' Angela was shocked.

'Jack, I told you not to use that word.'

'That's not okay, Jack,' Alex said.

'Dad said it.' Jack looked a little sheepish, having been told off by his aunt and uncle.

'Well, your dad is an idiot for saying it. It's not true and it's a nasty thing to say.' Angela didn't mince her words.

James wanted to shout, Finally!

'Angela is right, Jack,' Alex agreed. 'That's a really unfair and untrue thing to say. I know your dad may have said it, but it's wrong. I know you won't say it again because you're a good kid. Right?'

Jack nodded, looking upset.

'He didn't mean it. He's just repeating silly things he heard his dad say.' Anna, as usual, defended Jack.

Thank God for her siblings, James thought.

'Well, he knows now,' Angela said firmly.

Grace came over. 'I've been looking for you everywhere. We need to go, Mum. The cars are leaving for the graveyard.' To James and Bella, she said, 'Hi, I didn't see you in the church.'

'Two teenage girls in the house, poor you, mate.' Alex patted James on the shoulder.

'To be honest, the girls have been great, haven't they, Anna?'

'Uh, yeah, more or less,' Anna muttered.

'I only have one and she's wrecking my head,' Alex said. 'I keep telling her to be more like her cousin Grace. Our genius Grace is the one we all want our kids to be like.' Alex winked at his niece, who blushed.

'Grace really is fantastic,' James enthused.

'Bella has the lead part in the school musical,' Anna said.

'Yeah, while Grace is changing the world I'm singing "You're The One That I Want". Go, me!' Bella rolled her eyes.

They all laughed.

'Hey, now, speaking as someone who wanted to play Maria but got stuck at the back of the stage playing one of the nuns in *The Sound of Music*, I know how hard it is to get a lead role,' Angela noted.

Anna giggled. 'You were so sure you were going to be Maria and you're such a bad singer.'

'Our Angela was always a bit delusional.' Alex laughed.

'I was not delusional, just a little over-optimistic.' Angela winked at Bella. 'Anyway, good luck with it all. I suppose you've loads of rehearsals?'

'Yes, it's pretty full-on.'

'Mum, we need to go,' Grace reminded her.

James kissed Anna and held her close. 'Good luck at the graveyard. Let me know if you need me to do anything later.'

'Thank you, darling,' Anna said, gazing into his eyes.

'Oh, God, you two are so annoyingly in love,' Angela said.

'Tell me about it,' Bella said.

'It's lovely to see you so happy, sis,' Alex said.

'They fight lots too,' Jack piped up.

'Jack!' Anna said.

'Well, you do. It's either kissing or fighting.'

James was embarrassed. He didn't need Anna's family to know what went on behind closed doors.

'They're not fights, Jack, they're just little tiffs as we all figure out how to live together.' Anna tried to smooth it over.

'Exactly. They're usually silly arguments about logistics.' James wanted to reassure everyone that things were good with him and Anna.

'Speaking of logistics, I hope you're sleeping in your own bed every night, Mister. Anna and James need theirs to themselves. Are you, Jack?' Angela looked at him.

'Most of the time,' he muttered.

'It needs to be all of the time. You're too old to be climbing in with your mother,' Angela said.

'You used to be my favourite aunt but you're not now. You're all narky and giving out. I'm going to find my dad.' Jack slumped off.

'Go easy on him, Angela,' Anna said, while James resisted hugging his step-sister-in-law.

'Can I go now too?' Bella said. 'I have rehearsals.'

'Absolutely. Thanks so much for coming, Bella,' Anna said.

'Sure.' Bella shrugged. 'Your family are actually pretty cool.' She waved goodbye to them all and walked off.

'Anthony is waving frantically at us so we'd better go,' Alex said. 'Nice to meet you again, James.'

'Bye, James.'

James felt warm and affectionate towards Anna's family. At least they had witnessed how difficult Jack could be, and maybe through their eyes Anna would also see that he needed a firmer hand.

Conor rolled up the edge of his tight T-shirt to show off a little more of his arms. He splashed on some aftershave and gelled his hair so it was sitting just right. He slapped his cheeks and tried to pump himself up. Pete and Jimmy had said they were up for a big night. Conor loved big nights. He lived for them, but since Anna had left and he had all the time in the world to go out, he found he didn't want to. Sod's law, he thought. When I get nagged about going out, I'm desperate to go, but now I can do what I want, I don't want to.

'Come on, this will be a good session. You'll have fun with the lads. No nagging wives, just the three of us giving it socks,' he said, into the mirror. They were going clubbing after the pub. Conor just needed a few drinks to get going. He'd be fine. This was good. He grabbed his jacket and headed out of the door.

Pete and Jimmy waved him over. They had pints and shots already lined up. They drank and chatted and teased each other, and Conor felt himself relax. This was good: he was with his mates. It was nice not to be alone in the apartment playing video games or watching Netflix. He was sick of being on his own. He missed the kids. He missed Anna. Freedom was overrated.

'How are the kids?' Jimmy asked.

'Good, yeah. Grace is flying it with her science project. She's really independent. She pretty much does her own thing. But Jack is finding it hard. He rings me a lot. He can't stand living with your man.'

'Must be nice, though, having the place to yourself and the kids every second weekend,' Jimmy said.

No, it isn't. It's lonely as hell, Conor thought. He wished he'd pushed to have them every second week instead of only every second weekend. He was an idiot. He'd been so furious with Anna that he'd wanted her to have to look after the kids more so that she'd have barely any time alone with her new man. He'd wanted to make sure the professor got all Anna's baggage shoved right in his face. But he'd been an idiot. He missed the kids. He wanted to change the arrangement, but he'd signed the bloody custody papers.

'Yeah, it's good, you know, do what you want when you want,' Conor faked.

'I'd love a week off. Five kids is just too much. They never stop. I was at three football games, one basketball match and a hip-hop competition today.' Jimmy knocked back his shot.

Lucky bastard, Conor thought. I went to the gym and sat around wishing the day away.

Pete ordered another round and another, and then they headed to Insomnia.

The music was loud and Conor could feel it beating in his chest. The alcohol had taken effect and he was feeling good. Jimmy headed to the bar while Conor and Pete hit the dance-floor. Conor loved dancing and knew he was good at it. He danced away his loneliness and his regrets. A cute, sexy girl caught his eye. She was small and curvy with a great cleavage and a gorgeous smile. He danced over to her. They moved opposite each other. She was a sexy dancer.

When the song ended, Conor asked if she'd like a drink.

'Sure. I'm Milly,' she said.

'Conor,' he answered.

'You're very fit.' Milly squeezed his arm.

'I do my best.' He winked at her. 'You're pretty hot yourself.'

'I do my best.' She winked back.

Conor asked her what she wanted to drink. 'Coke Zero, please.'

'With what? Vodka?'

Milly shook her head. 'I don't drink.'

'Seriously?'

'Yep. Alcoholic dad, so . . .'

'Oh, well . . .'

'Yeah.'

Conor ordered a Coke Zero and a bottle of beer.

Jimmy came stumbling over to them. 'Con*oooooor.*' He threw his arms around his friend.

Conor gently pushed him back. 'This is my friend, Jimmy. He doesn't get out much – he's got five kids – so he's a bit over-excited.'

'Hi, Jimmy.' Milly held out her hand.

'Whash your name, love?'

'Milly and lose the "love".'

Jimmy looked confused. 'What?'

'Women don't like being called "love" by strange men,' Milly explained firmly.

'I don't understand.'

'Just call me Milly.'

'Okay, love, I will.'

Conor mouthed, 'Sorry.'

'I think I gonna go. I'm *soooo* drunk.' Jimmy swayed.

'Good idea,' Conor said.

'Do you think I'll gesh a ride from the wife tonight?' Jimmy asked.

Milly cracked up laughing. 'Fat chance.'

'Ish been ages.' Jimmy looked forlorn. 'My balls are gonna fall off.'

'I dunno, Jimmy, call me crazy but I'd say staggering home pissed out of your head at two a.m. and trying to throw the leg over your sleeping wife is not the best way to go about it. Maybe taking her out to dinner and having a coherent conversation with her might work better.' Milly grinned at him.

Conor burst out laughing.

'You're mean.' Jimmy pointed at Milly.

'No, just honest.'

'I'm gonna find Pete and go.' Jimmy stumbled off towards the exit. Conor saw Pete holding him up as they left the club.

'Do you look younger than you are, or do you hang around with older guys?' Milly asked.

'What age do you think I am?' Conor loved asking people this question. They never said thirty-seven. They always guessed younger.

Milly squinted and looked at him closely. 'Thirty-six.'

'What?'

'Older?'

'No. Well, yes, but people usually think I'm in my late twenties.'

'I'm a make-up artist. I know by looking at someone's skin how old they are. You look good, though, for an old guy.'

'How old are you?'

'Twenty-three.'

'You look good for a young one.'

'So are you married? Are you one of those guys who slips off his ring when he goes to nightclubs to prey on younger women?'

'No.'

'No, you aren't one of those men, or no, you aren't married?'

'Not married.'

'Kids?'

'No,' Conor lied. He didn't want to get into it. He wanted sex, she was cute, and she didn't need to know his history.

'Cool. So are you going to kiss me?' Milly asked straight out.

'Jeez, you young ones are very direct.'

Milly grinned. 'We know what we want and, right now, I want your lips on mine.'

Conor leant in and kissed her.

*

Conor opened his eyes and blinked. His head throbbed. He heard sounds outside the door and sniffed: someone was cooking. He began to piece together his night. He remembered Milly, coming home, having very good sex, and then he must have passed out asleep. He'd thought she'd be gone. But apparently, judging by the smell, she was cooking bacon.

He was tired and hung-over and he really didn't want to have to make awkward, post-sex conversation with a one-night stand over breakfast. He'd pretend he had to go to work, then grab a bacon sandwich and a coffee in the café around the corner. He dragged himself out of bed and threw on a pair of jeans, a T-shirt and trainers.

Milly turned when she heard the bedroom door open. 'Morning, sleep well?'

'Uh, yeah.' She was dressed, showered, her long blonde hair wet and piled on top of her head in a knot, and she looked as fresh as a daisy. She wasn't quite as gorgeous as he remembered, but she sure was sexy. Her bum looked great in her tight black trousers. She grinned at him and her face lit up. Killer smile. She wasn't pretty like Anna, but she was cute and sassy and he wanted to put his arms around her and drag her back to bed. He never felt like this after one-night stands. He usually couldn't wait to get rid of them.

'Right, well, your fridge is a disgrace. Nothing to eat here at all. I nipped down to the local shop and got bacon and eggs and fresh orange juice. You hungry?'

The food looked and smelt delicious. Conor's stomach rumbled. He could make conversation for half an hour. He sat down to fluffy scrambled eggs, crispy bacon and cold, fresh orange juice.

'Have you lived here long?' Milly asked.

'Five months,' Conor said.

'Bachelor pad, yeah?'

'Yeah.'

Milly eyeballed him. 'D'you know what I hate more than anything?'

'No?'

'Liars. You told me last night you didn't have kids. I wake up and see photos of your kids and a kids' bedroom with bunk beds in it. I was going to leave but then I thought, No, Milly, make him explain his lies and face up to his deceit. So, Conor, what the hell is going on?'

Conor put down his fork. He was too tired to lie and, besides, what was the point? She'd caught him out. 'I'm separated. I have two amazing kids, Grace is fifteen, Jack is just ten. My wife left me for another guy, an older dorky professor.'

'Ouch.'

'Yeah, it hurt like hell.'

'Do you think you could ever get back together?'

'No.' It was the first time he'd admitted it to himself. He'd held out hope, even when Anna had pushed him away after Grace's parent–teacher meeting. He'd still thought there was a slight chance. He reckoned she'd get bored with the professor. But who was he kidding? Sitting here in the cold light of morning, he knew it was over.

'Were things bad before she left?' Milly asked.

Conor was sick of lying to himself. Something about Milly's directness and the way she looked at him, almost through him into his soul, was making him be honest. Things had been terrible for years before Anna left. They barely spoke to each other.

'Yeah, we were like strangers.'

'Were you still surprised when she left?'

Yes, he was. He'd been shocked to his very core. He'd never thought she'd be the one to leave. He'd always thought Anna would be with him for ever. He knew he wasn't husband of the year, he knew he'd had a few slip-ups, but Anna didn't know about those one-night stands and, besides, she was so solid.

186

Anna was the rock. She held them all together. She had always been the more serious, sensible one. Anna would never do something crazy like have an affair and leave him. It was unthinkable. She wasn't that kind of person. She was a stayer, a keeper. She'd never upend their lives for another man . . . or so he'd thought.

To his friends Conor had never admitted how broken he was by Anna's leaving, but this morning he wanted to be honest – he needed to be. It wasn't just his ego that had taken a battering, it was his heart too. He'd realized too late that he'd taken Anna for granted. He'd let her slip away by not being there, by always wanting to be somewhere else.

'I was devastated. I never saw it coming, and when she told me, I thought it was just a fling. But . . . well, she's gone now.'

Milly reached out and patted his hand. 'It'll get easier.'

Conor dipped his fork into some scrambled eggs. 'Yeah, I know. I'm still angry, though.'

'Anger will just suck you dry. Sure, what good will it do you? You need to focus on the now and the future. You can't change your past.'

Conor raised an eyebrow. 'You sound like one of those therapists.'

Milly nodded. 'I did a year of therapy to get my alcoholic dad out of my head. It worked. I'm free of him now. I don't feel angry with him any more. I feel sorry for him.'

Conor certainly didn't feel sorry for Anna. She was in a four-bedroom house with a garden and was all loved up. In fact, she was glowing. Conor hadn't seen her look so good in years. Things had worked out pretty well for Anna.

'The other thing I learnt in therapy was that you have to own your own stuff.'

Conor looked up.

'You can't blame everyone else for life not turning out the way you planned it.'

Conor had never really planned his life at all. He'd assumed he'd be a pro footballer and when that failed, he'd just kind of fallen into things. He'd got married young, and they'd had Grace, and he'd worked as a mechanic, and then they'd had Jack . . . and life had just sort of slipped by.

'Like, I blamed my dad for me not finishing school, but it wasn't his fault. I'm the one who dropped out. So I stopped looking back and feeling sorry for myself and I focused on making things happen. Now I have my own business doing hair and make-up, and I'm working on bringing out a line of hair extensions of my own. I'm not going to let life pass me by. I'm going to grab it with both hands.'

Conor was impressed. For a twenty-three-year-old, Milly was very together. Maybe he should go to therapy. 'Perhaps you're right. I dunno. It's complicated when kids are involved.'

'It's only as complicated as you make it,' Milly retorted.

Conor held up his hands. 'Do you have an answer for everything?'

Milly grinned. 'Pretty much. I listen to loads of podcasts on psychotherapy and human behaviour, how to live your best life and not sweat the small stuff. I love all that psychology chat.'

Conor put his hands over his face. 'Oh, God, Milly, it's too early for this. My head is pounding.'

'You shouldn't have drunk so much,' she said. 'I feel great.'

'You look pretty good too.' Conor winked at her.

Milly stood up. 'Before you get any ideas, I've got to go. Any chance you could give me a lift to my car? I've got a wedding party to do hair and make-up for at eleven.'

'Sure. I'll just grab my keys.' Conor was disappointed Milly was leaving.

'What are you up to today then?' she asked, as they drove to her car.

Conor shrugged. 'Not much. Might hit the gym or go and

watch the football in the pub.' He realized he wanted to do neither of those things. He wanted to spend the day with Milly. He wanted to be around her positive energy, chat to her more and, truth be told, get her back into bed.

'Do you like being a mechanic?' Milly asked.

'It's fine. I guess I kind of fell into it,' he said, shrugging. 'I didn't try at school so university was never an option. I like cars so I thought being a mechanic would be cool.'

'And is it?'

Conor sighed. 'No, it isn't. It's boring. It's not like I'm taking an old car and making it into a cool racing car for myself. It's just changing batteries and tyres and brake pads and panel beating. Same thing over and over.'

Milly turned in her seat to face him. 'So what would you really like to do?'

No one had ever asked Conor that before. Anna had just nagged him to take on more work, and when he'd said he didn't really like being a mechanic, she'd told him to suck it up: they had bills to pay and two kids to look after.

'I think I'd be a good personal trainer. Keeping fit and doing weights is the one thing that I've always been consistent at. I love it. I need it for my sanity.'

'Well, it's worth it. You look hot, for an old guy.' Milly grinned. 'So why don't you become a personal trainer? My cousin did a course online – it only took about nine months. You've got more time now that you're separated. Why not use it to change your career?'

Conor stopped at the lights and turned to Milly. She was so full of energy, optimism and possibility. She saw the world through bright, clear eyes. She saw no barriers to change.

Was she right? Should he do a course online and change things up? Why not? He did have more time on his hands, and the nights and weekends without the kids were long and lonely. It would be good to have a focus and he did love training. He reckoned he'd be good at it too. He'd make a success of it and show Anna that he wasn't a loser, that he could be successful.

'Well?' Milly probed.

'You're right. I should do it and now is a good time.'

'Yeah!' Milly cheered. 'I'll get the name of the one my cousin did and text you.'

'Thanks,' Conor said. 'Not just for the course details, but for the encouragement.'

'I saw my dad drink his life away, partly because he hated his job as a security guard. He was bored out of his mind and miserable. I reckon if you like what you do, it'll help you get through life's ups and downs and keep you focused.'

'How did you get to be so wise so young?'

'I guess I'm just special.' She winked.

As they pulled up to her car, Milly clicked off her seatbelt and kissed his cheek. She went to open the door when Conor stopped her. 'I can't believe I'm saying this, but I'd really like to see you again.'

Milly laughed. 'Sod off.'

Conor frowned. 'What?'

'Do you honestly think any woman wants to hear *I can't believe I'm saying this, but* . . . Like you're shocked that you actually might want to see me again?'

'I didn't mean it like that. Not at all. I meant that I never usually want to see women again, but I do want to see you, I really do. I haven't dated anyone since Anna, I just normally . . . well . . .'

'Shag and run?'

Conor winced. 'Kind of, yeah.'

'Lovely.'

'But I feel different about you. I would really like to see you again.'

'Just so we're clear, I'm the catch here, mate. You're separated, have baggage, drink too much, and your apartment needs a good scrub. I'm young, hot and ambitious.'

Conor smiled. 'Very hot.'

Milly grinned. 'Yes, very hot.'

'So, any chance you'd consider seeing an older drunk with two kids and a smelly apartment again?'

Milly leant over. 'Luckily for you, the sex was great and, although you need a lot of work, I think you have potential. Sign up for that course and maybe I'll take a chance on you. Let's see how our next date goes. It better be good.'

Conor felt elated. He actually wanted to punch the air. It was ridiculous – he barely knew her but there was something about her. She was like a beam of sunshine bursting through his crappy life. 'How about tonight?'

'I'll be tired after work, not up for a big night.'

'We can chill, watch a movie and order takeout.'

Milly opened the car door and stepped out.

Oh, no, I've come on too strong. Conor was gutted.

Milly put her head into the car. 'I will agree on two conditions. First, you clean that apartment properly. I want to smell bleach when I come back. Second, you get off your arse and cook me dinner. I'd like roast chicken, roast potatoes and peas. For dessert I'd like banoffee pie. I'll see you at eight, and if you let me down or try to buy the food in, I'll know.'

Conor agreed readily and Milly kissed him goodbye, a long, lingering kiss.

Conor admired her bum as she sashayed over to her car. He was buzzing. He hadn't been excited about anything in ages. It felt really good.

24

Anna woke James up with a cup of strong coffee. He rubbed his eyes.

'Anna, we can't keep having this conversation. This has to stop. Jack has to sleep in his own bed. That is the last time I'm sleeping on the couch. It's been four months now, enough is enough. Even your own sister thinks it's ludicrous.'

'I know, I know. I'll have a serious chat with him today.'

'Promise?'

'Yes, I promise.'

'Please don't back down again. I need to be able to sleep in my own bed with my partner. He's going to have to get used to it. You're too soft with him – he needs a firmer hand.'

Anna immediately felt annoyed. What did he mean 'a firmer hand'? Why was it always her fault? James wasn't helping. In fact, his 'handling' of Jack had made things worse and more complicated. She was disappointed that he hadn't bonded with her son. She'd naïvely thought they'd get on well in time, but all they did was clash. And that didn't look like changing any time soon.

'Well,' Anna said, 'on the subject of firmer hands, you need to have a word with Bella about snapping my head off when I asked her to take her headphones off while I was trying to talk to her.'

James put down his cup. 'She was trying to learn lyrics. Look, she's a bit wound up at the moment because of the pressure of being the star in the musical. Now is not the time for me to give her a lecture. I'd rather wait to talk to her when the musical is over.'

The famous musical wasn't on for another five weeks. James was being ridiculous.

'I don't think a quiet word in her ear about being polite is going to traumatize her, James, and I would appreciate it.'

'Fine. You get Jack out of our bed and I'll speak to Bella.'

'Fine.'

James went up to have a shower and Anna headed to the kitchen to make the school lunches. She reheated the leftover spaghetti from the night before and put it into three Thermos holders.

'What's that?' Bella was watching Anna from the kitchen door.

'Your lunch.'

'What's in it? Tell me it's not that disgusting spaghetti.'

'It is the spaghetti and it's not disgusting.'

'I don't eat carbs,' Bella snapped.

Anna twisted the top tightly on the Thermos. 'You ate it last night.'

'Because I was starving and there was nothing else on offer. From now on I am not eating any carbs. So you can put that away. I'll just have fruit.'

'You can't last all day on fruit. You need carbohydrates, Bella. They're not bad for you. I know a lot of teenagers think that carbs make you put on weight, but they don't, not unless you eat enormous amounts of them. They're an important part of your diet.'

Bella rolled her eyes. 'I don't remember asking you for a lecture, and since when did you become a dietician?'

'I'm a nurse, Bella, and believe it or not, we know a lot about health.'

'Mum says nurses are people who failed to get into medical school.'

Your mother is a thundering bitch and an intellectual snob. 'That's not true and I love my job, thank you very much.'

Bella made herself a cup of black coffee. 'Whatever. Can you tell your kids to hurry up? I need to be in early for rehearsal.'

James walked in, smelling of shower gel and looking less grumpy than he had earlier.

'Morning, beautiful daughter.' He kissed Bella's head. Then he walked over and put his arms around Anna. 'Morning, you. Sorry about being grumpy earlier,' he whispered.

Anna kissed his smooth cheek. 'Me too.'

'Oh, God, can you please not do that in front of me?' Bella groaned.

James laughed. 'Sorry, but it's hard to keep my hands off Anna.'

'Try harder,' Bella said. 'Besides, you have a whole kid-free weekend coming up to grope each other.'

'Yes, please wait until we're gone.' Grace sat down at the table.

'Grace!' Anna giggled.

'Seriously, Mum, it's too much this early in the morning.'

'Agreed.' Bella fist-pumped Grace.

Jack walked in, went straight up to them and shoved James out of the way. 'Mum, I can't find my jumper.'

'Easy there, Jack.' James tried to keep his voice even.

'Go away. I need my mum.'

James gave Anna a pointed look.

'Jack, don't be rude,' Anna said.

'I need you, Mum.' He tugged at her arm.

'Let me finish my coffee.'

'*Muuuum.*'

Bella glanced at her phone and threw her hands into the air. 'It's twenty to eight! Jesus Christ, Anna, will you help him find his bloody jumper or I'll be late for rehearsal.'

'Ah, now, Bella, there's no need to snap,' James said.

Was that it, 'Ah, now, Bella'? Come on, James, crank it up a bit. How about 'Bella, do not ever speak to Anna like that again' or 'Hey, Bella, if you're rude to Anna again, I'll take the phone you have permanently glued to your face' or even 'Bella, you're a nasty cow and I'm going to send you to boarding school.'

Stop it, Anna, calm down. She took deep breaths as she followed Jack up the stairs to find his jumper, which was on the floor of his bedroom under his tracksuit. They were heading back downstairs when they heard Bella bellowing: 'COME ON!'

'Put a sock in it. You're giving me a headache,' Grace grumbled. 'Calm down.'

'Oh, so it's okay for everyone to run around getting *you* to school early for your science project, but *I*'m supposed to be chill about being late for my musical rehearsal?'

'Actually, Bella, I remember you holding us up and not caring that I had to get to school early. God, do you ever just shut up?'

Anna was delighted that Grace was giving as good as she was getting. She usually just ignored Bella and stayed out of her way. A small part of Anna was tempted to say she was still looking for Jack's jumper just to wind Bella up, but she pushed aside the temptation and ran downstairs to her grouchy step-daughter.

Anna was writing a list of things Conor needed to do over the weekend, and places the kids needed to be dropped to, when the doorbell rang. Jack raced out to open it.

'*Daaaaaad!*' he shouted.

'There's my sports-star boy and my genius daughter.'

Anna got up, and as she was heading to the hall to give Conor his detailed instructions, she heard, 'Guys, this is Milly.'

What was going on?

She walked out to find Conor standing in the hall with a woman. A young woman. A very young woman. A very attractive young woman.

'Hi.' Anna raised her brows as she caught her ex's eye.

'Hey, this is Milly.'

'Hi, Anna, nice to meet you.' Milly held out her hand and firmly shook Anna's.

What the hell? Was this Conor's girlfriend? He'd never mentioned her, and the kids clearly hadn't met her before. Was she some random young one he was shagging?

Anna studied the way Conor was looking at Milly. No, this wasn't some casual thing: he was gazing at her like a loved-up teenager. But how long had they been together and why was she here, in Anna's house?

'Hello . . . are you . . .?'

Milly nudged Conor.

'What?'

'I think your ex is wondering who I am, you dope.'

'Milly's my girlfriend.'

'Okay. How long have you guys been dating?' Anna asked.

'Long enough.' Conor wasn't giving Anna an inch.

'Could I have a word with you in private?' Anna asked Conor.

'Why?'

'Go on, you two have a chat. I'll help the kids with their bags.' Milly pushed Conor gently towards Anna. 'Very nice to meet you, Anna,' she called over her shoulder.

Anna walked into the kitchen and Conor followed her.

'What the hell is going on, Conor?'

He crossed his arms. 'What are you getting so wound up about?'

'Who is Milly and why is she picking up our kids?'

'Milly is my girlfriend and she's picking up my kids because she's with me.'

'How long have you been together? I've never heard of her before today.'

'I think you'll find, Anna, that it's none of your business.'

'Conor, I don't want my kids spending time with some bird you met last night.'

196

Conor chuckled. 'It's not a good feeling, is it, Anna? Seeing your kids walking off with a stranger? Now you know how I felt when you landed the professor on me.'

Anna tried to keep her cool. 'James and I were together for months before I introduced the kids to him. You've known Milly for all of about ten seconds.'

Conor leant back against the kitchen table. 'I may not have known Milly that long, but she's a diamond. I really like her and I wanted her to meet my kids.'

Anna clenched her hands into fists to stop herself slapping him. 'This isn't about you, Conor, you stupid fool, it's about our kids and how they are going to feel with you shoving some random woman on them. And, by the way, what age is she? Twenty? Seriously, Conor, it's really bad for the kids.'

'Get off your high horse, Anna. The kids will love her, and her age is, again, none of your business.'

'What kind of example are you setting for our kids? Meet Milly this week and who will it be next week? Molly?'

A smug smile spread across Conor's face. 'Wow, Anna, you're really bothered by this. And the funny thing is, there is absolutely nothing you can do about it. You can't control me any more. You walked out on me and you think you can still boss me about? Your professor is welcome to you.'

Conor strolled out of the front door, swinging his car keys. Anna was incensed. How dare he bring some woman he'd picked up in a bar into their kids' lives? She followed him out. She could hear Milly chatting to the kids.

'Messi, my arse, it's Ronaldo all the way, mate. He should have won the Ballon d'Or.'

'Exactly!' Jack was jumping up and down.

'I love your hair colour. I have girls paying me a fortune to get that exact tone,' Milly said to Grace.

'Let's roll,' Conor said, as they all went to get into the car.

'Hold on!' Anna called.

'What?' Conor glared at her.

'I just . . . I . . .'

Milly took a step towards Anna. Quietly she said, 'I know this must be weird for you, but I promise I'm a good person and I'm not trying to stand on anyone's toes or get in the way. I like Conor, but it's very early days. I won't try to become best mates with your kids and I'll respect their feelings and yours.'

Anna was taken aback. 'Oh, right, well . . . I mean . . . thank you. That's actually reassuring.'

'Milly, get your cute arse in the car or we'll all be late for the movie.' Conor beeped the horn.

Milly giggled and climbed in.

Anna watched as they drove off. She could see the kids laughing in the back. She felt . . . not angry . . . hurt. She felt hurt. But why? Conor was going to see other women, she knew that. But Milly was so young and gorgeous and lively, and the kids seemed drawn to her after only a few minutes in her company. She had real charm about her. Would they love her more than Anna? Would they want to be with their dad more now? Was Conor going to fall in love with her and have kids with her? Would he be the partner to Milly that Anna had wanted him to be to her? Would Milly be the person Grace confided her problems to and Jack wanted to watch movies with? Was Anna going to lose her kids to Conor's new girlfriend?

Stop it, Anna, you're being ridiculous. It won't last. It's a brief fling. She forced herself to take a deep breath to calm down. Then she walked back into the house to pour herself a large glass of wine and push down the emotions that were threatening to overwhelm her.

25

James reached his arms above his head and stretched. He felt so good. A full night's sleep in his own bed, sex with Anna and a lie-in. Best of all, her kids were with Conor, and Bella was with Ingrid. They were alone.

Beside him, Anna slept soundly, her hands under her cheek, like a little kid. It had been so good to reconnect. They'd badly needed the dinner, the sex and to sleep in the same bed. He was worried they were drifting apart. All this bickering about the kids and discipline and trying to be good step-parents was sucking them dry. He missed the romance, the cuddles, the intimacy, the 'us' time.

Anna rolled over and opened her eyes. 'Morning.' She gave him a sleepy smile.

'Morning, beautiful.' James kissed her.

'Do you hear that?' Anna said.

'What?'

'Exactly.'

James laughed. The silence was bliss.

'Is it bad that I'm thrilled our kids are not here?' Anna asked.

'I was thinking the same thing,' James admitted.

'Are we terrible people?'

'I think everyone is entitled to enjoy quality time with their partner without guilt.'

Anna snuggled into his chest. He loved the feel of her close to him.

'God, this is so nice. We're okay, aren't we, James?'

He held her tight. 'Yes, darling, we are.'

'I know it's all a lot more challenging than we thought, but we're strong, right?'

'Yes.'

'We'll figure it out, won't we?'

'Of course we will,' he said, wanting to believe it was true.

'I love you.'

'I love you too.' He kissed her.

And he did. He really did. He would do everything in his power to make this work. He'd put up with her irritating son and he'd suffer insults from her awful ex. Anna was worth it, and in a few years' time the girls would have moved out and hopefully Jack would be spending most of his time with his friends and his dad. They just had to get through this hard bit first.

'I know it's only been five months since we moved into this house, but sometimes it feels like five years,' Anna said.

'It certainly hasn't been dull.'

'No.'

James thought about the 70 per cent failure rate of second marriages and relationships that had the baggage of children. He'd been so smug when he'd first read that. So confident of his and Anna's bond. So completely sure that they would sail through combining their families and living together. He had certainly underestimated it . . . by a long shot. Now he could completely understand why so many relationships faltered and fell by the wayside. It wasn't easy.

'I'm so glad I met you,' Anna said, kissing his neck. 'I used to wake up beside Conor and feel sick. I was so miserable with him those last few years. But when I wake up and see you, I'm so happy.'

James wanted to point out that most mornings when she woke up, it was her son's face she saw because he was stuck on the couch, but he didn't want to break the romantic moment.

'Me too, although I used to wake up to an empty pillow, which I imagine was probably better than Conor.'

They both laughed.

'I was thinking,' Anna said.

Uh-oh. Whenever she said this, it usually meant some kind of plan for him to 'bond' with Jack. James braced himself.

'We have all the kids here next weekend, so why don't we take them camping? We can make bonfires and toast marshmallows and play cards and go on hikes. I think it would be a really good way for us all to come together as a family. No phones, no iPads, just us and nature. There's a lovely spot about a two-hour drive from here that we could go to. Wouldn't that be good? I think it's really important for us to be alone with each other as a family unit. We need to come together more as a family to help us move forward.'

Camping? Was she serious? James could think of nothing he'd hate more. He had been forced to join the Scouts briefly as a child, had gone on one God-awful camping trip and hated every second of it. Why on earth would you choose to sleep in a damp tent on uneven ground with spiders and worms everywhere and sit around a miserable little camp-fire waiting five hours for one sausage to cook? Christ, he'd rather nail his balls to the mast of a sinking ship. But she was right: they did need to connect more as a family. They were not united. They were all pulling in different directions and things weren't getting better. They needed to act before things got worse.

'James?' Anna sat up and looked down at him. 'What do you think?'

'Uhm, I . . . well, I . . .'

'I know.' Anna patted his arm. 'You're worried about Bella not wanting to go, but I actually think it would be really good for her. She needs to get away from her phone and engage with the rest of us. And I know Jack will absolutely love it. It'll be good for you and him. The two of you can go off collecting wood and building fires and doing all that stuff.'

James needed Anna to stop talking. The camping-trip idea was getting worse by the second.

'What about a hotel with a swimming pool and a kids' club where Jack could hang out with kids his own age?'

Anna shook her head firmly. 'No, James. A hotel will have TVs and Wi-Fi and restaurants and all that. We need to get the kids out into nature where there are no distractions and we all have to come together as a team.'

James nodded, buying time before speaking. He managed to croak, 'Okay,' as he tried to stop his blood pressure rising. Forty-eight hours in a tent with Jack? Shoot me now.

Angela poured a splash of brandy into the coffee cup and handed it to her sister. Anna took it gratefully.

'I'll have some of that too, thanks.' Anita held out her cup.

'You don't need it. Anna does.'

Angela lifted the brandy bottle back into a high cupboard and put a lock on the door handle.

'What are you doing?'

'Jason is sixteen. He's started drinking on the sly and he's not getting his hands on my good brandy.'

'Has he really started?' Anita asked.

'I caught him out. Sure he came in the other night trying to act sober and hugged me. He wouldn't hug me in a blue fit sober. And a stick of Wrigley's chewing gum can't disguise the stink of beer.'

'What did you do?' Anna asked. Grace was sixteen in four months' time: was she going to be drinking then? She knew a lot of kids started drinking young, some at only thirteen, but Grace was different, so smart and mature for her age. Anna really didn't think she'd start any time soon.

'I confiscated his phone for two days and it was torture. He followed me around begging for it back and telling me it was a violation of his human rights not to be able to communicate with the outside world. I lasted twenty-four hours and gave in. It was a violation of my human rights to be stalked and harassed every second of the day.'

The sisters burst out laughing.

Anita tapped Anna's arm. 'Right, come on, tell us all. What's Conor's new bird like?'

'Very young,' Anna admitted.

'Good-looking?' Angela asked.

'Super-sexy.'

'You're young and sexy,' Anita reminded Anna.

'No, I amn't.' Anna looked down at her scrubs.

'Well, okay, not in your work gear, but when you're done up you are.'

Anna thought about Milly and tried to figure out how to explain that she oozed sexiness.

'She's twenty-three,' Angela told them.

Anna was surprised. 'How do you know?'

'I asked Tom to bump into Conor accidentally on purpose in the gym and ask him about his new squeeze.'

'What did he say?'

'He said she's twenty-three, has her own hair and make-up business and he really likes her.'

'Oh.' Anna put down her cup.

A look passed between Angela and Anita.

'Anna, he was always going to meet someone and you can't stand him, remember?'

'I know.'

'But it still bothers you?'

Anna nodded. Why was she so put out by this new relationship? It was the kids, really: their reaction had made it so much worse.

'Grace and Jack came back from the weekend at his place full of how great she is and how much fun she is and how cool she is, and how Conor cooked them dinner and he'd painted their bedroom and . . . I asked him for years to paint our bedroom in the old house and he never lifted a finger. Now he's working and painting and cooking, and Grace told me he's signed up to do a personal-trainer course. I mean, what the hell?'

How come Milly, in the space of a few weeks, was able to get him to do things Anna couldn't in years?

'Hang on a minute. He's in the throes of lust. All men do this. They're all gung-ho in the beginning. He's putting on a show for her. It won't last. The lazy git won't be able to keep it up,' Anita assured her.

'And in a way it's kind of a – dare I say it? – good thing. If he's getting off his arse and doing things and making an effort, that's good for the kids,' Angela added.

'I know, but how would you like it if your kids came back and were raving about some other woman who was a girlfriend or whatever she is?'

Angela emptied a packet of chocolate fingers onto a plate.

'Jesus, the fingers are out now. This is royal treatment,' Anita noted.

Angela ignored her sister and popped one into her mouth. 'Look, Anna, I understand it's hard having a woman you don't know –'

'A hot, younger woman you don't know,' Anita interrupted.

Angela glared at her. '– a woman you don't know spending time with your kids. But at least she seems to be a nice person and your kids like her. Surely that's better than someone who isn't nice to them and makes them feel unwelcome or uncomfortable.'

'That's true.' Anita tucked into a biscuit, while Anna played with hers.

It was true: she'd be devastated if Conor was with someone who was mean to the kids but . . . well . . .

'Come on, spit it out,' Angela said.

Anna tried to push back the emotion rising in her. 'How

come they like her so much after one weekend and they still don't like James? How come Jack thinks Milly rocks because she likes football and he hates James? How come Grace thinks Milly is the coolest thing ever? How come it's always so bloody easy for Conor and so hard for me?' Tears rolled down her cheeks.

She had been tying herself in knots for months trying to make Grace and Jack like James, while Conor had picked up some random woman in a club and they loved her instantly. Anna was upset and annoyed: she desperately wanted her kids to like James and to have a happy home life where everyone got on well.

'Maybe you need to stop trying so hard to get James, Jack and Grace to like each other and just let them figure it out,' Anita said.

'I've tried that. Grace is polite but distant, and Jack just avoids James or argues with him. They're no closer than when we first moved in. In fact, Jack probably dislikes James even more now.'

Anita pulled the sleeves of her jumper up and propped her chin on her hands. 'I avoid Leanne like the plague and she's my own daughter. She's a thirteen-year-old viper, full of hormones and narky all the time. If you look at her sideways, she'll start an argument with you. Kids aren't easy, even with their own parents.'

'I guess so.' Anna bit the top off her biscuit and felt the sugar rush.

Angela got up to put on the kettle. 'Anna, is the camping trip a good idea? I know you have this vision of James and Jack being hunter-gatherers together, and you, Grace and Bella roasting marshmallows, but James doesn't strike me as a camping kinda guy, and nor does Bella.'

'I know, but if we go to a hotel everyone will just do their own thing. I saw this programme where they took a bunch of troubled teens camping and they all really benefited from being in nature and away from their normal life. They had to talk to each other and they had to help each other with cooking and building fires and all that. It was amazing how much they connected. I really think it's the only way to force us all to be together as a unit, relying on each other.'

'I understand your reasoning, but it feels a bit forced,' Anita said.

'I have to do something to break the tension between us all. I'm kind of dreading the whole thing, but I have to try.'

'I think it's good to try this, but you can't fake or force things, Anna. You need to be honest with James and tell him you're struggling.' Angela filled the teapot with boiling water.

'I'm afraid to,' Anna admitted. 'I'm afraid to rock the boat in case we all fall out into the sea and drown. We're in a delicate place. I reckon I'll just fake it till we make it. If I can pretend we're a happy family, then maybe we'll become one.'

'With all the will in the world, you can't make people like each other. It takes time,' Anita pointed out.

'Time, and bonding experiences like camping,' Anna said firmly. 'This will force us to be together to talk and create our own new family memories.'

'Okay, but don't set your hopes too high, it may not be the happy weekend you're imagining.'

Anna laughed. 'I'm not totally delusional. I'll take a weekend when no one shouts at each other as a success.'

'What about Bella, though?' Anita grinned. 'I'd pay to see her on a camping trip. What did she say when you told her?'

Anna chuckled. 'I got James to break the news to her, but I could hear her reaction through the wall. She freaked.'

Bella had refused to go. Anna had listened, wincing, as she shouted and screamed at her dad. Eventually, James had bribed her.

'James is paying her a hundred euros to come. He doesn't know that I know he bribed her.'

'Just like he doesn't know that you hate camping,' Anita said, gazing pointedly at her.

'I know it seems wrong to be lying to each other, but we're doing this for the good of our family and sometimes you have to stretch the truth a bit to make things happen.'

'Please take pictures of Bella in her fake tan and high heels in the tent.' Anita giggled.

Anna grinned. 'I can't wait to see what she brings with her as "essential".'

'You're a brave woman, Anna,' Angela said.

Brave or nuts? Anna wasn't sure. But she had to do something to shake them into a better place as a family, and she felt that a camping weekend was worth a try. It was different and none of them had really done it before, so it would push them all out of their comfort zones. That might be a good thing. Yes, she was dreading it, but she'd suck it up and be a cheery camp leader. She was going to blend this family together, even if it killed her.

26

Bella sat in the back seat wedged beside Jack, who kept wriggling and squirming.

'Jesus, can you stop it!' she snapped, as he elbowed her in the side for the tenth time.

'You're just a narky cow.' Jack shuffled around, trying to get comfortable.

'God, can you both just shut up!' Grace sighed and curled her body towards the window, putting her head back into her book.

'Guys, come on, let's all be nice to each other. We're going to have a fun weekend,' Anna said.

Fun? Was she having a laugh? The only reason Bella had agreed to go was because, one, her mum was away and she couldn't stay with her, and, two, her dad was paying her. Camping was her idea of utter hell. When she'd told Portia and Saffron, they'd actually gasped in shock.

'Camping as in glamping?' Saffron asked.

'No.'

'One of those big mobile homes that are like an actual house?' Portia asked.

'No.'

'OMG, are you staying in an *actual* tent? Like sleeping on the ground?' Saffron was appalled.

'Yes! Apparently my psycho step-monster thinks it will be a bonding experience for us. Even my dad doesn't really want to go, but he's afraid to tell her because he doesn't want to hurt her feelings.'

'I can't even . . .' Portia's eyes were wide.

'Will there be a hotel nearby for food and bathroom and stuff?' Saffron asked.

'Oh, no, we're going all out. We'll be peeing in the woods.'

'Oh, my actual God. That's, like, inhumane. You should probably call social services,' Portia said.

'I've thought about it.'

'Your step-monster must be a total freak,' Saffron said. 'How can she actually think pooing on the ground is going to bond you? I mean, seriously? It's so gross.'

'What will you eat?' Portia asked. 'Are you going to hunt for your food? Will you have to skin rabbits and cook them over a fire?'

Surely not. Anna couldn't be that crazy, could she? Bella was really worried now.

'On the good side, you'll probably lose more weight. I mean, you're not going to eat disgusting camp food,' Saffron said.

'You've lost loads already – you're nearly as skinny as Saffron and me,' Portia said.

'Not exactly. She's not a size eight yet.' Saffron was competitive about her weight. 'And her thighs will never be skinny. It's not your fault,' she said to Bella, with faux-sympathy. 'It's just your basic shape.'

Bella tried not to mind Saffron's stinging comment. She was right: her thighs – the stupid thighs she'd inherited from her mother – would never be skinny, but the rest of her could be. She was determined to be size eight by the time the musical opened. She was going to be a slim Sandy and look hot in her tight black trousers in that famous final scene.

Portia said nothing, but that didn't surprise Bella. No one ever really stood up to Saffron. It wasn't worth it. She'd just freeze you out and make you work to be in her good books again. It was kind of exhausting. Sometimes Bella wondered why she bothered being friends with her, but Saffron was cool and gorgeous, and being her friend gave Bella status that she would not otherwise have had.

'I want live Insta story updates of the trip,' Portia said.

'Oh, did I not mention? We're not allowed to bring our phones or iPads.'

Her two friends were struck dumb. A weekend with no phone was unfathomable.

Now Jack's bony elbow dug into her side.

'Ow.' Bella shoved his arm down.

'Ouch!' he cried.

Would this poxy journey ever end?

They pulled up to a field in the middle of nowhere. James tried to think positive thoughts about the forty-eight hours ahead, but none came. Anna had been told by one of her patients, who was an avid camper, that this place was a great spot. It was beside a stream, where you could get fresh water; the clearing was big enough to pitch two tents easily; and it was close to a wood, where you could gather logs and twigs for the camp-fire.

They climbed out of the car and James began to unpack the boot. He had borrowed a tent from a colleague and Anna had borrowed another from one of the doctors in her surgery. One tent was a two-man, the other for four. The plan was to put the kids in together and for Anna and James to sleep in the other.

They placed all of the many bits and pieces on the ground and Anna said, 'Why don't you and Jack get going on putting up the tents and I'll go and gather wood with the girls?'

Brilliant, James thought. I'm left with Jack, who will be no bloody use, to put up tents I have no clue how to assemble.

'Great. Okay, Jack, let's do this,' he said, in the most enthusiastic voice he could muster.

Anna gave him a thumbs-up and an encouraging smile.

'Maybe you should change your shoes, Bella,' Anna suggested.

'Your lovely runners will get very muddy.' Bella was wearing bright white flatform trainers.

'The only others I brought are my furry sliders.'

'You're not serious?' Anna asked.

'Yes, I am. I've never been camping and I didn't expect to have to trudge through revolting mud all day.'

'What did you think it was going to be like? We're sleeping in a field.' Grace sounded exasperated.

'News flash, Grace. I've never slept in a field before because I'm not a farm animal.'

From beside James, Jack roared, 'Yes, you are, Bella! You're a cow.'

Grace giggled and James saw Anna hide a smile. Not fair. They can't all gang up on Bella. 'Okay, that's enough,' he said. 'Bella can clean her shoes when we get home.'

The girls headed off into the woods with Anna, and James turned his attention to the tents. All he could see were poles everywhere. He could feel a headache forming already. He pulled out the instructions he'd snapped on his phone.

'No phones, Mum said,' Jack reminded him.

'No phones for you kids. Mine is necessary because it has the instructions on it.'

'Don't you even know how to put up a tent?' Jack asked.

'It's my first time.' James glanced down at the list his colleague had texted him.

1. Spread out the groundsheet.
2. Match the poles to the grommets on the tent body and the footprint.
3. Attach the tent body to the poles.
4. Lay out the rain fly on top of the tent.
5. Stake out the tent.

Christ, it was all double Dutch. Jack was watching him closely.

'Right, let's get the groundsheets down and match the poles to the grommets.'

'What's a grommet?'

Fecked if I know. James stared at the tent fabric and looked for signs of what a grommet might be.

'These must be them.' Jack pointed to the holes in the side of the fabric.

'Brilliant. Well done, Jack.'

They spread out the groundsheets and began to try to match the poles to the grommets. Nothing seemed to fit.

James tried to look confident but Jack saw through him fairly quickly. 'You're crap at this.'

James threw down a pole. 'Yes, I am.'

'Like, really crap.'

'Yes.'

'I went camping with my friend Owen and his dad put up the tent in a few minutes.'

'Good for him. Do you happen to have his number?'

'Why would I have my friend's dad's number? That's weird.'

'I was joking.'

'Your jokes are rubbish.'

God, this kid was hard to love, or even like. James bit his tongue and continued trying to figure out how to put up the sodding tent. Eventually, through trial and lots of error, it began to take shape.

Jack stopped insulting him and began to help. Soon they were working side by side and the first tent was up. James could see that it was slightly lopsided, but it seemed stable enough and he wasn't starting again.

'Good job, partner.' James held out his hand to high-five Jack.

'Only nerds high-five. We can fist-pump.'

They did so. 'Well done, and thanks for your help.'

'We've only done the little one. We still have to do the big one.'

'I think we deserve a break. How about a cup of hot chocolate?'

'Okay.'

James switched on the camping stove and filled the pot with milk from the cooler box.

They sat on the ground and waited for the milk to boil. Jack kept staring into the pot.

'Why is it taking so long?'

'It'll be ready soon.'

'When?'

'Soon.'

'I'm bored.'

'So am I, but we'll be busy soon, putting up the second tent.'

The milk began to bubble and James carefully poured it into two mugs and mixed in the chocolate powder.

They sipped in silence.

'This is actually really nice,' Jack said.

'Good. I appreciate your help, Jack. I think the girls are going to need our help this weekend,' James said. Anna had told him to lay on the 'You and me are the men of the camp' talk during the trip. He wasn't sure he could pull it off, he was hardly Bear Grylls's long-lost twin brother, but he'd do anything for Anna.

Jack shrugged, but didn't shoot the comment down, which was progress. James decided to use the opportunity to talk to him.

'I know it's been hard on you, with your mum and dad separating and then me coming into your life. I just want you to know that I think you're a great kid and I'd like us to get on and be friends, or like an uncle and nephew kind of relationship.'

Jack played with his cup. 'I have uncles and they don't live with me. I have friends, too. You're just Mum's boyfriend. That's it. Not my uncle or my friend.'

'Okay. Maybe they were bad examples. What I'm trying to

say is that I want us to get on for your mum's sake. I really love her and I want to make her happy. I know you love her too and want her to be happy. Right?'

Jack nodded.

'So then let's try to be . . . uhm . . . mates?'

'No.'

'Pals?'

'No.'

'What then?'

'Housemates,' Jack said. 'That's what we are, housemates.'

James smiled. 'I like that. It's a good way to describe us.'

'Don't get all excited. I still don't like living with you, but I'll try for Mum.'

James nodded. It was good enough. A small step, but at least in the right direction.

Anna plonked down an armful of wood, followed by Grace. Bella put down the few twigs she was carrying. She kept one in her hand and used it to try to scrape mud off her not-so-white trainers.

'Is that my tent?' Bella asked.

'No, that's the two-man for me and Anna. We're going to put yours up now. Jack is a terrific help.'

'Well, we did it together,' Jack said.

'That's brilliant,' Anna gushed. 'Wonderful.'

James shot her a warning look. If she overdid the enthusiasm, she could make Jack back off again. Anna caught his expression and gave a slight nod.

'And James made me a really nice hot chocolate. You should have one, Mum.'

'I'd love one, thanks.' Anna beamed at James.

James smiled back and winked at her. 'Jack, we need to get a start on the big tent now. Are you up for it, housemate?'

'Yep.'

Jack and James went over to sort out the big tent, Anna beaming at them. But she said nothing, thankfully.

'Can you hurry up? I'm cold,' Bella complained.

'Me too.' Grace shivered.

'Why don't you help them put up the tent? It'll keep you warm,' Anna suggested.

'I'll wait in the car. Call me when you're finished.' Bella held out her hand to her father for the car key.

James reached into his pocket for it.

'Hang on, why don't we all help with the tent? A team effort.' At another look from Anna, James shoved the key back into his pocket.

'Can I have a hot chocolate first?' Grace asked.

'Of course. Bella?' James asked.

'No way. There's far too much sugar in it. I'll have a black coffee.'

James made Anna and Grace hot chocolate and Bella a black coffee.

'This tastes so good,' Grace said.

'Told you James made good ones,' Jack said.

James noticed Bella looking longingly at Grace's hot chocolate. 'Are you sure you don't want one, Bella?' he asked.

'One hundred million per cent,' Bella said sourly.

James decided to let it go. 'Right, let's get this tent up.' He clapped his hands together.

James, Anna, Jack and Grace put the tent up. Bella stood in the background, looking bored, and did nothing.

'Good job, team,' Anna said. 'It's a big tent, too. Plenty of room for all three of you.'

'I'm going to sleep in the car,' Bella said.

'No. You're all sleeping together in this tent,' Anna said firmly.

'Dad?' Bella looked to James for support.

Oh, Christ, James thought, yet again caught between his

daughter and his partner. Bella was scowling at him and Anna was gazing at him pleadingly, wanting him to take her side. Talk about a lose-lose situation.

'Now, Bella, we're all sleeping in tents just for these two nights. We have big blow-up mattresses for everyone. You'll be comfortable, I promise. We've two doubles and two singles. Why don't you take the other double?'

'I think the fair thing to do would be to draw straws for the second double mattress,' Anna said. 'It's not fair to pick one of the children to give it to.'

'Well, I just thought as Bella is used to sleeping in a big bed . . .'

'James,' Anna said, 'we're drawing straws because that's the decent thing to do.'

James held up his hands. 'Okay, fine.'

Grace stood beside the tent in her jeans and old black trainers. 'She can have the double mattress. I don't care.'

'Me neither,' Jack said.

Hallelujah, thought James. Peace at last.

'But it's not right that Bella just gets it,' Anna said, clearly determined.

'Mum,' Grace raised her voice slightly, 'we don't care.'

James could see that Anna was furious and about to say something else, so he cut in quickly. 'Good. That's sorted, then. Thank you, Grace and Jack, you're very kind, aren't they, Bella?'

Bella gave a small nod. Anna looked like she wanted to kill him. God, this was exhausting.

Anna suggested a game of Thirty Seconds. Grace was paired with James, and Bella was with Jack and Anna. Grace stole a look at her watch. Five o'clock. They'd only been there three hours and it felt like for ever. She just wanted to get this weekend over with and go home. She knew how much it meant to her mum and she wanted to help her out, but she also knew it was a waste of time. No one was going to bond. No one wanted to be there, not even Anna, even though she was putting on a good show.

Bella was trying to explain a person to Anna and Jack without saying their name: 'So, he's like this Black guy. I think he's American, but he could be English.'

'Barack Obama?' Anna shouted.

'No. He's, like, way older than him and I think he might be dead, but I'm not sure. He was really into walking and stuff.'

'Walking?' Anna was puzzled.

'Well, yeah, walking or maybe running.'

'Carl Lewis?' Anna said.

'Who?'

'Famous American athlete.'

'Not him. He's like . . . I dunno, super-famous.'

Grace knew it was Martin Luther King. She knew that Bella was thinking of marches, not walks or runs. Was she seriously that stupid? Did she never listen in history class? There was a whole chapter on Rosa Parks, Martin Luther King and the civil-rights movement in their history book.

'Michael Jordan?' Jack asked.

'No.'

'Jay-Z?'

'No, I didn't say he was a singer, did I?'

'Linford Christie?' Anna asked.

'No, whoever that is.'

Bella's time was up. James was giving her extra but Grace didn't know why he was bothering: she was even worse than Jack at this game.

'Time,' Grace said.

James looked over at her. 'Well, only just, yes,' he said.

'Who was it?' Anna asked.

'It was Martin Luther King, wasn't it?' Grace said.

'Was it?' James asked.

'Yeah.'

'Bella!' Even her father was shocked. 'Martin Luther King was not a runner! He was a famous civil-rights activist. He made that speech, *I have a dream*, he –'

'Please do not start giving me a lecture on history. It's bad enough that we're in this dump and I have to sleep on the ground. I don't need a lecture on top of it.'

'Well, it's a good thing your mother isn't here. She'd be shocked,' James said, shaking his head.

'Well, she isn't, and you'd better not tell her,' Bella snapped.

James said nothing and picked up a card for his turn. Grace guessed four of his list of five.

'Right, Jack, you're up. Come on, let's get a good score here.' Anna rubbed her hands together.

Jack picked up his card and read it. 'So it's, like . . . uhm . . . this is a footballer who is really famous.'

'Ronaldo?' Anna guessed.

'No.'

'David Beckham?'

'No.'

'Uhm . . . whatshisname . . . Robbie Keane?'

'No, way more famous.'

Anna turned to Bella. 'Help me out here.'

'I hate football. It's a bunch of losers chasing a stupid ball. Who cares?'

'Football is brilliant!' Jack shouted.

'It's boring,' Bella said.

'No, it isn't. You're boring!' Jack yelled.

'And you're an annoying little shit.'

'Bella!' Anna gasped.

'Well, he is and someone needs to tell him.'

'Leave him alone,' Grace said. She was so tired of Bella and Jack constantly sniping at each other.

'He is not,' Anna said. 'Apologize immediately.'

'For what? Telling the truth?' Bella hissed. 'Your stupid son drives everyone mental, including my dad.'

Anna glared at James. 'Would you like to jump in here?'

'Bella, you're out of order. You should apologize to Jack and Anna,' James said.

Bella put her hands on her hips in defiance. 'You always say it's important to be honest, Dad. Well, I'm being honest.'

'You drive me mental and my mum hates you.' Jack kicked Bella hard in the shin.

'You little shit!' She slapped him across the cheek.

Grace was utterly shocked. She couldn't believe Bella had actually hit Jack. This was a new low.

'How dare you hit my son?' Anna roared, and pulled Jack into her arms. 'Jesus Christ, James, will you bloody well *do* something!'

'She shouldn't have slapped him but neither should he have kicked her. They both need to apologize,' James said, and he looked just as furious.

'He's ten!' Anna shouted.

Grace felt like she was hyperventilating. Her breathing almost hurt her chest. The tension that had been building was getting on top of her and making her feel ill. She was so, so sick of this. It was living in a toxic bubble all the time. She wanted to get up and run and keep running and not look back. This was her life, and she hadn't chosen it. She had no control over it and she hated it. The pent-up emotions of the last five months crashed down on her and she felt almost dizzy with rage.

'WILL YOU ALL SHUT THE HELL UP!' Grace screamed at the top of her lungs.

Everyone turned to stare. She couldn't believe that that noise had come from her. Her face felt hot and her hands were clenched.

'I am so over this. I am sick of you all bitching and arguing. I hate this. I hate our life. I wish I could live on my own. I don't want to sleep in a tent. I don't want to pretend we're a family when we're not. Mum and James, stop trying to force us to like each other and bloody *bond*. It's all fake bullshit. I'm sick of all of you. I have had it.'

'So the mouse has a voice.' Bella grinned. 'I agree with Grace. This is bullshit.'

Grace ignored her and turned to her mother. 'Open the car. I'm not staying here.'

'Grace, come on, love. Let me make you another hot chocolate.' Anna talked as if she was still six years old. It grated on Grace's taut nerves.

Grace looked directly at her mother. 'I do not want a fucking hot chocolate. Open the car right now. I am done. End. Of. Discussion.'

'But, Grace –'

'OPEN THE BLOODY CAR.' She was sick of them all. She was fed up being the nice one, the accommodating one. She hated this stupid blended family set-up every bit as much as Bella and Jack did. She wanted to go home, lock her bedroom door and FaceTime her friends. She was sick of trying to please everyone. They were never going to be a family. They all needed to accept that. She was done pretending.

27

Conor felt a finger digging into his back. 'Go away, Milly.'

'Get up, you lazy git.'

'What time is it?'

'Eight thirty.'

'Jesus, Milly, it's Saturday. Let me lie in.'

Milly put her face close to his. 'You've only worked two days this week. Get your arse out of bed. We're going for a run and then we're going to do a shop. I'm going to work and you're going to cook your kids a proper meal.'

'I spent the other three days working on my personal-trainer course.'

'What do you want – a medal? Come on, lazy bones.'

Conor pulled the duvet over his head. It smelt like fresh flowers. Milly had made him buy new washing powder that made everything smell really good.

He felt a sharp pain in his back as Milly jumped on top of him. 'Up, now.'

He knew she wouldn't stop until he got up, so he gave in. Besides, he had no hangover because they'd stayed in and watched a movie the night before. Milly had cooked a gorgeous chicken curry and only allowed him to drink two beers.

He'd always hated Anna telling him what to do, but with Milly it was different. He wasn't sure why. Maybe it was because he felt she was doing it because she believed in him. She wanted him to be happy and to succeed. He knew that Anna had stopped believing in him long ago. He was always letting her down and messing up. It was a pattern they'd fallen into. Anna was the one with the steady job and he was the let-down. He put his needs first, he went out late, he worked sporadically, he was selfish, he was a bad husband . . . In the end, if he was being honest, he'd played up to his role. Nothing he did could please her, so why bother?

But Milly seemed to think he had potential. She liked him and fancied him and wanted him to do more with his life, to find fulfilment. She wanted to build him up, not knock him down, like Anna did.

Conor wanted to impress Milly and show her that he could be a good dad and a good partner. She worked non-stop and had all these plans for her future. It was infectious. She was so excited about life's possibilities and that made Conor feel positive, too. He'd signed up to the personal training course the day Milly had sent him the details and he was loving it. He was good at it and found it really interesting. His confidence had been boosted. He felt less like a failure. Conor was determined to complete the course and shake up his life. He wanted Milly to keep looking at him with pride, not like Anna did, her eyes filled with disappointment.

Conor dragged himself out of bed and headed off for a jog with Milly. He enjoyed it, and enjoyed even more staring at her sexy Lycra-clad bum as they did laps of the park. They stopped after three to catch their breath.

'You're not bad for an old fart,' Milly joked.

'Thanks. Watching your bum was a good incentive.'

Milly giggled. Conor loved making her laugh. He hadn't made Anna laugh in years.

'If you play your cards right, you may just get to see it naked later.'

Conor picked her up and swung her over his shoulder. Milly laughed. 'Put me down, Rambo. Come on, we need to get some groceries for that empty fridge.'

They pottered around the local supermarket, Milly telling Conor what to put in his basket. She'd planned for him to cook a pasta dish.

'It's not complicated but it has chicken and vegetables in it, so the kids will be properly fed. No more takeout pizzas. I'll text you instructions. It'll be delicious, and make sure you save some for me because I'll be starving after doing this photo-shoot. It's going to be a long day.'

The strange thing was that when Anna had told him what to cook he'd felt emasculated, but with Milly it felt like encouragement. Everything with her was different – and better.

When they got home, Milly helped Conor unpack all the bags, change the kids' bed linen and clean the bathroom.

'Right, the place is hygienic and presentable now. I'm off.' She reached up to kiss him.

Conor put his arms around her and held her close. 'Thank you,' he whispered into her ear.

'For what?'

'For coming into my life and making everything better.' Conor found he was choking up. Jesus, get a grip, man. He'd scare her off if he started blubbing into her hair after only a month of dating. But she'd got under his skin and he was smitten.

'That's the nicest thing any bloke has said to me.' Milly kissed him on the lips. 'You older blokes are much nicer to your girlfriends.'

'Less of the "older blokes".' Conor was glad to be able to joke and side-step his emotions.

'Older but fit.' Milly winked. 'I'll be putting your heart rate to the test later, babe.' She pinched his bum and headed out of the door.

Conor laughed and waved her off. He felt like a kid again. Happy. This was what it felt like to be happy. He hadn't felt like this in so long he'd forgotten. He felt light, full of energy and hope. It was brilliant, absolutely bloody brilliant.

There was a knock on the door and Conor rushed to open it.

'Hey, kids,' he exclaimed, hugging them.

Behind them stood Anna. What was she doing here? She usually dropped them downstairs and left.

Anna looked around the apartment. 'The place looks great,' she said, sounding surprised.

'It's Milly,' Grace told her. 'She made Dad clean up and buy cool new cushions, plus this amazing rug.'

The rug was a lovely mixture of shades that lifted the whole living area, and the cushions gave the grey couch a much-needed pop of colour. Milly had given them to him as a present. 'It's thanks for having me as your almost permanent new room-mate,' she'd said.

'I really like it,' Anna said. 'She has great taste.'

Anna's eyes then rested on the big corkboard in the kitchen area. It was covered with photos of the kids.

'Dad and me and Milly did that the last time we were here,' Jack said. 'Look, Mum, there's a photo of me in my first football boots.'

Anna followed Jack over to look at the photos. Grace went into the bedroom to put her weekend bag down. Conor stood back, watching Anna taking everything in.

'I'm starving. Can we get takeout for dinner?' Jack asked his dad.

Conor shook his head. 'Nope. I'm making chicken pasta primavera,' he said, putting on an Italian accent.

'But I want pizza,' Jack grumbled.

'This is going to be delicious. You can help me cook. You can be my sous-chef.' Conor pulled Jack into a playful head-lock. Jack laughed.

'I'm sorry, did I hear that right? You are cooking a meal from scratch?' Anna asked.

Conor tried not to be irritated by her shocked tone. 'Yes, Anna, I'm cooking.'

'Wow, clean apartment, fresh flowers in a vase, and now you're cooking . . .'

'Your point is?'

Anna smiled, but not a nice, open Milly smile, a kind of sneery smile. The smile Conor had grown to hate.

'I'm just taken aback. I can't remember the last time you cleaned and cooked.'

'Well, I guess when you're with someone who encourages you, rather than puts you down, you want to do more stuff.'

Anna flinched. 'That's not fair and you know it.'

Conor leaned back against the counter and folded his arms. 'Isn't it?'

Jack slipped out of the room and went in to join his sister in the bedroom.

'I didn't put you down.'

'Yes, you did, all the bloody time.'

'Oh, I get it, you meet some young, innocent, clueless woman who thinks you're God's gift and now suddenly I'm the bad guy.'

'Milly is young, but she is not innocent or clueless.'

'I did not put you down, Conor. I just got sick and bloody tired of watching you sitting around scratching your arse while I worked day and night. What was I supposed to do? Congratulate you for being lazy? Tell you what a great guy you are?'

Anna the martyr, Conor thought. Always the bloody victim. 'I dunno, Anna. Maybe if you'd stopped being such a bitter bitch all the time I'd have done more.'

'How dare you call me that? I was young and carefree when you met me, but you ground me down. Living with you made me deeply unhappy. I think I was pretty close to having a nervous breakdown when I met James. I'd forgotten that being happy was possible, but now I'm really bloody happy.'

'Are you, Anna? Because you don't look it.'

'Yes, I am. Blissfully,' Anna snapped.

'Well, so am I, so that makes two of us.'

Anna snorted. 'You barely know her. It's hardly love, Conor.'

'Who made you an authority on love? What gives you the right to tell me whether I'm in love or not?'

'Are you seriously trying to tell me that after a few weeks of shagging, you're madly in love?'

Conor paused. Yes, he was. He was head over heels about Milly. It was quick, it was sudden, and it was very unexpected, but he was. 'Yes, I am.'

Anna laughed. 'Oh, Conor, you'll never grow up. This is an infatuation. I give it another month.'

Conor put his mouth close to Anna's ear. 'I don't give a rat's arse about your opinion. Now please take your toxic energy and leave.'

Anna looked startled, then turned on her heel and left without another word. He felt a brief stab of guilt, but then he thought, No, she is toxic and I don't have to put up with that any more. She'd pull down his new sense of self if he let her, and he wasn't going to let that happen.

They were about to sit down to dinner when Milly arrived back. Conor opened the door to her, and when he saw her gorgeous smile, he put his arms around her and held her close. This was the face he longed to see, not Anna's disapproving one. All this time he'd thought he missed Anna. What a joke.

'Well, hello to you too.' Milly laughed.

Conor pulled back and grinned at her. 'Sorry, I'm just glad you're here.'

'Well, I am kind of fabulous.' Milly giggled.

She put her big wheelie suitcase full of her make-up, hair products and tools against the wall in the hallway and they went into the living room-kitchen area.

'Hey, guys,' Milly greeted the kids and plonked herself into a chair beside Jack. 'Something smells good. I'm starving.'

Conor handed her a plate of chicken pasta.

'Is this any good, kids?' Milly asked.

'It's actually delicious,' Grace said.

'Oh, good. It's my favourite recipe. I told your dad to follow the instructions carefully so he wouldn't mess up.' Milly shovelled a large forkful into her mouth and chewed. 'Mmm, good job.' She reached over to fist-pump Conor.

'There are too many vegetables in it,' Jack complained.

'My brother's the same as you, doesn't like his veggies. Next time your dad can make it with just peas and have extra veggies on the side for anyone who wants more. How does that sound?'

'Much better.' Jack smiled.

Milly chatted to the kids with an ease that Conor loved. She told them funny stories about crazy clients she'd done make-up for, and wedding stories, and jokes that made them laugh.

'A good one I heard was this. It's more for Grace, though.' Milly winked at Grace. 'Right, so this couple, John and Jenny, get married and go off on their honeymoon. When they get back, Jenny phones her mother who asks her how the honeymoon was. "Oh, my God, Mum," Jenny says, "the honeymoon was wonderful. So romantic and beautiful . . ." But then Jenny bursts into tears. "But as soon as we returned home John started using the most awful language . . . saying things I've never heard before! I mean, all these terrible four-letter words! You've got to come get me and take me home . . ."'

'"Calm down, Jenny," the mother says. "Tell me, what could be so awful? What four-letter words?"'

'Still sobbing, Jenny whispers, "Oh, Mum . . . words like 'dust', 'wash', 'cook' and 'iron'."'

Milly cracked up laughing, and so did Grace.

'Never let a man tell you what to do, Grace.' Milly wagged her finger. 'Mind you, you're far too smart and beautiful for that. Your dad told me about your science project. He's dead proud of you. I think it's incredible. You're going to take over the world of science, and this rascal,' she playfully pinched Jack's nose, 'is going to play striker for Liverpool.'

Grace and Jack beamed at her, basking in the light of her genuine enthusiasm and praise.

'Oh, I've just remembered another good story.' Milly imitated a very drunk father of the bride making a terrible speech. Grace and Jack roared laughing. Her sense of fun and her complete lack of awkwardness were infectious.

Conor fell even more in love with her that night.

28

It was Sunday night and they were back home from Conor's. Grace was listening as James and her mum argued about Jack and Bella yet again. They seemed to forget that her bedroom backed onto theirs and the walls were thin. So, not only did she have to suffer their headboard banging against her wall when they were having sex, but she also heard them when they were fighting, which was a lot lately.

Since the disastrous camping trip, things had got worse. Grace felt a bit guilty for freaking out, but if she hadn't, Bella was bound to at some stage. It was never going to work. You just could not force people to get on. But at the same time she didn't want her mum and James to split up because that would mean more upheaval and Grace had had enough of that to last a lifetime. The way they were arguing now made her think of her mum and dad in the months before they had parted, which worried her.

That was the weird thing about families, even your own actual family. You might not like your sister or brother or mother or father because you didn't choose to be in their lives. You were born and you were stuck with these people for eighteen years until you could get away. Some people got lucky with their family and others didn't. And if your parents split up, you were forced to live with a whole other family you hadn't chosen.

Grace loved her mum and dad and Jack. James was fine and Bella was okay too, in very small doses, but she was counting the months until she could get away to study in America and choose the people she shared a place with. And the beauty of it was that if her flatmates annoyed her she'd just move out and find other people to live with. She wouldn't be stuck. Once she was eighteen, just over two years away, she'd be able to choose her own housemates. She couldn't wait.

Thankfully, James and Anna were going out tonight, and she hoped they'd have a nice time and stop arguing. Grace was hoping that her own plans for the evening would work out. She just needed to get Bella onside.

Anna popped her head around Grace's bedroom door. 'Hi, love, we're off now. I've left money for pizza. Will you watch a movie with Jack, so he's not left on his own all evening?'

'Sure.'

'Hopefully Bella will leave you both alone and stay in her room,' Anna whispered.

'It's fine, Mum, go and have a nice time.'

Anna smiled. 'Thanks, I'm looking forward to it. James and I need a night out.'

'Bye.'

'Bye, and thanks, Grace.'

'Minding Jack is hardly a big deal.'

'I mean for being an amazing daughter. Honestly, when I see Bella and how difficult she is, it makes me appreciate you even more than I already did.'

Grace smiled. 'Go on, Mum, you'll be late.'

'Love you.' Anna blew her a kiss.

As soon as the taxi had driven off, Grace took off her track-suit and put on her skinny black jeans and a pink crop top. She applied her make-up, trying to remember the tips Milly had given her.

'Less is more, babe,' Milly had said. 'Especially when you're young and beautiful.'

She finished off her make-up using the mascara Milly had given her. Wow, it really did make her eyelashes look longer and fuller.

Grace pulled on her black boots and her faux-fur black jacket and headed downstairs. Bella was eating a bowl of broccoli at the kitchen table, watching *Gossip Girl* on her phone.

She glanced up. 'You look amazing.'

'Thanks.'

Bella's eyes narrowed. 'You didn't get this done up to stay in, though, did you?'

Grace chewed her lower lip. 'No. The thing is, my friend has a free house and she's invited a few people over and I was thinking of popping round for, like, just an hour. Is there any chance you'd keep an eye on Jack?'

'No way.'

'Look, all you have to do is order him a pizza and let him watch a movie. You don't even have to sit in the same room as him. Please, Bella.'

'How come you get to go to a party and I get stuck with your freak brother?'

'He's not a freak. Don't say that.'

Bella rolled her eyes. 'Fine. Annoying little monster.'

Grace sighed. 'He's a ten-year-old kid who's had his life turned upside-down. You of all people should understand how that feels. Give him a break.'

Bella's eyes flashed. 'Speaking of break, he destroyed my new lip gloss. Apparently, Einstein thought it was glue and smeared it all over his copybook, then wondered why the picture wouldn't stick. Clearly you got the brains and he got . . . Well, I guess that's yet to be decided, right?'

Grace wanted to tell Bella to sod off and leave her brother alone, that she wasn't exactly Mensa material herself, but she needed her help, so she swallowed her anger and remained calm.

'Bella, I've been working on my project for months. This is the first night out I've had. Please do me this one favour.'

Bella paused. 'I'll tell you what. I'll do it if you write my French essay.'

'Deal.'

'I want to get over ninety per cent. It'll keep my mother off my back.'

'You'll get it. Now, I have to go. The money for the pizza is there. He likes a plain margarita. Don't tell him I've gone out. Just say I'm not feeling well and I've gone for a nap.'

'I'm not planning on talking to him at all.'

'Fine, I won't be late.'

'Be home before your crazy mother. I'm not having her interrogating me on where you are.'

Grace could hear the music before she rounded the corner to Sofia's house. She could see lots of her classmates through the window, drinking and dancing. She pushed her way through the packed hall and into the kitchen.

Sofia was sitting on a chair, bending backwards, while a very fit older boy poured vodka down her neck. Most of it was spilling over her top and onto the floor. When she saw Grace, she stood up and threw her arms around her friend.

'Gracie, you're here.' Sofia was already drunk. 'This is my cousin, Tom. Tom, this is my best friend, Grace. She's, like, *suuuuuu*per-smart. Like a genius. Like a science geek, but not a geek.'

'Hi, geek-who's-not-a-geek.' Tom grinned at Grace, who tried not to blush. 'Do you want a shot?'

Grace hadn't really drunk alcohol before. She'd been in situations a few times when her friends had been drinking beer or vodka they'd stolen from their parents' houses, but she had only ever taken a few sips.

'Come on, live a little. If you're truly not a geek, then you'll do a shot,' Tom taunted her. He held out his hand and pulled her towards him.

God, he was gorgeous. Grace felt her heart racing. She tried to appear calm.

'I promise to be very careful pouring it into your hot mouth,' he murmured into her ear.

Grace's knees almost buckled. She sat down to steady herself, but Tom took it as a sign that she was ready for shots. Before she knew it, she was tilted backwards and vodka was pouring into her mouth. All around her everyone cheered.

'Go, Grace!'

After swallowing two large mouthfuls, she sat up. Tom high-fived her. Grace could feel the effects of the vodka hitting her toes, then shooting straight up to her head. It felt good. In fact, it felt bloody brilliant. She felt lighter than she had in months. She felt more carefree. She wanted to dance and have fun, forget all about her parents and their endless issues, her step-sister and all of them. Grace ran towards the music and threw her hands into the air.

Later, as she sat up from another shot, the room started to spin.

'You're a badass geek,' Tom whooped.

But the fun feeling of freedom was gone. The lightheaded, warm, fuzzy feeling was no more. Grace felt dizzy, disoriented and sick. She stood up and stumbled. She staggered through the mass of people, at least half of whom were strangers who had crashed Sofia's party and were currently spilling drinks and cigarette ash all over the carpet.

Grace used all of her willpower to concentrate on not vomiting. She tripped on the front doorstep and landed hard on her knees. She dragged herself up and tried not to cry as her knees throbbed and blood trickled down her legs. Home, she had to get home.

Bella was watching *Wonder Woman* with Jack. He'd kept wanting to go up and check on Grace, to see if she was feeling better, and Bella had needed to distract him, so she'd sat down with him to watch the movie. It actually wasn't bad and she was quite enjoying it. They were close to the end and Jack had barely drawn breath the whole way through.

'Seriously, how about we watch the film without you commenting on every single thing that happens?' Bella said, rolling her eyes.

'I'm just telling you about the other DC superheroes. The original seven members of the Justice League are Aquaman, Batman, Flash, Green Lantern, Martian Manhunter, Superman and Wonder Woman.'

'Well, the only one I'm remotely interested in is Wonder Woman. I don't care about some stupid Green Lantern or Flash. I mean, what kind of superheroes have dumb names like that?'

Jack's jaw dropped. 'They're really important members of the League.'

'Yeah, well, in my opinion the only one that counts is Wonder Woman. Look, Jack, women are superior to men. That's a fact. We're smarter, we know how to get what we want, we're stronger mentally and we can manipulate men.'

Jack stared at her. 'No way! Look at Superman.'

'Superman is only Superman because of Lois Lane. She makes him great.'

'No, she doesn't.'

'Yes, she does. I'm doing you a favour here. I'm giving you a life lesson. Women rock. They're better than men in every way. Accept it and your life will be much easier.'

'What about Batman?'

'He's just a –'

They heard the front door bang and someone falling. Bella jumped up.

'Mum?' Jack called. He stood up to go into the hall.

'No! You stay here just in case it's a robber.'

'Do you think it is?' Jack stepped back from the door.

'No – but it could be and I'm a woman, and as we just saw, women are badasses.'

Bella opened the door and saw Grace lying passed out in the hall. Jesus, how much had she drunk? Right, she needed to manage this.

She closed the door. 'Something's fallen over in the hall and smashed. I need you to stay in here while I clear it up. Do not move.'

'What fell? What is it? Who came in the door?'

'No one. Your mum mustn't have closed the front door properly and it slammed shut and something broke.' Bella was impressed with her quick thinking.

'What thing broke?'

God, he was persistent.

'A vase.'

'But there aren't any vases in the hall.'

'Well, a glass or something, but I need to sort it out. Do not move from here. Sit down and watch the end of the movie. I'll come back in and tell you when you can come out.'

'Then you'll miss the end. I'll pause it for you.'

'No, it's fine, it's getting late. Go ahead and watch the end and you can tell me what happened. Okay?'

'Okay.'

Thankfully, he sat down and Bella slid out of the door, closing it firmly behind her.

Grace was lying on the floor, groaning. Bella heaved her up and dragged her up the stairs and into the bathroom.

'Feel sick,' Grace croaked.

'Do not even think of puking on me. These are new Nike trainers.'

Bella sat Grace on the floor, beside the toilet. She rolled up a towel for Grace to kneel on and held her hair back. Grace heaved, then threw up over and over again into the toilet bowl.

Bella rubbed her back as the poor girl emptied her insides. She handed Grace a wet facecloth.

'Thank you.' Grace wiped her mascara-streaked face.

'Seriously, dude, how much did you drink?'

Grace rinsed the facecloth and rubbed her eyes with it. 'I don't know. It was vodka and I was doing shots.'

'Oh, my God.'

Grace examined her blotchy face reflected in the mirror. She began to cry. 'I'm such an idiot. I was trying to impress this older guy, Tom.'

Bella sat Grace down on the side of the bath and took out her cleansing products. She cleansed Grace's face and eyes, then patted moisturizer and eye cream on her face.

'That feels so good,' Grace muttered. 'Thanks for being so nice. Please don't tell anyone. I'm so embarrassed.'

'Who am I gonna tell? Your mum? My dad? Are you nuts? Besides, give yourself a break. Everyone makes mistakes. You've just never made one before. Saint Grace is human after all. To be honest, I'm relieved. It was getting really annoying living with Miss Perfect.'

Grace snorted. 'I'm not remotely perfect. I just hate confrontation, so I avoid it.'

Bella threw the used cotton wool into the bin and lowered the toilet seat. She sat down and faced Grace. 'I should probably do the same, but I can't seem to keep my big fat mouth from saying what I feel and think.'

'It's supposed to be healthier to express yourself than keep everything in.'

'Yeah, but it gets you into a lot more trouble.'

Grace played with the towel on her lap. 'Can I be honest?'

'You've just puked in front of me so we can be honest with each other, yeah.'

'I think you're very tough on my mum. She's actually a very nice person. I know she's trying too hard, I know it's annoying, but maybe give her a chance, try to get to know her.'

'She's *very* annoying, though.'

'She usually isn't, but with you it's like she's making such an effort to get you to like her that she's coming across all weird and needy. Your dad is really awkward with Jack too and it just doesn't work.'

Bella dabbed eye cream on her own eyes. 'You're right. Poor Dad just has no clue how to relate to Jack. He's trying way too hard and then he gets frustrated and your mum gets involved and it all escalates.'

Grace nodded. 'It's hard on all of us, living together, isn't it?'

'Yep.'

'Much harder than I thought it was going to be.'

Bella looked directly at Grace. 'I wish they'd never met. It was so much better when it was me and Dad in the apartment alone.'

'But when you see them together and they're getting on, and you see how happy they are, I guess . . .' Grace tailed off.

'It's true,' Bella conceded. 'Dad is so in love.'

'I've never seen my mum like this,' Grace admitted. 'She's so happy with him.'

'So is my dad. Mind you, they're arguing a lot lately.'

'I know. It's non-stop, these days. I'm worried about their relationship. But it's always about the same thing – you and Jack. If you could get on with Mum and Jack could get on with your dad, I think life would be easier all round.'

Bella put the top back on her eye cream. 'The good news is that I'll be rehearsing day and night for the musical over the next few weeks, so Anna will barely see me.'

'That's a Band-Aid, not a solution. You have to figure out how to get on with her.'

Bella groaned. 'Why couldn't Dad just randomly shag women? Why did he have to fall in love?'

Grace started giggling. 'He's so selfish.'

'The cheek of him to have feelings.' Bella laughed. The two girls cracked up.

There was a bang on the bathroom door.

'What's so funny? I want to hear the joke,' Jack shouted. 'Open up, I need to tell Bella what happened in the movie.'

'Shoot me now.' Bella covered her face with a towel.

29

James kissed Anna. 'You look beautiful.'

'Thank you. I'm looking forward to a good night out for all of us.'

'Me too. I like your family. They're fun. Well, the ones I've met are – there are so many of you!'

'Brace yourself because Anita has invited every single cousin and relative we have.'

James took a deep breath. 'Okay. I may have to ditch the car and drink heavily.'

Anna laughed. 'Do. It'll be a fun night. Anita loves a party, so she'll definitely have gone all out for her fortieth. We can pick the car up tomorrow.'

'Come *ooooooon*, hurry up,' Jack shouted from the front door.

'Go ahead and ring the bell,' Anna called to him, as she made her way up the path, Grace following.

He did so, and the door flew open. Anita stood there in a bright pink party dress, a tiara on her head. 'Welcome! I'm forty years young today,' she announced, giggling wildly.

'I see you've been at the Prosecco already.' Anna hugged her sister.

'Just one or two.' Anita winked.

She kissed James on the cheek, and hugged Grace and Jack. 'Come on in and fill your boots.'

They walked into a house stuffed with balloon arches, streamers, banners and tables sagging under the weight of the food.

'Oh, my God, Anita, the place looks amazing,' Anna said.

'Bit over the top, but what the hell?' Her sister grinned.

'Anna!' Her brother Anthony wrapped her in a bear hug, followed by Albert, Alex and Adam.

They all shook James's hand and slapped him on the back.

'So how's life, sis?' Adam asked.

'Good, thanks.'

'Yeah? How's it been with the two families living together? Can't be easy.'

'Well, no, we've had some teething problems, but we're getting there,' Anna admitted.

'I honestly don't know how you do it. I can't stand my own kids most of the time. I couldn't deal with anyone else's.'

James laughed. 'It's been an adjustment for all of us.'

Anna wanted a night off from talking about their family set-up. She wanted to have some fun with James. They both needed a break.

'James, let's get a drink,' she suggested and moved him towards the kitchen where the bar had been set up.

They poured themselves a large gin and tonic each.

'Anna!' Her cousin Gavin rushed over to hug her, elbowing James out of the way.

Anna tried to introduce James to Gavin, but three more relatives pushed past to say hi to her and James was nudged out of the kitchen door.

While Anna caught up with her extended family, she kept an eye on James, who spent most of the party drinking gin and chatting here and there with family members, who all made an effort to talk to him.

Anna tried to get to him a few times but kept being side-lined by people she hadn't seen in ages. Then she saw James sit down beside her cousin Keith and knew he'd be all right. Keith taught computer engineering at the Institute of Technology and was one of those people who could chat about anything under the sun. She knew he and James would get on like a house on fire. She relaxed, refreshed her gin and enjoyed the chat.

It was when she went out to the garden to cool down after dancing with her mad cousin Sarah that she heard Angela talking to Grace. They were out of view behind Anita's garden shed but she could hear them clearly.

'. . . so I'm only applying to universities in the US.'

'What about here or the UK?' Angela asked.

'No, I want to get as far away as possible and for a long time.'

'Ireland's not so bad.'

'It's not Ireland, it's my family. I'm sick of Mum and Dad arguing, James and Mum arguing, Mum and Bella arguing, and James and Jack arguing . . . It's never-ending, Angela. I thought when Mum left Dad that things would be better, but now she and James fight all the time too.'

Oh, no. Anna hadn't known Grace was feeling that bad about everything. She didn't want her to run away to America for ever.

'Well, I'm sorry to hear that. I'm sure it'll get better, though. Time always heals things.'

'I don't care any more. I'll be gone as soon as I can and I am never, ever having kids.'

'Ah, now, don't say that.'

'I mean it. If you have kids, every decision you make affects them. Adults are fundamentally selfish. They do what makes them happy, and their kids just have to suck it up.'

Anna was struck by the note of bitterness in Grace's tone – she sounded fifty, not fifteen. It hit her hard that their living situation was making Grace see life in this way. The guilt rose up inside her and she felt sick.

'Hold on a minute now, Missy. Your mum was incredibly unselfish for years. She stayed with your dad and tried her absolute level best to make it work. I'd have been long gone. She did that for you and for Jack. So now she's found happiness, I think she deserves it. I get that it's hard for you kids, but life isn't always straightforward, Grace, and what doesn't kill you makes you stronger. You're an amazing girl and you have a brilliant future ahead of you, but never forget that you have the best mum in the world, one who made a lot of sacrifices for you over the years.'

Thank you, Angela, Anna thought. Thanks for seeing what I tried to do and for letting Grace know that it wasn't easy.

'I know. I love my mum. I just hate the new house and the set-up. It's really hard.' Grace's voice shook.

'Ah, pet,' Angela said gently. 'It's been a tough few years. And you're brilliant and we're all so proud of you.'

Anna walked around the corner to where her sister and daughter were chatting.

'Hi.' Angela's eyes widened.

Grace wiped a stray tear from her cheek.

Anna put her arms around her daughter. 'I overheard you, and I'm sorry, Grace. I'm sorry you've had to put up with so much upheaval in your young life. I'm sorry that your dad and I didn't work out and that you hate living in the new house. When you had your meltdown on the camping trip I could see you were struggling and I've been trying to figure out how to talk to you and make things better for you.'

'It's okay, Mum. It's not your fault.'

'It's no one's fault,' Angela said. 'It's just the way things have turned out.'

'I tried so hard to keep us together as a family with your dad, but I just couldn't do it any more. It was killing me.' Anna began to get upset. 'I lost myself in that marriage, and the last few years were really tough. But please know that I tried.'

'I know you did. I saw how hard you tried. I told you to leave, remember?' Grace was crying now too.

'I never thought us all moving in together would be so difficult. I was stupid and naïve and, yes, Angela, I know you warned me.'

'Ah, sure, lookit, it would have been complicated even if you had waited longer.'

'James is such a good man, I presumed you and Jack would just love him,' Anna went on. 'And I presumed I'd love Bella. I know it must sound so ridiculous, but I honestly did. I thought we'd all be so happy together.' Anna tried to control the tsunami of emotions welling up.

'James is fine, it's just . . . Jack and I and Bella didn't choose any of it. Bella was happier when it was just her and James, and I think it would have been easier if it was just you, me and Jack living together.'

'Yes, but your mother fell in love and she deserves love. Mums are people too, Grace. And Anna has had it tougher than most. I'm not going to slag your dad off because that's not fair to you, but he was no picnic.'

'Would you be happier if I left James and we moved in just us?' Anna asked.

Grace gave her a teary smile. 'No, Mum, because you would be miserable and broken-hearted and that would be worse. I don't want you to give up the man you love. It's just hard, but I'll be gone soon.'

'I don't want you to run away. I don't want you to dread coming home.'

'All kids run away from home as soon as they can,' Angela reminded her. 'We all did. And then you realize that home isn't so bad after all.'

'I won't dread coming home, but I am looking forward to choosing my housemates.' Grace smiled.

'Grace, I want you and Jack to be happy. You are my priority, always. If living with James and Bella is really making you miserable, we'll move out.'

'Stop that now. It's like musical chairs in this family. You all need to stay where you are and get on with it. Jack needs to behave and Bella needs to keep her mouth shut and you'll all be grand,' Angela said. 'No family is straightforward, none.'

Grace rubbed her mother's back. 'Mum, I don't want us to move out. I'm genuinely so glad that you met someone you love and it's lovely to see you happy. I'm just blowing off steam.'

'Promise?'

'Yes.'

'And promise when you do leave that you'll come back?'

'I promise.'

'If you don't, I'll stalk you. You know that, right?'

'Yes, I do.'

'I love you, Grace.'

'I love you too, Mum.'

'Ah, stop, I'm nearly crying here myself. Come on, this is supposed to be a party. Back inside now and let's have some fun.' Angela shooed them towards the house.

They could hear music coming from the lounge. Everyone was crowded into the room and there was a lot of whooping and cheering. While Angela went to get a drink, Anna and Grace peered over the crowd of heads to see James at the piano, playing 'Bohemian Rhapsody'.

My God, he must be very drunk she thought, trying not to laugh. James was banging out the keys and singing at the top of his voice.

'Mum, look.' Grace pointed at Jack, who was standing to James's left singing along.

It was one of Jack's favourite songs. He'd heard it in school at music class and become obsessed with it.

'This is a miracle,' Anna whispered.

'I wish Bella was here. She's not going to believe it. I have to take a video for her.' Grace whipped out her phone.

Anna stared at the two men she loved most in the world, one big, one small, singing a duet. Miracles did happen.

Around them, Anna's family joined in and soon the roof

was almost lifted off the house with everyone singing. Best of all, James and Jack were smiling at each other and singing together. Anna went from devastation about Grace to euphoria.

Her brother Anthony leant over and grinned at her. 'James is actually a bit of craic. I thought he was dry, but I was wrong. He's good fun.'

'He's the best.' Anna fell more in love with James than ever.

She watched James stand up from the piano stool, put his arm around Jack and they both took a bow. Everyone cheered loudly. Anna caught James's eye and blew him a kiss. He grinned widely.

Grace giggled. 'I can't wait to send this to Bella.'

'More!' Anna's relations shouted.

James sat down again and, for the next two hours, played every request that was asked of him.

In the taxi on the way home they sang 'Bohemian Rhapsody', and even though Grace rolled her eyes, she was smiling.

Anna prayed that this night was a turning point for all of them.

30

Anna hovered outside the bathroom door. She knew that if she knocked, Bella would bite her head off, although she had been a little less rude to her lately. She'd been watching Bella over the last couple of weeks, and she'd noticed how little she ate, and how whenever she did eat a meal, she would lock herself in the bathroom afterwards. Anna had dealt in her surgery with a lot of young girls who had eating disorders and knew the signs all too well.

She had to do something before it got worse. She decided to talk to James when they were in bed, the house was quiet, their phones were off and there were no distractions.

James climbed in and sank into the mattress.

'Bliss.' He sighed with pleasure. 'Here's hoping Jack sleeps through the night again. I've really enjoyed being in my own bed this week and getting to have lots of sex with my gorgeous girlfriend.'

Anna swiped his hands away. 'Hold on there, tiger. Before we get all hot and bothered, I need to talk to you about something serious.'

'Oh, God, really? Now? Can't we just have sex and go to sleep? Can't it wait until tomorrow?'

Anna shook her head. 'Sorry, darling, but no. It's about Bella.'

James sighed. 'What's she done now?'

'Nothing. She's actually been almost civil to me lately. I'm just worried about her, James. I think she may have developed an unhealthy relationship with food.'

'Bella? No. She's actually trying to be healthier. You've got the wrong end of the stick.'

'James, she's lost quite a bit of weight and I've noticed that she frequently goes to the bathroom after eating. In the surgery, these are red flags for an eating disorder.'

James looked at her, eyes wide. 'Bella? An eating disorder? No, you're wrong, Anna. I know you see things in work, but this is Bella we're talking about. She's far too sensible to go down that route.'

Anna took a deep breath. 'Parents often think their child couldn't possibly develop a problem like this, but many young people do, James, particularly girls. I know the warning signs and I'm sure I'm seeing them here in this house.'

He shook his head. 'I hear your concern, Anna, and it's nice of you to worry about Bella, but I'm afraid you're simply wrong on this. She's just eating a more considered diet, which is normal for her age. And she wants to look her best for the big performance. But she's grand.'

Anna realized he couldn't hear what she was saying. She'd seen this before. She'd tell a parent about their child's eating disorder or a mental-health issue, and they'd flatly deny it. Denial was a coping mechanism, and it was hard to break past it – especially before it was too late.

'Come on, Anna,' James said. 'You're so focused on parenting well, you're just seeing a problem that isn't really there. I love you for caring, but there's really no need to worry. I'd know if there was an issue with Bella.'

Anna nodded, her heart heavy. How could she make him see? The problem was, he couldn't see it if he didn't want to. She opened her mouth to press him again, but then stopped. There was no point. Much as the idea filled her with dread, she realized that her best bet would be to approach Ingrid. Mothers usually understood issues around food better than fathers. Ingrid might even have an inkling already. And if she didn't, knowing how she operated, Anna reckoned she'd have the best people lined up to help Bella within minutes.

'It's all right,' she said, smiling. 'I'll keep an eye and come back to you if I feel it's necessary.'

'You do that,' he said, pulling her close.

There was nothing for it: she'd have to go into the lion's den and take this up with Ingrid. God knew what reception she'd get, but it was too important to let it slide or for her fear of confrontation to stop her. Anna had seen how fast eating disorders could take hold and devastate teenagers' lives.

The tan, the make-up, the nails, it was clear that Bella was trying to keep up with the girls at school and project a certain image, and Anna knew that being thin was a huge part of that. She couldn't pretend it was anything other than it was. James might be able to live in denial, but this was Bella's life and well-being, and there was no way Anna was going to sit back and watch her spiral downwards. She had to act and act fast.

Anna stared into her open wardrobe. What do you wear when you're visiting your partner's ex-wife at work? Trousers and a shirt? Smart day-dress? Or just go casual, jeans and a jumper?

This was ridiculous. Anna pulled out a pair of black capri trousers and a baby blue jumper. She looked smart, but not like she was trying too hard. She was a thirty-seven-year-old woman: why did Ingrid intimidate her so much? 'Shoulders back,' she said to herself in the mirror, 'and just get on with it.'

Ingrid's response to Anna's text asking to meet for a coffee had been icy: *I'm up to my eyes but if you call into my office at 1.30 I could spare fifteen minutes.*

Spare? As if she was doing Anna a great favour when, in fact, it was the other way round. Maybe if Ingrid got her head out of her emails, she'd notice her daughter was in trouble. Still, Anna knew she had to tread carefully. No one wanted someone else telling them that their child had a problem. She'd seen it in the surgery time and again: parents got very defensive, angry or upset. Somehow Anna reckoned Ingrid would be firmly in the former category. She just hoped she could talk her round and make her see they had to get past shock or denial and act fast.

Anna parked her car and walked through the huge glass revolving doors into the vast lobby of Ingrid's office building. She took the glass lift up to the top floor and told the receptionist she was there to see Ingrid White.

'Please take a seat,' the perfectly groomed receptionist said.

Anna sat down in a plush dark green velvet chair and waited . . . and waited . . . and waited.

After half an hour she'd had enough. At this rate she'd be late to pick up Jack and Grace. Bella was staying late at school for rehearsals.

She dialled Ingrid's mobile.

'Yes?' Ingrid barked.

'Ingrid, it's Anna. I've been sitting in your reception for half an hour. I have to go soon. I thought we were meeting at one thirty?'

'My conference call with New York ran over. These things happen. I'm free now. My secretary will come and get you.'

God forbid you'd get off your high and mighty arse to come and get me yourself. Anna threw her phone into her bag.

A glossy secretary turned up to bring Anna to Ingrid's office. It was huge, with wall-to-ceiling glass windows that gave panoramic views of the city. In the middle sat a large chrome-and-glass desk. Anna tried to look nonchalant, but the office was incredible. Compared to the small room Anna shared with the other nurse in the clinic, its small window overlooking the car park, this was a palace.

Behind the oversized desk sat Ingrid, typing furiously on her laptop. She acknowledged Anna's presence with a curt nod, not bothering to get up or stop typing for five seconds.

'Have a seat,' she barked. 'I just need to finish this email.'

'Can I get you anything, Ingrid?' the secretary asked.

'An extra hot soy latte.'

'And you?' the secretary asked Anna.

A Valium and a large glass of cold white wine.

'I'm fine, thanks.'

The secretary left the room and there was silence.

'So, how can I help you?' Ingrid had finally stopped typing, but her eyes were still zoned in on her computer screen.

Like mother, like daughter. Ingrid clearly liked staring at screens as much as Bella did.

'You can't help *me*.' Anna didn't appreciate being treated like some kind of client. 'It's Bella who needs help.'

Ingrid finally looked up. Her eyes bored into Anna through her designer glasses. Ha! Anna had her attention now.

Ingrid frowned. 'What on earth do you mean, Bella needs help?'

Anna took a deep breath and plunged in. 'I have noticed recently that Bella has lost a fair bit of weight and that she's eating less and less. I've also heard her vomiting after meals. I'm worried that she's developing a very unhealthy relationship with food that could be dangerous.' Anna tried to put it as delicately as possible and purposely avoided using the words 'eating disorder'.

'What exactly are you implying? That Bella is anorexic?' Ingrid didn't mince her words, which was encouraging.

'Not anorexic, no. But I think she may be heading towards an eating disorder. I see a lot of young girls with eating disorders in the surgery and it's something that can escalate into a dangerous zone very quickly.'

Ingrid's eyes narrowed. 'You're hardly an expert in the field of eating disorders because of a few patients.'

Ouch. 'Not an expert, no, but someone who has years of experience.'

'Experience as a nurse. You're not a qualified psychiatrist.'

Anna gripped the handle of her bag. 'No, Ingrid, I'm not a psychiatrist, but I've been living with your daughter for over six months now and I've seen some very worrying behaviour. I'm bringing it to your attention to make sure she receives any help she may need.'

'A few months' living part-time together hardly makes you an expert on her behaviour. Bella is my daughter. I think I'd know if there was anything wrong with her.'

'Sometimes we can miss what's right under our nose. It happens to parents all the time.' Anna continued to be diplomatic despite her rising rage at her concerns being belittled and disregarded.

'I don't miss anything,' Ingrid said brusquely. 'When Bella is with me, she eats perfectly well. There is no rushing to the bathroom after dinner or vomiting.'

James had told Anna that Bella spent a lot of nights eating dinner in the penthouse alone, while Ingrid and Denis entertained clients. So maybe Ingrid was genuinely clueless as to what was going on.

'Bella told me she's trying to be healthier and lose a few pounds for this musical she's so involved in,' Ingrid went on. 'I don't see anything sinister with that. Frankly, I'm a lot more concerned about all the study time she's wasting on rehearsals than the fact that she's choosing to eat a few salads.'

'Well, I think vomiting after dinner is worrying.' Anna was done with being subtle. She was sick of Ingrid's patronizing attitude. Her daughter was in trouble, and if Ingrid would just get her head out of her arse for a second, she just might notice.

'How many times have you actually discovered her vomiting?' Ingrid asked.

'Six or seven.'

'Well, she never does that when she's with me. Maybe she doesn't like your cooking.' Ingrid raised one of her plucked eyebrows.

That was it. Anna had had enough. She'd come here in good faith, to share a genuine concern, and she was being treated like a pariah.

She stood up. 'I won't take up any more of your valuable time. I was worried about your daughter and I thought you should know. You seem adamant that there's no problem, so I'll say no more.' Anna walked towards the door and turned. 'And, by the way, I'm a damn good cook.'

Anna shook with rage the whole way down in the lift, through Reception and out onto the street. She stood outside the building and took deep breaths in and out. Clearly Bella had learnt manners from her mother.

Ingrid finished her soy latte, which wasn't hot enough, snatched up her phone and dialled.

'Hello, Ingrid,' James answered. 'I hope you're not calling to change Bella's schedule.'

'No, I'm calling to tell you to get your girlfriend to refrain from barging into my office and telling me that my daughter has anorexia.'

'What? Anna came to your office?'

James clearly had no idea that Anna had called. He'd sounded genuinely surprised. Ingrid rolled her eyes. Typical James, no idea what was actually going on. How had she ever married him? He let everyone run rings around him. That's what she loved about Denis: he was totally in control of everything. No one messed with Denis. No one did things that Denis hadn't agreed to. Denis was never taken by surprise. James was permanently taken aback by people and their behaviour. It was very irritating.

'Yes, James, she did and I did not appreciate it. I'm Bella's mother and you are her father. No one else is to get involved in her life. Denis wouldn't dream of turning up at your workplace accusing Bella of having problems. Bella is none of your girlfriend's damn business, James. I am perfectly capable of looking after my own daughter. Tell her to back off and focus on her own children, especially that awful boy of hers.'

'I didn't know Anna was going to visit you, but to be fair, Ingrid, she has Bella's best interests at heart. She's a very caring person.'

'Oh, please, spare me the my-new-girlfriend-is-so-much-nicer-than-you crap. She's interfering, just as Bella has always told me.'

'Now hang on, Ingrid, that's not fair,' James said. 'Anna cares about Bella, which is a good thing.'

'Bella doesn't need Anna's care.' Ingrid could feel her blood pressure rising. 'Bella has two parents. She doesn't need a third. And if your girlfriend wants to create drama, she can do it at home with you. I want no part of it or her. She is never, ever to come into my office again spouting rubbish about my daughter. Is that clear?'

'She is not creating drama. It's called genuine concern, Ingrid. I don't tell Anna what to do and I'm not about to start.'

'Well, maybe you should. Rein her in, James.'

'I'm not reining her in. She's not a horse, Ingrid. You're completely overreacting to a kind gesture of concern.'

Ingrid's secretary knocked gently on her door and pointed to her watch.

'I have to go. I have a meeting. This nonsense has taken up enough of my time. Control your girlfriend, James.'

'For God's sake, Ingrid, I don't *control* Anna. Nor would I ever want to.'

Ingrid hung up before he could say any more. She didn't need to hear James telling her how cold she was, or how controlling. She'd heard it all before, in almost every argument they'd ever had. Yes, she was controlling: that was how she'd risen to the top of her profession. Emotional, dramatic women didn't negotiate multi-million-euro deals. Soft, warm women didn't succeed in the corporate world. Ingrid was proud of her success. She pitied women who sat at home baking, making their children and husbands the centre of their universes. What happened when the kids moved out? What happened if your husband left you? What happened if he got sick and couldn't work? What happened if he dropped dead? That had happened to Ingrid's mother when her father died suddenly of a heart attack. Her mother had devoted her life to being a wife and homemaker. Feck all use that was when her husband died and they had no money. Her mother had taken to her bed with depression, and Ingrid, aged fifteen, had had to go out and find work to pay the bills. She had sworn then that she would never, ever rely on a man for money. She had worked tirelessly to be independent and secure, and she was bloody proud of herself.

She wasn't worried about Bella losing a few pounds. She was worried about her daughter not focusing enough on her studies so she could be a smart and financially independent woman. Bella needed to get a good degree and a good job so that she would always be able to support herself. Never rely on a man for your happiness or financial support. That was what she had always told her daughter, and she meant it. Ingrid was happy with Denis and the lifestyle they had was fantastic. But if he left her in the morning, she'd still have a wonderful life with no financial worries.

Ingrid stood up, put on her jacket and walked to the boardroom, shedding the irritation of Anna's interfering and her ex-husband's weakness as she went.

31

Conor settled into the corner of the couch with his feet up and switched on the football. He was looking forward to a day of chilling out after working four long days at the garage this week and studying every night for his course.

'What are you doing?' Milly bustled into the room, freshly showered and dressed.

'Relaxing,' Conor answered.

'Have you looked outside? It's a beautiful day. Come on, up you get. We'll make a picnic and take the kids to the park.'

'What? Ah, no, Milly. I want to take it easy, and the kids won't want to go to the park when they get here.'

Milly put her hands on her hips and stood in front of Conor, blocking the TV. 'Conor, all kids want their parents' attention. Jack might want to watch the football with you, but it's not fair on Grace. You can record the match and watch it later. But you are not spending this lovely day inside. Come on, let's make a really special picnic with all their favourite things. You can bring a football and play actual real-life football with Jack in the park.'

Conor really did not want to make a sodding picnic and sit in the park.

'What do the kids like? I know Jack's mentioned Mars Bar Rice Krispie squares – we can make those now, easy-peasy. What about Grace?'

Conor racked his brains. 'She likes flapjacks.'

'Okay, we'll make those, too, and we'll get a fresh baguette and some ham and cheese and make it all nice for them.'

Conor didn't want to make flapjacks and Rice Krispie squares, he was wrecked, but Milly was not going to back down and she had a knack of making everything sound like it was going to be fun – even baking.

'Come on, lazy bones. If we get it all ready early, we might even have time for some pre-picnic sex.'

Conor jumped up. 'Get your coat,' he said, laughing, as he pulled her towards the front door.

'Men.' Milly giggled. 'You're all the bloody same.'

Conor pulled her towards him. 'Can I help it if you're the sexiest woman alive?'

She kissed him. 'I've never been with a bloke who made me feel so good about myself.'

He kissed her back. And I've never been with a woman who made me want to be a better man and father, he thought.

Grace and Jack looked surprised when they arrived into the apartment and heard they were going out for a picnic.

'What do you mean, a picnic?' Jack wasn't impressed.

'Well, we'll go to the park and eat,' Conor answered.

'And you'll play football with your dad and me and Grace, if she wants to. And we've made all your favourites, Mars Bar Rice Krispie squares and flapjacks.'

'Did you bake these, Dad?' Grace sounded shocked.

'Yes, he did.' Milly grinned. 'He's not half bad when he tries.'

Conor beamed at her. 'Maybe now you'll all stop being so shocked when I cook. I'm not just a pretty face and muscle, you know.'

Grace laughed. 'You hid it well until now. Who knew there was a chef inside you?'

'Now, I wouldn't go that far,' Milly said, and the two of them burst out laughing.

Conor pretended to be offended. 'Come on,' he said, 'let's do this picnic before I change my mind and park myself in front of the telly instead.'

They headed outside, Conor carrying the picnic basket, and walked the twenty minutes to the park.

Milly picked a spot under a big tree. She unpacked the picnic and laid it on a red spotty blanket. Everything looked so pretty. There were napkins and cups, a big Thermos of hot chocolate and lots of food. Milly sat down beside Grace, pulled her hoody over her head and sat in her denim shorts and a vest top that showed off all her curves. Conor could see his daughter gazing at Milly. He felt the same – he could barely take his eyes off her.

After they'd eaten, Conor and Jack got up to play football.

'Are you coming, Milly?' Jack asked. 'I want to see if you can actually play.'

'Cheeky sod, I can play all right.' Milly grinned. 'I'll join you in a minute, but I just need to digest my food first.'

The boys kicked the ball around and Grace sat with Milly. It should have been awkward because Grace didn't really know her, and when she was left on her own with James it did feel a bit awkward, but Milly made everything seem normal.

'Those flapjacks were nice and the Mars Bar things, yum. I always feel sorry for those skinny models who never enjoy their food. I love my treats.'

'They were delicious,' Grace agreed.

'Your dad was being the sugar police when we were making them.' Milly chuckled. 'He kept saying they were too high in sugar. He's really got into the nutrition side of his course. But I think a few treats every now and then are a good thing.'

'Me too.'

It had been really nice to see her dad getting into his personal-training course. Grace had never seen him so focused. The last weekend they'd stayed he had studied – like, actually sat down with his laptop and worked. Grace had been in shock.

'Your dad was telling me you're going to California in a few months to the Global Science Fair. How do you feel about it?'

'I'm excited and nervous.'

'Your dad is dead proud of you and I'm proud to know someone who is so clever.'

'Thanks, but I'm not really clever. It's just a good idea.'

Milly sat up. 'Hey, now, don't do that. Don't play it down. It's an incredible achievement and you need to own it. I'd be walking around with a megaphone shouting about it if it was me. I'd get T-shirts made up. And posters.'

Grace giggled. She loved Milly's straight-up enthusiasm.

'It's great to find what you're good at when you're young. I always knew I was good at make-up and hair. Some people never figure out what their talent is. I'm so glad your dad's found his. I think he'll be a brilliant trainer. What would your dream job be?' she asked Grace.

'I'd like to work in scientific research and development.'

Milly picked up another flapjack and took a bite. 'Wow, good for you.'

They watched Conor and Jack playing football.

'Is there anything girly you'd like to do today? I could do your nails if you like, or is there anything else you'd like to get done?'

Grace could think of one thing she really wanted. Her mum said she had to wait until she was sixteen, but Grace didn't see what difference a few months made.

'Do you do highlights?' she asked.

'Of course. Would you like me to do some for you later?'

'I'd love it. Just a few, like, nothing mad.'

'Don't worry, I'll do subtle ones. Highlights would look amazing on your hair. I think a warm honey tone mixed in with your natural brown would be fab.'

'Would you really do them today? I mean, it's your day off.'

'I'd love to do them for you. You're drop-dead gorgeous as you are, but a few highlights will just enhance your beauty.'

Grace blushed.

'You're even cuter when you blush.' Milly smiled at her. 'It's a very lucky boy who gets you, Grace. Make sure you only go for a guy who makes you feel ten feet tall and appreciates how fantastic you are.'

'Okay.' Grace was embarrassed, but she also liked that Milly was giving her advice. She was so confident and cool that Grace wanted to be like her. She also liked the influence Milly was having on her dad. He never, ever would have taken them on a picnic or signed up to do a course if he hadn't met Milly. She really hoped he didn't mess up this relationship. Milly was so good for him.

Back at home later, Milly highlighted, washed, cut and blow-dried Grace's hair and then, when she had finished styling it, she handed Grace the mirror.

'Now, if you don't like them, I can change them, so don't worry.'

Grace took a deep breath and held the mirror up to her face. She gasped. 'Oh, my God, I love them.' The highlights were fantastic, and Milly had cut some layers into her hair too. It was gorgeous.

'Aw, I'm glad you're happy. You have amazing hair and the colours I added just enhance it, really.'

Grace couldn't stop staring at herself. She looked cooler now, older, more sophisticated. She felt more confident. She stood up and hugged Milly. 'Thank you.'

'For nothing. Sure I'm only delighted to do it.'

Grace spent the rest of the evening staring at herself in the mirror, swishing her hair about and taking selfies to send to her friends, who were all jealous and begged her to ask Milly to do highlights for them too. She hadn't felt this good about herself ever. It was a wonderful feeling.

Anna pressed the doorbell and thumped on the door.

'Okay, relax, I'm coming,' Conor's voice called.

He opened the door in his boxer shorts.

'About bloody time. I've been ringing the bell for ten minutes.'

'I was in bed.' He pointed to his almost-naked body. 'What are you doing here anyway? What's wrong now? Did I forget to pack Jack's socks or something?'

Anna was shaking with anger. 'This is serious, Conor. I'm furious. How dare your girlfriend dye Grace's hair without my permission? I told Grace that she could get highlights when she was sixteen. We've been talking about it for ages. It was going to be my gift to her on her birthday, but then she comes home with her hair all done.'

It had been her promise to Grace. They had agreed that she'd wait and that on her sixteenth birthday, which was still a couple of months away, Anna would book her in for highlights. She'd had it all planned out: she was going to take Grace for lunch afterwards and have a lovely girls' day out. But Conor's stupid girlfriend had ruined it and hadn't had the decency to ask Anna's permission.

Milly came up behind Conor. She was wearing a pair of black lace knickers and a T-shirt, her hair tousled. They must have been having afternoon sex. Anna hadn't had afternoon sex in ages. For some reason, this enraged her even more.

'What's going on?' Milly asked.

'Anna's doing her nut because you put a few streaks in Grace's hair. It's the usual overreaction she has to everything.'

'I'm not overreacting. I'm just very annoyed that you didn't ask my permission to put highlights in my fifteen-year-old's hair.'

Milly's voice was husky when she spoke – could this woman ooze any more sex appeal? Anna felt like a frump beside her in her jeans and sweatshirt.

'I'm sorry. I didn't think you'd mind. Grace asked me to do them yesterday and she was really happy with the result.'

'That's not the point. You can't just do everything Grace asks you to. She's fifteen, for goodness' sake.'

'Right, yeah, I get it. Sorry, I'm new to all this. I've never had a boyfriend with kids before.'

That's because you're practically a kid yourself, Anna thought.

'Don't apologize, Milly.' Conor put his arm around her. 'You made Grace really happy. You've nothing to be sorry for. My ex is just being her usual control-freak self.'

Anna resisted the urge to punch Conor.

'No, babe, I get it.' Milly rubbed his arm, then turned to Anna. 'I can dye it back, no problem. I can come over now and do it, if that's what you'd like. I'm really sorry. I honestly didn't mean to step on anyone's toes.'

Anna was taken aback by Milly's genuine remorse. It was disarming. She wasn't going to get her to dye Grace's hair back, that was ridiculous, and Anna would be the big bad witch if she did. But it was nice of her to offer.

'I don't think that's necessary. But, in future, can you please check with me before doing anything?'

'Absolutely.'

'Bollox to that. Milly doesn't have to call you to ask your permission to do anything. I'm Grace's father and if I say something's okay when Grace is with me, we don't need your clearance. Go home, Anna. Go home and boss your boyfriend around. I don't have to listen to your crap any more and don't ever tell Milly what to do again.'

'Hang on, babe. She's just being a protective mum. I get it.'

'Thank you, Milly.' Anna ignored Conor's sharp words. 'I'm glad you see where I'm coming from. Right, I'll leave you to it.'

Anna turned to leave and as Conor slammed the door behind her, she heard Milly say, 'I know what'll make you feel better,' and a low, sexy giggle.

They were off to have more sex. Lovely afternoon sex. Lucky

them. Anna and James had been drifting again lately. There had been a lovely patch after Anita's party, when Jack had settled in his own room and they'd felt like a real couple for a change. But then Jack had started insisting on sleeping in her bed again, and that was that: James back on the sofa, tension back, arguments back, the sinking feeling that they were running out of options to make their family work. The fun had gone out of their relationship. When did they last have sex? Too long.

As Anna walked away from Conor's apartment block towards her car, she thought about how much she missed the high of their initial romance. Everything was stressful now. She'd underestimated how difficult it was going to be. She'd been stupidly optimistic, as usual. It was her Achilles heel, thinking everything would work out well. She should have learnt by now.

Anna felt tired. She was weary from trying and failing to connect with Bella, from worrying about her vomiting, from knowing that Grace wanted to get away from her family as soon as she could, from trying to get James and Jack to find common ground and from dealing with her difficult ex-husband. On top of all that, now she had to deal with feelings of jealousy that would not go away. She was jealous of how much her kids liked Milly. There she was, trying and failing miserably, and there Milly was, grade bloody A girlfriend, winning at everything. What was Anna doing wrong? Was it because Milly was so young and cool? Was there a way for her to have fun with Bella? How? She couldn't give her highlights or a make-over. All she could give her was a smear test or a flu vaccine, and that somehow didn't sound like a recipe for bonding.

Anna felt stupid and defeated. It wasn't working. Their family wasn't a family. It was a mish-mash of people of different ages who barely tolerated each other. And she had no more ideas for what to do about that.

32

Bella sang 'Hopelessly Devoted To You' but missed the high note.

'Come on, Bella, you sang this perfectly yesterday. What's going on?' Mrs Long asked.

Bella was tired and hungry and furious. Because psycho Anna had told her dad that she wasn't eating properly, he had forced her to eat a big breakfast. She'd had to wait until she got to school to puke it up because she could hear her dad prowling outside the bathroom at home. It had been hard to vomit and Bella had had to shove her fingers down her throat over and over again. Her throat felt raw and sore now and she couldn't hit the high notes. Damn her stupid step-monster, she hated her. She was ruining her life.

'I can sing it,' Saffron offered.

What the hell? Why was Saffron asking to sing Bella's part?

'It's fine. I just need some water,' Bella cut across her.

'I'm happy to stand in, Mrs Long.' Saffron kept pushing. 'Bella, your voice does sound very off today.'

'Thank you, Saffron, but Bella is perfectly capable of reaching the notes. Take five, Bella, and we'll try again.'

Bella made damn sure she hit all her notes after that. She was not giving up her role to anyone.

After rehearsal, they sat outside to eat lunch. Bella drank from her bottle of water. Saffron was nibbling a stick of celery. 'Do you want one?' she offered.

Bella shook her head.

'Aren't you having any lunch?' Saffron asked.

'No, I had a big breakfast.'

'You've got so skinny,' Portia said.

Bella smiled. She was thrilled to hear that.

'Being too thin is gross,' Saffron snapped. 'No guys fancy girls who are like skeletons.'

'I think Bella looks amazing,' Portia said. 'She's as skinny as Olivia Newton-John was in the film.'

'Am I?' Bella said, looking down at her body. It didn't look that good to her.

'Totally.'

'Olivia Newton-John had tanned skin, blue eyes and blonde hair. Bella looks nothing like her.' Saffron chewed a grape.

'When you're all dressed up in costume, you'll look just like her,' Portia said.

'No, she won't. Stop being such a lick-arse, Portia. Are you trying to suck up to Bella because she has the main role in some stupid school musical that no one actually cares about?'

'Jeez, Saffron, relax. Why are you so narky?'

Saffron flicked back her long blonde hair. 'Because I'm bored. You two are boring me to death. Can we please talk about something interesting?'

'Like what?' Portia asked.

'Anything but Bella's stupid weight loss and *Grease*,' Saffron snapped. 'Oh, forget it.' She stood up. 'I'm going back in.'

They watched her stomp off. Portia turned to Bella. 'She's jealous of you.'

'Really? Why?'

'Saffron has to be the prettiest and the thinnest and the centre of attention. Now you've lost weight and got the main role in the musical. Watch out, she can be a real bitch when she's jealous.'

Saffron was jealous of her? Wow, Bella was thrilled. She'd never imagined that could happen.

Ingrid talked on the phone while Bella took a photo of her green chicken salad and posted the photo on Instagram *#Piggingout #bestsaladever #fivestarfood*

Ingrid finished her conversation and hung up. She sat down beside Bella at the dining table. 'Is that all you're having for dinner?' she asked her daughter.

'Yeah, I had a big lunch.'

Ingrid looked at Bella properly. Not the usual cursory glance, but a long look. Bella had lost weight, quite a lot.

'Bella, are you eating properly? I know you're trying to be healthier, but you've got thin and it's important to fill your body with all the food it needs at your age.'

'I am eating, Mum. I've just cut out sugar and junk. I feel much better for it.'

'Fine, but make sure you eat well. You need a good, solid diet for your body and your brain too. It's not just about the body. And some girls can get carried away with ridiculous diets.'

'I know, Mum, but I'm not one of them.'

Ingrid nodded. 'Yes, I know. But I had a little visit recently from your dad's girlfriend.'

Bella's eyes widened. 'What? Anna came to see you? Why?'

'Oh, yes. She barged into my office and told me that you have an eating disorder.'

'She what?' Bella's face went bright red. 'Oh, my God, she is such a freak.'

Ingrid laid her hand on Bella's arm. 'It's okay, darling. I told her to back off.'

'I can't believe it, Mum. She's unreal.'

'I was pretty taken aback myself. She's one of those overly emotional women who makes a drama out of everything, it seems.'

'So, what did she say?'

'Oh, that you've been vomiting and not eating, and that you're in danger and on and on. Thankfully I had a meeting to go to, so I got rid of her quickly. I wasn't happy to have some stranger coming into my office and telling me about my own daughter who lives with me half the time. I think I'd know if you had a problem. Really and truly, the cheek of her.'

'I told you she's a nightmare to live with.'

'Yes, but why did she say you were vomiting? Have you been?'

'I had a stomach bug. Saffron and Portia had it, too. Loads of the girls in my class got it. God, she's such a drama queen. I hate her.'

'I thought as much. There was a bug going around – my secretary had it too.'

'Can I please come and live with you full-time? I could stay here in the penthouse when you're in London. It's totally safe. Please, Mum?'

Ingrid did feel sorry for Bella having to live with the awful Anna, but James was her father and he had joint custody, so it was a pointless argument. 'Darling, you know that can't happen. I really do feel for you in your current situation, but your dad needs to see you too.'

'I hate it there.' Bella was getting upset.

'Bella, listen to me.' Ingrid needed to be firm. She didn't want Bella growing up thinking she could just click her fingers or, worse still, turn on the waterworks and get anything she wanted. At fifteen, Ingrid's life had been turned upside-down. Life could throw you curve balls at any time. Bella lived a life of privilege, and Ingrid was happy to provide it for her, but she did want her daughter to toughen up a bit too. 'I lost my father when I was your age and my mother fell apart. I had to fend for myself. I had a job at fifteen. I worked every single day after school and all weekend. You have two parents who love you and a very privileged life. I know you don't like living with Anna, and I can't say I blame you, but it is temporary. You'll be off to college in a few years and you'll never have to live with her again.'

'It's a long time living with a lunatic.'

'Just keep out of her way. She's bound to find some other drama to focus on soon.'

'God, I hate her. I'll give her hell for going to you and trying to cause drama.'

'No, don't do that,' Ingrid said. 'It will just cause a huge row and it won't achieve anything. I set her straight. I made it very clear that she is to back off and leave you alone. If you bring it up again it will just add fuel to the fire, which I have stamped out. Best to let it go now and hopefully she's got the message. Besides, Bella, she's your dad's partner so you have to find a way to live with her. My advice is to try to keep under her radar as opposed to confronting her. She will just create more drama out of an argument. Say nothing and keep out of her way.'

'But, Mum, is there no way I could live –'

Denis came barrelling out of his home office into the room. 'Ingrid, the contractors on the Chicago job have pulled out. We're having a crisis meeting in half an hour. Can you make sure everyone is on the call?'

'All right, I'm coming now. I'll set it up.'

Ingrid turned to Bella. 'Finish all of your dinner and make sure you eat properly in front of Anna. I don't want any more visits.'

Ingrid rushed out, her head already tuned to Denis and his needs, leaving Bella alone. That was why she didn't see her daughter go into the bathroom, didn't hear her throwing up. The conference call ran to two hours, so she also missed witnessing Bella lie down on her bed, stomach rumbling, and cry herself to sleep.

33

James slammed the front door, thumped down the hall and threw his briefcase onto the kitchen floor.

Anna spun around. 'Are you okay? Did something happen?'

'Oh, yes, Anna. Something happened all right. I almost lost my job today.'

'Jesus, James, what happened? Sit down, talk to me.'

'*Muuuuuuuuum!*' Jack roared. 'I'm hungry.'

'Give me one second, James.'

'Sure, run to Jack, like you always do.' James opened the fridge, took out a bottle of white wine and poured himself a large glass.

Anna rushed into the living room. 'Jack, I need you to do me a favour. This is really, really serious. Do not come into the kitchen until I tell you. Do not ask me for anything. Do not shout or make a sound. Just play your game and zip it. Okay?'

'Okay, no need to be so narky. I just said I was hungry.'

'I'll get you food later. Do not move.'

'Fine.'

Anna closed the kitchen door and sat down opposite James, who was drinking wine like it was lemonade. 'Talk to me,' she said.

James narrowed his eyes as he refilled his glass to the brim. 'Let's see now. Well, it all started with another sleepless night on the couch. My third straight night trying to sleep on the couch while my step-son sleeps in my bed with my partner.'

'I'm sorry about that, he's just –'

'STOP!' James snapped. 'For once, please stop defending him.'

Anna stopped talking.

'The funny thing is, I thought Anita's party was a break-through for me and Jack, but clearly not. He was back looking for my spot in the bed within days. What did I get? Three or four nights in my bed before he was back?'

Anna opened her mouth to say something, but James held up his hand.

'Oh, I know you think he's upset about Milly. But he isn't, he loves Milly. He thinks Milly's great. He's just acting up and you, as usual, are giving in to his every whim. Every time we take one step forward, we end up taking three back.'

'I'm sorry you feel that way and I promise not to let Jack sleep in our bed.'

James rubbed his eyes, he felt more tired than ever before in his life. Today had been a disaster.

'Tell me what happened in work,' Anna gently probed.

'I fell asleep. I fell asleep and completely missed picking up Laurence Holland from the airport and bringing him to the university for a keynote lecture. He is one of the most highly respected and best-known economists in the world. I have spent months trying to persuade him to come to Trin-ity. It was a huge coup when he finally agreed. And then . . .' James laughed bitterly '. . . I fell asleep and left him stranded in the airport. I decided to have a fifteen-minute nap in the car to try to revive myself after yet another sleepless night, but I forgot to set the alarm on my phone. So, Laurence had to make his own way to Trinity, where there was no one to greet him. He eventually found his way to Benjamin Cross's office. He's our president. So, not only did I make a complete fool of myself in front of Laurence, but Benjamin got to hear all about it.

'I didn't even make it in time to introduce him before his lecture to my students. By the time I woke up, Laurence had already begun his lecture. Benjamin was furious at my lack of professionalism. I had to make up a bullshit excuse about Bella being sick.

'I was mortified and humiliated, Anna. I made a complete fool of myself and insulted a man I admire and revere, and I let down Benjamin and the university.'

'Oh God, James, I'm so sorry. That's awful. Were you able to apologize and chat to him after the lecture?'

James frowned. Had she not been listening? 'He was furious, Anna. He didn't want to chat to me. He went straight back to his hotel. My reputation has been really badly scarred. I don't make mistakes like this. I don't let people down. At least, I never used to. I can't continue like this, Anna. This is not working.'

Anna's eyes widened. 'We can fix it. I can make it work.'

'I really don't see how you can.'

'Please trust me, James. I can make things better. Step one is that you will never sleep on the couch again, I swear on my life. Step two, and I've been thinking about this, actually, I do half-days in work. Instead of working five days from nine till four and having to put Jack into afterschool study, I could work just from nine until one. It'll give me time to grocery shop, pick Jack up, make a nice dinner and help him with his homework. So, by the time you get home all of that chaos is done and dusted, the house will be calm and I can focus on you. It'll mean I'm earning less, but I can save money on groceries by buying in bulk. We can cut the Sky TV subscription, and save on heating . . . There are loads of ways to save money. I'm very good at budgeting. I've been doing it for years.' She was pleading with him.

He wanted to believe her. 'Would you really do that?' James knew how important the clinic was to Anna.

'Sure. I've been thinking about how to make things better for all of us and I was going to suggest it to you. I was waiting for the right time. I'm sorry I didn't mention it sooner.'

'I'm sorry too, but if you really mean it, I think it would help. I'd love to come home and not have to deal with Jack and his homework tantrums. I would also love to sleep properly, every night, in my own bed.'

'I promise on my life you will never sleep on that couch again, and I will make the house a calmer and more peaceful place to come home to. I know you hate the chaos.'

'Thank you, darling,'

'I'm so sorry I didn't say it sooner.'

'At least we've got a plan in place now.'

'I love you, James.'

'I love you too. Actually, I think I'm a bit drunk. Any chance we could sneak upstairs and celebrate our decision between the sheets?'

Anna grinned. 'Hell, yes.'

They snuck upstairs. Anna went into the bathroom first, and by the time she came out, two minutes later, James was passed out on the bed, snoring.

Anna boiled the kettle and waited nervously for Chrissie and Tony to arrive. She was exhausted. She had slept barely a wink. She'd been awake all night while James slept soundly beside her, worrying about this last-ditch attempt to make things work. She knew that if things didn't improve at home, James might leave. Bella was unhappy and now his job was on the line. She had to make it better. Anna had to fix their fragile family before it broke for good.

Chrissie and Tony strolled in, laughing about something. They had such an ease about them. Married for thirty years, they were best friends. They had chosen not to have kids. Anna laughed when she remembered she had felt sorry for them missing out on the wonders of parenthood. She was wrong: they hadn't missed out on anything, and were blissfully happy, while she and James, with their kids, were miserable.

Not that Anna would change Grace or Jack for the world, but the truth was that if she and James were childless, they wouldn't have any problems.

Anna took a deep breath and welcomed her bosses to work. She handed them a coffee each and a bag of pastries.

'This feels very like an early-morning bribe.' Tony was instantly suspicious.

'A very nice bribe.' Chrissie sipped her coffee.

'I'm buttering you up and I asked you to come in early because I need to talk to you about something,' Anna said nervously.

'What's up?' Tony asked. 'You're not pregnant, are you?'

'You can't say that to an employee.' Chrissie slapped his arm. 'Are you, though?' she asked Anna.

Anna shook her head. 'No. Jesus, two kids and one step-daughter is enough. I actually wanted to talk to you about the practice and about going part-time.'

'Oh, I see,' Tony said.

Anna needed to get the words out and she was terrified they might say no, so she kept talking. She had to make this work.

'The move with James has been more complicated than I anticipated. The kids aren't settling in that well and it's a lot of change. And then, well, James messed up in work because of lack of sleep and it's kind of my fault because I let Jack sleep in our bed and James had to sleep on the couch, and he's furious, and we had another row about my overindulging Jack and . . . well . . . something has to give. So I've decided that I need to go part-time and try to sort things out before they get any worse. Maybe if I'm around more for Jack, he'll act up less. I have to try because things are . . . well . . .' Anna paused to regain control of her emotions. There had been a coldness to James last night when he was talking to her, which Anna had never seen before. He was devastated about his work fiasco. She was going to lose him if she didn't act fast.

Chrissie stepped forward and hugged her. 'It was never going to be easy. Step-families always have trouble adjusting in the beginning.'

Tony hovered behind them.

Anna sniffed. 'I just didn't think it would be this hard. I thought the kids would love James as much as I do, and I naïvely presumed that I would love Bella because she was James's daughter.'

'That was naïve,' Tony agreed.

'Tony!' Chrissie frowned at her husband.

'Who really loves other people's kids, seriously? Who?' Tony asked.

'He's right,' Anna said. 'It's not easy. It's hard to love your own sometimes, never mind someone else's. I was so caught up with James and in love with him that I thought things would just fall into place. I was so stupid.'

'You weren't stupid. You were in the throes of love.' Chrissie tried to soothe her.

Anna shook her head. 'That's all very well when you're young and have no kids. When you have kids, you need to think with your head, not your heart.'

'I disagree. You can think with both,' Chrissie said.

'I thought so too, Chrissie, but I'm not sure any more. I'm not sure of anything any more.' Anna began to cry. 'I'm so sorry. I swore I'd hold it together and be professional.'

'If you want to go part-time for a while and see if it works, we'll support you,' Tony said.

Chrissie handed Anna a tissue and she blew her nose. 'Thanks so much. I have to fix this, and I think if I'm around for Grace and Jack and have more time to get to know Bella better, it might help to smooth things over. James is really supportive of me going part-time. We both feel, well, we hope, the kids, and both of us, will benefit from it. And the fact that James works, unlike my ex, means I can manage the drop in earnings. I'd do five mornings a week, nine till one. How does that sound?'

Anna stared at her two bosses, willing them to agree. They could easily replace her with someone full-time and with less baggage. Anna loved working with them and they had been so supportive of her through all of her ups and downs. They had been really good friends to her as well as employers. The practice had grown over the last few years and they now had three other GPs on board, a physio and a second practice nurse, Gemma. That should mean her doing less hours wouldn't cause too much of a problem. She wasn't leaving them in the lurch.

'It's kind of ironic, isn't it? I used to ask you for overtime and now I'm looking for part-time. I'm sorry, guys, I don't mean to mess you around. You know I love working here. And once I get my family on a better track, I can come back full-time.'

Chrissie smiled at her. 'We'll figure it out. You deserve a break. I've never met anyone who's worked as hard as you have, and now you need to focus on your family.'

Tony nodded in agreement. 'I'm just worried that our patients will be gutted you're not always here for them. They're very loyal to you but, as Chrissie said, we'll figure it out. We want the best for you and the kids.'

Relief flooded through Anna's bones and she threw her arms around them. 'Thank you. I really appreciate this and everything you've done for me. Honestly, this job and you two have got me through the last few years.'

Chrissie kissed her cheek. 'Enjoy the time with the kids. It'll be good for all of you.'

Anna knew it would be good for Grace and Jack. She wasn't so sure about Bella. But she had to make this work. This was her last chance to knit the family together. She'd love-bomb Bella and win her over with kindness. She'd talk to Jack about sleeping in his own bed for good and, if need be, she'd bribe him to sleep in it.

Her relationship was at crisis point and she needed to do whatever it took to bring it back from the brink. She had not caused all of this upheaval for nothing. That couldn't happen. She was going to make this family dynamic work, no matter what.

34

Conor ordered two oat-milk lattes from the young guy behind the counter.

'Seriously, Conor? Can I just have milk?'

'Nope, oat milk is way healthier.' He kissed her cheek. 'You'll get used to the taste.'

'I'm regretting pushing you to do the personal-trainer course. You're becoming a health nut. Can I at least have one small chocolate to go with my coffee?'

'Only if it's seventy per cent cocoa.'

Milly groaned. 'What have I created?'

Conor smiled. 'A very happy man.'

They kissed, and when Conor pulled back he saw someone staring at him.

'Chrissie?' It was Chrissie from Anna's clinic.

'Conor? I thought it was you. How are you?'

'Never better,' Conor said, putting his arm around Milly. 'This is my girlfriend, Milly.'

'Nice to meet you.' Chrissie proffered a hand.

'Chrissie works with my ex,' Conor explained.

Milly shook Chrissie's hand. 'Yes, I work with Anna. We'd be lost without her.'

'Anna's a nurse, right?' Milly asked.

'Yes.'

'I think nurses are angels. When my mum was sick, the nurses in the hospital were amazing to her.'

Chrissie laughed. 'I agree with you, and Anna is one of the best. Our patients love her. She's so kind to them.'

'I'm glad she's kind to someone,' Conor said.

Chrissie looked directly at him. 'Anna is kindness to her core, Conor, and she's having a tough time. Go easy on her.'

'Tough time in her big house with her fancy professor?'

'Blending two families is not straightforward. Anna is trying to make everyone happy, as usual, and is wearing herself very thin. She needs support right now.'

Conor shrugged. 'Every decision has consequences.'

'Some decisions are made for you by other people's behaviour.' Chrissie glared at him.

Milly cleared her throat. 'Well, I hope she takes some time for herself. We all need to mind ourselves, don't we?'

'Yes, we do,' Chrissie agreed. 'I'm glad to say Anna has decided to go part-time for a while, just until everyone is settled in the new home. I think it will be good for her to have some breathing space.'

'Sounds like a great idea,' Milly said.

Chrissie's order was ready. She picked up her coffees. 'Well, nice to see you, Conor, and lovely to meet you, Milly.'

'You too, Chrissie.' Milly waved goodbye.

'See you,' Conor said.

They sat down to drink their coffee. Milly was quiet.

'What?' Conor knew she wanted to say something.

'I think you should lay off Anna,' Milly said.

'What do you mean?'

'I mean, you should stop being so angry towards her. You said yourself your marriage was bad for the last few years. She's met someone and now so have you. You're both happy, so why drag all this anger and resentment around? Just let it go.'

'It's not that easy, Milly. She really hurt me.'

'I know, but all you're doing by holding on to your anger is hurting yourself and your kids. You need to think about them. They hate seeing you fight with Anna, and no kid wants to hear their dad criticize their mum. You need to park it, Conor. When you're with me you're so loving and chilled and kind, but when you're around Anna you're a bit of a dickhead, to be honest, and it's really off-putting.'

Conor sighed. 'She just winds me up. She drops the kids over with a list of instructions, like I'm incapable of looking after my own kids.'

'Well, instead of getting the hump about it, show her how capable you are and she'll back off. You have to try harder to get on with her for your kids' sake, Conor. Take yourself and your bruised ego out of it. They come first, end of.'

Conor reached over and pulled Milly close. 'How did you get to be so wise?'

She shrugged. 'A crappy childhood?'

'I love you, Milly. Like, I really, really love you.'

Milly blushed. 'You're not half bad yourself.'

Conor leant in and kissed her. She was right: he needed to try to let the anger towards Anna go, but it wasn't that easy when it was so deeply embedded.

Grace stood with Milly while Conor paced up and down the side of the football pitch, shouting encouragement at Jack's team.

'Nice pass, Luke . . . Tackle, Harry . . . Hard luck, John . . . *Shoooooot.*'

Milly pulled her faux-fur coat closer around her body. She looked effortlessly glam and cool, as always. Grace studied her style. Baggy ripped jeans with fishnet tights underneath, black biker boots, a bright orange polo-neck and a black faux-fur bomber jacket. Grace could never pull off that outfit. Milly just had 'it' – a way of wearing clothes that makes everything look good. If anyone else wore that outfit, they'd look dumb, but Milly rocked it.

'Your dad gets very into the footie, doesn't he? He'll be running on to play in a minute.' She giggled.

Grace laughed. 'He can be so embarrassing at times, especially when he shouts at the referee. He was asked to leave once because he was giving out to the referee about giving a "fake penalty" to the other team.'

'I like that he's passionate. You see some dads who come to the games and look at their phones the whole time or just drop their kids off and don't even stay to watch. Give me a Conor any day.'

Milly was right: Grace's dad was passionate in a good way.

'So, Grace, how are things with you? What's going on in Grace's world?'

'Nothing much, really. It's all about Bella at the moment. Her school musical is coming up – she's playing Sandy in *Grease*. Thank God it'll be over soon. She's so wound up about it she's driving us all mad.'

'Oooh, a diva in the house. To be fair, that's a big deal for her, starring role and all. In a way, it would be less pressure to star in a musical that was not in your own school being watched by your classmates and their parents. I hope she does well.'

'I think she will. She has a really good voice. I just . . . I . . .'

'What is it? Come on, spit it out.'

Grace hesitated, she didn't want to create drama but she was worried and her mum was stressed enough, so she didn't want to burden her with it but she needed to talk to someone. 'I think Bella's trying to lose weight in an unhealthy way.'

'Like what? Not eating? Throwing up her food?' Milly said it straight.

'I've only heard her puking a few times, but she's eating less and less. I met a few of her friends at her party and their Instagram posts are all about being skinny and hot. They post loads of photos in bikinis and underwear, and all the comments are about how amazing they look because they're so thin. Bella's lost weight and she keeps saying it's because she wants to look good for the play and be healthy, but I think it's more than that.'

Milly clapped as Jack's team scored a goal and Conor jumped up and down cheering.

'Maybe you should mention it to your mum and she could talk to Bella's dad,' Milly suggested.

Grace sighed. Her mum and James were not getting on well, and things were so tense in the house right now that she didn't want to rock the boat.

'It's a bit tricky at the moment. Mum and James are . . .' How could she say 'getting on badly' without being disloyal to her mum?

'Having a bit of a bump in the road?' Milly suggested.

'Yes.'

'All couples have bumps, and it can't be easy having two families in one house. Don't worry, Grace. There's nothing you can do anyway. They have to sort out their own stuff. You just get on with your own life and let the adults do their thing. I grew up in a mad house and if there is one thing I learnt it's that you can't control what goes on around you. You can only control how you react to it and how you let it affect you. At the end of the day, always remember you have a mum and dad who absolutely adore you, and that's pretty great. A lot of kids don't have that.'

Milly was right. Grace couldn't control what went on at home. Still, though, it was hard to see her mum and James arguing so much. She just wanted everyone to be happy and for things to settle down.

'If I was you, I'd keep an eye on Bella, and if you hear her puking again, get your mum on a quiet day and mention it to her.'

'Thanks, Milly, I will.'

'You're a fantastic girl, Grace, honestly. I wish I'd been as copped on as you when I was fifteen. I was drinking in bushes and kissing all the wrong boys.'

Grace thought that sounded a lot more fun than worrying about everything and everyone all the time.

35

Bella stood at the bottom of the stairs, waiting impatiently. What the hell was her dad doing? He knew how important today was. He knew she had to be in early.

'*Daaaaaad!*' she hollered up the stairs. 'Come on, it's my last rehearsal. I can't be late.'

'*Grease, Grease, Grease.*' Jack shuffled down the stairs, rubbing sleep out of his eyes. 'That's all you ever talk about.'

'Shut up, squirt.'

'Shut up, yourself.' He shoulder-nudged her as he walked by.

Bella held him by the arm. 'If you need to stop an asteroid, you call?'

'Superman,' he replied.

'If you need to solve a mystery, you call?'

'Batman.'

'But if you need to end a war, you call?'

'Wonder Woman.' Jack grinned.

'Exactly, because women rule the world and I'm going to own that stage tonight.'

'Sandy's a dork,' Jack shouted and ran away, giggling, before Bella could catch him.

Bella smiled and called her dad again.

Anna appeared at the top of the stairs. She beckoned for Bella to come up. What now? Bella thought grumpily.

'Your dad's not well. He's been up all night. He seems to have viral gastroenteritis.'

'What?'

'It's a very bad stomach bug,' Anna explained.

Bella looked into the bedroom. Her dad was lying in the bed with a bucket beside him and a towel across his chest.

Anna was wearing a face mask and handed Bella one. 'It could be contagious, and you don't want to catch it today of all days.'

Bella put on the mask and went in to her dad. He looked awful.

'I'm so sorry, Bella,' he croaked. 'I wanted to bring you in early. Anna has kindly offered to do it.'

'But are you going to be able to come to the show later?' Bella asked.

'Yes, I'll be there.'

'Okay. Get well, Dad.'

'Thanks – and, hey, break a leg. You're going to be fantastic.'

'I hope I don't forget my lines,' Bella mumbled.

'You won't. You've always been a star in my eyes,' James said. 'And now everyone's going to see you shine.'

Bella smiled. 'Thanks. See you later, Dad.'

She hoped he'd be okay. Stomach bugs usually only lasted a day, and if he'd been sick all night, he'd probably be fine by lunchtime. Right?

Anna followed Bella out. 'I'll drop you in.'

'But Jack's only having his breakfast now, I'm going to be late.' Bella began to panic.

'It's okay. We'll go now and I'll come back for Jack and Grace.'

'But by the time you drop me and get back, they'll probably be late for school and you'll be late for work.'

Anna grabbed her coat from the hook inside the front door. 'I know, but it's your big day and I understand how important it is for you to be in early for the dress rehearsal. I've called the clinic to explain I'll be late.'

'Oh . . . well, thanks.' Bella was touched. She had barely said two words to Anna since coming back from her mother's, and here was Anna being nice to her. She knew she should probably offer to wait and arrive late for her rehearsal instead of putting everyone else out, but it was too important and she was too nervous. She needed to be in school with the cast ASAP.

On the way in the car, they listened to the radio. For once, Anna wasn't harassing Bella with questions and trying to chat. She didn't tell her to put her phone away. She just drove and left Bella in peace.

Bella's phone buzzed. It was a message from her mum.

What time is the play?

Bella sighed and typed, *7pm*. She'd told Ingrid at least ten times already.

My flight lands at 7. I should get the second act.

Bella cursed under her breath.

'Everything okay?' Anna asked.

'It's just my mum. She says she's going to be late for the musical.'

'Oh, I'm sorry. I'm sure the school is recording it, though, aren't they?'

'Yeah, and Dad can record it too. But, like, I told her a million times the date and time.'

'She's a very busy lady.' Anna tried to be tactful. She paused, then added, 'Listen, Bella, I'm going to do everything I can to get your dad to the play, but he might be too sick. If he doesn't improve significantly, he can't go and pass the bug to everyone else.'

Bella bit her lip. Her dad had to come. He'd always been so encouraging of her love for acting and singing and had always taken her side when her mum had said it was all a waste of time. 'Please help him get better,' she begged.

Anna gently patted her arm. 'I promise you, I'll move heaven and earth to get him there.'

Bella clicked off her seatbelt. 'Thanks, Anna, and I appreciate the lift.'

Anna looked surprised. 'Oh, you're welcome. And good luck.'

Inside, Bella checked herself in the full-length mirror that was perched in the corner of the classroom. Around her there was chaos, with some girls getting into costume and applying make-up while others from the older classes helped the teachers stick sideburns onto the faces of those who were playing male roles. There were clothes and bags and make-up everywhere.

Bella smoothed her skirt and tightened the belt around her cardigan another notch. She looked good. Skinny. Sandy was skinny and now so was Bella.

'You look *amaaaaazing*,' Portia gushed.

'Have you lost more weight?' Saffron's eyes lasered in on Bella's waist.

'Yeah, a little bit,' Bella admitted.

'Having such a skinny waist just highlights your chunky thighs. You looked much better before. Now you're all out of proportion.'

Bella looked down. Was Saffron right? Did her thinner waist make her legs look even bigger? No matter how little she ate or how much she threw up, Bella could not make her thighs skinny.

'I disagree. I think you look hot,' Portia said. 'If we were doing this play with an actual boys' school, they'd all fancy you.'

'Your tan looks really fake – your legs look orange,' Saffron said. 'What brand did you use?'

'The one you told me to get. Bronze Goddess.'

Saffron shrugged. 'Well, it doesn't look orange on my legs.'

Bella looked down at her legs. They did look a bit orange. But it was too late to fix them now. She started to sweat. Damnit. Now her make-up would run. She tried to calm down.

'OMG, Saffron, can you, like, stop freaking Bella out?' Portia sounded angry. 'She looks fab.'

'It's called honesty, Portia. Real friends are supposed to be honest with each other. If I looked a state, I'd want Bella to tell me.'

Bella felt rage, anxiety and tension rise inside her. She snapped, 'You're right, Saffron, we should be honest with each other. You are being a complete and utter bitch right now.'

Bella turned and walked over to Heidi, who was playing the part of Danny. She could hear Saffron shouting, 'How dare you call me a bitch?' but she chose to ignore her.

'Did you just call Saffron a bitch?' Heidi giggled.

'Yes.' Bella grinned.

'Good for you. I don't know why you and Portia are friendly with her. She's awful.'

Bella nodded. Heidi was right, Saffron was awful. But she usually directed her nasty comments and her sharp claws at other girls. Saffron was funny, too, when she criticized them and made a joke of it. It was only when you thought about what she'd said that you realized how cutting it was. But now that Bella was on the receiving end, she saw her so-called friend for what she truly was: a mean, nasty cow.

Later that day, in the small gap between rehearsals and the live performance, Bella went into the bathroom to have a moment alone to decompress. Okay, deep breaths. She needed to be calm before going on stage. Channel Sandy, she told herself. Sweet, innocent Sandy.

She was feeling calmer when her phone buzzed.

Missed flight, next one not until 8pm. Won't make your play. Sry. Mum.

Bella's hands shook as she dialled her mother's mobile. 'What the hell?' she shouted. 'How could you miss your flight?'

'My meeting ran over and then the traffic was horrendous.'

'You know how important this is? You promised you'd be here,' Bella raged.

'Calm down. I understand you're upset, but it's not exactly

the end of the world. It's a school play. Tell James to video it for me.'

'It's not a play.' Bella's voice began to break. I will not cry, she told herself sternly. She fought back tears. She would not ruin her eye make-up. Portia had spent ages applying it and it looked brilliant. 'It's a musical. It's a musical that I am starring in and it's a huge deal for me. Everyone's parents are coming. Even girls who have no lines. You always put work before me. I'm sick of it.'

'Bella,' Ingrid's voice was sharp, 'it's a school musical, not your graduation ceremony. It has taken up far too much of your time and energy. Singing and dancing won't get you into university. Now go and enjoy your night and call me later to let me know how it went. Break a leg.'

Bella hung up and pressed her fingers into the corners of her eyes to stop tears escaping. She had so wanted her mum to be there to see her shining. She wanted her mum to see that she had talent. She was never going to be brilliant at maths and accountancy, but she was good at this.

She shook out her arms and legs, then rolled her head to loosen her tense neck.

'You will shine,' she said to her reflection.

She texted her dad. *Where are you sitting?* But there was no answer.

She texted Anna.

We're nine rows back to the left.

Is Dad here? Mum missed her flight.

Oh, no, sorry to hear that. Yes ur dad's here.

'Phew.' Bella went to turn her phone off, just as another text from Anna came through.

You'll be fantastic. Go out and shine!

A standing ovation. An actual standing ovation. Bella and Heidi stood out in front of the audience and bowed again and again.

It was magical. Bella felt as if she was floating on air. The whole performance had passed in a flash. She'd remembered every line and hit every note.

Bella held her hand up to her eyes to block out the stage lights, but she couldn't see her dad. She bowed again and then the curtain came down. The cast hugged each other and whooped and cheered. Then everyone raced down into the hall to see their parents. Bella couldn't wait to see her dad and hear what he had to say.

Anna was gobsmacked. Bella was like a professional up on the stage. She *was* Sandy. She had all the moves and her voice, wow. She'd hit every high note and hadn't missed a beat. Anna saw a whole new Bella. She looked like she belonged on the stage. She looked happy up there.

'She's really good,' Grace whispered.

'I know,' Anna replied. 'What a revelation.'

'Like a professional.' Grace gazed up at her step-sister in admiration.

'I'm bored,' Jack huffed.

'Sssh, not long to go.' Anna handed him another sweet. She'd had to bribe him with a bagful to come and by lying about how long the musical would last.

But while Jack was restless, Anna could have watched it all night. The performers were brilliant, putting heart and soul into every number. She enjoyed every minute of it.

When the play was over and the standing ovation had ended, they put their coats on and waited for the cast to come out. Anna spotted Bella searching for her dad. She felt bad about lying to her, but she hadn't wanted to upset her right before her performance, especially when she'd texted Anna that Ingrid had missed her flight.

Anna couldn't understand it. How could Ingrid not prioritize such an important night in her daughter's life? What possible meeting or work issue could trump seeing your flesh and blood performing onstage? Anna had never missed an important event in her kids' lives and, to be fair, neither had Conor. He wasn't good about homework or helping with the educational side of life, but when it came to sport or school plays or Grace exhibiting at science fairs, he'd never missed one.

And poor James was at home, utterly devastated. He'd tried to get up three times and his legs had given way each time. Anna had rushed home from work at lunchtime and pumped him full of fluid to try to get him well enough to attend, but he had a really nasty bug and he was completely flattened. He'd been in tears about missing Bella's big night.

Anna had asked Grace and Jack to come with her to support Bella. All around them, parents were telling their children how wonderful they were. Anna waved over at Bella. She caught her eye and Bella came rushing over.

'Where's Dad?'

Anna handed Bella a bunch of flowers she'd bought in a garage on the way over. 'I'm so sorry, he was just too sick. He tried so hard to be here, but he couldn't even stand up.'

Bella's face crumpled. 'So . . . so . . . no one saw it?'

'We did,' Jack announced. 'It was a bit boring, but you were brilliant. I never knew you could sing so good.'

'You were amazing, Bella,' Grace said. 'Honestly, you stole the show.'

'We're all so proud of you. My goodness, Bella, you are so talented. Your voice, your acting, just incredible,' Anna said. She hadn't thought it possible, but she actually wanted to hug Bella. The poor girl was so upset that her parents had missed it.

'Thanks.' She fought back tears.

Anna reached over and took her into her arms. Bella didn't push her away.

'We got you these too.' Jack handed his step-sister a box of chocolates. 'Sorry, but I opened them and took two. I was starving.'

'Jack! You had loads of your own sweets,' Anna scolded him.

'I know, but you lied about how long it was, it went on for ever. I got hungry.'

Bella tousled his hair. 'No problem and thank you.'

'Grace recorded all your solos so your dad can watch them,' Anna told her.

'Thanks.' Bella tried to smile.

'Honestly, Bella, you were a shining star tonight. You really have a talent. I was blown away,' Anna said. 'When you hit that high note on "Hopelessly Devoted", the woman beside me actually gasped.'

Bella smiled, a real smile. 'Did she?'

'Yes! It was amazing,' Anna said. 'I was looking at you in awe.'

'I missed it a few times in practice, so I was worried, but thankfully I hit it tonight.'

'You must be so proud of yourself.' Anna squeezed her arm.

Bella shrugged. 'I guess. I'm kind of rubbish at everything else.'

'You're not rubbish, you just don't have the same focus because you don't love that other stuff. But this, Bella, this is your thing. You came alive on that stage. You looked like a different person up there. I just really wish your mum and dad could have made it, but I'm sure you'll be cast in other shows based on that performance.'

'Well done again, you were the star of the show.' A girl came up and hugged Bella.

'Thanks, Portia.'

'Hi, Grace, I remember you from Bella's party. My cousin is still talking about how hot you are.' Portia grinned.

'Oh, well . . . umm, thanks, I guess.' Grace blushed.

'My mother said she couldn't hear you at the back, that your voice didn't carry,' the girl standing behind Portia said.

'Saffron!' Portia stared at the girl.

'Your mother must be deaf,' Grace piped up. 'We were half-way down and we could hear perfectly.'

'Yeah, Bella was the best,' Jack said.

'What would you know about musicals?' Saffron dismissed him.

'I will fight for those who cannot fight for themselves,' Jack said.

Bella laughed and high-fived him.

'OMG, a boy who quotes Wonder Woman!' Portia exclaimed. 'How cool is that?'

'A freak boy,' Saffron muttered.

Before Anna could say anything, Bella turned on her. 'How dare you insult my step-brother? You're just a sad, jealous cow. Piss off, Saffron.'

Anna's eyes stung with tears. Grace had defended Bella, Jack had stood up for Bella, too, and now . . . now Bella had just defended Jack. Maybe there was hope after all – for their family, and for her and James.

36

A uniformed crew member came over and set down hot coffee, hot milk, soy, low fat and almond milk, plus freshly made mini chia-seed scones.

'Thank you, Anya.' Ingrid smiled at her.

The young woman nodded and retreated discreetly. Their skorts and striped Breton tops were cute, but Ingrid felt the skorts could have been a few inches longer. There was a lot of leg on view. The male crew wore shorts that landed almost to the knee, while the women's skorts were more mid-thigh.

When Ingrid had met Denis and he'd invited her for a trip on his boat, her heart had sunk. She hated boats. She wasn't a strong swimmer and boats made her nervous. But then they'd arrived on the *Fairweather*, and she'd realized that Denis's 'boat' was, in fact, a floating hotel. Six double bedrooms, with marble bathrooms en-suite. A crew of twenty, including a Michelin-starred chef, a swimming-pool on the actual boat, a gym, an office and a screening room . . . It was incredible. Too much for two people, though. Ingrid felt uncomfortable with all the staff buzzing around for just her and Denis.

At least this time there were five of them on board. Although Ingrid found Claire, Denis's daughter, difficult and was not impressed with her latest boyfriend, Toby, at least the crew had more people to look after.

The best part was getting to spend time with Bella and make up for missing her play. Ingrid really hadn't thought it was that big a deal, but when she'd heard that James hadn't made it either and had seen how upset Bella was, she knew she had some making up to do. She'd also received an incredibly irritating, gushing text from Anna, telling her how wonderful Bella had been and how talented she was and how Ingrid 'must be feeling so upset about having missed it all' and attaching videos of Bella's solos.

Ingrid had to admit that Bella was impressive in the role but, still, it was a hobby that was taking up too much of her time.

'Coffee, love?' Ingrid asked Bella.

'Yes, black, please.'

'No milk?'

'No, I drink it black now.'

'Okay.' Ingrid poured coffee into a pretty white china cup with a blue anchor on the side.

Denis scrolled through his emails and Claire lit a cigarette.

'Would you mind not smoking at the table?' Ingrid asked, as a cloud of smoke blew into her face.

'Oh, for goodness' sake, we're outside, Ingrid. Dad doesn't mind, do you, Dad?'

Denis looked up. 'What?'

'You don't mind me smoking on deck?'

'Not really, no.' Denis went back to his phone.

Claire smiled smugly at Ingrid, who tried not to look as annoyed as she felt. She got up and moved seat.

'What would you like to do today?' she asked Bella.

Bella shrugged. 'Chill in the sun, try and get a tan, maybe work out in the gym.'

'Well, you shouldn't waste the whole day. How about going ashore to Santorini and visiting Akrotiri? It's a Bronze Age settlement and one of the most important archaeological sites in Greece.'

Claire snorted. 'Wow, Ingrid, that sounds like so much fun for a fifteen-year-old girl. Whoopee-doo, a visit to look at old stones. Lucky you, Bella.'

Ingrid gripped her coffee cup and tried not to mind Bella giggling at Claire's comment. 'I think it would be an incredible thing to see,' she said.

'I think Bella would rather poke her eye out with a fork.' Claire was not letting go. 'Why don't you go and visit your boring stones and leave Bella here to hang out with me and Toby and have some actual fun on her holiday?'

'Bella?' Ingrid looked at her daughter.

'I don't want to visit a Bronze Age site. I'm tired from all the rehearsals and the musical. I want to chill out. You go.'

Ingrid wanted some quality time with Bella on her own and it was stupid not to go and see an important site when you were so close by. But she didn't want to push Bella. She knew she was on thin ice.

'Denis, will you come?'

He glanced up. 'I might be able to later. I have a conference call now that could run on.'

'No, Dad, you can't go later. You're coming jet-skiing with me, remember?' Claire reminded him. 'You promised me, Dad, no backing out.'

'Sorry, Ingrid, looks like I'm fully booked.'

Ingrid tried not to mind Denis choosing to spend time with Claire over her. She was his daughter after all, and he was very good about having Bella to stay every second week and holidays. But it was the way Claire lorded it over Ingrid that bothered her. She made sure that Ingrid knew Denis would always prioritize her. Ingrid was aware that he spoilt his daughter out of guilt for never having been around when she was younger: he had had an affair and broken up with her mother when she was only six years old. After he left, Denis admitted to her that he had buried himself in work and seen Claire only once a month. On the days they were together, he didn't really know what to do with a young child, so he just bought her things, anything she wanted.

Thank God she was an adult and didn't live with them. Ingrid didn't think her relationship with Denis would have lasted six weeks if she'd had to live with Claire.

Claire put out her cigarette and waved over a crew member. 'I'd like a latte with oat milk, please, and make sure it's extra hot. The last one was barely warm.'

'My coffee was perfectly hot,' Ingrid said. 'Maybe you left yours too long before drinking it.' She hated the way Claire was so rude to the crew.

'No, I didn't. Considering this is my father's boat and he's paying these people a lot of money to work here, I'm entitled to get my coffee the way I like it.'

Ingrid wouldn't have blamed the crew if they'd spat in Claire's extra hot coffee.

'Dad?' Claire put her arm around Denis's shoulders.

'Yes, pet.' Denis beamed at her.

'Toby and I are going ashore to do some shopping later this afternoon. They have some amazing shops in Santorini. I may need to borrow your credit card.'

'What's wrong with your own?' Denis asked.

Claire kissed his cheek. 'Don't get cross, but I may have maxed it out when we were in New York last weekend.'

'What are you like? You spend money like water.'

'I know, Dad, but I was having so much fun and I kind of bought myself an early birthday present.'

'Your birthday is four months away.'

'But the bracelet was one of a kind and I was afraid it would be sold to someone else. You'll love it when you see it. They're adjusting it and I'm flying over to pick it up next week. Look.'

Claire showed Denis a photo of the bracelet on her phone. 'Isn't it incredible? Every time I wear it, I'll think of what a brilliant dad you are.'

Denis smiled. 'It is a nice piece. Okay, but take it easy with the shopping today.'

'Of course I will, Dad.' Claire hugged him. 'You're the best. Doesn't my dad rock, Toby?'

'Totally,' Toby drawled. 'I wish mine was more like him.'

It never ceased to astound Ingrid that a man who was so clever, driven and single-minded could be such a pushover when it came to his daughter. Ingrid was determined that Bella would not grow up to be entitled, spoilt and manipulative. She worried that having been exposed to so much wealth early in her life, she might come to view it as 'normal'. But no, between Ingrid and James, they'd keep her feet on the ground.

She really didn't want Bella spending a lot of time with Claire and Toby, but she couldn't force her daughter to come sightseeing either. So, Ingrid got up and went to organize for the crew to bring her ashore.

Bella stood up and rinsed her mouth. The taste of vomit disappeared quickly. The yacht was amazing and the food was so delicious that it was hard not to eat. Still, she'd only let it sit in her stomach for five minutes so that was okay. When she reached seven stone she'd stop throwing up. Only half a stone to go.

She went outside and lay beside Claire on the huge sunbed overlooking the ocean. Toby was smoking a cigarette with a very strong smell.

OMG, was he smoking weed?

Toby passed the joint to Claire, who inhaled and held the smoke inside before exhaling slowly. It was weed.

Claire held out the joint to Bella. 'Want some?'

Bella froze. She didn't want to seem like a stupid kid in front of Claire, but she also didn't want to get high.

'Come on, live a little. You don't want to end up like your uptight mother,' Claire said.

'That woman is so wound up. Like, does she ever just chill the fuck out?' Toby's voice dragged, like it was an effort to speak. 'She needs some serious Xanax.'

Bella thought Toby was a bit of an idiot. He talked a lot of nonsense. He had a really posh accent and talked about working 'in the family business'. But when Ingrid had asked him what he did, he was really vague and said, 'Oh, a bit of import–export.' Bella could see that her mother thought he was full of crap. Now, Bella wondered if his 'import–export' business was drugs.

Claire laughed. 'Maybe I'll spike her wine tonight with Xanax and she'll stop being such a killjoy.' Claire lowered her sunglasses and looked at Bella. 'How do you stand being her daughter? She's such a ball-breaker. Like, does she ever stop banging on about education, hard work and interesting books to read or things to see?'

Bella knew her mum could be a pain. She was furious with Ingrid for missing the musical and hadn't forgiven her yet, but even though her mother was in her bad books, she still didn't like other people slagging her off.

'She never stops talking about her job too. It's pretty fucking boring,' Toby said. 'Like, I know your dad does, too, but he's a hugely successful property developer. She's just his accountant.'

'One of his accountants,' Claire corrected him.

His main accountant and his right-hand woman, Bella thought. But, still, they were right, her mum was obsessed with her job and Bella was sick of it. Her mum had let her down. She hadn't seen her as Sandy.

She reached over for the joint and inhaled deeply.

'Bella . . . Bella . . . Bella . . .'

Someone was calling her name. Bella wanted to answer, but her face felt numb. She couldn't form words. She opened her eyes. Her mum was standing over her, shaking her shoulders and calling her name.

What the . . . Where was she?

Bella felt herself being pulled into a seated position. Her body felt floppy and her mind was fuzzy.

'Bella, can you hear me?' her mum asked.

She nodded.

'Jesus Christ, how much did she smoke?' Ingrid snapped.

Bella saw Claire and Toby standing behind her mother.

'Chill out, Ingrid, she only had a few drags. She just passed out because she's not used to it.'

'Not used to it?' Ingrid shouted. 'No, Claire, my fifteen-year-old daughter is not used to smoking drugs. How dare you give her weed?'

'She wanted some. I'm not her mother. I was smoking weed at her age. It's not a big deal.'

'You could have damaged her brain. You could have brought on psychosis. How could you be so casually reckless with my daughter's life?'

'Let's all calm down.' Denis appeared in Bella's eyeline. 'I understand you got a fright and Claire was very foolish to give her a joint, but Bella is fine, Ingrid.'

'She's not fine, Denis. I came back and found her passed out on the sun lounger. Your wonderful daughter and her boyfriend were inside watching a movie while my young daughter was drugged out of her mind.' Ingrid's voice shook with emotion.

Bella reached over and put her hand on her mother's arm. 'Mum, it's okay. I'm fine. I feel a bit fuzzy, but I'm fine.'

'She just needs to sleep it off,' Claire said.

Ingrid glared at her. 'I do not need any advice from you. I want you and your drug-dealing boyfriend to leave.'

Claire laughed. 'It's my father's boat. I'm not going anywhere. If anyone should leave, it's you. I'm family, Ingrid, you're just an employee.'

'Are you going to let her speak to me like that?' Ingrid looked to Denis for support.

Bella's mind was clearing from the fog. The tension in the room was insane. She held her breath.

Denis looked uncomfortable. Outside work he hated confrontation of any kind. He just wanted an easy life. But Ingrid didn't give a damn about his feelings right now.

'Denis?' she snapped.

'Claire, Ingrid is my wife. Have some respect, please. I think everyone needs to calm down,' Denis said.

'I do not need to calm down, Denis. My drugged-up daughter could have gone swimming and drowned or choked on her own vomit. Anything could have happened.'

Claire snorted. 'If Bella was going to choke on her own vomit, she'd have done it by now. She's puked up every meal since we've been on the boat.'

What? Bella was alert now. Damnit, how did Claire know?

Ingrid stared at Claire. 'Excuse me?'

'Oh, come on, you're telling me you haven't noticed that your daughter has lost a load of weight and is throwing up all her meals?'

'Bella has slimmed down, but she was on a health drive for her school musical.'

Claire slow-clapped. 'Wow, Ingrid, you really are mother of the year, aren't you? You don't even know that your daughter has an eating problem and you have the neck to give me a hard time for letting her have a few puffs of a joint?'

'What? How dare you speak to me like that?'

'The truth hurts, Ingrid. Why don't you ask Bella yourself?'

Ingrid turned to Bella. 'Is this true?'

Bella felt tired, really, really tired and hungry, hungry to her bones. She didn't have the energy to lie. She nodded.

'Oh, Bella.' Ingrid put her arms around her daughter and held her.

It felt nice. Bella snuggled in.

Turning to Denis, Ingrid said quietly, 'Can you please get everyone out of here? I need to talk to Bella alone.'

'Of course. Call me if you need anything.' Denis ushered Claire and Toby out and closed the door.

Ingrid sat beside Bella and held her hand. 'How long have you been vomiting up your meals?'

'About four months.'

'Oh, Bella. Why?'

'I wanted to look like Sandy in the musical but also . . . also . . .' Bella's head was still fuzzy, but she could feel all the words she'd been pushing down for so long rising up. She was tired of it all, and lonely too. She needed her mum to know, she needed her to understand how hard it all was. She was sick of pretending to be okay when she wasn't, she wasn't at all. She felt completely lost and alone.

'Also, I wanted to be in control of something. When you left Dad, everything was turned upside-down and then I got used to it. But then Dad met Anna and everything was upside-down again but worse, because I had this new family, with kids my age, and I hated it. I hate other people controlling my life and making me live where I don't want to live or have siblings I don't want. I feel like an outsider in Dad's house. And I'm sick of moving from house to house and trying to fit into a family that isn't mine and . . . and . . . you're always busy, you're always working, so I'm on my own most of the time when I'm living with you . . . and you missed my musical, Mum. It was such a big deal for me, but you put work first, as always. Everyone's parents were there except mine. I was so hurt.' Bella felt a wave of emotion overwhelm her. A sob escaped from her mouth and she began to bawl. She cried and cried as her mother held her.

'Oh, Bella, I'm sorry, pet.'

Bella tried to stop crying but she couldn't. She felt years of hurt, worry, confusion, frustration and angst pour out of her from deep inside.

'Why do you always put work first?' Bella sniffed.

Ingrid sighed. 'Because I'm terrified of not having enough money. When my dad died, my mum fell apart and we had nothing. Fear of poverty has followed me around my whole life and it drives me to work harder, earn more, save more, so that

I can be safe and secure and look after you and never be left destitute. Your life can change in a second and I never want you to have to go through the fear of not knowing if there's going to be enough money for food or rent. It never leaves you.'

Bella had heard her mother talk about not having a lot growing up and how important it was to earn your own money, but she hadn't realized she'd worried about having enough food to eat. 'Did you really not have food sometimes?'

Ingrid nodded. 'We moved into a tiny flat and lived on bread and beans for months until I got a part-time job. My mum just kind of fell apart and couldn't cope, so even though I was still at school, it was up to me to earn money to keep us going. I've never told anyone this, but I stole food from my classmates' bags sometimes.'

'Seriously?' Bella couldn't imagine her mother stealing.

'Only when things were very bad but, yes, I did.'

'I'm sorry, Mum. I didn't know things were so awful for you.'

'I'm sorry too, Bella. I've made enough money never to have to worry again. But I still work day and night and it's not okay. Work is just so crazy and there's always some crisis to manage. But you'll be gone in a few years and I'll have missed all this time with you. I promise to try to be more present.'

'I just wish you could work a little bit less when I'm there. You're always on your phone, and when Denis says he needs you, even if you've planned to do stuff with me, you just cancel.'

Ingrid winced. 'I do, and it's wrong. I suppose that when Denis needs me to sort out serious business issues, I feel I can't say no. I've got into the habit of never saying no, but of course I can. I suppose I'm a bit of a control freak and I don't want anyone else doing my job, not even for one afternoon.'

Bella grinned. She couldn't believe her mother had just admitted she was a control freak.

'What are you grinning at?' Ingrid asked.

'A bit of a control freak?' Bella giggled. 'Mum, you're the biggest control freak ever.'

Ingrid laughed. 'I suppose I am.'

Bella leant into her mother's shoulder.

'Bella, did you smoke the weed to get back at me?'

'Yes.'

'Have you ever smoked before?'

'Never, and I never, ever, ever, ever will again.'

'Good.'

'I'm sorry. It was so stupid.'

'Yes, it was, and dangerous, but you've learnt your lesson. Now we need to talk about the eating and vomiting. I'm going to get you help with that. I'm going to find you the best person to talk to and help you to overcome that urge. And I will help you in every way I can.'

'Thanks, Mum.'

Ingrid let out a groan.

'What?'

'I've just remembered Anna coming to my office to tell me she was worried about you. I was so sharp with her. But she was right. Your dad's girlfriend knew you were in trouble before I did. Claire's right. I'm a terrible mother.' She pulled Bella in close. 'I promise I'll try harder to be there for you. I love you, Bella.'

'I love you too, Mum.' Bella smiled as she closed her eyes and drifted off into sleep.

37

Anna picked up one of the scatter cushions from the couch and plumped it up for the tenth time. The house had never been so clean. She'd scrubbed it from top to bottom. The trestle table she'd rented was covered with her best white tablecloth, and the two vases of yellow tulips looked lovely against the white. She had yellow candles, and she'd put little yellow chicks along the centre of the table.

On every plate was an Easter egg. She'd got posh artisan-type ones for Ingrid and Denis, and the rest were the usual bog-standard ones. Bella seemed happier and healthier in the weeks since she'd come back from her mid-term holiday with Ingrid. Mind you, who wouldn't be happy after a week on a luxury yacht? It sounded like bliss to Anna. She had spent the mid-term week doing smears, blood tests, changing dressings and giving vaccines, then coming home to mind Grace and Jack and be a housewife. A week of luxury on a yacht sounded like heaven.

Jack was in the garden, kicking a football into a goal over and over again. He was covered with mud despite promising to stay clean in his new jeans and T-shirt that Anna had bought especially for Easter Sunday lunch. Sod it, she thought. At least he wasn't running around the house knocking things over.

Anna had decided, after James and Ingrid had missed the musical, the awful camping trip and the constant bickering and tension in the house, that it was time to get everyone together in one place and try to smooth things over. She'd invited Conor and Milly, as well as Ingrid and Denis, and she hoped that, maybe, today would show the kids that everyone could get on and they could be a kind of, sort of, big family.

She'd been surprised by Ingrid's *We'd love to come* text in response to her invitation. She'd expected an *I'm far too busy in my big important job to come to your silly lunch* text, but Ingrid had replied immediately and almost sounded warm. Conor had also said yes and asked if he could bring anything! Milly was clearly working magic on him. Anna hoped the lunch would go well. She wasn't expecting miracles, but a nice, uneventful, calm lunch would be great.

James came in carrying an ice bucket with two bottles of white wine cooling inside. He placed it in the middle of the table and came over to Anna. Kissing her, he said, 'The table looks wonderful. You're amazing for doing this.'

'Let's hope everyone behaves,' she said, crossing her fingers.

'Hopefully there'll be safety in numbers,' James said.

BANG. Jack's football smashed into the window. James jumped.

Anna rubbed his back. 'Breathe. The glass is reinforced and it's better to have him outside than running around knocking over glasses in here.'

'How about we pour ourselves a glass before everyone arrives?' James suggested.

'Good idea.'

They sat side by side, sipping wine. They could hear Bella and Grace getting dressed upstairs. They were playing music loudly and going in and out of each other's rooms, trying on outfits. 'I think they're getting on,' James whispered.

'Yes,' Anna replied.

'Maybe we're finally getting somewhere,' James said.

'I think we might be.' Anna smiled.

'Things have definitely improved since you went part-time. I'm getting regular sleep in my own bed, the house is less chaotic and now you're hosting big family lunches. Thanks for everything.' James kissed her.

Anna decided not to admit to paying Jack twenty euro every week that he slept in his own bed.

'I love you, Anna.'

'I love you too.'

They were kissing when they heard, 'Gross!'

Jack was standing at the window, covering his eyes.

'Short but sweet,' Anna said, and James laughed.

Ten minutes later, the doorbell rang. Anna answered it to Conor and Milly. Conor had never been punctual in his life, yet here he was, dressed smartly in dark jeans and a shirt and bang on time. Milly was wearing a midi-length figure-hugging red dress that showed off all her assets. She'd changed her hair: it was now platinum blonde and cut into a shaggy bob. She was holding a large bunch of flowers. 'Thanks so much for having me.' She handed Anna the flowers.

'They're lovely, thank you.' Anna stepped back to let them in.

Conor leaned down and pecked her on the cheek.

'I like your hair,' Anna commented. It was very short on the sides with a bit of length on the top that was gelled to one side. He looked like a different person. Smart, fresh and put together.

Conor smiled. 'All down to Milly. She cut it last week.'

'I think it suits him – he's even hotter now.' She winked.

Anna wasn't sure what to say. If she agreed, did that sound like she thought Conor was hot? She decided to smile and say nothing.

They moved into the living room.

'Oooh, the table looks lovely. You've gone to so much trouble,' Milly said. Then, seeing James, she held out her hand. 'I'm Milly, very nice to meet you, James, thanks for having us over.'

Us, thought Anna. So Milly and Conor were an 'us'.

Conor and James shook hands and muttered hello.

'Can I offer you a drink?' James asked.

'I'd love a sparkling water,' Milly said.

'Do you have any Heineken Zero?' Conor asked.

What? Conor was asking for a non-alcohol beer? Anna was shocked.

'Oh, uhm, I'm not sure,' James said.

'No, we don't. Sorry. I presumed you'd be drinking,' Anna said.

Conor sat back in the couch, with Milly close beside him. 'No, I'm driving. I've got an exam next week so I need to keep a clear head. I want to ace it.'

Who are you? Anna wanted to shout. Where is Conor? Where is the man I married who always put himself first? When did you ever not drink because of work or study? When did you ever behave so responsibly? What *had* Milly done? Had she put a spell on him?

'Well, can I get you a soft drink, then?' James asked.

'Sure, thanks, I'll take a Coke.'

'And if Conor's driving, will you have a glass of wine, Milly?' James asked.

'No, thanks. I don't drink. Alcoholic dad, a very Irish story.' Milly laughed. 'Never had much of a tolerance for alcohol when I did drink anyway.'

'There you go, Milly.' James handed her a glass of sparkling water and refilled Anna's wine glass, which was already empty.

Milly took a sip. 'Thanks, James. So, I hear you're an economics professor. How brilliant is that? I bet your students love you. Handsome professors aren't that common.'

Anna observed James blushing. Milly had disarmed him within minutes of meeting him. She was something else.

'Well . . . that's, uhm, kind of you. I'm lucky I have some really bright, enthusiastic students this year.'

Milly waved her hand in the air. 'I love enthusiasm. I think it's a brilliant trait.'

'So do I,' James agreed. 'It's an underrated virtue in my opinion.'

'Milly is the most enthusiastic person I've ever met.' Conor looked at her adoringly.

Bloody hell, there was certainly no lack of enthusiasm in this room. There was a full-on love-in taking place. Anna took a long sip of her wine.

Grace and Bella came in. Grace went straight over to her dad and Milly.

'Hey, gorgeous, I love your skirt. Is that River Island?' Milly asked.

'Yes. It's the one you said I should get.' Grace gave a little twirl.

'I was right. It looks absolutely amazing on you.'

Anna didn't know that Grace had bought the skirt because of Milly. She'd never said. But it was gorgeous on her.

'Hi, Bella, I'm Milly. How are you? That top is stunning. Is it Michael Kors?' Milly asked.

'Yes.'

'Well, it looks even better on you than it does on the model in the ad.'

Bella grinned. 'Thanks. Is that dress Zara?'

'Sure is, got it yesterday.'

'It looks incredible on you.'

'Thanks, babe. They have some great new combats in. The khaki ones would be fab on you.'

Anna was speechless. Here was Milly, chatting to Bella as if they were old pals. Bella was smiling, engaging and being really nice. Unbelievable. Anna wanted to stamp her foot and shout, 'Hang on a bloody minute! I've broken my back trying to get Bella to talk to me and to get to know her and you just swan in and disarm her in one bloody second. It's not fair!'

She also felt very out of the clothes loop that was going on all around her. She was wearing a red pleated midi skirt and a fitted cream cardigan with red pockets. I bought my outfit in Next, in case anyone cares, she wanted to announce. Hello, I also like clothes and am interested in chatting.

Jack came barrelling into the room and jumped on top of his dad on the couch. Conor wrestled with him and they fell to the floor laughing.

They scrambled up and Jack went over to Milly. 'Did you see Woodburn's goal last night?'

'Did I? Wasn't he brilliant? The way he curled the ball in. Unreal.'

'Amazing.'

'I reckon he's going to be the new Salah.'

'Me too.'

'He's got the speed, the footwork and the skills,' Milly said. 'He's got a bit of swagger going on, too. You need that to be a striker, I reckon.'

'Do I have swagger?' Jack asked.

'Dude, you are *all* swagger.' Milly held out her hand and Jack fist-pumped her, grinning from ear to ear.

Anna tilted her head back and drained her wine glass.

Ingrid handed her coat to James and hung back while James showed Denis into the living room. She tugged Anna's arm and pulled her back into the hall.

Anna turned to face her. 'Oh, hi, welcome,' she said. 'Is James getting you a drink?'

'Yes, thanks. Look, Anna,' Ingrid lowered her voice, 'I wanted to thank you.'

'Not at all. It's nothing fancy, just a casual lunch,' Anna said.

'No,' Ingrid replied, 'I wanted to thank you for noticing that Bella had a problem and for trying to tell me. I'm ashamed that I missed the signs.'

'Oh.' Anna was gobsmacked. She reckoned apologies weren't

something Ingrid did often. 'Well, these things aren't always easy to spot and you're very busy so –'

'Being busy is not an excuse for missing something so important. I'm trying to cut back on work and spend more time with Bella. I've neglected her and I can see that she needs me now more than ever. I think the break-up of my marriage, me moving in with Denis and then James moving in with you has been a lot harder on her than I realized.'

Anna patted her arm. 'I feel the same way. I've actually gone part-time in work because I'm so worried about Grace, Jack and Bella. Being a parent is not easy.'

'I didn't understand that,' Ingrid said. 'You make it look easy.'

Anna laughed. 'I fail miserably at it ninety per cent of the time.'

'I appreciate you didn't say "I told you so." I was pretty sharp with you that day. I'm sorry.'

'You were,' Anna said, 'but it's very hard to have someone else come in and tell you something about your own kid. I tried to tell James, too, and he didn't believe me either. You're not alone, Ingrid. Accepting that your child has a problem is really difficult for any parent.'

'Well, thank you. The problem is Denis. He relies on me so much. Our personal lives are completely intertwined with our work. He's a workaholic and expects the same from me. I love my job, but I do know that I need to focus more on Bella now.'

'Well, if it's any comfort, I promise I'll keep an eye on her when she's here and I'll call you if I see anything that worries me. How does that sound?'

'Great, and I really appreciate you looking out for her.'

Anna smiled. 'Sure we're all family now. A patchwork, but a family.'

Ingrid watched every bite Bella put into her mouth. It wasn't a lot, but at least she didn't leave the table to throw up. Baby steps, the therapist had told Ingrid. She'd reassured her that they'd caught it early and that Bella spoke very positively about missing food and wanting to have a healthy approach to it again. She had admitted that she'd gone too far. The therapist felt that these were all positive signs that Bella would recover well, although she had cautioned Ingrid not to force her to eat or make mealtimes a battleground, but rather to encourage her gently. Ingrid was doing her best to obey those instructions.

Milly was holding court, telling an amusing story about one of her Bridezilla clients. Everyone was hanging on her every word, except Denis, who was checking his emails, and Anna, who was glaring at Milly.

Interesting, Ingrid thought. Was she jealous? Were Milly's youth and magnetic personality threatening to Anna?

Ingrid watched Anna's reaction when the whole table burst out laughing at Milly's punchline. She looked positively thunderous.

Ingrid thought Conor and Milly looked much more like a couple than Conor and Anna did. Conor looked and acted younger than he was and Milly must only have been in her early twenties. Conor was wearing a very tight-fitting shirt that stuck to his muscles, and Milly was in a tight dress that showed off her cleavage and her curvy bum. They matched.

Anna dressed more conservatively and, while very pretty, looked like a woman in her late thirties. She was far more suited to James than to Conor. So why was she looking so put out? She had left Conor, so it seemed futile to be annoyed that her family liked Milly. Wasn't that a good thing?

Milly leant over and placed a hand on Denis's arm. 'So, Denis, what do you do, then? I hear you're minted.'

Denis laughed, disarmed by her candour. 'I'm in property.'

'What age were you when you made your first million?'

'Twenty-nine.'

'My goal is to make my first million from my hair extensions in the next four years, so I'll be twenty-seven.'

'I like your confidence.'

'No point being a wilting violet in the world of business. Am I right?' Milly grinned.

'Yes, you are.'

'I'm working on perfecting my products right now. They have to be exactly right before I can start selling them. You only get one chance to impress people. If I do someone's hair and they don't like it, they'll never book me again. So if I try new hair extensions and I don't rate them, I'll never buy them again. It's all about the quality of the product and the price point.'

'Yes, but people will always pay more for good quality,' Denis said. 'Don't forget that.'

'Oh, I know, Denis, you're dead right there. Better to have one really good lipstick than three cheap ones.'

Denis laughed. 'I don't know much about lipstick, but I know that my hotels are renowned for having the most comfortable beds. I spent more money than I had at the time, sourcing the best-quality beds for my first hotel, and I've never regretted it.'

'OMG, the beds are amazing,' Bella said. 'Grace, you have to experience sleeping in them. You should come over sometime.'

Ingrid was surprised. Bella had always said Grace was quiet and seemed to think they were too different to be friends. Clearly, that had changed. It was a good thing. Grace was a bright, hard-working, focused girl who was going places. Ingrid was delighted they were getting closer.

'We should book in for a night.' Milly winked at Conor.

'We could certainly test out those mattresses.' Conor grinned.

'Dad!' Grace made a *eww* sound, but she was smiling.

'What?' Jack asked.

'Nothing,' Anna snapped, and stood up abruptly to take everyone's plates.

Milly jumped up to help her.

'Sit down,' Anna barked. 'You're a guest. James can help.'

Milly quickly sat down again and looked to Conor, who rolled his eyes and put his arm around her. 'She's in a mood, just ignore her,' he said quietly.

Denis tucked his phone into his pocket and stood up. 'I'm afraid I have to go.'

'We haven't had dessert yet. Just wait another fifteen minutes and I'll come with you.' Ingrid wanted to stay until the end of lunch. Anna had gone to a lot of trouble and she did feel she owed her for keeping an eye on Bella – and, truth be told, she was enjoying watching the dynamics at the table.

'Sorry, darling, I need to go now. I'll send the car back for you.'

Ingrid sighed. There was no point in arguing with Denis. He had always, and would always, put work first.

'Okay, send George back to pick me up in half an hour.'

'Stay longer, Mum?' Bella asked.

'Okay, an hour.'

Anna came back in and plonked the dessert on the table with a bang.

38

Anna was flinging dishes into the dishwasher and muttering under her breath.

'The lunch is going really well, don't you think?' James placed the dirty cutlery in the basket.

'Well, Milly's a big hit anyway. Everyone's mad about Milly.'

James didn't get it. Why was Anna annoyed that everyone liked Milly? She was great. She was making a huge effort to get on with everyone and was keeping the conversation flowing with funny stories and easy chat. She also seemed to be a really good influence on that tosser Conor. He was behaving like a human being and hadn't said or done anything to wind anyone up or insult them.

'What's wrong, darling? For once everyone's getting along and having a nice time. I thought you'd be pleased. Even your ex is behaving.'

Anna stood up, holding a dirty plate. 'I can see that,' she hissed. 'I can see that Conor is a changed man. He barely got out of bed for me, but in a few short months he's changed completely for her. What kind of magic wand does she have? Why did I get the crappy Conor and she swoops in and gets the good one?'

James wasn't sure what to say. Anna was shaking with rage. Was she jealous? Did she see this new version of Conor and regret leaving him?

'It's good that he's improving, isn't it? And that the kids like her?'

'Oh, the kids love her. It's all Milly this and Milly that. Every-one loves Milly.'

'Come on, Anna, try to see this as the positive it is. Conor is happy and your kids like her. If Milly was some awful woman the children loathed, you'd be really upset.'

'I know it's a good thing. I just don't need her shoved in my face.'

'But you invited her.'

'I know I bloody did, but I didn't think she'd have everyone eating out of the palm of her hand, including you, by the way.'

'I . . . well . . . I was just being friendly.'

Anna rinsed a plate under the tap and placed it in the dishwasher. 'It's hard, James. It's hard when a much younger, gorgeous woman swoops into your life and everyone is besotted with her. When you see your ex growing into the person you begged him to be. When you see your kids rushing over to hug her and chat to her. When she makes step-parenting look so bloody easy while I find it so hard. I just need a minute to process it all. Okay?'

James nodded. He got it now. Milly did make it all look effortless. She had Jack adoring her while he himself was still struggling to connect with the boy. And he could see that Grace and even Bella were mad about her.

James put his arm around Anna. 'You've changed me and made me a better man.'

Anna rested her head on his shoulder. 'No, I haven't. You were lovely when I met you. I'll be fine. I'm just a bit jealous of how easy Milly makes it all look.'

'It's early days. Her shine may wear off.' James grinned. He kissed her cheek. 'Come on, let's go back out and have some of that cake you flung on the table.'

Anna giggled. 'I was having a moment.'

'I'll pour you a large glass of wine. It'll help take the edge off.'

'I've had three already.'

They both burst out laughing.

'I'll be an alcoholic before this day is over,' Anna said, as she stepped back into the room.

James picked up a large knife to cut the cake with and headed back to the table.

'I want to cut the cake,' Jack shouted. 'Mum hid money in it. I want to find the money.'

'No, Jack, it's a very sharp knife. Let James do it,' Anna said.

'No way, mate, you could chop your finger off.' Conor pulled Jack back, but he wriggled away.

'Come on, James – please?'

James spotted an opportunity to be the non-strict parent. He could say yes and prove himself to be on Jack's side for once. 'Okay. Be very careful, though.'

'Thanks, James.' Jack beamed at him and grabbed the knife.

Jack put his left hand on the cake and pushed down to feel for the hidden money and with his right hand he stuck the knife into the cake.

'*Arrrrrrgh.*'

'Jack!' Anna screamed.

James froze. Conor leapt up and yanked the knife from Jack's hand.

Blood spurted everywhere. Ingrid grabbed a napkin and handed it to Conor, who wrapped it around the bloody finger.

'The tip. You have to find the tip!' Milly shouted. 'They can sew it back on.'

Anna dug her hand into the cake and produced the tip of Jack's index finger. 'Ice. Grace, get me some ice or a bag of frozen peas or something.'

Grace raced off and came back with a bag of frozen broccoli.

'Hold it tightly,' Anna told Conor.

Jack was sobbing hysterically in his father's arms.

'You're okay, big man, it's going to be okay. I promise,' Conor tried to soothe him.

'I'm sorry, Jack, I –' James tried to apologize, but Conor cut across him.

'You bloody moron. Stay away from my kid,' he roared. Then, turning to Anna, he said, 'Hold the finger tight and get him into the car. I'll drive.'

'I'll come with you,' James said.

Conor spun on his heels. 'Get the hell away from me and my son.'

James looked to Anna. She had blood all over her top and she was crying.

'I told you not to give him the knife. Why didn't you listen? For God's sake, James, he's ten.' She turned and walked out of the room with Conor.

James stood at the front door, feeling sick, and watched them drive off. He felt a hand on his shoulder. It was Milly.

'Jack'll be all right, kids bounce back, and Anna and Conor will calm down. They just got a fright.'

James wasn't so sure about that.

Milly clapped her hands. 'Right. Let's clear this up so Anna comes home to a nice clean house.'

James watched as Milly went over to Grace and put an arm around her. 'You okay? It was a shock to see that.'

Grace nodded. 'Will they be able to sew the tip back on?'

'Of course they will. He'll be like new. My cousin ripped half his finger off when the car door slammed on it. They sewed it back on and you wouldn't even notice. Why don't I make you a sugary tea for the shock? Sit down on the couch.' She looked around. 'James, I think you need a stiff drink. Sit down there beside Grace and I'll get you one.'

Milly delivered their drinks and then got to work.

She, Ingrid and Bella were a great team. They had the table cleared, dishwasher filled and running, pots steeping and the hired table and chairs folded and stacked in the hall within an hour.

315

'Grace could help a bit. I think she's okay now,' Bella said, as Grace lay on the couch with her feet up.

'No. I'm still suffering from shock,' Grace said, winking at her.

'Liar.' Bella threw a cushion at her.

'I'd like a chocolate biscuit for my shock.' Grace grinned.

'Sod off.' Bella laughed.

James was still genuinely in shock. Grace got up to get her own biscuit and Bella sat down beside him.

'It wasn't your fault, Dad,' she said.

'Oh, Bella, it was. I should never have given him the bloody knife. I was trying to be nice.'

'That's your problem, James.' Ingrid sat down opposite them, a tea-towel in her hand. 'You always try to be nice.'

'Mum,' Bella said sharply, 'he's upset.'

'I know he is. Look, James, the boy is a walking car crash. If he hadn't cut himself with the knife, he'd have injured himself some other way. He can't sit still. Giving him the knife was not your finest moment, but they can't blame you.'

James rubbed his eyes. 'Unfortunately, I think they very much do blame me.'

'They're just upset. They'll calm down when they see it's only a small injury.'

'Mum, to be fair, he cut the top of his finger off.'

'It's not a big deal really, Bella,' Ingrid continued.

'It is when it's your child,' James said. 'Come on, Ingrid, if Denis had handed Bella a sharp knife, aged ten, and she'd cut her finger off, you'd have been furious.'

Ingrid sat back in the couch and folded the tea-towel. 'True, but after the initial shock I'd have got perspective.'

'I hope so. Jesus, step-parenting is hard going.' James rubbed his eyes.

Ingrid smiled. 'I'm so glad Claire had left home by the time I met Denis. I don't think we'd have lasted a week if she'd lived there full-time.'

'Really?' Bella was surprised.

'God, yes, she's a royal pain in the arse.'

'Claire isn't that bad,' Bella defended her step-sister.

'Yes, she is.'

'I suppose, if I'm being honest, Anna probably doesn't find me that easy,' Bella admitted.

James smiled. 'You could definitely try harder.'

'I guess.'

'Anna is a good person,' Ingrid said.

James was shocked. 'I'm glad you can see that Anna's a good person,' he said to Ingrid. 'I got the impression you didn't like her.'

'I was too quick to judge.'

'So unlike you.' James grinned.

'Sod off.' Ingrid laughed. 'It's not as if you and Denis are best pals.'

'It's hard to get close to someone who spends their life with their head in their phone. He's worse than any teenager.'

Ingrid sighed. 'He's obsessed with work. And, yes, I know I am too, but he's on a whole other level and it's got much worse since he expanded the business to America.'

'I like Denis. He never bothers me and he's super-generous,' Bella said loyally.

'Anna is a very special person too,' James reminded her. 'She deserves a chance, and respect.'

'I know. I'm getting there with her. Baby steps, Dad,' Bella said.

Ingrid reached over and took James's phone from his hand.

'Speaking of phones, stop calling and texting Anna. Give her some space to sort out her son. She'll call when she can. She knows you feel bad. Don't crowd her, James.'

'I just want to make sure Jack is okay.'

'I know you do, but sending her fifteen messages is just going to annoy her. Let her focus on Jack. She doesn't need to deal with your guilty feelings right now.'

'You're right. I'm going to have a shower. I'm covered in blood.' He held out his hand for his phone. 'I promise to stop calling.'

While James was upstairs, Milly, Ingrid and the girls finished tidying up the last bits and pieces. Ingrid had called the driver, George, and told him not to come. She'd let him know when she was ready to go.

'Wow, the place looks tidier and cleaner than ever,' Grace said. 'Mum'll be thrilled.'

'It'll be nice for her to come home and put her feet up,' Milly said.

Grace's phone beeped. 'It's a message from Mum. Jack's having the tip sewn back on and apparently everything is going to be okay.' Grace beamed.

'That's great news. What a relief. Sit down, girls. I'll make us all tea,' Ingrid said.

Bella and Grace sat at the kitchen table. Bella listened to her mum chatting to Milly. Ingrid was giving Milly advice on setting up her business. Milly was listening closely to everything she said. Bella felt proud that her mum was so clever and that she was offering to help Milly.

'I wish I'd listened more in maths class,' Milly said. 'You're brilliant.'

'I'm good with figures, but I haven't got a creative bone in my body,' Ingrid admitted. 'I've had the same haircut and worn the same clothes for years. I'd love to have a bit more style, like you.'

Milly studied Ingrid. 'Would you consider shaking things up a bit? You'd look ten years younger if you cut your hair into a sharp bob and threw in a few highlights.'

'Really?'

'Yep. No offence, but you have a terrible haircut and you need to change your hair colour. It's too dark for your skin tone. I could sort it out for you right now. I have all my gear in the boot of the car.'

'Go on, Mum.' Bella was excited. She'd love her mum to be cooler. Her hair was so boring – dark brown, shoulder length, cut straight across. No layers, no colour, no shape.

Ingrid put her hand up to her hair. 'Well, I don't know . . . I suppose I could.'

'Do it, Ingrid,' Grace said. 'Milly is the best. She did my highlights for me.'

Ingrid examined Grace's hair. 'They do look lovely.'

'I'd recommend some caramel highlights for you,' Milly said, as she studied Ingrid's hair.

'I'm not sure about that. I don't want to look ridiculous.'

'Mum, just do it. You'll look so much better,' Bella urged.

Milly put her hands on Ingrid's shoulders. 'Trust me, you'll be happy with the result.'

'Oh, what the hell, let's do it.'

'Woo-hoo!' Bella was thrilled. Her mother never did anything spontaneous and she was so conservative in her look. She was dying to see what Milly would do.

Ninety minutes later, Ingrid looked like a different person.

'OMG!' Bella squealed, when Milly finished blow-drying Ingrid's hair. 'You look incredible.'

Ingrid walked over to the mirror above the mantelpiece. She turned, twisted and ran her hands through her hair.

'Do you think she likes it?' Milly whispered to Bella.

'I don't know, but I think it's fab.'

'She looks so much younger.' Grace gazed at Ingrid's transformation.

Ingrid turned around slowly and beamed across the room at Milly. 'You are a genius. I love it!'

Milly threw her hands into the air. 'Phew! I was worried there for a second.'

'I should have done it years ago.' Ingrid laughed. 'It's fantastic.'

'You look amazing, Mum,' Bella gushed.

'I feel younger and fresher and lighter. Thank you, Milly.'

Milly gave a little bow. 'Right, I'm knackered. I need a chocolate brownie to give me a boost.' She picked a large one from the plate. 'Yum,' she said chewing. 'I probably should have taken the smaller one, but what the hell? I love brownies and, besides, no man wants to be with a toothpick. What's sexy about that? We women need something to wiggle.' She wiggled her own bum. 'Am I right, ladies?'

'Absolutely.' Ingrid reached over for a brownie. Grace tucked in to one too.

Bella thought Milly was gorgeous and super-hot. She was right: being skinny wasn't sexy. The brownies looked delicious. Bella reached over and picked up the smallest. She was sick of being hungry.

39

Jack lay in the double bed while Anna fussed around him. He held up his bandaged finger like a beacon, shouting, '*Ooow!*' whenever she got within a foot of it. James tried not to roll his eyes.

Taking a deep breath, he asked cheerily, 'How are you feeling today, Jack?'

'Wrecked. I didn't sleep well.'

Neither did I on the bloody couch that's ruining my back, James thought. 'Oh dear. Maybe you'd sleep better in your own bed,' he suggested.

Anna, who was pulling the covers up around Jack's chest, spun around. 'No, James, I want to keep an eye on him. Jack needs to be minded. He's been through a lot.'

And it's all my fault. How many times did he have to apologize? He'd told her and Jack that he was sorry a million times. *He* hadn't sliced the bloody kid's finger off: Jack had done it all by himself.

Anna had been icy since the accident. In the three days since it had happened, she'd barely spoken to James.

'Jack, pet, keep your hand up on the pillow. Remember, you need to keep it higher than your heart for a few days to reduce the swelling.'

Jack grumbled and put his hand on the pillow.

'Well, I'm off to work. Jack, is there anything you'd like me to bring home later? Any special treat?' James asked.

'I don't want anything from you,' Jack said. Then, clearly seeing a wasted opportunity, he said, 'Actually, get me a big bag of M&Ms and a big bag of Gummy Bears.'

'James!' Anna snapped.

'What?' What had he done now?

Anna pulled him outside the bedroom onto the landing and shut the door behind her.

'For God's sake, he doesn't need you buying him lots of junk to make him hyper. I'm trying to keep him calm and quiet so he doesn't do any further damage to his finger. He's already scarred for life.'

'I don't think a few sweets will do much harm and he seems to be recovering well. It was only the tip.'

'Only the tip?' Anna hissed. 'Your fingertips are full of nerves and extremely sensitive. It's a very painful injury. His finger will be sensitive now and could be painful for months.'

'Anna, I didn't mean to sound flippant, but you said yourself the doctor reckoned that Jack will be fine. He's a strong boy, and he'll bounce back in no time.'

'Eventually. I'd like to see how you'd be if I cut Bella's finger off. My God, Ingrid would probably sue me for negligence and Bella would be lording it over me for life. But I'm supposed to be fine about this after barely three days?'

James sighed. Nothing he said was right. 'Anna, I'm sorry it happened. I wish I could go back and change it, but I can't.'

'No, you can't.'

'What can I do to make it up to you?'

'You don't have to make it up to me. You need to make it up to Jack. He's the one who lost his finger.'

The tip of his finger. 'I'm trying to, Anna.'

'Buying him junk isn't going to cut it, James. You need to spend time with him.'

'I've tried to talk to him, but he tells me to get out every time I go into the room.'

'Suck it up, James. Your daughter did the same to me for months. But I kept trying and now Bella and I are getting on better. Not brilliantly, but better. You have to keep trying.'

I am bloody trying. But how the hell am I supposed to get to know a kid who roars at me to go away every time I see him?

'I will.'

'Good, because you have a lot of work to do to earn his trust again after the whole incident.'

Trust? He hadn't hacked Jack's finger off. It was an accident!

The doorbell rang. James went down to answer it. It was Conor.

'There he is, the man of the moment, the child-stabber. The gobshite who maimed my son. All that time spent studying and you're too stupid to keep a sharp knife away from a kid.'

James gripped the door handle and forced himself to resist the urge to slam the door in Conor's incredibly irritating face.

Conor pushed past him. 'Where's my boy? Jack, where are you?'

Lolling about in my fucking bed, James almost said, but managed to restrain himself.

'Up here, Dad,' Jack shouted.

Anna came down the stairs. 'Hi, Conor.'

'How is he?'

'Better, but still very sore.'

'Poor thing. I'll hang out with him now if you want to go to the surgery or get a bit of time out.'

'That'd be great, thanks.' Anna smiled at her ex. 'I need to change the dressing now, so if you could help me distract him, that'd really help.'

'Of course. I'll have him so distracted he won't even notice.'

They walked up the stairs, chatting about their son.

James stood in the hall feeling like an outsider in his own home. 'Bye, Anna,' he said quietly and left for work.

Anna listened as Grace told her all the 'cool things' that Milly and Conor had planned for the weekend.

'Milly's taking me with her on a photo shoot and then she got tickets through a client for the pre-screening of the new movie with Harry Styles. How cool is that? Milly is the best.'

'And on Sunday Dad's taking me to see Milly's cousin playing football. He's brilliant. He plays for Shamrock Rovers,' Jack piped up.

Anna gripped her mug of tea. Milly. Milly. Milly. 'Are you sure you feel up to a football match? I don't want anyone bumping into your finger.'

'I'm fine, Mum. It's been a whole week,' Jack said. 'It's not even that sore any more.'

'Okay, I'm just worried about you.'

'He's fine, Mum. Stop fussing,' Grace said. 'Dad and Milly will look after him.'

'I feel a bit sorry for Milly,' Jack said.

'Why?'

'She has nightmares.'

'What?'

'She screams sometimes and shouts Dad's name. Conor, CONOR!' When I said it to Dad, he said she has nightmares and sometimes wakes up and shouts his name because she's so scared.'

Grace snorted into her hand.

'It's not funny, Grace. Nightmares are scary,' Jack said.

Bloody hell, they were obviously at it all the time. Anna and James hadn't been intimate in ages. James had been on the couch again since Jack's accident and he was extremely grumpy about it, which Anna thought was unfair considering it was kind of his fault that Jack had cut himself.

The doorbell rang.

'It's Dad and Milly!' Jack raced out to answer it, followed by Grace.

Anna followed them and felt like crying when Jack hugged

Milly tightly. He had never hugged James and, if she was being honest, she didn't think he ever would.

'Hi, guys, are you ready for a fun weekend?' Milly said.

'Yes!' they answered.

'It's going to be epic.' Conor grinned at them.

'I just need to talk to you about the football match you're taking Jack to,' Anna said. 'I'm worried about him being jostled.'

'I totally understand,' Milly said, 'so I've organized for us to meet three of my cousins who are all big strong lads and they're going to stand around Jack to protect him as well as Mr Muscles here.' Milly pinched Conor's arm and giggled.

'Okay, and what's this photo shoot you're taking Grace to?'

'Anna,' Conor snapped, 'it's all fine. Relax, will you? Stop giving Milly the tenth degree.'

'No, babe, it's okay. I'm happy to tell Anna more. It's a shoot for *Image* magazine. I thought it'd be a bit of fun and Grace seems keen.'

'I am!' Grace beamed.

Anna felt a wave of emotion rising inside her. They were all so happy and excited and she suddenly felt so alone. Her kids wanted to be with their dad now, not with her and James. Bella didn't like her, and she was arguing with James all the time. She wanted to be wrapped up in Conor and Milly's bubble of happiness.

'Okay, well, have fun,' she managed to croak.

'Oh, we will.' Conor picked Jack up and swung him over his shoulder. Jack roared laughing. Grace linked Milly's arm and chatted about the photo shoot. They looked like a family, a happy one.

Anna closed the door and went upstairs to cry into her pillow.

'ARE YOU KIDDING ME?' Bella stormed into her bedroom.

Anna quickly wiped her face and turned around. 'What's wrong now?' she asked wearily.

'I'll tell you what's wrong. Jack has used all of my Chanel Coco Mademoiselle foaming shower gel.'

Was she seriously having a meltdown about bloody shower gel? Anna sat up. 'Bella, there are people dying of hunger and disease. It's shower gel.'

'What do hunger and disease have to do with this? I'm pissed off, Anna. I am sick of your idiot son using my stuff.'

'Don't call him that, Bella.'

'Well, he is.'

'No, he isn't. He's a kid who just grabbed the shower gel he saw first. He didn't do it to annoy you. If your shower gel is so important to you, leave it in your bedroom.'

'He came into my room yesterday looking for a highlighter. He has no boundaries. I hate this house. I have no privacy and it's a dump.'

'Oh for goodness' sake, calm down. Do you always have to be so dramatic about everything? You're just not used to sharing, and you know what? It's good for you to learn, Bella. It'll make you less selfish.'

'This isn't sharing, this is abuse of my things. He didn't take a bit of my gel, he used the whole bloody bottle. And as for calling me selfish, that's rich. My dad is sleeping downstairs while Lord Jack sleeps in his bed. Jack gets away with murder in this house and you treat him like some kind of prince. Maybe if you said no to him more often, he wouldn't be such an annoying little shit.'

'Enough! Do not speak about Jack like that and do not tell me how to parent my child. Your dad is sleeping on the couch because Jack is traumatized by what happened and is in serious pain.'

'Oh, please, it was the tip of his finger, not his arm. Now who's being dramatic?'

'Go away, Bella.'

'Not until you promise to tell Jack to stay the hell away from my room, me and my things.'

Anna stood up and tried to control her fury. 'Bella!' she shouted. 'You live in a house with two great kids. You're lucky to have them as your siblings. The whole world doesn't revolve around you. Stop being such a selfish, self-centred cow, cop on and leave me alone. I'm not in the mood for your bullshit, so shut up and get out.'

'You might need to calm down, Anna.' James was standing in the doorway.

Shit, shit, shit. How much of the conversation had he heard? Anna's stomach sank. She had lost her cool and now James had witnessed it.

'I'm calling Mum to see if I can stay with her.' Bella stormed out of the room.

Silence.

Anna tried to think of something to say, but nothing came to mind. She wasn't sorry she'd snapped. Bella had pushed her too far too often, and she needed a swift, sharp shock to knock her out of it.

James pulled off his tie, hung up his jacket and leant against the dressing-table in the corner of the room, as far away from Anna as he could get.

'We need to talk,' he said quietly.

Anna nodded. They did, and she knew it wasn't going to be pretty.

40

The sun rose behind them, sending beams through the kitchen window. Anna and James sat opposite each other, holding hands. Anna was sobbing.

'I think we need it,' James said gently. 'It's only temporary.'

Anna sniffed. 'I know, but what if you decide not to come back?'

James kissed the back of her hand. 'I will come back.'

Anna wasn't sure she believed him. They'd been up all night, talking in circles. But what they kept coming back to was that theirs wasn't a happy household. Every time they seemed to be making headway, something happened to scupper them again. It wasn't good for their children, they both knew that. They were making their children unhappy, that was the bottom line. And they could not in good faith continue to do that.

'I love you,' she sobbed.

'I love you too. That hasn't changed,' James reassured her.

'I just wish it wasn't so hard. What if you realize you're happier without me and my baggage?'

James's eyes welled. 'I won't, I'm not.'

'Maybe it's just the wrong time for us,' Anna said. 'Grace and Bella will be eighteen in three years.'

'And Jack will be eighteen in eight years,' James said.

'So should we just have a really long break and meet up again in eight years?' Anna gave him a watery smile.

'Well, without the children, it would definitely be a hell of a lot easier. Remember how good and easy it was before we blended our families together?'

'I know. But we do have children,' Anna whispered, her voice breaking.

'I want to be with you, Anna.'

'And I want to be with you.'

'But can we do it if our kids aren't happy? Bella's asked me so many times if she can move in with Ingrid full-time. I'm her dad, and I need to be there for her. And Jack, well, he fundamentally hates me no matter what I do, and I don't see that changing.'

'He doesn't hate you,' Anna said, for the millionth time that night. 'He just hasn't got to know you properly yet.'

'It's been eight months, Anna, and I've tried, I really have.'

'I know, but he's still young. He'll be more mature soon and you'll get along better.'

'He thinks I broke up your marriage and he resents our time together. I don't want him to think I'm pulling you away from him.'

Anna wiped her eyes. Jack did resent James. He blamed him for everything, the break-up with Conor, the house move, the new sibling, the finger . . . everything.

But if James didn't come back, Anna couldn't afford the rent on the house. She'd have to move again, and that would be more upheaval in their lives. She'd have to go back to work full-time, too. She could move into town, closer to their schools and to Conor. It would probably make the kids happier, but what about James? She loved him. Did having kids mean you had to give up on love? Did you have to sacrifice your own happiness for them? It didn't seem to mean that for Ingrid or Conor, so why for them? Anna had spent her whole life doing everything for her kids. Can't I have this, God? she thought. Can't I have love in my life *and* be a good mum?

Apparently not. None of their children were happy. The idea that Grace was just waiting until she could go to university, get away from her and Conor and all their drama, burnt Anna to the core. She didn't want her daughter wishing her life away. She wanted her to enjoy her time at home. She wanted Grace to have happy memories of her childhood. She wanted Jack to be happy, too. Had this whole love affair been a horrendous mistake?

James reached over and stroked her cheek. 'You know, over seventy per cent of second marriages and relationships fail when there are children involved.'

She nodded. 'I don't want to be a statistic, though.'

'We had an uphill battle from the start.' James took his glasses off and rubbed his eyes. 'It's not our fault. We've thrown the kitchen sink at it.'

'Maybe parents with kids just don't get to have a romantic life until the kids are adults,' Anna said.

'I don't know,' James said. 'I thought it would have fallen into place by now.'

'I don't want to be alone.' Anna felt herself getting upset again. She loved James, she wanted to be with him, but not with all the drama. She wanted it to be like it was before, romantic and passionate and loving. She knew passion faded – she'd been married to Conor for long enough to grasp that – but she really loved James and she knew he loved her too, deeply and truly. But once they'd blended their families, it had felt like they were trying to push a rock up a mountain.

'I want to be with you, Anna. Let's take this time to see if we can figure out a way to make it work where everyone is happy. Well, happy-ish.'

'I'd take happy-ish.'

James stood up. 'I'm going to pack a bag and then we can tell the kids. I'll drop Bella to Ingrid for her week.'

Anna felt her stomach drop and her heart ache. 'Oh, God.'

'I know.' He held her close. 'It's so bloody hard.'

'So we can't communicate at all, right?'

'I think that's the best thing. A full break to clear our heads. See how the kids respond to it. See how we respond to it. It should give us some clarity. I hope.'

'Okay. So we meet up in a month's time and see where we're at?'

'Yes.'

James went up to pack his bag.

The kids were sitting around the kitchen table. Jack shovelled cereal into his mouth, Bella stared at her phone while eating yogurt and blueberries, and Grace spread peanut butter on a bagel.

Anna felt as if she was going to throw up. James dropped his suitcase at the front door and came into the kitchen.

Clearing his throat, he said, 'Kids, we have something important to talk to you about.'

'Oh, my God, if this is another lame family camping trip, I'm telling you right now that I'm not going,' Bella drawled.

'Me neither, unless it's a trip to Disneyland. Is it, Mum?' Jack asked.

Anna shook her head.

'Can it be quick? I have early-morning sport today.' Grace bit into her bagel.

'Well, the thing is, you may have noticed that Anna and I have been arguing a bit lately and . . . well . . . combining the families has been more complicated than we first thought. You kids don't seem to be very happy, and while we thought things would settle down after a time, it hasn't really happened like that. So, we've decided it's best that we take a break.'

'What do you mean, take a break?' Grace asked.

'I'm going to move back into my apartment with Bella for a month and you'll stay here with your mum, and we can all have the space to think about things.'

'It's for the best,' Anna said, holding back tears. 'We don't want you kids living in a house where everyone is constantly arguing. It's all been much more challenging than James and I thought. We were probably naïve and I'm really sorry, to all of you. I know that this is hard for you, guys, but I promise we didn't take this decision lightly.'

'So are you breaking up or is it a break? I don't get it,' Bella said.

'We're taking some time apart to think about how to move forward, or whether that's an option.'

'So you're moving out?' Jack said.

'Yes.'

'I'm taking Bella's room,' he shouted.

'Jack!' Grace glared at him.

'What?'

'Mum's upset.'

'Are you, Mum?'

'Yes, love, I am. I'm upset about making everyone turn their lives upside-down and then it not working out the way I thought it would. I'm sorry that you and Grace and Bella haven't been happy here. I wanted this to be a happy home, somewhere you could come home from school and feel warm and loved. But it didn't work out like that and I'm sorry.'

'We've really tried,' James said. 'And maybe, with some space, we'll be able to find a way back.'

'So what do I do about all my stuff in my bedroom?' Bella asked.

'We'll figure that out,' James said.

'I'm sorry, Mum,' Grace said.

'It's okay, sweetheart. It's just life. It's complicated and messy sometimes.'

'I'm sorry too,' Bella said. 'But maybe it is for the best. You guys are arguing a lot these days.'

'I'm never getting a girlfriend. All couples do is fight,' Jack said.

Anna swallowed the lump in her throat. What was she teaching her kids? That relationships were toxic? The whole reason she'd left Conor was so that she could be in a healthy, equal, loving relationship with James. But even with all the love they had, they'd ended up arguing all the time.

'Right, well, we'd better go.' James kissed Anna. 'I'll see you in a month.'

She nodded, unable to speak. What was going to change in a month? They'd still have kids, they'd still have step-children who didn't like them. She felt all hope drain from her as she watched James and Bella walk out of the door.

41

Conor's slice of toast hung in the air.

'What?'

'Mum and James have broken up,' Jack repeated.

'No, Jack, they're taking a break. They haven't split up,' Grace explained, trying to make it sound less dramatic than it actually was.

'Oh, no,' Milly said.

'I'm glad.' Jack reached over and spiked another sausage with his fork.

'Well, well, the big romance is not so perfect,' Conor said, grinning.

'They were fighting all the time,' Jack said.

'So where is James now?' Conor asked.

'He's gone back to his apartment, with Bella,' Grace said.

'Wow, interesting. So the professor has legged it back home.'

'Conor,' Milly snapped.

'What?' He shrugged. 'I'm just saying.'

'It's sad. I hope they can work it out,' Milly said.

'I hope they don't,' Jack said. 'I've got Bella's room now and it's *waaay* bigger than mine.'

'Good for you, Jack.' Conor fist-bumped him.

'How is your mum doing?' Milly asked Grace.

'She's pretty upset, thanks for asking.' Grace glared at her father.

'Well, I think it's a good thing for all of you, including your mum,' Conor said. 'None of you liked James and you all hated his daughter, so it's better that they split up. No point dragging it on.'

'It's not over, Dad, it's just a break, and I don't hate Bella at all.'

'I did in the beginning, but then she was kind of okay,' Jack said.

'Breaks rarely work,' Conor said.

'Well, this one might.' Grace was furious with her dad. Her mum was in bits and he had no empathy.

'Hopefully it will.' Milly patted her arm.

'Maybe Anna's just better on her own,' Conor said. 'Some women are. She's independent and strong and likes things her own way, so maybe she'll be happier now.'

'Just because she's independent and strong doesn't mean she doesn't want or deserve love in her life,' Milly said. 'I consider myself independent and strong and I'm with you.'

Go, Milly, Grace wanted to cheer.

'And your own daughter is strong and independent. Do you think she doesn't deserve to have a partner too?' Milly drove her point home.

Conor put down his fork. 'Jesus, Milly, keep your hair on. I'm just saying that some people aren't cut out for relationships and maybe Anna is one of them.'

'She was married to you for almost twenty years. I'd say she's pretty damn good at them,' Milly reminded him.

'I want to see my kids happy, and if Jack's happy they've split up, and he's got the big bedroom, then so am I.'

'Yeah!' Jack cheered.

'Well, I'm not,' Grace said, although in a way she was. For her, it meant less conflict in the house and more peace. But for her mum it meant heartbreak. It was so confusing to know how to feel.

'Look, all you kids can do is be nice to your mum and support whatever decision she makes,' Conor said. 'As long as it's the right one. Look at me and Milly. When you're with the right person, there's no hassle – it's just easy.'

'Yeah, but I don't have kids, Conor, so that makes it way less

335

complicated,' Milly reminded him. 'If I had a kid, we'd have had to get a bigger place and you'd have had to step-parent my kid, whether you liked them or not. It's not easy.'

'Well, then, maybe Anna needs to find someone with no kids.'

'You need to work on empathy, babe.' Milly wagged a blue fingernail at him.

'I don't know about that, but I do need to study for my next exam. Did I tell you that I aced the anatomy and physiology module?'

'He came top of the class,' Milly told them.

'Wow, Dad, that's so cool. Will you train me?'

'Course I will. You'll be as big as The Rock when I'm finished with you.' Conor playfully punched his son's arm.

'Well done, Dad.' Grace was delighted to see her father, for once, focused on his career. Milly really had worked wonders with him.

Milly parked outside Anna's house and helped the kids with their bags. She hesitated, then made the decision to go up to the front door with them. It felt wrong to just drop them off and drive away when she knew Anna was upset. Conor's lack of sympathy had really bothered her – it was a side of him she really didn't like – so she'd offered to drop the kids home. The last thing Anna needed was to see Conor and for him to say the wrong thing or put his big foot in it.

Anna opened the front door and Milly got a shock. She had aged five years. She looked exhausted, sleep-deprived. She had purple circles under her eyes and her whole body sagged as if the weight of the world was on her shoulders.

She smiled for the kids. 'Hi, guys, I missed you.' She hugged them tightly. Jack wriggled out from under her arms and ran into the house. Grace followed her brother.

'Thanks for dropping them back, Milly. Where's Conor?'

'He has an exam tomorrow so he's studying.'

'Wow! Who would have thought of Conor and studying in the same sentence?' Her voice held a hint of bitterness.

Milly thought it best to change the subject. 'Look, I hope you don't mind but the kids mentioned that things were a bit tough with you and James and I just wanted to say I'm sorry and I hope you work it out. That day you had the lunch here, I thought you seemed lovely together.'

Anna's face crumpled. 'I thought so too.' She sobbed. 'God, I'm a mess. I can't stop crying.'

'Here, let me make you a nice cuppa. You look like you could do with some company and I'm a good listener. Come on.' Milly took Anna's arm and led her into the empty kitchen. The kids had disappeared upstairs.

Milly put the kettle on and bustled around making tea and put on some toast, which she buttered thickly and cut into squares.

'Now, nothing like tea and toast when we're struggling.'

'Thank you,' Anna croaked. She picked up the toast and chewed slowly.

'So, have you been in touch with James at all?'

Anna shook her head. 'We said no contact for a month and then we'll meet up and decide what to do.'

'That's hard.'

'Yep, it sure is. When the only person you want to talk to about your problems, your best friend, is actually the person you can't call. I've gone to call him a hundred times, but I know we need to take the time to figure things out. We've been going around in circles for months. Things will be bad and then they'll settle a bit and I'll think, Yes, we can make it work, and then they kick off again. It's been so hard. I want this to work so badly, but the kids aren't happy. I've failed to give my two the happy home I'd imagined and it breaks my heart.'

Milly chose her words carefully. 'Anna, I grew up in a house

337

full of conflict. My dad was an alcoholic arsehole. But I always knew my mum loved me and that was enough. All kids need to know is that they're loved. Whatever happens between you and James, your two kids know they're loved by their mum and dad. A lot of kids don't get that lucky. Your kids are brilliant. They're happy, well-balanced children. You've done a great job, and Bella has that too. She's loved by two parents. So all of your kids are going to be fine.'

'Thanks, that's really nice of you to say. But if James and I break up, I'll have put my kids through all of this upheaval for nothing. I would have left Conor anyway, I was long done with that marriage, but I could have moved in nearby and not subjected them to a new neighbourhood, far away from their friends, a new step-dad and step-sister. I did it all because I fell in love. My sisters warned me that I was being too rash, acting too quickly, but I ignored them because I was all loved up in my little bubble of happiness and just presumed everything would slot into place. I was so stupid.'

Milly ate the toast that Anna had pushed aside. 'You weren't stupid, you were optimistic. What's wrong with that? If we all made decisions thinking they'd fail, sure we'd never do anything. You fell in love, you took a chance – you followed your heart. There's no crime here, Anna. Stop beating yourself up, and who knows? Maybe this break will give you and James the space to figure out how to make it all work.'

Anna sipped her tea. 'How do you make it look so easy?'

'What?'

'The way you've connected with my kids. I've tried so hard with Bella and we're still locking horns eight months later. How do you do it? I'm not going to lie, I feel a bit resentful of how easy you make it look.'

Milly smiled. 'First of all, let's be honest, I'm almost closer in age to the kids than I am to their parents. Second, I don't have any kids, so there's no baggage with me. And, third, I don't live

338

with your kids. I see them every second weekend and it's all fun and games. I don't have to get them to do homework or make lunches or pick up from school or give out to them for bad manners. I just get to be Fun Milly. You have the hard job of parenting. I don't.'

'I'm glad Conor met you. I'm glad my kids like you – it makes it easier for me when they're with Conor. I don't know what spell you've cast over him, but since he met you he's a much better dad, so thank you and please don't ever break up with him.'

Milly blushed. 'Well, thanks. I'm no magician, though. I think timing has a lot to do with Conor pulling up his socks. When you left him it gave him a real kick up the arse and I met him when he was ready to change. He's no picnic, though. We do have our tiffs.'

Anna shrugged. 'Tiffs are fine. Arguments are different.'

Anna's eyelids were drooping. It was time for Milly to go.

'I'll leave you to get an early night. I really hope you guys work it out, and if I can do anything, let me know. Grace has my mobile.'

Anna reached up and hugged her. Milly squeezed her back. She'd never imagined when she first met Anna that she'd be bear-hugging her in her kitchen. Life was strange and full of surprises.

42

James ordered a glass of white wine and loosened his tie. The restaurant was typical Ingrid – sparse, sterile, full of corporate types tapping furiously on their phones.

He put his into his pocket, and when the waiter handed him his wine, he sipped it slowly, savouring the crisp, cool feel of it slipping down his throat.

He felt tired right down to his bones. He had a constant knot in his stomach. He missed Anna so much it physically hurt. After ten days apart he was feeling worse, not better. He yearned to talk to her, to hold her, to tell her he loved her and that they could make it work, but he knew that was a lie. How could they make it work? They'd tried so hard and yet they'd failed.

His ex-wife arrived with her phone glued to her ear, as usual. She sat down opposite him and mouthed, 'Dry white wine.' James ordered her drink and waited patiently for Ingrid to finish her call.

'Sorry, hi.'

'Hi. So . . . why is a psychologist calling me to rearrange his appointment with our daughter and why was I not aware that she was seeing a psychologist, Ingrid?' James's tone was harsh: he was furious. They had always co-parented well. They didn't keep things from one another and Bella's happiness was always their mutual priority. But then, out of the blue, James had taken a call from a psychologist and was completely blindsided.

Ingrid thanked the waiter for her drink and took a long sip. 'I didn't tell you because I wanted to try to sort it out, and I hope I have. I honestly think she's going to be fine. But,' she sighed, 'Bella has been struggling with weight loss and food issues and vomiting.'

'What?'

'She's been vomiting up her food and not eating properly. She's developed an unhealthy relationship with food and her body. But the psychologist is confident she'll make a good recovery. She's already eating better, has put on four pounds and hasn't freaked out about it. The psychologist said that Bella began by wanting to lose a few pounds for the musical, then saw it as a way to have control over something when everything else in her life was changing. New home, new step-mother, new step-siblings and all that.'

James's heart sank. Anna had warned him. She'd seen the signs and he had dismissed her concerns. Oh, God, how had he missed that his daughter was struggling so much?

'Anna spotted it, but I didn't believe her.' James groaned, covering his face with his hands. He'd been so self-righteous, telling Anna, 'I think I know my own daughter better than you . . .' Poor Anna. All she'd wanted to do was help.

Ingrid leant forward. 'You're not alone. Remember, Anna came to my office and told me that she was worried about Bella and that she felt something was wrong. She told me that Bella was throwing up. I thought she was being interfering and overly dramatic. I was quite rude to her.'

James could just imagine how chilly Ingrid had been.

The waiter served them their food, soup for James, salad for Ingrid.

'How did we miss it?' he asked his ex-wife.

Ingrid put down her fork. 'Let's be honest, I probably had my head in my phone and my focus on work.'

James was shocked. He'd been thinking that was exactly how she'd missed Bella's problems, but he was very surprised to hear Ingrid admit to it so readily.

'And I've been distracted with Anna, trying to get to know her kids and struggling with Jack.'

'We've failed her, James,' Ingrid said.

'Yes, we have.'

'I've promised her that I'll try to pull back on work when I'm with her, and I think you need to be more present, too. Of course, it'll be easier for you to do that now you're back in the apartment alone with her and not dealing with step-children. I was sorry to hear about your break-up. Anna is a very nice person, but the situation was untenable.'

James frowned. 'It wasn't untenable, it was just complicated.'

'So is this a temporary break or permanent? I think you need to make a clear decision either way. It's not good for Bella to be in limbo. I always knew it wouldn't work out because you rushed into it. Moving in with Anna and her children so quickly was madness, but you wouldn't listen.'

Jesus Christ, he didn't need a bloody lecture on his decision-making. Ingrid could be so patronizing.

'It felt right at the time and it's still what I want. But, yes, I admit that I thought it would be easier than it proved to be.'

Ingrid placed her knife and fork together on the side of her plate and picked up her wine glass. 'How could you think that combining two families who barely knew each other was going to be easy?'

'I didn't think it was going to be easy,' James snapped, 'just not as difficult as it has been.'

'You fell in love and didn't think things through or listen to advice.'

James felt the hairs on the back of his neck prickle. Ingrid was so quick to judge. 'Well, Ingrid, you walked out on me and Bella when you met Denis and that wasn't the greatest of ideas either.'

Ingrid leant forward. 'Our marriage was long over by then and I didn't inflict a set of siblings on Bella. She only had to see

Claire once every few months. You, on the other hand, dumped our daughter into the middle of someone else's family and expected her to slot in.'

'Bullshit. Bella wasn't dumped into anyone's family. She became part of a joint family.'

'And how is that working out, James?'

James didn't want to admit to his ex-wife that he lay awake at night worrying that he'd rushed into it. That he was wondering if he'd made a huge mistake. But he needed to talk to someone.

'It's just so much more complicated than I could ever have imagined. I don't know if . . . if we're going to be able to fix it and get back together.'

'Do you still love Anna?'

'Yes.'

'Do you want to be with her?'

'Desperately.'

'Well, you look a mess, exhausted and miserable, so clearly you're not thriving without her.'

'I'm devastated.'

Ingrid sighed. 'Bella told me you've been very down. She's worried about you. Look, James, you need to figure out what you want, make a concrete decision and stick with it. This uncertainty is bad for everyone involved. Bella needs stability in her life. Do you really think you love Anna enough to take on her kids long-term?'

'I'm crazy about her.'

'Well, then, make it work. Stop wasting time fretting about it and figure out a way to fix it. After all the upheaval you've both caused your families and all the effort you've put into this relationship, you need to salvage it. All this chopping and changing is a disaster. Sort it out, James, for everyone's sake.'

Ingrid glanced at her phone and stood up. 'I have to go. Keep a close eye on Bella and make sure she stays on track with her eating.'

'I will.'

'I'm going to send you the psychologist's report so that you're fully in the loop. She also sent some recommendations for books we could read on the subject and I'll include those. The better armed we are, the better we can help Bella.'

'Okay. I'll read everything. And I'll tread softly with Bella.'

He watched as Ingrid tapped furiously on her phone. He felt weary. It was all very well for her to bark at him to 'fix it' and 'make it work', but it wasn't easy. But, then, if he did break up with Anna for good, it would all have been for nothing. All the disruption and the stress would have been pointless. He couldn't do that to Anna, or to her kids, or to Bella. He had to figure this out. Ingrid was right: the best way forward for all of them was to make one clear decision and stand by it. James's head throbbed as he paid the bill and walked slowly back to his office.

43

'Ouch. My goodness, Anna, what's wrong with you today? That was much sorer than my usual blood tests.'

Anna pulled the needle back and put the cap on the vial of blood. 'I'm sorry, Harriet, I didn't mean to hurt you.'

'Well, it wasn't that painful, but it wasn't your usual delicate touch. Are you all right? You look very peaky.'

'I'm fine, just slept badly,' Anna said, for the millionth time. All of her regular patients had commented on how pale she looked, how tired she seemed, how down in the dumps she was . . . What was wrong? They wanted to know, but she couldn't explain. It was too painful, and she didn't want to hear their advice because there was nothing anyone could say to make it better.

She had failed and that was that.

She looked at the schedule. Her next patient was Beyoncé Carter. Was someone having a laugh? She opened the door to ask Nadine what was going on, only to see her two sisters sitting in Reception.

'Beyoncé?' Anna asked.

'Yes,' Angela said, and strutted past her, followed by Anita.

Anna closed the door and her two sisters sat up on the patient bed, facing her.

'What's going on?'

'You tell us,' Anita said, crossing her arms.

'You refuse to meet us, you're avoiding our calls, you're always too busy to talk and we know you're miserable,' Angela stated.

'We're here to help.'

'No one can help,' Anna said. 'It's just an impossible situation.

I rushed into it, I was stupid. I was wrong to think that because James and I loved each other our kids would too. And you can say, "I told you so," at any time here.'

Anita pulled out a huge bar of chocolate from her bag. 'I didn't bring alcohol because you're in work and I don't want you to kill anyone, but you need chocolate.'

'You're not stupid – a bit impulsive maybe, but not stupid,' Angela said. 'You did rush into it, but sure you were in love and you thought everything would fall into place. Unfortunately, life isn't that simple, and kids can be right little feckers.'

'But it's our job to look after them, though, so until they leave home, you're stuck with them,' Anita added.

'That's so true,' Anna said. She sighed. 'If you decide to have children, you have to be prepared to sacrifice yourself for them. Their needs, wants, happiness and health come before yours. If they aren't happy, you aren't happy. They didn't choose to be born. We decided that so it's our responsibility to care for them and do everything in our power to give them a good life. That's the truth.'

'Yes, but you deserve to be happy too, Anna. Being a mother doesn't deny you the right to happiness,' Anita said.

'But if her happiness leads her to make decisions that make her kids unhappy, what does she do?' Angela wondered.

'She talks to her kids and tells them that she wants to be with James and asks them to be good about it. Or to suck it up,' Anita said.

'Would you say that to your kids? How do you think they'd respond?' Angela asked.

Anita sighed. 'Badly, and they'd make my life hell. But does that mean we can't live with the man we love if our kids don't like him?'

'Unfortunately, yes,' Angela said.

'You could just keep dating him and wait until Jack leaves home, then move in with him?'

'Kids don't move out until they're in their mid-twenties, these days,' Angela said. 'And that's if you're lucky.'

'Just another fifteen years then.' Anita sighed. She handed Anna more chocolate. 'Here, you need this.'

Anna held the chocolate in her hand. 'I've really messed up. I used to worry the kids were going to be badly affected by my arguing with Conor, but then I moved them out and away from their neighbourhood, into a house with a strange man and his daughter, and it was all for nothing. I tried to force Jack to like James and the whole thing was a disaster. I'm really worried that I've damaged the kids even more.' Anna began to cry.

Anita clicked her tongue and broke off a big piece of chocolate. 'Stop that. You haven't damaged anyone. You just put yourself first for once in your life and things were trickier than you'd hoped.'

'Grace and Jack are brilliant kids, with a great mum and a half-decent dad. They're fine,' Angela agreed.

'But what about you and James?' Anita asked. 'Is it definitely over, or are you still hoping?'

'We agreed to have one month with no contact, just time to think and see how it was panning out, then meet up and make a final decision. So I'm seeing him Wednesday week.'

'Right, that's a good plan,' Angela said. 'So there's definitely still hope. I reckon you'll set eyes on each other and realize you just have to be together and you'll have another crack at it. You're mad about each other.'

'But, as you've just pointed out, our love for each other isn't really enough to carry us all through. It can't carry a whole family.'

'Well, how are the kids taking it? Are they secretly missing each other? Do they realize the house is quiet and they actually preferred it the other way?'

'I wish,' Anna said. 'Nope, they seem very happy just the three of us. And obviously I'm not in touch with James, but

347

I can easily picture Bella being blissfully happy back in her nice, uncluttered apartment and only James to contend with. I'm sure she's thanking her lucky stars every day. I can't see her suddenly realizing she likes us lot and misses us. No chance.'

'You never know,' Anita said. 'Angela's right – you two are mad for each other. You'll probably decide it's all worth it.'

'Maybe,' Anna said doubtfully.

'I'm really sorry this has happened to you,' Anita said. 'Especially after the awful time you had with Conor.'

'Me too,' Angela said. 'You deserve to be happy.'

The two sisters put their arms around Anna and squeezed her tight, hoping that their love for her would infuse some comfort into her weary heart.

Grace woke up. It was dark and she was cosy under her duvet, but she needed to go to the toilet. She shouldn't have drunk that glass of water before bed. She crept out of her room and nearly jumped out of her skin when she saw a figure standing motionless outside her mother's bedroom, ear pressed to the door. She gasped and the figure turned around. It was Jack.

'What are you doing?' she whispered.

'Shush,' he said, putting his finger to his lips. 'Listen.'

Grace quietly moved towards him and she listened. She could clearly hear her mum crying, big sobs, but it sounded muffled, like she was pushing her face into the pillow.

'Come on,' she said to Jack, gently pulling him away. Reluctantly, he moved back from the door and allowed her to manoeuvre him into her room. 'Wait here a minute,' she said, tucking him up in her bed. 'I'll just run to the loo and come back.'

When she got back, Jack was fidgeting with her alarm clock, pressing buttons and rattling it.

'Stop, Jack,' Grace said. 'You're messing up the time.' She fixed the clock and put it out of his reach.

'Mum's crying,' he said. 'I hear her every night. I hate it. Is she crying because James is gone?'

Grace nodded. 'She misses him and it makes her sad.'

'But she's got you and me,' Jack said. 'It's nice being just us, isn't it?'

'It's okay,' Grace said. 'I didn't mind James, he was nice. And I was starting to get on with Bella. She was nicer than I first thought.'

'Yeah,' Jack said. 'She was good to watch movies with and she could be funny too.'

Grace didn't say anything.

'Is it over?' Jack asked. 'Are they never going to be boyfriend and girlfriend again?'

'I don't know.'

'I feel bad that Mum is sad, but I kind of hope James and Bella don't come back,' Jack admitted to his sister.

'But what if that means Mum is heartbroken, Jack? What about what makes her happy? When she met James, she was super-happy. Don't you remember how smiley she was?'

'Yeah,' Jack said, shrugging his shoulders. 'But when Mum was happy, Dad was sad. And now Mum is sad and Dad is happy with Milly. My head hurts. Why couldn't Mum and Dad just have stayed together in the first place?'

'Sometimes two people just aren't meant for each other, no matter how much they wish they were. Mum and Dad are very different. Dad and Milly are good together, don't you think? And Mum really loves James,' Grace said. 'He's good for her, Jack. He makes her happy. She worked really hard for years and never had any time for herself. It's lovely for her to be with someone who loves her and looks after her like James does.'

'Dad loves her.'

'Do you ever remember Mum and Dad laughing together or going out together or hugging or kissing or having fun?'

'Not really,' he said.

'Mum has all that with James.'

'I guess. I just find James . . . annoying.'

Grace put her hand on his shoulder. 'I know you do. Look, I hated moving here too. I hated having a step-sister. But Bella isn't so bad and James is actually nice. And if they break up for good, Mum is going to be heartbroken.'

'I don't want her to be heartbroken,' Jack said, looking tearful. 'But maybe she'll only be sad for a little bit. Like when I lost my favourite football boots and I cried for a few days but then I was okay.'

Grace shook her head and smiled at him. 'Jack, love is not like football boots.'

'So, you think she'd be sad for ever?'

'Not for ever, but for a long time.' Grace glanced at her clock. 'Now, time to go back to your bed. I need sleep.'

'I can't bear Mum being sad,' he said, as he climbed out of the warm bed.

'I know you can't,' Grace said. 'That's why we have to think about Mum, not just about ourselves.'

'So you think I should tell her I want James and Bella back?' he asked.

'I think you and I shouldn't really interfere,' Grace said. 'But whatever Mum and James decide, let's do our best to be happy for them. I mean, you're happy for Dad and Milly, aren't you? You don't mind Milly being around.'

Jack grinned. 'No, I love Milly. She's great.'

'Well, James and Bella aren't the worst. So if they say we're trying again, let's agree that you and I will try our hardest, for Mum.'

Jack looked doubtful, but he stuck out his little finger. 'Okay. Pinkie promise?'

Grace hooked his finger with hers. 'Pinkie promise.'

'Goodnight, Grace.'

Grace sighed. This stuff was so complicated, and it was even harder to explain it to a little kid. She looked at the clock: 3:23 a.m. She really hoped Anna would get some sleep. Her mum looked like she was about to keel over from tiredness at any moment. Something had to give.

44

Anna stood outside the bar and smoothed down her dress for the zillionth time. Her phone beeped. A text message.

Good luck, sis. We're rooting for you. Love conquers all. A&A

She smiled. Angela and Anita had helped her choose her outfit for the day. A dark green dress with high black shoe boots – 'You need to look sexy,' Anita had said – and a black velvet blazer. She felt a bit overdressed for a Wednesday evening at 6 p.m., but she did want to look good. She wanted James to remember how good she could look.

And she did look good, and most of that was thanks to Milly, who had kindly offered to do her make-up and hair and had done an amazing job. She'd insisted on coming over that afternoon and had spent ages making Anna up and styling her hair. She had somehow converted Anna's under-eye bags and lifeless skin into glowing, dewy radiance. Anna's hair was glossy and shiny. She looked as good as she possibly could.

She spotted James straight away. He was at a corner table, fidgeting nervously with a coaster. Seeing him made her catch her breath. He looked so handsome. He was wearing her favourite shirt, the blue one that brought out his eyes.

Inhaling deeply, Anna straightened her shoulders and walked towards him. His eyes lit up when he saw her.

'Anna.' He jumped up to greet her.

She leant into his arms and it felt so right. It felt like home.

'God, it's so good to see you,' he muttered into her hair.

'You too. I've missed you.'

'Oh, me, too.'

James gently pulled back and they sat down opposite each

other. He reached naturally for her hand and held it in his warm one. Anna ordered a glass of wine from the hovering waiter.

'You look beautiful,' James said.

'You look good too.'

'I've barely slept.'

'Me neither.'

'I miss this. I miss us,' James said, his voice breaking.

'So do I, so much.'

'I love you, Anna.'

'I love you too.'

'I've thought a lot about us over the last month and I know one thing for sure. You are the love of my life.'

Anna felt a tear roll down her cheek. She was so relieved he felt the same way. Maybe they could work it out. 'And you're mine.'

The waiter placed her glass of wine down and she quickly rubbed the tear away.

'How are the kids?' James asked.

'Okay. Bella?'

'She's fine.'

'So . . .'

'So . . .'

'What do we do now?' Anna asked. 'How do we fix this?'

'Actually . . . I'm . . . I think that . . . Oh, Jesus.' James took a large gulp of his drink.

'It's okay, take your time.'

James composed himself. 'I thought I'd made a decision until I saw you. God, this is so difficult.'

'I know. I hate being apart too.'

James ran his hand through his already messed-up hair. 'The thing is, if I'm being honest, Bella is happier now, living with just me, than she was in the house. How are Jack and Grace finding it?'

Anna's heart sank, but she had to be honest too. 'They seem happier too.'

'But I'm utterly miserable without you,' James admitted.

Anna nodded. 'So am I.'

'But . . .' James paused '. . . we have to think of our kids, and Bella is definitely happier and . . . and I have to admit that I don't miss the chaos and conflict. It was pretty bad towards the end.'

'Oh.' Anna felt her heart begin to crack as hope poured out of her.

'I'm miserable without you but . . . we might just have to put aside our happiness for the kids. And as unbearable as this is for us, they're the kids, we're the adults.'

Anna squeezed her hands together. She whispered, 'I can't bear not to be with you.'

'I feel the same way, but we tried, Anna, and we failed.'

'Maybe we could try again in a few years, when they're older?' Anna grasped at straws.

'I guess so. I'll wait for you, Anna, you know I will.'

'But in the meantime, do I not get to see you?'

'It's too hard, Anna. It's too hard to see you but not be with you. The kids are always going to come between us.'

'I want to be a good mum, but I also want to be happy.'

'Me too. They always say parenting is the ultimate sacrifice.'

Anna nodded. He was right. Deep down she knew it. The kids had to come first. 'You're only as happy as your least happy child, and Jack was miserable,' she admitted.

'Oh, Anna. I wish things were different.' He reached for her hand.

She pulled it away. 'Don't. Don't say or do anything nice. I'm holding on by the thinnest of threads here.'

She knew if she let him hold her or if she looked into his eyes that she would fall apart. 'I think I'd better go.'

'No, not yet.'

'There's nothing left to say, James. It hurts too much.'

'I'm sorry.'

'Me too, sorrier than you'll ever know.'

'I love you, Anna.'

'I know you do and I love you, but I guess this time, love just isn't enough.'

Anna stood up abruptly and ran out of the bar and down the street, letting her emotions cascade out of her. She sobbed and sobbed as her heart shattered.

Jack was telling Grace about his friend, Ted, getting into trouble for farting in class. 'The smell was so bad that Mrs O'Reilly said it wasn't normal and he was to go outside if he ever felt the need to fart again, so he kept going outside and making loud farting noises.'

Grace was laughing so hard she had to put her glass of water down.

Anna watched them from the cooker. They were happy. That was what mattered. They'd be fine about the break-up, delighted to know they were going to move back closer to school, their friends and Conor. She was a mum: her kids had to come first. She'd made the right decision. She was doing this for them. Feeling somewhat calm for the first time in twenty-four hours, she cleared her throat.

'Kids, I need to talk to you about something.'

'Oh, no. Are you getting back with James?' Jack asked.

'Jack,' Grace said, 'we talked about this.'

'It's okay if you are,' Jack mumbled.

'Well, the thing is I'm not. We have decided that it's best for all of us if we remain apart. So we'll have to move again, I'm afraid. I'm really sorry about that. We can get a smaller place nearer to your dad and school. So, you'll be pleased about that.'

'Yes!' Jack said. 'I'll be able to play with my mates after school.'

'Yes, and it'll just be the three of us, so that's all good.'

'Are you okay, Mum?' Grace asked.

'Absolutely. It's for the best.' Anna spun back to face the cooker as tears filled her eyes.

'Mum, we want you to be happy too,' Grace said.

Anna blinked away the tears. 'A mother is only as happy as her least happy child. If you guys are happy, then so am I.'

'Well, I'm sorry you broke up.'

Anna could feel herself losing control. She had to get out of there before she started bawling.

'It's fine, honestly.' She rushed from the room as a sob escaped from her mouth.

45

Bella rolled her eyes at Saffron's latest selfie. She was such a try-hard. There were only so many bikini shots anyone could take. She wasn't Kendall Jenner, for goodness' sake. Like, seriously.

She logged out of Instagram without liking or commenting on the photo. She'd pulled back from Saffron since the night of the musical, when her real bitchiness had come to light. It had been pretty cool, though, the way Grace and Jack had jumped to her defence.

Bella put down her phone and opened the fridge. Her dad hadn't been to the shops again and he'd promised. He forgot everything these days. Bella was worried about him: what if he forgot important things in work and got fired?

She went online and ordered Thai takeaway for them, otherwise they'd starve and she was done with starving. She had missed food and was enjoying eating properly again. Talking to her therapist had made her realize she was really crying out to her mother for attention. It wasn't so much about her dad, Anna and moving to the crappy house. It was more about her mum's lack of attention, which she was craving. Mind you, now she had Ingrid's full focus it was pretty intense. Her mother called her five times a day and was all over her constantly. Still, she needed her more than ever now that her dad was such a basket-case.

She could hear her dad in the bedroom. He was playing the same song he had played on repeat since he'd talked to Anna. It was doing Bella's head in. If she had to hear Adele sing 'Never mind, I'll find someone like you' one more bloody time, she'd go nuts.

She knocked on his door. 'Dad?'

'What is it?'

'First, can you turn that song off, please? Second, I've ordered food for us.'

The music ended and James opened his bedroom door. He looked like hell, unshaven, dark circles under his eyes and a crumpled shirt that he must have slept in. Bella handed him a bunch of laundered ones.

'What's this?'

'Clean, ironed shirts, Dad. You can't go around looking like a hobo. I told Mum last week that I was worried about you and she suggested using the hotel's laundry service. So, from now on, every Sunday evening you'll have five fresh shirts delivered to your door.'

James pulled her in for a hug. 'Thanks, Bells, that's really thoughtful. Sorry about dinner. I meant to go to the shops after work but I just . . . forgot.'

'It's okay, Dad. We'll have nice Thai food.'

'I'm not very hungry, but I'll sit with you.'

Bella led her father to the couch and sat beside him. Holding his hand, she said, 'Dad, you have to eat and sleep, stop listening to that sad song and try to get on with things. I know you're sad, but I'm genuinely worried about you.'

James patted her hand. 'I'll be fine. Don't worry about me. I'm very resilient. I'm just a bit raw. But I'll bounce back.'

Bella wasn't sure he would. He'd been a mess since they'd left and he was even worse since he and Anna had decided to call it a day. She had told her mum that she was afraid to leave him on his own in case he didn't eat or get out of bed. So Bella had stayed almost a month straight with him. Her mum had been very nice about it. She came over often for dinner and checked in on James all the time.

Bella was surprised that her dad and Anna had broken up. She'd thought he'd come home and say they were moving back in, but instead he had looked grief-stricken and told her in a voice that didn't sound like his that it was over, then tried to pretend he was happy about it.

On the one hand, she was delighted not to be living in that suburban house with Anna, Grace and Jack, but it was awfully quiet in the apartment. She'd got used to the chaos and even, sometimes, missed the chat in the bathroom at night when she and Grace would brush their teeth side by side. She even missed Jack telling her every single thing that had happened to him during the week she'd been staying with Ingrid. Most of all, she missed seeing her dad happy, smiling and laughing.

When the food arrived, James played with his while Bella tried to coax him to eat more. It was kind of ironic that she was worried about his eating. How the tables had turned. But her dad had no appetite.

'I'm sorry, Bella, I'm not much company these days. I'm just really tired. I'll head to bed early and, hopefully, I'll have more energy tomorrow. And I promise not to forget the groceries. Night, I love you.'

She hugged him. 'I love you too.'

Bella was in a deep sleep when she heard her phone vibrating. It was probably Portia sending dorky gifs or TikToks. She pushed her phone under the pillow beside her to muffle the noise.

It vibrated again, and then again. Oh, for God's sake. She yanked it out from under the pillow. She had five missed calls from . . . Grace.

Maybe she was drunk again and needed help. Bella pressed redial. Grace picked up on the first ring.

'Jack's missing,' she screamed into the phone.

'What?'

'He's missing and we can't find him. Did he contact you?'

'No.' Bella double-checked her messages, just in case. 'Nothing.'

'Oh, God, where is he?'

Bella could hear Anna shouting in the background, 'I don't know, Conor, I just found his bed empty.'

'Conor and Milly are on the way – he's not there either. Oh, my God, Bella, where is he? What if something's happened to him?'

'Okay, calm down, he's a smart kid. He'll be fine. He may have fallen asleep in the garden or the neighbour's shed or something. I'll wake Dad. We can come over and help. It'll be okay, Grace, we'll find him.'

Bella shook James awake and he got dressed in ten seconds flat and drove like a maniac over to the house.

Milly let them in. Conor and Anna were in the living room, both crying.

Conor was shouting, 'Did he say anything to you, Anna? Think.'

'No, I told you already, nothing.'

James and Bella stood in the doorway.

'Hi.' Grace went over and hugged them both.

Anna looked up. 'Hi, did Jack contact either of you?'

They shook their heads.

'Did you double-lock the front door, Anna?'

'Yes, I bloody did, Conor. He must have gone out the back. The key is gone.'

'You should have hidden it.'

'He's never done this before.'

'He could be dead.' Conor was getting hysterical. 'He could be dead on the side of the road.'

'Babe, breathe. We'll find him,' Milly said.

'Did you say something to upset him?' Conor persisted.

'No.' Anna was crying. 'I just told him that James and I had decided to break up, but he seemed relieved, to be honest.' Bella noticed Anna looking away from James.

'That wouldn't upset him. I'd say he was delighted. But did

you say it was his fault, did you blame him? Make him feel guilty or responsible for the break-up?'

'No, I didn't!' Anna cried.

'Stop harassing her, Conor. It's not helping.' James stepped in.

'Mum didn't blame anyone, Dad. She'd never do that,' Grace snapped at her father.

'Conor, cool it. I think we should divide up and search the local area. He probably just wandered off. Maybe he's sleep-walking,' Milly said.

'Good idea, Milly.' James snapped into action. 'I'll go with Bella. Conor, you and Milly go in your car, and Grace, go with Anna. We can take three cars and split up. We'll take the N11, you take the N7, and, Anna, you head west on the N9.'

They all rushed towards the door. Bella saw Anna go up to her dad. 'Thanks for coming.'

'I'll always be here for you,' he whispered.

'Come on, let's go,' Conor roared from the door.

They were running down the driveway, about to head off, when Anna's phone rang. It was an unknown number. Every-one froze.

'Hello?'

They all leant in.

'Mum.'

'Oh, Jesus! Jack, are you okay?'

'Yeah, I'm fine. I came to see James and Bella, but they were out, so I rang their neighbour's buzzer. This is her phone. I'm cold and tired, Mum. I want to come home now.'

'Oh, Jack.' Anna began to sob.

Conor grabbed the phone. 'We're on our way, mate. You sit tight and do not move.'

'Okay, Dad.'

Conor handed Anna back her phone and threw his arms around her. 'He's okay, he's okay.'

Bella tugged her dad's arm. 'Let's go and see what he wanted to talk to us about in the middle of the night.'

James rang Mrs Prendergast's buzzer. She stood there in her nightdress, with Jack beside her.

'I'm so sorry about this,' James said.

'Well, I did get a bit of a shock,' she said. 'The poor lad seems a bit upset. He said he walked the whole way and it took over two hours. I've given him a hot chocolate and he seems a bit perkier.'

'Thank you so much. I'll take him now.'

Bella tugged Jack towards her and gave him a big hug. He looked small, young and frightened. 'What the hell, Jack? You scared the life out of us.'

'Thank God you're all right. Everyone's been so worried about you.' James rubbed his back.

'What are you doing wandering around in the middle of the night, you dope?'

'I wanted to talk to James and . . . well, you too, I guess.'

'JACK!' Anna ran up the last flight of stairs and threw her arms around her son. Bella jumped out of the way so she didn't get crushed. 'Don't ever do that again, I was so scared. We all were.'

Grace hugged him too and cried into his hair.

Conor came panting up behind them. 'Come here to me.' Jack moved from his mum and sister to his dad. Conor held him tightly. 'If you ever do that again, I'll kill you. Do you understand? It's not okay to go wandering around at night. What the hell were you thinking?'

'Maybe leave the lecture until tomorrow. He's worn out,' Milly suggested.

Jack pulled away from his dad and went back to James. 'I need to – to tell you something.' Jack stumbled over his words.

'It can wait. You can call him tomorrow.' Conor nudged Jack towards the stairs.

'No, Dad.' Jack pushed him back.

'Let him speak, Dad, it's obviously very important.' Grace spoke up.

James put a hand on Jack's shoulder. 'Okay, Jack, take your time, tell me what you need to say.'

Jack opened his mouth and blurted out, 'Mum is, like, super-sad and crying all the time and I know it's because you broke up and I feel that maybe . . . well, maybe it was a bit my fault. I was mean to you and that wasn't very nice and I feel bad about it. I want Mum to be happy and smiley again and I've tried to make her smile but she's just sad all the time. I think you're the only person who can make her happy again. I know I said mean things and I was rude and I'm sorry. I really am very, very sorry. I just wanted my mum and dad to get back together, but I know they won't. Dad likes Milly now and he's happy. So . . . so . . . will you be my mum's boyfriend again? I love her so much and I hate seeing her so sad.' Jack began to cry. He buried his face in his arm.

James reached over and pulled him close. 'Oh, Jack, you're incredibly brave to come here in the dead of night to tell me that. I completely accept your apology and I'm sorry, too. I should have been more patient with you. I'm just not used to boys and I should have tried harder.'

'So will you come back?'

James hesitated. 'It's complicated, Jack. Your mum and I are trying to do what's best for all of us, especially you kids. We believe you're happier living without a step-family.'

Jack wiped his tears with the sleeve of his hoody. 'I won't stay in your room, Bella, you can have it back, and I won't kick my ball against your bedroom wall, I promise.'

Bella smiled at him. 'Hey, I was a pain in the arse to your mum and I'm older than you. I should know better. And I wasn't brave enough to do something crazy, but also very cool, like sneaking out and walking across a city at night to apologize and try to get Anna and James back together. You rock, dude. You're like a mini superhero.'

'Really?'

'Totally.'

'If I try to be nicer to James and Bella tries to be nicer to you, Mum, could that work?' Jack asked.

Bella looked at Anna, who was struggling not to cry. 'Sweetheart, it's not that easy. We've tried so hard, and it just wasn't working.'

'But you always say if you really want something you have to try very hard and not give up.'

'Oh, Jack, this is more complicated and there are five people involved. We want everyone to be happy, most of all you kids.'

'But I want you to be happy, Mum, and you're not.'

'It's because it's only just happened. I'll be okay.'

James crouched down. 'Jack, we really tried to make it work. Honestly, your mum and I did everything. But it's okay, because we feel we made the right decision for you and Grace and Bella. We're sad, and I'll always love your mum, but as she said, we'll be okay. It's just all very raw right now. I don't want you to worry about your mum or me or anyone. Just have fun and enjoy life.'

'Come on, it's late, let's get you into bed,' Conor said.

Bella poked Jack in the back. 'Hey, squirt.'

'What?'

'I actually kind of miss you.'

He grinned. 'Me too.'

'Jack, *The world is not ready for all that you will do,*' Bella quoted from *Wonder Woman*.

Jack grinned. 'Bella, *If no one else will defend the world, then I must.*'

'Dude, you tried your best and I think you're a badass.'

Bella watched Jack, Conor and Milly leave. Grace hugged her step-sister goodbye. 'I'll message you.'

'Cool, I'd like that.'

Anna lingered. 'Well, thanks, both of you, for helping. I really appreciate it.'

'Of course we'll always help you guys.'

'I guess I'd better go and look after my son, make sure he doesn't escape again.'

'He's a brave kid.'

'Yeah, he is. I . . . I just wish . . .'

'I know, me too.' James's face was full of pain.

Bella's heart wanted to break for them both. It was agony to witness, so she looked away.

'Goodbye, James.'

'Goodbye, Anna.'

46

Milly answered the door to Grace, Jack and Anna, flapping her nails to dry them.

'Sorry about the smell of nail polish, but I had to do them, they were a disgrace. Come on in, your dad's just made beetroot brownies. They're actually not as gross as they sound.'

Jack hugged Anna goodbye. Grace hesitated. She felt bad leaving her mum on her own all weekend. She was so sad.

As if sensing what Grace was thinking, Milly said, 'Anna, you have to come in and taste them too, come on.' She hustled Anna in and sat her down at the kitchen table.

Grace smiled at Milly and whispered, 'Thank you.'

'She needs a bit of minding, poor thing,' Milly whispered back.

Conor was cutting his brownies into even squares.

'Did you actually put manky beetroot into them?' Jack asked.

'Yes, and they taste brilliant. Go on, try one.'

'No way. I hate beetroot.'

'I'll try it.' Grace put out her hand and Conor placed a brownie in her palm. She took a bite. 'Actually, not bad.'

'Anna?' Milly asked.

'What?'

Grace looked at her mum. She was miles away. She'd been like this a lot lately, always switching off, living in her head.

'Would you like a brownie?'

'Oh, uhm, sure, why not?'

Conor handed Anna a plate.

'Conor cooking brownies, how times have changed.' Anna took a bite.

Grace saw her dad bristle.

'Well, Jack, how are you after all that craziness last weekend?' Milly cut across the tension.

'Fine. I'm sorry for scaring everyone. Mum got me a phone so she can always know where I am.'

'Nice one. I'll have to give you my number in case you're ever stuck or can't get hold of your dad.'

'Thanks, Milly, that would be great,' Anna said.

'And how are you?' Milly asked Anna gently.

Grace watched her mother trying to be upbeat.

'I'm fine, thanks.'

'Can I play the Xbox?' Jack asked.

'Sure,' Conor said.

Jack left the table. Milly leant over and took Anna's hand.

'You look very peaky. Are you sleeping?'

Anna shrugged. 'It's been a difficult time, but I know it'll get easier. Break-ups are hard.'

'It will get better, but it's not easy for you. You need to look after yourself,' Milly said.

Conor sat down at the table. 'You've no one to blame but yourself, Anna. If you hadn't rushed into it, none of this would have happened. You moved our kids in with him way too soon. I told you it wouldn't work.'

Grace was annoyed with her dad for being insensitive.

'I realize now that I may have been a bit hasty,' Anna admitted.

'You were in love. You thought everything would work out. There's no crime in that,' Milly said.

Conor put the remaining brownies on the plate into a Tupperware box. 'Yeah, but she dragged our kids into it. Moved them across town, away from me and their mates. They were miserable, and then James causes Jack to nearly lose his finger. And all for what? A failed romance.'

'Jesus, Dad, she didn't plan for it to fail,' Grace said.

'No one goes into a relationship thinking it won't last.' Milly glared at Conor.

'No, he's right, it was stupid. It is my fault and I feel terrible that I put the kids through so much.' Anna fought back tears.

'It's okay, Mum, we're fine,' Grace tried to reassure her.

'You might be, Grace, but Jack isn't. He hated living there, he was miserable and then he cut his finger off and ran away in the middle of the night – he could have been killed. And all this could have been avoided if your mother hadn't been so selfish and only thought about herself and what she wanted.'

'Conor!' Milly snapped.

'Dad!' Grace watched her mother's face fall.

'It's the truth and Anna knows it. The whole thing was a mistake. She put herself first and you kids second.'

'Stop, please.' Anna's face collapsed. She jumped up from her chair and sprinted out of the apartment, tears streaming down her face.

'Why did you have to say that?' Grace ran after her mother, but Anna was too quick. By the time Grace got to the lobby, Anna was gone.

She rang her phone, but it went to voice-mail. Grace slowly climbed back up the stairs. She felt sick. The front door to the apartment was open. She could hear Milly's voice: 'What kind of a person kicks someone when they're down?'

'I just said the truth.'

'No, you didn't. You just said your version of the truth. Your angle, your biased opinion.'

'Relax, Milly. Anna has been criticizing every decision I've made for years. She dragged my kids into her mess and I'm annoyed about it. I don't want to see my kids upset.'

'Your kids are fine. James was a nice man. What they're upset about is that their mother is heartbroken. You sticking the knife in and upsetting her even more is disgusting.'

'Disgusting? What – am I not allowed an opinion now

because Anna's upset? When I was left on my own in this apartment while she ran off with James and took my kids with her, did she come over and ask me how I was? Did she show me sympathy? No, Milly, she didn't. She just ran off with James and to hell with me.'

'That's bullshit, Conor, stop rewriting history. You told me yourself that your marriage was long over. Anna didn't run away with anyone. She left a bad marriage. She fell in love with someone else, just like you have now too. Anna and James are mad about each other. They only split up because the kids found it hard to adjust. It's the ultimate sacrifice, their love for their kids' happiness. I think she's amazing and you should be supporting her, not putting her down.'

'Oh, come on, it's not bloody *Love Story*. She'll be fine in a few weeks. She's laying it on thick so that we'll all feel sorry for her and no one will remind her that this was all her doing.'

'Do you know who you sound like right now?'

'Who?'

'My arsehole of a dad. He liked to kick people when they were down. He had no empathy or compassion for anyone.'

'Jesus, Milly, calm down. I only spoke the truth.'

'That's what he used to say. Sometimes you need to shut up and keep your harsh and brutal opinions to yourself, Conor. That woman is broken. She needs to be held up, not knocked down.'

'Chill out, Milly, you're totally overreacting. Besides, you don't really know what you're talking about. I know Anna a lot better than you. She'll be fine. She's made of steel.'

'Did you see her? She's shattered.'

'She messed up and she feels guilty about it. She'll get over it.'

'Wow. You have shown a really nasty side of yourself tonight. You're cold and heartless. I'm not staying with someone who behaves like you just did. I am out of here.'

'What?'

'I'm going home.'

'You're being ridiculous.'

'You need to take a long, hard look at how you treat the mother of your children. It's wrong and you need to apologize to her. I can't even look at you right now.'

'I do not need to apologize to Anna for speaking the truth and for being annoyed that my kids got dragged into her mess.'

'Cop on, Conor, before you push everyone away.'

Milly stormed out of the door, sweeping past Grace, who called after her, but Milly was not stopping.

'Gotta go, sorry, Grace,' she called, over her shoulder.

First Mum and now Milly. Grace felt rage boil up inside her. Rage such as she'd never felt before. She went in and slammed the front door.

Conor jumped. 'What the hell, Grace?' he snapped.

'I need to speak to you in your bedroom,' she hissed.

'Can it wait? I've just had a bollocking from Milly. I need a break.'

'NOW!' Grace roared.

Jack called, 'Stop slamming doors and shouting. I can't concentrate.'

Conor followed Grace into his bedroom. She shut the door.

'What has got into you? Don't tell me you're going to have a go at me too? Jesus, I can't get a break today.'

'Sit down and shut up. For once in your life, just shut the fuck up and listen.'

Grace was thoroughly sick of it all. She was sick and tired of her father behaving like a child.

Conor stared at her, open-mouthed. She never shouted and she never cursed either. But Grace wanted to scream and curse at the top of her lungs now. It felt good. Rage coursed through her veins.

'You were a pig to Mum tonight, a total pig. Have you no heart? She is devastated. How could you be so mean? She has been so good to you. You screwed up your marriage to Mum and now you're messing up a relationship with Milly too. Congratulations, Dad, you are a total arsehole. All you ever do is blame other people when things go wrong. You blamed Mum for walking out on you when everyone – and I mean *everyone*, including me – couldn't believe she'd stayed with you for so long. Then, by some miracle, you meet Milly and now you're going to fuck that up too. What is wrong with you?' she yelled.

She had no control. The words were flying out of her mouth and she didn't care if they hurt him. In fact, she wanted to hurt him.

'When will you grow up and behave like an adult? When will you be a proper father and husband and human being? When will you stop sitting around waiting for women to save you? Get off your lazy arse and go to work, finish your course, look after your children, be a man. When will you stop calling James a home-wrecker and slagging him off in front of Jack? Do you have any idea how much that messed with his head? You constantly knocking James made his relationship with Jack impossible. You poisoned him against James and that hurt Mum and James's relationship, but it also hurt Jack. Don't you see? If Jack and James could get on, things would have been easier for everyone. It's pathetic. You've behaved like a stupid child. I've had it, Dad. I'm sick and tired of it.

'If you don't cop on, you'll end up a lonely, bitter old man. I'll be gone soon, and after me Jack will go, and what will you have then, Dad? Nothing. Just a sad, empty life with no respect from anyone because you, and you alone, messed it all up. You have two kids who, despite your being so selfish and self-centred, love you. You have an amazing ex-wife, who gave you half her house when she sold it, and you have a fabulous girl-friend. But it looks like you're going to lose her too.'

Grace stopped to catch her breath. She was shaking with emotion and anger. Conor covered his face with his hands.

'Jesus, Grace, I'm gutted you feel that way about me. I know I'm not father of the year, but . . . but I thought I was doing okay. I mean, look at you, you're amazing, winning prizes and all.'

'Who sat with me and helped me with my science homework? Mum, not you. Who worked night and day to pay the mortgage and the bills? Mum, not you. I don't respect you, Dad. I was beginning to, because since you met Milly you've got your life together and I was proud of you doing your personal-training course, but tonight you treated Mum like crap in front of me and you're a total dickhead. How do you think it makes me feel to see you being horrible to Mum when she is so low and so sad? It makes me hate you.'

'Stop, Grace, please. I'm sorry. I . . . You're right. I was a dickhead, I'm just angry with your mum about a lot of things, but I should never have spoken to her like that. And you're right, she is a brilliant mum. I'm really sorry I've hurt you and let you down. I am trying to be a better man and dad. I'm not proud of how I let your mum carry the brunt of the earning and the worry. I was a lazy git. I want to make it up to you. I want to finish my course and set up a business and be able to give you a better life.'

'We don't need money or things, Dad. We need you to step up and show up and be a good person and a responsible person, and treat our mum with respect and kindness.'

Conor's voice broke. 'I'll try harder, I promise. You and Jack are my world. I hope you know that. I bore the faces off the lads talking about how brilliant my kids are. I can't believe you're mine, to be honest, especially you. You're so smart and bright and gifted. I just look at you in amazement. You've achieved more in your fifteen years of life than I ever have.'

Grace felt her anger turn to emotion. She suddenly felt tired and tearful. She sat down on the bed beside her dad.

'You and Jack are the best things in my life,' he went on. 'Your mum was too, except I was too stupid to realize it. She was always too good for me, to be honest. Anna should have met someone like James, smart, together, well-educated. She got stuck with me and she did her best. I think, in a messed-up way, I always felt like I wasn't good enough and that's why I behaved badly sometimes. As if I was proving to myself and everyone else what they already thought. Anna married down. Anna could have, and should have, done better.'

Grace swallowed tears. Her dad was right. Over the years, Grace had often overheard her aunties saying, 'Anna should never have married him', 'He's useless', 'She could have done so much better' . . . But until now, she'd never realized that her dad felt that too. It can't be easy always to feel that you're not good enough.

'But why didn't you try to prove them wrong, Dad?' Grace asked.

Conor sighed. 'Because I'm an immature, stubborn bollox and because I believed them.'

'Do you think that about Milly, too?'

Conor nodded. 'Yes. She's way too good for me. All I ever wanted to do was be a professional footballer and I really thought it would happen. So when I got injured, my whole life and all my dreams were shattered. I didn't know who I was if I wasn't Conor the footballer. My whole purpose in life was gone – I was nobody without football. I got lost and wallowed in self-pity. I guess I never bounced back, really. But then I met Milly and she didn't know about my past and my failures, and she looked at me like I was someone special, someone with potential, and it made me feel so good about myself. I started believing that maybe I could turn my life around. I'm trying to step up, do my personal-training course and be a better dad and stuff. I'm sorry I've let you down. I really am.'

Grace nudged her father with her shoulder. 'You're not that bad. You have some redeeming qualities.'

'Like what?'

'You can be funny and fun, spontaneous and loving and proud. And, let's face it, you're obviously charming because you have a way of making fabulous women fall for you.'

'And then screwing it up.'

Grace smiled and patted his hand. 'Milly loves you, Dad. Call Mum and apologize to her, then go and talk to Milly and tell her you're sorry for the way you treated Mum and you realize you were out of line. Own it, Dad, own your mistakes. Tell Mum how sorry you are and be kind to her. Then go and find Milly. She's amazing – don't you dare let her go.'

They both stood up. Conor reached out and pulled Grace in for a hug. 'Thank you.'

'For roaring and cursing at you?' Grace muttered into his shoulder.

Conor laughed. 'Yes, actually. Thank you for telling me how you feel and giving me the kick up the arse I needed. I never want to let you down. You're my world, Gracie.' His voice shook as he kissed the top of her head. 'Can you look after Jack while I go and grovel to the two most important women in my life – apart from you, obviously?'

'Yes.'

Grace waved her father off. She felt lighter than she had in months. The knot in her stomach had released. It wasn't gone, she was still worried about her mum, but it had definitely loosened. It had felt so good to be honest with her dad for once. And, to be fair to him, he had taken it on the chin. She felt closer to him today than she ever had before. She crossed her fingers and hoped he'd work things out with Milly. At least then she'd have one happy parent.

47

WhatsApp - New Group - We Need to Talk
Admin - Bella
Invite - Grace
Invite - Jack

B - Hey, guys. Jack, congrats on finally getting a phone, it only took running away in the middle of the night to get it. Nice work! Welcome to your first WhatsApp group.

J - Hi, this is cool!!!

G - Hey, Bella, how's it going? What do we need to talk about? I'm curious.

B - Our parents! My dad is having a nervous breakdown before my eyes. He walks around like a zombie. What is your mum like?

G - Similar. Zombie-esque here too.

J - Mum is sad all the time when she thinks we're not looking but fake happy when we are.

B - I'm seriously worried about Dad. I've never seen him like this and he's not getting better. He's getting worse. It's like watching heartbreak in real time. Freaky.

G - Same. I feel so bad for Mum. I'm worried she's going to make a mistake in work and give someone the wrong injection or medicine.

B - I wonder do judges give you a free pass if you kill someone accidentally because your heart is broken?

J - WHAT?? Is Mum going to kill someone?

G – No! Of course not.

B – She's joking (kinda!).

G – Jack, it's fine. Mum is not going to kill anyone.

J – So can we fix them?

B – There is only one way to mend a broken heart.

G – Move to the other side of the world?

J – WHAT?? Are we moving to Australia?

B – Jeez, I thought I was the drama queen. RELAX, we're kidding.

J – I don't get your jokes!

G – The only way to fix this is for us to get them back together.

B – That means we all have to live together again.

J – I'll do it. I kind of miss you, B.

B – I want my room back, squirt.

J – Done.

G – I'll do anything to stop seeing Mum so miserable.

B – Ditto re my dad. So now we need to come up with a plan.

J – What does re mean?

B – It doesn't matter. Focus on the solution.

G – Let's meet up and discuss.

B – I'm in the penthouse this weekend and Mum and Denis are out all day
Saturday. Can you guys come over?

G – Yep. We're staying with Dad so we can just tell him we're coming to
see you.

B – Great.

J – Can I order room service?

B – Maybe.

J – Coooool!!!!

G – What time?

B – 2 p.m.? We can order late lunch.

J – Yes!

G – Okay, let's all have ideas to discuss.

J – What if I can't think of one?

B – No room service.

J – Okay, okay. I'll think hard.

B – Ciao!

G – Hasta la vista.

J – What does that mean?

B – OMG, you're even annoying on text!

48

'Hey, come on in.' Bella stood back to let Grace and Jack in.

Grace tried to be cool and not gasp at the amazingness of the penthouse suite.

Jack, on the other hand, whooped, 'This is a*maaaaaazing*.'

They followed Bella into the living room. Grace's feet sank into the plush cream carpet and she was blown away by the gorgeous furniture and the view. The place was like something from *Gossip Girl*.

'You are so lucky to live here,' she said.

'I feel like a celebrity.' Jack lay back on the couch.

Bella grinned. 'What do you want to order? Drinks? Food?' She handed them menus.

Grace would have liked to order everything, but she didn't want to appear greedy so she stuck with a latte and a scone. Jack settled for a burger, fries, a milkshake and a brownie with ice cream. Bella picked up the phone on the table beside her and ordered for them all, with a latte for herself.

'Aren't you eating anything?' Grace said. 'Bella?'

'Don't you start! My mum and dad are bad enough. Mum had lunch with me – she's only just gone. I'm fine, honestly. The therapist has been amazing and, besides, I really missed food. I was miserable being hungry. I love my nosh. I know I'm lucky that it was caught early, before it got bad. My cry for my mother's attention is over and now she's stalking me. Be careful what you wish for.' She laughed.

Grace noticed that Bella had put on some weight, and looked so much better. She also seemed happier and calmer. Having Ingrid focusing on her was clearly making a big difference.

Bella tucked her bare feet under herself and snuggled a cushion to her chest. 'So, is your mum as miserable as my dad?'

'Is your dad spending most of his time locked in the bathroom or bedroom crying?' Grace asked.

'Or crying into her pillow all night long?' Jack said.

'Not quite, but he's doing a lot of wandering around looking heartbroken, not saying much, not eating much and generally behaving like someone in a semi-coma of misery.'

Grace kicked off her trainers and sat cross-legged opposite Bella. 'Snap. She's as miserable as him.'

'Are they better off apart, do you think?' Bella asked. 'I mean, they were fighting a lot.'

'Yeah, but it was always about us kids.'

'You mean me and Jack.' Bella grinned. 'You're the perfect child, the one who doesn't cause any trouble.'

'Saint Grace.' Jack rolled his eyes.

'I just keep out of the way because it makes life easier. And, let's be honest, you have been a total bitch at times to my mum.'

'I'll admit that I've had my moments, but she doesn't make it easy to like her when she zones in on me all the time and tries to inflict her dopey rules about phones on me.'

'She was a bit over-eager in the beginning, but she is also the one who noticed you were puking up your food and the one who came to your musical. She's very caring and kind.'

'Why are you puking up your food? Who does that?' Jack asked.

'Thanks, Grace,' Bella glared at her.

'Sorry.'

'Jack, why don't you go and watch TV? You can choose a movie from the list and use the noise-cancelling headphones.'

'*Cooooool!*' Jack ran over to the other side of the vast room and put the headphones and TV on.

'Sorry, I kind of forgot he was here,' Grace said.

'It's okay. I'm over all that now. I hated being hungry. And your mum was right to tell my mum even though I was furious at the time because I felt she was spying on me. I know she had good intentions and I did really appreciate how nice she was – how nice you all were – about the musical.'

'She really loves your dad. When they first got together, I'd never seen her so happy.'

'Likewise. Dad was high on life when he met Anna. I'd never seen that side to him. He was giddy.'

'But I know he struggles with Jack, and Jack struggles with him.'

'Yeah, he does,' Bella agreed. 'To be fair, Jack is incredibly annoying, but I feel that I had a breakthrough with him the night I babysat and you went out and got pissed.'

It was Grace's turn to blush. 'Oh, God, don't remind me. You were great that night.'

Bella shrugged. 'It could happen to anyone. But watching that movie together gave me and Jack common ground and he was easier to deal with after that. Dad needs to find something like that to connect with him. And he was a superstar for coming over to talk to Dad in the middle of the night. The kid has balls.'

Their food arrived on a beautiful silver tray, served on china plates.

Grace put Jack's in front of him and he gave her the thumbs-up. He was immersed, happy, and didn't want to be interrupted.

Grace went back to Bella and laced her freshly baked scone with butter and jam. She took a bite. 'Mmm! It's so good, do you want some?'

'Go on then.' Bella reached over and took a chunk of scone. 'Yum.'

Grace took a sip of her delicious latte. 'Okay, so we've established that our parents only really argue about you and Jack. Different parenting styles, different rules and all that. When they were dating, and we weren't all living on top of each other, they were madly in love.'

Bella drained her coffee. 'True.'

'So, for the sake of your dad's happiness, can you be nicer to my mum?'

'I can, if she stops nagging me and trying to make me bend to her rules, which are totally different to my own mother's rules.'

Grace put down her cup. 'But that's life, Bella. Jack and I can do things in my dad's place that we can't in Mum's. They have different rules and parenting styles, too. I'm sure it's the same when you're here with Ingrid and Denis.'

'Well, kind of, I guess. But neither of my parents is nearly as strict as your mum and she can't expect me to live by her rules. She's not my parent.'

'Yes, but you're living in her house.'

'But it's my dad's house too and his rules are different from hers. Like the no-phone-at-the-table rule your mum has – it drives me absolutely nuts.'

'Yes, but equally your dad is constantly on Jack's back about tidying up his stuff and calming down. That nagging drives Jack crazy,' Grace pointed out. 'Do you think if we all sat down and calmly tried to come up with a set of rules for our joint household, rules that everyone can live with, that could work?'

'Maybe.'

'If Mum and James stop having arguments about you and Jack, they could go back to focusing on themselves and their love bubble, and they'd be less focused on us, which would be a good result all round.'

Bella nodded. 'True, but your mum is going to have to compromise on some of her rules.'

'And your dad is going to have to chill out about living in a messy house and get used to living with a hyper ten-year-old.'

'So, how do we work this out?' Bella asked. 'Come on, Einstein.'

'Everyone sit down and discuss it together?'

Bella rolled her eyes. 'Too dry and boring. I think we should do something bigger. How about we show Dad and Anna that we want them to get back together? We could organize something romantic for them.' Bella clapped her hands. 'I know! I can ask my mum if we can book a room for them here at the hotel and have rose petals on the bed and champagne.'

'It's a great idea,' Grace said, 'but we also need them to know that we three kids want them to get back together and that we're all willing to try harder to get along. It can't be just about one romantic night.'

'Hang on. I'm getting to that part.' Bella got up and paced the room. 'How about we make a video of us at home? Like, a funny video of Jack being messy and me being rude and that's the *Past* part, and then we can act out how things are going to be, the *Future* part. We'll video Jack being super-tidy and me being really polite, and then we can all say how much we want them to stay together and be happy or something like that. We can write a script and make it look professional and we can film it when Anna's at work one morning.'

'Wow! I'm impressed,' Grace said, grinning at her. 'That's actually a really good idea. The video would show we're willing to try going forward, and the romantic night would give Mum and James the chance to reconnect. I love it. Let's do it. Let's work on the script now.'

Bella smiled. 'Okay. I'll grab my laptop and we can take notes.' As she was leaving the room, she turned back. 'The best part for you and me is that we only have a few more years of this. You'll be in some American university saving the world and I'll be in London in drama school, if I can persuade my mother that I'd rather poke my eyes out than study accountancy. But Jack has at least eight more years to go, and five of those will be living in the house by himself with Anna and my dad, the poor sucker.'

'Don't you mean "those poor suckers"?' Grace said.

They cracked up laughing.

'By the way, my dad is onside now too,' Grace said, 'so it'll make things much easier. He won't be bitching about Mum or giving out about James in front of Jack any more, so that will help Jack adjust his attitude.'

Bella looked at her. 'And did you have anything to do with that change?'

Grace smiled. 'I may have had a few quiet – or not so quiet – words with my dad.'

'My turn to be impressed,' Bella said. 'That's seriously good going, Grace. It really will make a difference. All that home-wrecker stuff was awful. Well done, you.'

Bella went off to get her laptop and Grace lay back on the luxurious couch. Maybe, just maybe, they could make this blended family work.

49

Milly arrived with a big bunch of red roses. Conor followed her, carrying a huge teddy bear holding a love heart.

'Hello, everyone. Hi, Ingrid, you look great, the hair looks good.'

'I love it. I want to book you in for another cut and colour. I must get your number.'

'Sure, happy to. Oooh, this looks fab.' Milly took in the gorgeous suite that Ingrid had organized.

'Isn't it amazing?' Grace gushed. 'Mum's going to love it.'

Jack climbed up on the bed.

'DOWN!' Bella ordered him. 'Do not even think about bouncing.'

'Jeez, no need to rip my head off.'

'I am channelling my inner Wonder Woman.'

'I noticed,' he said.

'Hey, Jack, why don't we leave the ladies to it and go downstairs and get a Sprite?' Conor said.

'Don't give him Sprite, Dad. We don't want him all sugared up when they arrive,' Grace said.

'You're right, as always.' Conor winked at Grace. 'I'll get him a juice.'

They left. Ingrid, Grace, Bella and Milly pulled out the rose petals and scattered them over the bed and the floor. Milly placed the bear in the middle of the bed.

'I tell you what, I'd fall in love in here.' Milly looked around the room. 'Petals, scented candles, champagne, chocolate strawberries. It's like a movie set. You girls have done a brilliant job.' She hugged Grace, then Bella.

'It was Bella's idea.'

'Yes, but you were the one who said we needed to do something to save them,' Bella said.

'You both deserve huge credit and arranging this romantic night is a really thoughtful and mature thing to do,' Ingrid said. She put her arm around Bella. 'I'm proud of you.'

'Well, you gave us the room and the champagne,' Bella said.

'Yes, thanks again, Ingrid,' Grace said.

'I hope it works out. I want your dad to be happy. He's a good man and Anna is a great mother,' Ingrid noted.

'Oh, me too. I'm a sucker for romance,' Milly said. She pulled Grace in for a big hug. 'You girls are amazing.'

Ingrid looked at her watch. 'They'll be here soon.'

Bella placed the laptop under the television and set it to play the video with just one click.

They exited the room, scattered a final line of rose petals through the sitting room to the door and left the suite.

Anna walked into the hotel lobby in the black dress that Grace had told her to wear. She'd had her make-up done and her hair blow-dried by one of Milly's friends. She had no idea what was going on, but she suspected it was a sweet gesture by Grace to cheer her up, probably involving her sisters. Anna's eyes felt puffy under her concealer. She hadn't known it was possible to cry so much. It had been a month of hiding in her bedroom and the toilet at work sobbing into towels and pillows so the kids and her colleagues wouldn't hear her. She was exhausted, emotionally and physically. But Grace had begged her to dress up and come out, so she had agreed.

She walked into the bar and the first people she saw were Conor and Jack. Oh, God, no: Grace had organized a family dinner. Anna didn't feel like sitting with her ex and trying to be chatty. They were on good terms after his profuse apology, but she was too tired to make an effort tonight. She wanted to turn and run back to the sanctuary of her pyjamas and her bed-room, but Jack raced over to her.

'Hi, Mum.'

'Hi, love.'

He jumped up and down in front of her.

'Did you give him a fizzy drink?' she asked, walking over to Conor.

'No, just apple juice.'

'Guess what?' Jack hopped from one foot to another.

'What?' Anna asked.

'You're gonna be happy tonight.'

'Jack,' Conor warned his son, 'let your mum have a drink. You look lovely in that dress, Anna.'

'Thanks. What's going on?' Anna asked suspiciously. 'Has Grace organized a family dinner?'

'Something like that, yeah,' Conor answered. 'What would you like to drink?'

'I'll just have sparkling water. I've got a splitting headache,' she said. Probably from being dehydrated with crying.

Conor ordered her a glass of champagne.

'Conor!'

'You need it. You've had a tough few weeks and I want to treat you. You deserve to be spoilt.'

Anna felt tears well up again. How did she have any left? When did you dry up? How long did you have to cry before your tear ducts packed it in?

Conor told Jack to go and find Grace. He handed Anna the glass of champagne.

He must feel really sorry for me if he's forking out for cham-pagne, Anna thought.

'I'm really sorry you're having such a hard time, and once again, I'm so, so sorry that I was mean to you when you were in the apartment. As I said to you that night, I'm sorry for so many things. The list is very long. You're an amazing mum and woman. I just want you to be happy because you deserve it.'

'Thanks,' she said, dabbing at her eyes with a cocktail napkin. 'Your apology that night and again now means a lot. I just want us to get along. And I'm glad you have Milly. She's lovely and the kids are mad about her. It makes it so much easier when . . .' Anna gulped back tears '. . . when the kids like your partner.'

Conor reached over and held her hand. 'Hey, you never know what can happen, and kids are more willing to adapt than you think.'

Anna wished that was true, but in her experience when your kids didn't like your partner, and his kid didn't like you, and you struggled to like each other's kids, it made things impossible.

Grace came into the bar, her face flushed, followed by a still bouncing Jack.

'Hi, Mum.' She hugged Anna. 'You look amazing.'

Anna gazed at her family. She needed to stop feeling sorry for herself. She had two fantastic kids and she was getting on well with her ex for the first time in years. She had a job she liked. She'd go back full-time, move into a cheaper place and figure it out. Love wasn't on the cards for her and she had to accept that.

'Finish your drink, I need you to come with us,' Grace said.

Anna knocked back her champagne and felt it hit the tips of her toes. She hadn't eaten much in the last month and she felt light-headed from the bubbly alcohol.

She followed Grace, Jack and Conor into the lift. It was sweet of them to plan a family night out to cheer her up. She was touched.

They zoomed upwards, then followed Grace out of the lift. She led them to a door that said 'The Langham Suite'.

'Wow, fancy. Did you win the lottery, Conor?' Anna joked.

Grace opened the door with a key card and stood back. The

room was dark, lit only by candlelight. Anna stepped in, and as her eyes adjusted, she noticed the rose petals.

'What's going on?' she asked, confused.

'Anna?'

They turned to see Bella leading James down the hotel corridor. He was all dressed up in his best navy suit and a red tie with little navy polka dots.

Anna's stomach flipped. He looked so handsome.

Ingrid and Milly walked out of the suite and stood in front of them.

'Anna and James,' said Ingrid, 'your daughters and Jack have organized a night in the hotel for you. They set up everything. It was completely their idea. Conor, Milly and I just helped with logistics.'

'We wanted you to have a night on your own, with no annoying kids around,' Bella said.

'A romantic night with no interruptions,' Grace added.

'And no me in your bed.' Jack giggled.

'We're sorry you broke up,' Bella said.

'We want to show you that we are *all*,' Grace said, 'willing to work hard to make this blended family work.'

'Dad loves Milly now, so he's not sad, and we don't want you to be sad either, Mum,' Jack said.

'And Mum has Denis and you've been miserable without Anna, Dad. I want you to be happy and I want you both to know that I'm going to try very hard to be nicer to live with.'

'And Grace said I have to find stuff to do with you. I don't want to talk about boring books or go for boring walks so maybe you can learn Minecraft,' Jack suggested to James.

Anna watched as James's face melted into a smile. 'I'd love that, Jack.'

'Right, well, let's leave them to it,' Conor said, pulling Jack towards him.

'There's a video on the laptop. Just press Play. It shows you how we used to live together in the past and how we're planning to live together in harmony, hopefully, in the future.' Bella grinned.

'We want to make this family work,' Grace added. 'We want you to get back together and be happy.'

Anna tried to find the words. She opened her mouth, but no sounds came out.

James reached for her hand. 'This is incredible, thank you.'

'Go.' Ingrid hustled them into their suite. 'Close the door and enjoy yourselves and I'll send breakfast up in the morning.'

Anna turned to face her broken, glued-together family. 'Thank you, from the bottom of my heart, for giving us this chance to make it work. I love you all.'

'Even me?' Bella laughed.

'All of you.' Anna smiled.

'Thanks, everyone. Now, if you'll excuse us, we have some catching up to do.' James reached over and closed the door.

Bella and Grace looked at each other. 'What do you reckon?' Bella asked.

'I'm hopeful,' Grace said.

'Yeah, me too,' Bella agreed.

Ingrid, Milly, Conor and Jack were walking ahead.

'Mum,' Bella called.

'Yes, love?'

'Can Grace stay the night?'

'If her dad's okay with it, sure.'

Conor looked to his daughter. 'Do you want to?'

'Absolutely.'

'Okay, then. I'll pick you up tomorrow. Call me when you're ready.'

Grace and Bella linked arms and headed towards the lift.

'What about me?' Jack was upset. 'I want to stay with you guys too.'

Bella nodded. 'Okay, but you're not allowed to be annoying and we're watching a chick-flick.'

'Fine. Can I have chips?'

'Yes,' Bella said.

'And ice cream?'

'Don't push your luck.'

'Please?'

'Okay, fine.' Bella ruffled his hair and put her arm around his shoulders.

The three of them continued towards the lift, arm in arm. Siblings of a kind, a family of sorts.

Acknowledgements

Families have changed form and format over the years and I wanted to write about the challenges so many parents and children face when two families become one.

As always, a book is not a solo project but a team one.

Thank you to:

My editor Rachel Pierce, who always, without fail, makes all of my books better with her brilliant editorial skills.

Patricia Deevy, who has been by my side since my very first book, guiding me and supporting me.

Michael McLoughlin, Cliona Lewis, Carrie Anderson, Brian Walker and all the team at Penguin Ireland for their continued support and help.

My agent Marianne Gunn O'Connor for her thoughtfulness, loyalty and support through thick and thin.

Hazel Orme, for her wonderful copy-editing and for being such a positive force.

My fellow writers, it is so lovely to have you in my life because you understand the world of writing and you just 'get it'.

My mum, sister, brother and extended family. Thanks for always cheering me on and being so generous with your support.

All of my friends – I'm so lucky to have you in my life. You're the best bunch of mighty women.

Hugo, Geordy and Amy – lights and loves of my life.

Troy, I couldn't do this without you. You are my rock.

And finally, a huge thank you to all of the booksellers, librarians and to you, the readers. Thank you, always.